Also by John Wessel

This Far, No Further
Pretty Ballerina

kiss it goodbye

john wessel

simon & schuster

new york   london   toronto   sydney   singapore

SIMON & SCHUSTER
Rockefeller Center
1230 Avenue of the Americas
New York, NY 10020

This book is a work of fiction. Names, characters,
places, and incidents either are products of the
author's imagination or are used fictitiously. Any
resemblance to actual events or locales or persons,
living or dead, is entirely coincidental.

Copyright © 2002 by John Wessel
All rights reserved,
including the right of reproduction
in whole or in part in any form.

SIMON & SCHUSTER and colophon are registered trademarks
of Simon & Schuster, Inc.

Book design by Ellen R. Sasahara

Manufactured in the United States of America

10   9   8   7   6   5   4   3   2   1

Library of Congress Cataloging-in-Publication Data

Wessel, John, 1952–
Kiss it goodbye / John Wessel.
p. cm.
1. Harding (Fictitious character : Wessel)—Fiction. 2. Private
investigators—Illinois—Chicago—Fiction. 3. Chicago (Ill.)—Fiction.
4. Ex-convicts—Fiction. I. Title

PS3573.E8149 K57 2002
813'.54—dc21   2001041160

ISBN 0-684-87063-0

For my sister Carol,
with love and admiration

Acknowledgments

Every author knows that books are not written, they're rewritten. My former editor, Bob Mecoy, got this one started before moving on—thank you, Bob, for all you did for me; I'm very grateful. Marysue Rucci is my editor now and I am very lucky to have her. Her suggestions were invaluable. She kept throwing the manuscript back at me, and it got better each time. I'm hoping she wasn't throwing it against the wall in her office as well. The same goes for my wonderful friend and agent, Molly Friedrich, who read so many drafts I'm sure she's sick to death of it, and me. Molly knows what I'm trying to do better than anyone. I'm blessed to have the benefit of her judgment, taste, and intellect, all far superior to what I can bring to the table; I would be lost without her. Thanks to everyone at Aaron Priest, and everyone at Simon & Schuster. Finally, thanks to my wife, Susan, who read the same drafts as Marysue and Molly but mercifully never threw them back, preferring to encourage and inspire me as only she can. Thank you, thank you, Susan. I promise the next one will be shorter.

Her pure and eloquent blood
Spoke in her cheeks, and so distinctly wrought
That one might almost say, her body thought.

—John Donne, *Of the Progress of the Soul*

It is an isle under Ionian skies,
Beautiful as a wreck of Paradise.

—Percy Bysshe Shelley, *Epipsychidion*

part one

my friend Alison and I are sitting in a South Side bar discussing white holes and the big crunch, the existence of God, monogamous guilt-free sex—all theoretical subjects at the University of Chicago. It's a slow-moving Saturday afternoon in early December, a perfectly lazy day. We've got an hour to kill before we're due at Bond Chapel for Beth Reinhardt's wedding.

Beth teaches Western Civ and she's had bad luck with men; by my count, this is marriage number four. There are restraining orders on two of the former husbands—the third is still in Stateville—and the bride herself has just declared bankruptcy so with Christmas just around the corner it should be a very festive occasion.

Alison's known Beth since childhood—they grew up on the same block, went to the same schools—but my own knowledge of Beth is much more fragmentary. I know her taste in martinis (very dry), religion (lapsed Catholic), and men (nondenominational). I know she returned to Hyde Park from Berkeley three years ago, swapping one assistant professorship for another, divorcing one man while swearing off all others, and that Alison helped her through this period, taking her to exercise classes, jogging with her along the lakefront, shooting pool in Wicker Park, baby-sitting her kids. (Beth did her dissertation on the medieval church, and her kids, who adore her, often show up on our doorstep on Halloween dressed as Thomas Aquinas, Peter Abelard, or various generic Franciscans.) I know she smokes too much, has published too little, has a fondness for old MGM musicals and vintage clothing, and once tried to climb whatever mountain you climb before you climb Everest. I don't know if she made it to the top. All that really matters to me is that she's Alison's friend.

I've decided to prepare for the wedding by drinking single-malt scotch. Alison's preparing for an Ironman triathlon next spring; she's drinking water laced with creatine. She looks very hot today dressed in a tight black dress, with matching industrial jewelry and lineman's boots. Her fingernails are painted flat gunmetal-gray. The dress drops very low in the back. She's drawing lots of stares each time she leaves the table. I make a mental note for the wedding: *Sit in the last row.*

"Thanks for dressing up," she says, giving my tie a life-threatening tug. She's not crazy about anything I'm wearing today—formal black Chucks, a corduroy jacket with faux faculty elbow patches, a tie with flying toasters and dive-bombing bread slices that came free with an old screen saver. There's some strawberry jam on it, too, saved from breakfast. I don't have many ties. But corduroy, I feel, never really goes out of fashion.

"What's the lucky bastard's name again?" I say, savoring the scotch. "This guy who's marrying Beth? Bachelor number four? Charlie something?"

"Charles, not Charlie, okay, Harding? He's not one of your wise-guy friends. This is a good, decent man, a poet, a scholar. He doesn't have a rap sheet. Maybe that's hard for you to relate to, but Beth finds it refreshing." She swirls the cloudy water in her glass. "He's a romantic; he proposed to her on her birthday. He *remembers* her birthday. He loves her kids. And his last name's Muller. Charles Muller. Why is that so hard to remember?"

"I'm not sure. It might have something to do with his personality. Or lack thereof. Let's face it—middle-aged guys who drink tea and write rhymed couplets don't make the most forceful impression."

"Middle-aged guys who are still single can be hard to find, Harding. He's very stable."

"He's very dull."

"Maybe that's what Beth needs right now. Especially after her first three. Sometimes dull sounds damn good to me, too. There are nights when dull would be a real change of pace." She checks her watch. It's guaranteed waterproof, SEAL approved, but if you ever wore the damn thing in the water, you'd sink like a stone. "Besides, Charlie's not really dull, he's just quiet. Still waters, you know? His poetry's pretty far out there, makes Ashbery look simple, and he's gotten all sorts of awards—and now you've got me doing it, calling him Charlie."

I reach out and push her hair behind her ears. She has her contacts in, a sure sign that it's a formal occasion. "Let's hear that résumé again."

"Visiting professor, English," she says, "tenure-track potential, currently at Colorado. Doesn't drink. Doesn't smoke. Doesn't talk a whole lot. Robert Lowell expert. Tall, stoop-shouldered—he's got sort of a Lowell thing going himself, minus the lithium. Beard thing under control. Published. Genius grant. First marriage, no kids, minimal baggage. Beth's crazy about him."

"Beth goes crazy like this every two or three years, Alison. The registry at Field's should give out frequent fliers." It occurs to me that I myself am a middle-aged guy. I'm still getting used to forty. "And he comes with just a tad of baggage, doesn't he?"

"Like what?"

"Like does your good friend Beth know that you roomed with Charlie back in college in that commune on Hyde Park Boulevard—"

"Here we go," she says, amused. "Now we get to the heart of the matter." She likes to play at being upset, but it takes more than this to get under her skin. "This is why you don't like him? We didn't room together, Harding—I shared a house with him and nine or ten others. That's all. And you know about the house. I've told you about the house. It was just a dorm—Grand Terrace wasn't a commune. Don't be so Neanderthal."

It was a strange sort of dorm, though, a tall, ramshackle house jammed between apartment buildings, far away from the main quadrangle. It wasn't listed with student housing, not officially, though advisers sometimes guided second- or third-years there. It attracted artists, writers, other social outcasts. The residents called it Grand Terrace because of the missing second-floor porch, which fell off during a three-keg party one summer. The four-by-six supports still hung in midair like a skeleton.

"You didn't answer my question," I say. "Does Beth know about you and Charlie?"

"Of course she knows. But there's nothing to know. Charles was postgrad, I was a sophomore. He was older than me, much older—"

"He's nearly my age, Alison—"

"—I meant to say *much, much* older—and people were always moving in, transferring out—he lived in the penthouse, I lived on the first floor. We had different classes, different friends, I had that part-time job waiting tables at the Blue Gargoyle, he was teaching freshmen at Circle and reading manuscripts at the *Chicago Review*—"

"You remembered him well enough to recognize him at that stupid Mensa convention last spring."

"He remembered *me,* Harding. I'm apparently hard to forget. Can I help it? Is that my fault?" She shakes her head. "Come on, let's not fight, we're gonna have a good time tonight. Weddings are just big parties. Lots to eat and drink. If you're good, I'll introduce you to some of my clients, faculty wives with good muscle tone, you'll love them." She owns PowerFemmes, a women's fitness center on South Woodlawn. I'm a silent partner. It's a serious gym, hard-iron, no-frills, no-nonsense, a lot like Alison. There are free weights, squat racks, benches, mats. No sauna, no pool, no health café. No Jazzercise. "Just do me a favor, okay? Look, don't touch. There's a lot of repressed sexuality in that bunch, I wanna keep it that way. It helps with the workouts. Just be civil. You're not marrying Charles, you don't have to like him."

"I don't like him now."

She sighs. "I put up with your friends, Harding. Like Boone. And Donnie Wilson. And your lowlife clients, *none* of whom has good muscle tone." She mixes some protein powder with her water, turning it mossy green. It reminds me of a science-fair experiment I did in ninth grade. "Speaking of which . . . you're not still driving out to see Donnie tonight, are you? I want you with me at the reception."

"I won't miss the reception. I'm not meeting Donnie till much later." Donnie Wilson runs a corporate security firm; he often hires me for jobs too sensitive for his own firm to handle. In this case "sensitive" usually means illegal. Donnie himself, according to his ex-wives, is not a particularly sensitive guy.

Alison takes a large vitamin pill from a very small purse, washes it down with what's left of her water. It must be one of the high-fiber kind. It smells like mulch. I tell her that I should be the one taking vitamins and protein powder.

"What in God's name was that move you tried on me last night?"

She grins. "You liked that?"

"I loved it, baby. I can hardly walk."

"It was nothing, just a variation on the scissors. I teach it in self-defense class."

"That wasn't self-defense," I say, draining the scotch.

"You couldn't move, could you?"

"I wasn't trying to move, Alison. The last thing in the world I wanted to do was move."

"That's the point, lover," she says. "It's called death ecstasy, I think, in sociobiology—the wounded prey surrendering to a far superior force. . . ."

"Wonderful. How civilized."

"Welcome to the animal kingdom," she says, and heads for the bar, drawing more stares. She's very tall, has long black hair, a boyish figure. Whenever she helps me on a case—her photography skills come in handy and she works cheap—her surveillance reports are

written in black ink on cream-colored paper. They are models of cal-
ligraphy, filled with detail. "Subject wore a yellow raincoat with
matching galoshes," she'll write. "Umbrella didn't match."

She brings me another drink. I think she's freshened up her water. It's hard to tell. The scotch I'm drinking is usually for after dinner.
It tastes just fine after lunch.

"Isn't that Detective Crowley?" she says, sitting down, crossing
her long legs. "The guy in the trench, looking lost by the front
door?"

"You're right." I hold my glass aloft until Terry Crowley sees us.
He's a CPD detective in Violent Crimes. Our paths have crossed a
few times, but we're not exactly friends. He's aging rapidly. I think
cop years are like dog years. He has liver spots on his hands. He has
spots of mud on his topcoat, which he throws over a chair at our
table. And he has a new scar on his left cheek, a perfect circle, as if a
tentacle from some underwater beast had grabbed him and held on
tight.

His sport coat's even older than mine, with frayed lapels, torn
pockets, and at least two bullet-size holes, more likely from late-
night cigarettes than a 9mm. His scruffy brown wingtips have
slightly mismatched laces and are dotted with salt. He fits right in
here at the Cove Lounge, one of the darker, seedier Hyde Park bars
known mostly for a good jazz jukebox. He says hello to Alison, eye-
ing her dress and her legs. He doesn't seem surprised to see us.

"What are you doing in Hyde Park, Terry?" I say. "Hassling students? Rousting the homeless?"

"I'm working out of the Twenty-first," Crowley says. "You
didn't know?"

"I don't read *CopNews*," I say. "I lose track of your promotions."

"It's just temporary. The watch commander's on leave." He's
looking around as though there might be a waitress. It's not that
kind of place. "Plus I'm sort of easing back into things. Working
part-time."

"You were sick?" He does look like he's lost a lot of weight. And his face has a chalky color that I'd attributed to the Cove's mood lighting.

"They cut something out," he says with a shrug. "I had a little work done." He might be talking about putting in a new patio. "So I've been at a desk, cleaning up some odds and ends. Dead-end shit. Nothing real exciting. Sort of like your job, Harding."

A girl at the next table smiles at Crowley. She's young, blond, dressed to kill or at least turn a profit—sheer blue blouse, short vinyl skirt, ankle-strap heels. Either she's a student or a hooker or a student dressed like a hooker. Maybe she's a hooker going back to school.

"Can you drink? Let me buy you a drink, Crowley."

"I'm on duty."

"Which means?"

"Just a beer," he says. "Maybe a shot."

I fight my way through the crowd and get Crowley's drinks. When I return, he's wearing bifocals the same color as the liver spots. There's a stack of pictures on the table. Alison is looking at me, eyebrows raised. It's never a good sign when cops take out pictures.

"You two going somewheres later?" Crowley says, peering over his glasses. "Or do you dress up like this for the crowd here at the Cove?"

"We've got a wedding. Faculty members, friends of ours."

He nods. "Thought we might have dinner. Catch up on old times." He doesn't really sound like he means it. And I'm not sure what old times he's referring to. Crowley was the first Chicago cop I ran into after prison. He wasn't real friendly. He didn't take me to dinner. He lights a cigarette, spins an ashtray painted like a roulette wheel—LIGHT UP YOUR LIFE AT HOLLYWOOD CASINO—and rolls the match onto twelve black. It's not one of my lucky numbers.

"Maybe I should show you this first," he says, unfolding a piece of paper. It's a fax of business cards, arranged like a collage. The Xeroxing turned bent corners and folds into wrinkles. There's a card from a dry cleaner, one from a faith healer, one from an insurance agent—another kind of faith healer, I guess. There's one from an herbalist. And one from a doctor.

DR. WILLIAM WOKOWSKI
MICHAEL REESE HOSPITAL
Practice Limited to Ear, Nose, and Throat

"I'm running them down for a friend of mine. Two of them were dead ends," Crowley says. "The faith healer has so far eluded my grasp. I'm not planning on going door-to-door. The herb guy I'm checking out next. The card says Hyde Park Boulevard, but that's just 51st Street, isn't it?"

I nod. I'm noticing the typeface on the Wokowski card—Helvetica Bold? Geneva?—and remembering the dizzying array of choices that the River North printer offered me when I ordered them nine or ten years ago. I felt I was letting him down, buying the cheapest design. He had endless fonts, colors, styles. Endless pen-and-ink drawings of endless ears, noses, and throats.

"This last one—I guess they checked with Reese," Crowley says. "Nobody ever heard of the good Dr. Wokowski. Which is surprising; it's usually easy tracking down a doc. They called the state board, the AMA. Nothing. But the name's real enough. And so are the phone numbers—or they were, years ago. So I'm thinking somebody borrowed the name. Which is a pretty stupid thing to do." He grabs a handful of peanuts. "Funny thing, when I saw this, right away I thought of this guy played lineman beside you in high school, Harding. Big, red-haired guy, built like Butkus. Missing a couple of teeth. Wasn't his name Wokowski?"

"You remembered that?" I'd forgotten that Crowley played high school ball in the Catholic League a year or so ahead of me. It seems like a long time ago. It seems even longer when I look at the lines on Crowley's face. Are we really the same age?

"He ran over me enough times. He was all-city, his picture was in the goddamn paper every year when I looked for mine—and he got a scholarship, he played college ball at Kansas. Did you know that?" I shake my head. "Well, it wasn't much of a career. A vein popped somewheres. An artery. An aneurysm. I guess you didn't send him no flowers." He takes a long drink of beer, fingers the fax.

I'm trying to remember when I last used that business card. I often carry half a dozen of them in my wallet. It's a cheap way to fake an ID; the M.D. impresses people, and most of the time nobody stops to wonder why a physician would bother to carry business cards around.

But it's been years since I used this one. I don't even remember why I used that particular name. Maybe I thought it was cute. It was definitely lazy. And in my profession things done in haste—or carelessness—have a way of coming back to haunt you.

"Where did you find them?" I say.

"The cards? With the girl," he says, tossing me a photo like a banco dealer in a Bond flick. "Take a look."

I turn the picture over.

"Her name's Tracy Lawrence; she washed up on a rock last month in East Dubuque. The case is going nowhere. A buddy of mine retired from Area One Burglary runs the department out there; I'm helping him out."

"Jesus," Alison says, staring at the photo. She doesn't turn away. The girl was in the water a long time, but that's not what's so awful. Her neck doesn't quite reach her shoulders. Her hands are placed near her wrists. The cops put her back together for the picture. I'm not sure why they bothered.

"One of the locals found her in a trash bag. It got hung up on a rock or who knows, it might've ended up in New Orleans, made somebody's Mardi Gras." He shakes his head. "They should really have the feds involved, you want to know the God's honest, especially on something this nasty, and this was real, real nasty"—Crowley spreads out a row of pictures worse than the first—"but nobody wants to share the glory. And nobody wants the FBI or the state police stomping on their cozy little bed-and-breakfasts. You ever been out there, Harding? For a weekend maybe?" He looks at me. I think he's forgotten Alison's even here. "They say it's very scenic."

"East Dubuque?"

"Galena."

"I thought you said she washed up in East—"

"She did, she did, but she was staying in Galena." The blonde bumps Crowley's chair; she giggles, gets to her feet a little unsteadily, and takes the long way to the bathrooms. I can't tell if it's the beer or the platforms that make her walk such an adventure. Crowley's watching her like a crossing guard. She's awfully young for this place, but I don't think Crowley's gonna check her ID. "They're not making a whole lot of progress out there. She was Jane Doe until last week. Then they got lucky with a couple of things. I guess she's from Missouri, but she lived in Hyde Park, went to school here eight or nine years ago. You sure you never been out there, Harding?"

"No." Galena is a tourist trap in western Illinois, the kind of idyllic small town I do my best to avoid. It's possible I passed through it—my memory of my drinking years is filled with more holes than Crowley's jacket—but right now all I can think about is the pictures and the way the different angles expose the wounds. They are jagged in a way I've never really seen before. Unless something got to her in the water. Her flesh looked like it'd been pulled apart.

"You should go sometime," he says. "They say it's scenic as hell."

The fax sits on the table like a used napkin.

"I'm sorry, what did you say about the business cards?" Alison says. "They found the cards on her?"

"Not on her, no, Alison," he says with a slow smile. "They're slow out there in East Dubuque, they're not quite that fucking slow. They found her wallet. I can't tell you where."

"How did she die? I mean . . . was she alive . . ."

"You mean was it the knives, was she alive when it—no, she was strangled."

"Was that all?"

He shrugs. "It seems like enough to me."

"Was she raped, Detective?" she says, a different timbre in her voice.

"She was assaulted, yeah."

Alison nods, sits back in her seat. She avoids my eyes.

"East Dubuque is upriver from Galena," I say. "Do they know where she was killed?"

"I think they know which way the river runs, Harding. But no, they don't have a crime scene, just reservations at the DeSoto House that nobody claimed last weekend of October. Happy fucking Halloween. The rest of it . . . who the hell knows. It's not even my case."

"You're just helping your buddy," I say. "Running a few names."

"The ones connected to Chicago," he says, nodding. "My primary concern is I'm hoping the guy who borrowed Wokowski's name has gotten smarter since then. And learned to make up the fucking names before he goes around putting them on cards and handing them out to every dame he meets in a bar."

"He might have been on the job, working a case, missing persons, Terry. Just trying to make a buck."

"That's one scenario," he agrees. "One I've been thinking of. Purely as a matter of coincidence. You were working the South Side eight or nine years ago yourself, weren't you, Harding? Right after you got out of the pen?"

"You know I couldn't work then, Terry. I didn't have a license."

"You don't have a license now, Harding. That doesn't seem to stop you from working." He refolds the fax and puts it neatly in his pocket. His fingers are covered with wrinkles, or maybe they're scars from fine cuts, the wear and tear of homicide paperwork. "East Hyde Park Boulevard—that's close to heres, right?"

"Four or five blocks," Alison says. "You could walk it. I used to, twice a day when I lived down there."

Crowley gives Alison a blank look, which turns into another

small smile. I'm not sure which part intrigues him more—her familiarity with the street or the suggestion that he should walk for no reason.

"Alison used to live on Hyde Park Boulevard," I say. "When she was in college."

"Yeah? You know this building?"

"Not by the number. And that area's changed, it was nicer when I lived there. But it's not a bad walk, if the storm doesn't hit. They're not very good at clearing the snow in Hyde Park."

"Me, I don't mind the snow," Crowley says. "Never did, even when I was walking a beat. If you ask me, this city's meant to be under a foot of snow. Like a postcard. Spring is the fucking problem—spring hits, the fucking snow melts, you've got nothing but dog shit. The ice thaws . . . you've got bodies." He tugs on his thinning hair, a nervous habit I don't remember him having. "God only knows what a herbalist is. A cook? A gardener? And East Hyde Park Boulevard—that's just a fancy name for 51st Street, isn't it?"

I nod.

"Then why the hell don't they just call it 51st Street?"

"I don't know, Terry," I say. "I guess they think it's more scenic."

Crowley smiles. "It's a scenic fucking world, isn't it? That's my impression, anyway. I'm beginning to think the whole fucking world is nothing but flowers and candy."

He smiles at me and then leans forward on his elbows. I'm supposed to listen closely.

"What I'm hoping here, Harding, is that if there did happen to be any more of these cards lying around, it would be nice if the guy would have the good sense to get rid of them. Before they cause him or anyone else that might know the guy any more needless aggravation. On a nice Saturday. That's what I'm thinking."

"I can understand that."

"You don't think any more are gonna surface?"

"I don't see how they could," I say, "if the guy took care of that personally."

"He'd have to have gotten smarter by now, wouldn't he?"

"He couldn't get much dumber."

He nods. "That's what I'm thinking."

He finishes his beer and stands to leave. He pushes his chair back in neatly, like a child leaving the dinner table. The blonde scoots her chair in, turns to smile at Terry. He smiles back. It reminds me of Gene Hackman in *French Connection* when he picks up the little girl on a bicycle. Roy Scheider has to uncuff Gene from the bed the next morning. Love is a many-splendored thing.

It's getting late. The jukebox is getting mellow: Della Reese with lots of strings.

So love me as I love you in my reverie . . .

"Detective?" Alison stands to face him. She's an inch or two taller. "Where was she living when she died? Galena? Hyde Park?"

"They don't know. They don't have a current address. They're working on it." Crowley picks up the shot of Daniel's, which he must have been saving for dessert. There's a tremor in his fingers I've never noticed before. His face looks like rolled-out pastry dough. "Go to your wedding," he says. "Enjoy the beautiful weather. Give my regards to the sanctity of marriage."

Alison watches him leave. She waits until he's all the way out the door and on the street before she sits down and looks me in the eye. There's something sad on her face.

I can tell she's upset. Because she's doing what she often does when she's distracted or worried—exercising, pushing against something. Testing herself. Her boots are pressing hard against the oak table legs. Leg extensions. I can see her thighs extending through her stockings. The wood's creaking like my knees did last night.

"It's nothing," I say. "I don't know her."

She must have known me though. She might as well have had that Wokowski card pinned to her like a dry-cleaning ticket.

"We've got time for one more drink," she says, handing me her empty glass. The light's gone from her eyes. It could just be the storm clouds throwing shadows in the room. "Get me something stronger this time. Vodka. Hold the water."

"He shouldn't have brought those damn pictures."

"I'm okay. Just get the drinks."

"I don't know her, Alison. Really."

"I know, Harding," she says. "But I do."

2

at four o'clock Alison and I are in the last row of Bond Chapel, waiting for Beth Reinhardt's wedding to start.

The chapel seats three hundred; it's a favorite campus spot for both weddings and funerals, and right now it's SRO, filled with an extended family from three failed marriages and ten years of teaching—friends, faculty, students. Everyone's here except the groom. He's late enough that each time the wind rustles the creaky rear doors three hundred heads swivel, hoping to catch a glimpse of the embarrassed suitor or Beth in her white-icing gown—but all they see is Alison fixing my tie or pushing my hair back. They're necessarily disappointed. Meanwhile the late arrivals tiptoe in like thieves, smile at me like old friends, and nod expectantly. They want my seat.

We got here late ourselves, after driving to campus and spending a good ten minutes hunting for a parking place. The traffic was murder. There's still a foot of snow on the ground from last week; half the parking spots have disappeared. When we finally did manage to squeeze the 4Runner into a very tight spot on the Midway, we weren't much closer to the chapel than if we'd just left the car at the Cove.

We sat there for a minute. I was listening to the Blackhawks, waiting to hear the score. Play had been stopped. There was blood on the ice. Alison was bundled up in her coat. She hadn't said much since we left the Cove.

I didn't feel like pressing her. I talked about the weather, I asked about Beth's wedding gown, about Charlie's tux, about the wedding gifts and the honeymoon plans. I knew the answers already. She was slumped in her seat, her head turned to the glass. She'd been crying, something she rarely does. Her contacts were out. A box of Puffs was cradled in her lap. Her feet were pushing hard against the floor mat.

When she finally spoke her voice was a hoarse whisper.

"I've been thinking about the Laundromat," she said, blowing her nose, wiping her eyes. "Clovernook Cleaners, the one by Power-Femmes? You think it does much business?"

I shrugged. It wasn't number one on my list of questions. A long black Cadillac with vanity plates—KEWL ONE—pulled alongside, waited until I waved him on. I could sell this parking spot for twenty bucks easy.

"They don't maintain it very well," she said. "The washing machines are always broken, filled up with water. The dryers are ancient, the floor's warped from all the flooding. . . ."

"It's pretty run-down," I agreed.

"Leon wants to retire. You know Leon, the owner?"

"I've met Leon."

"Well, that's all he talks about. Retiring, moving to Florida, going to the dog races. If he did . . . if they moved out . . . then we could expand the gym, put in a whirlpool. Maybe a massage table."

Her eyes closed. You can only distract yourself with something like Leon and his Laundromat for so long before you start thinking of other things, like those photographs and the jagged cuts on Tracy's hands. . . .

She started drawing circles in the fog on the window. I got her wire-rim glasses out of her purse and slid them over her ears. Her cheeks were very pale. Her red eyes were filled with questions. "Who would *do* something like that, Harding?"

I turned the heat down a bit. "Someone who knew her, I guess. And lured her to that hotel in Galena. They'll have to trace her movements the last month or two, talk to her friends. Now that they have an ID, it shouldn't be too hard." I don't mention what's really bothering me. *Someone went to a lot of trouble dumping the body. And then somehow left her purse where it could be found. With my card in it.*

"Do you think Crowley knows more than he told us?"

"Sure."

"Why not tell us?"

"Right now, I don't think he cares all that much. That might change."

"Poor Tracy," she said.

"When did you meet her?"

"In college, sophomore year. We were in a women's fiction group, Tuesday nights at the Blue Gargoyle. We were reading Jane Bowles. She'd been living in Pierce. I'd just moved out of Hitchcock."

"I remember."

"You do?"

"Sure. The room with the view. Of somebody's air conditioner. Which made a noise like fingernails on a blackboard every time it was turned on."

"Right," she said, smiling.

"You wore your hair short then. With a streak of purple. Which drove your dad crazy when he saw it. And blue lipstick. And you had a little temporary tattoo, of a butterfly, on your left ankle."

"You remember all that?"

I shrugged.

It doesn't seem that long ago to me. I'd just met her, coming back from prison on a Greyhound. We were both heading home. I was wearing a ninety-dollar state-issued black suit. She was wearing torn jeans and sandals and a black sweater and she was just about the loveliest thing I'd ever seen. We had lunch together at a Woolworth's in Berea, Kentucky. She told me about visiting her father in Florida. I told her about prison. I'd done eighteen months for manslaughter after a case went south in more ways than one. That was ten years ago. The Woolworth's is long gone. The prison's gone, too, replaced by a corrections facility. I'm guessing Berea, Kentucky, is still there.

"And then I moved out of the dorms and into the house. Grand Terrace."

I nodded. The house, the famous house with the missing porch. I was dating her then, but I knew I wasn't the only one. I was trying to figure her out. It wasn't easy. I'd been through a rough time in prison, learned to keep things to myself, and Alison had a directness that I misread as a kind of style. I wasn't used to someone so honest. She kidded me about my long silences, my nervous replies. It might have been what attracted her to me. She might have misread that as a kind of style, too.

We stumbled into a relationship, discovered places where our South Side lives had intersected—Sundays at Comiskey Park, school trips, bars. The ward at Wyler Hospital where we'd had our tonsils out, ten years apart. Alison's parents were academics; her mother's dead, but I've met her dad, whom she's still close to, and when I picture him coming home it's to a house full of books, antique furniture, the smell of pipe tobacco. I can see him as he walks in the door—like in a fifties sitcom—tired and distracted but stopping to play with Alison, holding her aloft in his arms.

I grew up a few miles away—an hour by bus, you have to transfer twice—behind the ruins of the stockyards. My old man was a roofer. The house always smelled like last night's dinner. Other than a copy of *Hawaii,* which my mother was always starting, our library came from *Reader's Digest.* Our furniture came from Goldblatt's. And when my old man came home—if he did come home—we'd be in our beds holding our breath until he went to sleep.

Alison reached into my coat pocket and pulled out a handkerchief. The black Cadillac paused behind us once again, blinked its lights. I was starting to feel sorry for the guy. "We'd better get going," I told her, waving him on. She nodded, checked her makeup in the rearview, brushed her hair.

The Midway was quiet. We walked across North Plaisance to

59th Street. Students hurried through the cold toward Harper Library. Alison's spring coat was almost like a thin black bathrobe, two sizes too large, hanging to her boots, covering her hands. She didn't seem to feel the cold.

"Later that year Tracy lost part of her scholarship. She got a job waitressing at Jackson's, that bar on 53rd near Kimbark. The one where the McDonald's is now."

"I used to drink in there all the time."

"You used to drink everywhere, Harding."

"Maybe I met her."

"I don't think so."

"Maybe I gave her the damn Wokowski card myself." I was still trying to remember what case I might have been working on then. Crowley was right—I had been all over the South Side then, no license, no clients. Just hustling, working out of my car, handing out cards . . .

She shook her head. Her long black hair shimmered like sable.

"Why not? I didn't know her. Maybe I tried picking her up."

"She knew you. She knew who you were. Because we were friends."

"You and Tracy."

"Yes," she said. "And you and me."

"You never introduced us."

"There were lots of people back then I never introduced you to, Harding."

"Like Charlie."

"Like Charlie, yes," she said, sighing. "Or Tracy. Or a dozen others . . . There was a girl in the house who was part Eskimo, named Aioki. Did I introduce you to her or any of the others? No. So what's the big deal?"

"Aioki the Eskimo never washed up on the Mississippi shoreline, Alison. Whatever happened to Tracy?"

"She left after spring quarter, moved to the West Coast. She wanted to write. I got a letter from her once, she was living by the beach. After that . . . I don't know, I sort of lost track of her."

We passed through the archway connecting Wieboldt and Classics. There's an old stone here from the original University of Chicago, which was located at 34th and Cottage Grove and went bankrupt in the 1880s. I walked past here every day for five years without noticing it until someone pointed it out. I just didn't know where to look.

"She never came to any of the reunions?" I said. "Or sent you a Christmas card?" She shook her head. "What about her writing—you never heard about her getting published?"

"Like I said . . . I lost track of her. There was some campus magazine she might have written for, just small-time." She pulled her coat tighter. Her hands were buried in her pockets. "Remember that party I took you to at Bartlett Gym last year, with the models and the ice sculptures?"

"Vaguely." Alison dragged me to a lot of very bad parties—gallery openings, performance art shows—when she was into photography. I remembered the ice sculptures melting into the canapés, I remembered a live mermaid perched on the diving board. A friend of mine named Boone was there, running the open bar. I didn't remember much else.

Neither did Alison. "It might have been a launch party for a magazine. And Tracy might have been involved somehow. . . ." She shrugged. She didn't know the name of the magazine or the editor and she was clearly uncomfortable discussing it. It took me a minute to realize why—I'm slow at this sort of thing: She felt guilty about not staying closer to Tracy.

Ahead of us, people were streaming into Bond Chapel. It did indeed look like a perfect place for a wedding. As we joined the crowd, I remembered another night when I was much younger, much warmer, when I crossed the Midway in just the same spot and saw Alison playing Frisbee in a tank top and cut-offs and how sexy she looked. There were three or four other girls with her; perhaps Tracy Lawrence was one of them. Perhaps Charles was there, too.

Perhaps they all went back to Grand Terrace together afterward. There was a dead-serious deadbolt on the front door of Grand Terrace, but once you got inside things got a little looser. None of the bedrooms ever seemed to be locked. And the doors always seemed left open deliberately, just a few inches, as though inviting you to listen. . . .

Alison took my arm as we went inside. "Who would do such a thing?" she said again, shivering.

It's getting a little warm now in the chapel. People are fanning themselves with programs left from last Sunday's service. Alison is distracting herself by telling me about some of the faculty.

"The thin man with the goatee is Rossi, from Geology. Almost got canned, he sleeps with his students. Male students. Very young male students. The one in the cheap tuxedo is Kornovsky from Russian Lit . . . doesn't look it, I know, but he is quite the womanizer. If they still use that term. He sleeps with everybody. That little man in the expensive suit runs the university press . . . he once came up to a woman I know at a cocktail party and told her he could carry her on his shoulders to New Orleans."

"He was drunk?"

"We assume he was drunk." A slender man in a charcoal suit stops to talk to us, introducing himself as Dr. Henry Dahlgren. He's better dressed than most of the other men here—better shoes, better tie. Better haircut. He may be the only male in the room with mousse in his hair. He asks about Beth, expresses concern, holds my arm in an overly familiar way while telling a joke about orgone boxes that I laugh at but find incomprehensible. He seems to be having a good time. A lot of the faculty don't get out much. Maybe he's been hitting the sherry.

"Semi-shrink," Alison tells me when he excuses himself to take a call on his cell phone. "Big deal in corporate consulting. Henry was on the search committee, helped Charles get his appointment. Don't ask him about his research, he'll start telling you about monkeys he hypnotized in the war."

"Why was a shrink on the search committee?"

"They always do that, different disciplines. Somebody from History, somebody from Soc. Besides, Henry's an assistant dean now. And, oh my God, there's Moira." She must mean the woman Dahlgren's talking to, a pale, very thin redhead in a very slinky black dress. She's sitting with her legs crossed, hands folded on her knee. She looks bored. He may be running the orgone box joke by her.

"That's Henry's wife, soon to be ex—they've been separated for a year. . . . God, what is she doing here?"

A lady in a summer-stock straw hat turns to shush us. We're whispering, but Alison's whisper has a very authoritative timbre.

"Come on," Alison says. "Let's go see how Beth is doing. Right now she's probably dropping Xanax like gumdrops."

We get up and try to sneak out the back door. Three hundred heads turn to watch. I wonder if any of Beth's former husbands are here or if she even invited them. I don't know what the etiquette is for that. *RSVP if paroled.*

It's dark outside now. The campus is settling in for the night. Beth's in a small room in the next building. She's a bit older than Alison, early thirties, five feet two, with short blond hair. She's sitting on a folding chair at a long wooden table, holding her wedding dress up off the floor, smoking a Virginia Slims. Her legs are bare. It's sort of a Courtney Love look.

"Don't tell me," she says when she sees us. "I don't want to know—"

"Beth, relax, we haven't heard anything," Alison says. "I thought you'd like some company, that's all. And what are you doing with that cigarette? You promised me you quit."

"I'll quit when I'm married."

"Which should be any minute now," Alison says.

"Where is he, Alison?" Beth says. "Where?"

"He'll be here."

She nods. "But why isn't he here *now?*"

"Something silly happened," Alison says, patting her on the shoulder; they might be two sisters commiserating on prom night. "Something you'll laugh about tomorrow. He'll be here. You know Charles."

"I thought I did," Beth says. "I'm starting to wonder. Do we ever really know anybody in this world? Aren't we all really strangers?" The Xanax is really starting to kick in.

"I saw Henry Dahlgren out front," Alison says.

"I know, he came back here, too," Beth says. "He offered to go look for Charles. . . . He's very sweet. I didn't know what to tell him. Where would he look? I mean, if Charles is drinking again . . ." She puts out her cigarette and starts digging in the pack for another. "I guess Moira's here, too."

"I thought they were getting a divorce," Alison says. "I thought she was in the Caymans with her latest significant other."

"Did you see the dress she had painted on? Unbelievable."

"I know," Alison says. "I hope she's wearing underwear."

There's some kind of organ music drifting in, very mournful, just what we need right now. It sounds like something from *Bride of Frankenstein:* Procol Harum's "Repent Walpurgis."

"Maybe he stopped off somewhere," Beth says. "He gets absent-minded sometimes—we sent him out for pizza last week, he was gone two hours. He was telling me how back in college you guys once had to send out a search party for him when he made a beer run."

Alison shakes her head. "I forgot about that."

"He said you found him in Jackson Park writing a poem. Just sitting by the lagoon."

"That was the *old* Charles," Alison says. "The *new* Charles isn't that self-absorbed. There's got to be a reason for this. Right, Harding?"

I nod, though nothing comes to mind. "Does he have a car?"

"He doesn't own one," Beth says. "I mean, he did, but he sold it.

He was looking for a new one, something big enough for the kids. Should I have asked Henry to go look for him? Do you think we should call the police? Or the emergency rooms?"

"It's too early for that," Alison says. "Isn't it, Harding?"

"Probably."

"Isn't it?" she says, kicking me.

"Definitely. Way too early."

"Besides, Harding's going to go out right now and find him."

"He is?"

"I am?"

"Right now," she says firmly. "So there's no need to worry. He's very good at this. It's his job."

"That's the first I've heard you say that. Where would I look? Besides the Jackson Park lagoon?"

"He's been staying at a frat house on University. Start there."

"Alison—"

"Just find him." This kick lands squarely on my shins. If this conversation goes on much longer, I may need orthopedic surgery.

I suppose I could stop for a drink somewhere. If nothing else, I could storm into the bathroom at the frat house, asking where the old make-out king's supposed to be getting married.

Beth gives me a key to Charles's room. "Maybe you could check Starbucks. And Jimmy's," she says. "And the Cove. And Tiki. Just in case."

"I had that same thought. And I'll ask a guy I know at campus security if he's heard anything. You know, just in case."

"I suppose he could have had an accident," Beth says, "or a stroke or something."

"We'll keep a good thought," I say. She squeezes my hand. On my way out Henry Dahlgren hurries past me with a glass of something for Beth, saying, "Here we are, here we are, this will make you feel much better." He looks like he's used to being in charge, whether here or on his committees. Right now I'm guessing he wishes they'd expanded the search a little more.

Dahlgren's wife, Moira, is with a group of smokers huddled under the arch. She hasn't bothered to fetch her coat. She's wearing very little except that slinky black dress and a small string of pearls. Her hair is beautifully cut. Her evening purse is small and oddly shaped, hanging on a long beaded strap. Her shoes might be snakeskin. People don't dress like this very much in Hyde Park, but I think Moira would draw attention anywhere. She has a small black tattoo that's only visible when she turns to you, swinging her hair, as she does to me right now.

"Trouble in paradise?" she says, smiling. She acts like we have a shared history that I can't quite recall.

"Just a momentary lapse in reason." Her purse has a small French logo; her tattoo looks like a Chinese symbol. Her perfume smells like money. I watch her walk back inside. The crowd parts automatically. She's got the walk down pat.

I wish now I'd parked closer. The quads are empty. It's very cold, but seasons don't matter much here. There isn't a lot of grass; all the buildings are gothic gray. If you wanted to be optimistic, you could call them "slate" or "taupe," but that's just the aging of the stone.

I walk past shuttered tennis courts, part of the pleasing geometry of a campus based on quadrangles. Beside the courts are three greenhouses. Three bright triangles of glass—three snow-covered peaks, two valleys between them. Square box fans on both ends made of weather-worn tin. The buildings are charcoal gray, the sky is black. The only green anywhere is the painted link fence by the tennis courts, squares of asphalt buried beneath the snow. There are no nets.

an optimist would start at the frat house, hoping to find Charles in his bed asleep. I start at the nearest bar, Jimmy's, then make three or four other stops on 53rd Street. No one's seen Charles. I check the package stores, one or two restaurants, even talk to the cashiers at the Chalet to see if Charles bought some of the cheap Burgundy they keep near the front registers. A bartender at the Tiki remembers him but not from tonight. From the way he talks, Charles has been spending some time there.

"You wouldn't like to pay off his tab, I guess," the bartender says. I politely decline. So much for Alison's hopes that he'd stopped drinking.

The frat house is one of several along University Avenue. Greek life on this campus is atypical; there's no social scene whatsoever, and the residences are used more for alternate housing than anything else. I think Beth arranged for Charles's stay here, thinking it might be more conducive to writing than a Ramada. I went to a party here once in the late seventies, more beer than dope, with somebody trying to read Pound's *Cantos* on the couch. I half expect to hear Peter Frampton coming from old KLH speakers, but I think it's Radiohead.

The music's coming from a side room on the second floor, where two guys are blasting the stereo while watching *Space Ghost*. They're both in their underwear, drinking Mountain Dew, holding bowls of popcorn. Somehow they must have been left off the wedding invitation list. I ask them if they've seen Professor Muller tonight.

"The weird dude from upstairs?" says one. "He's a professor?" The idea strikes him as terribly funny. "No, I haven't seen him. You seen him, Max?"

Max says he hasn't seen him. "But maybe he's got another date with Professor Reinhardt."

"She's a babe," says the other.

"That dude gets lucky more than the rest of us put together," Max says.

"He's engaged," I say. "It's not luck when you're engaged."

it's very warm inside Charles's room, the radiator's hissing in the corner like a cat that doesn't like my smell. I turn on a small light near the bed. The covers and blankets are on the floor. At first I think someone's tossed the place, but then I see a pillow and an ashtray and I see that Charles has just been sleeping on the floor. It suits the image I have of him: austere, Zen-like. Or maybe he just has a back problem. I check the ashtray for something more than the nasty French cigarettes Charles is supposed to have quit, the ones I see him sneak in Beth's backyard after dinner. I check the few places in the small room where he could hide a flask or a bottle. If he's still drinking he might have taken them along, wanting them near. I know the feeling.

I remember an evening I spent with Charles just before fall quarter started, last September. We began at my apartment, discussing movies and music, favorite restaurants. He liked Eric Rohmer and Ravel; I liked Sergio Leone and Steve Earle. He raved about a sushi place in Denver; I mentioned a ribs place on 47th Street. We searched for common ground and found it when I took him for a drink at the Cove. I didn't know he was trying to quit, and he certainly wasn't about to tell me, not when I was buying. In a neighborhood full of academics and eccentrics, he didn't seem unusual. He wore a suit with badly frayed cuffs, walked with a kind of lumbering grace. We drank Wild Turkey, my brand, and he matched me drink for drink. The jukebox was playing John Prine.

> I'll be halfway to Heaven with Paradise waitin'
> Just five miles away from wherever I am

He begged me not to mention the evening to Beth or Alison, and I agreed. It didn't seem an unusual request. I never liked telling Alison when I was drinking. But I should have recognized the look in his eyes that night. God knows I've seen it often enough. He's an alcoholic the way some guys are Catholic—lapsed, with fitful conversions. Everyone returns to the church sooner or later.

I go through the drawers in an old pine desk and check the closet. Most of his clothes are still in his suitcase. There's no tux in the closet. I'm sure Beth meant well, putting Charles here—I know Alison thought it cute and romantic, staying apart before the wedding—but the longer I'm here, the more this room seems wrong for Charles. There's no phone, for one thing. He'd have to use the house phone, one floor below. And the eaves are tilted in, giving it a claustrophobic effect. Beth may have wanted him to write, and to be around students, but it's more likely he felt out of place, too old, and when he needed a drink, he would feel the walls closing in. . . .

A hardcover book on the floor, a biography of Anne Sexton, has reviewers' notes and publicity sheets enclosed. Charles must have been commissioned to do a review. There's a torn sheet of paper that's apart from the others, serving as a bookmark. A handwritten note across the top is in soft pencil.

> There is a poetry
> of death

Below there's dialogue, from a play or something.

> —you won't leave me hanging.
> —no, no.

—god, I'd like to see you in that peach dress.

—I'll wear it for you sometime.

—peach dress and white summer sandals . . . what else would you wear.

—a slip usually, with a bra and panties.

—no panties.

—all right.

—no slip and no panties, just bare brown legs. . . .

I leave the biography of Anne Sexton. I take the bare brown legs with me.

my 4Runner's exhaust system needs work; it coughs itself to life. I'm carrying a pager and a cell phone. Neither one has gone off. So I'm surprised that when I get back to the chapel I see Alison in the foyer, talking to Terry Crowley. There are two uniforms with them and a campus cop. The cops look a little hyper. Most of the guests have left. The few who've hung around look a little stunned.

Alison looks very calm. She's listening to Crowley, nodding, speaking in a whisper. If you didn't know better you'd think nothing was wrong. But as she talks, her hands reach behind her, absently searching for something to hold on to and push against. She finds a cast-iron railing. She grips it with both hands. She holds it for a count of ten. The veins stand out on her wrists.

4

This stretch of Hyde Park Boulevard has seen more scenic days. So has the tenement I'm in. The building's crumbling; the apartment sits at the top of six flights of stairs. There's no elevator. It's the only apartment on the floor, but it's not exactly a penthouse. The rooms are small. The floor's covered with cat shit and dime bags and needles. How the junkies make it up here is beyond me. There are uniforms and campus cops and evidence techs everywhere, each of them winded from the climb.

A handful are still on the stairs, pointing to a pattern of bloodstains.

"That's where we think it started," Crowley says, motioning toward the stairs. He's holding a notebook, but there's nothing written down. "There's a fight here, we're thinking, some sort of struggle. Not much of one, there's not much blood. He wasn't killed there. He hit his head or something. Then he was drug to the window. See how it's just the tips of the shoes being drug? It was somebody big at the other end."

Crowley's eyes follow the path the body took, two reluctant legs pulled like deadweight to the window, still open. The glass isn't broken. This was done very neatly. A neighbor found the body in the alley. "Ricky Lopez," says Crowley. "The former resident. The deceased herbalist." He didn't take the stairs.

Nobody saw him fall. But a man—tall, white, in a black coat—was seen entering the building around four. No one saw him come out.

"I was just puttering around here, Harding, when your girl-friend called me about Muller. I love the way these things work out, don't you?"

"You mean cops latching on to the first suspect they stumble upon? You can't be serious, putting Charles in this."

"How well do you know Mr. Muller, Harding?" Crowley shoves the notebook in his pocket. He's a little nervous about something, which I don't like. Nervous cops make me nervous.

"I don't know him at all."

He blows on his hands, as though that would warm them. The heat's off in the hallway. The radiator's been yanked from the wall. Alison's wrapped in her coat. I'm discovering the limits of corduroy.

"Sure you do," he says. "You were at his wedding. You're old buddies, remember?"

"I misspoke. I exaggerated. We were putting in an appear-ance . . . for Alison's health club. She's got a lot of clients on the faculty."

"So you were handing out business cards?" Crowley says, amused. "I heard something different. One of the in-laws says you're all old friends, real cozy, you go way back—"

"How did he die?" Alison says quietly. "This man, Lopez—"

"—the in-law says you lived across the street, all of you in some commune. You might have mentioned that to me, Harding, back in the bar, when you saw the address on the card—"

"Detective? How did he die?"

"Lopez? Broken neck," Crowley says, turning to her. "And there's some trauma from the fight. Whether the neck was broken in the fall or before, the M.E. will have to sort out." Crowley's a little distracted tonight. He may be unhappy about catching a homicide while on temporary duty. He may be thinking of the blonde in the bar. "Is that true, Alison, what the in-law said?"

"Not exactly."

"She said you were the matchmaker, you introduced them. You've known both of them a long time."

She finds a spot to stand in, away from the blood. Like a cop, she keeps her back to the wall. "I knew Charles in college, Detective. I saw him at a convention last spring, by chance. He seemed lonely, I thought of Beth, that's all—"

"Two of my favorite words, 'by chance.' Funny how often they come up in my line of work. When was the last time you talked to him?"

"Tuesday or Wednesday," she says. "On the phone, very briefly. He seemed fine, he was looking forward to the wedding. He seemed *happy*." She makes it sound like that's something new for Charles. "And there's no way he'd be in a place like this."

"He lives in Denver?"

"Yes."

"And he's moving to Hyde Park to take some sort of teaching position?"

She nods. "But there are people from the university who could answer these questions a lot better than we could—"

"I'll be talking to them," he says. "Right now I'm talking to *you*, Alison. Okay?" She nods. "What about you, Harding?"

"I know him through Alison. We had dinner once or twice. That's it." A slight exaggeration, but cops like absolutes.

"So you weren't working for him."

"Of course not."

Crowley's hand is in his jacket pocket. I think he's playing with the damn fax again, just to annoy me. I should buy him a couple of steel balls.

"What about the other guy, Mr. Lopez? You ever done any work for him?"

I shake my head.

"I really should be with Beth," Alison says, turning to go.

"In a minute," Crowley says. "I'll get a squad car to drive you over. I want some background on Mr. Muller first. So when the trustees start picking up the phone and complaining to my boss about how we can't keep drugs out of the neighborhood and how a professor can't even walk down the street on his wedding day, I don't sound like a complete dunce. Did Charlie have any personal problems you're aware of, Alison?"

"No," she says.

"Any substance abuse problems?"

"No. And his name's Charles, Detective."

"Right. I'll make a note of that. Did he just come to Hyde Park for the wedding? Has he been in Denver all year?"

"He was living in Denver," Alison says. "But he made a number of trips here since last spring to see Beth."

"What do you think, Terry?" I say. "Charles came in here dressed in his tux to buy drugs?"

"It wouldn't be the first time it happened. I've found johns in whorehouses dressed in nine-hundred-dollar suits. In crack houses, too."

"Come on."

"Okay, wise guy. You tell me what went down here."

"I doubt Charles Muller was even here."

"Let's pretend he was."

"Then he wasn't buying. If he's guilty of something, it's being dumb enough to walk to the wedding. Maybe he wanted a minute to himself. What you said before is true—he used to live across the street ten years ago. Maybe he wanted to see the old neighborhood. Which has gone downhill since then. Lopez or his partner grabbed him on the street. He looked like an easy mark. But whatever went down here, somebody else killed Lopez. Charles got caught in the middle."

"So where is he?"

"He panicked. He ran. It happens. He'll turn himself in tomorrow."

"The innocent bystander defense."

"He's an English professor, Crowley. He writes poetry. He doesn't throw pushers off the roofs of buildings."

"We've got two people saying a tall Caucasian came into the

building. Alone. Wearing a dark topcoat. About the time Muller didn't show up for his wedding. You know how many white guys come to a place like this?"

"Then he came in here to see someone else."

"We're checking the other tenants. Nobody was expecting Mr. Muller. To tell you the truth, from what I've seen, the rest of them aren't much different from Lopez. Half the units are empty. And there's no sign of any struggle until the top floor."

"This is absurd," Alison says impatiently. "Lopez was a junkie. Charles was probably fighting for his life. Have you checked the neighborhood? He could be hurt, he could be bleeding to death—and that's if he was even here. Why are we even talking about him being here—"

"Lopez wasn't a junkie, Alison. He was a dealer, very small-time. There's a difference. And he's got nothing violent anywhere on his sheet. The reason most people come into this building and walk up six flights of stairs is to buy what Mr. Lopez is selling."

"Bullshit," Alison says. "Charles, looking for drugs? He never did drugs. Never. He doesn't even drink anymore."

"He used to?" Crowley says.

"He had a little problem," she says, backpedaling. I can tell she's mad at herself for revealing even this much. "Which is completely under control."

"I thought you said you barely knew him."

"I know him well enough to tell you he wouldn't be looking for crack on his wedding day."

"Maybe not crack," Crowley says, pushing it now, sensing a weakness. "Maybe something to give his wedding night a little boost—but I guess you wouldn't know him well enough to tell me that."

Alison stares at Crowley. For a second I think she might take a swing at him.

"Maybe you're right," he says. "I'm willing to keep an open mind here. Lopez has ten other arrests on his sheet. Maybe we should be looking in another direction."

"Like what."

"Like the other ten busts. Which were for hustling," Crowley says. "Could you maybe help me with that one, Alison? Does Charlie go both ways?"

"Come on, Terry," I say. "Back off."

"I'm leaving," Alison says. "Now."

"One last fling, before he ties the knot? Lopez picks him up on the street, they come in separate, meet in the lobby where Charlie thinks he's gonna get his rocks off, but Lopez says, Let's go upstairs, I can do you much better there and, besides, you don't wanna be seen down here on your wedding day—"

"That's enough, Terry."

He shrugs. Alison steps over the yellow crime tape, avoids the techs, and heads downstairs.

"I hope I didn't hurt her feelings," Crowley says to me, watching her leave. "You know I've got nothing but respect for the institution of marriage."

A couple of the techs like this; they're smiling at Crowley. I sidestep the map of footprints they've drawn on the floor and walk to the window, now closed. There's a fire escape outside I hadn't noticed before. The alley below is fairly well lit. They've been predicting snow all day, but the sky's still clear. A Metra train rumbles in the background.

There's a woman on a neighboring stoop throwing clothes at a shirtless man, who's stumbling a bit in the front yard, shivering. I can almost read his lips: *baby baby baby.* Just another Saturday night.

"What are you gonna do about the business card now, Terry?" He's sitting down, lowering himself awkwardly to the steps, favoring his left side. No wonder he's grumpy. I like the way he waited until Alison left before showing how tired he was. I don't much like the way he talked to her.

"The Wokowski card? Now I gotta give it up, Harding. No way around it." He shifts his weight, trying to get comfortable. He used to be able to physically intimidate you in these situations. That doesn't mean he's helpless. "Which is a shame, because sooner or later they'll bring the feds in, you'll get called downtown . . ."

"What do you want, Terry?"

"Just a little legwork," he says. "Those pictures I showed you, the Lawrence girl. See what you can find out about her, just the local stuff. I've got the other end covered. You don't have to solve the fucking murder. Just give me something to pass along."

"What do you have on her so far?"

"Nothing very current." The index card he gives me has her date of birth, Social Security number, bits and pieces of her life: born in Michigan, parents dead, last known address four years out of date. "She has a car, an old Gremlin that hasn't turned up. Illinois registration, expired."

"You didn't find a license? Or some credit cards?" He shakes his head. He must know more than this, but he's not sharing it with me.

"See if there's anybody in Hyde Park still remembers her," Crowley says.

Alison's down in the alley now, stopping to see where the body landed, bluffing her way past the cops and the yellow tape, talking to a female uniform. It occurs to me that she would have made a good cop. Better than Crowley probably. He gets up slowly and walks over to me. He's watching her, too, but he's not studying her professional manner.

"You shouldn't let her out in public wearing a dress like that, Harding. Jeez. When she took her coat off before, half her rear was hanging out." The techs exchange laughs. "Don't laugh, boys. That is the future Mrs. Harding."

"We're not getting married, Terry."

Crowley goes inside the apartment and I follow him, taking my first look at the lifestyle of Ricky Lopez. The living room is dominated by a huge TV and an orange vinyl couch. A black cube holds his CDs; lots of dance, Spanish crossover, mainstream pop, especially boy groups. There's an unframed copy of Picasso's lovers that looks torn from an art book as well as an unhealthy stack of *Boyz-World* magazines. The kitchen walls are papered with calendar pin-ups, mostly male, though December is represented by both sexes. They make a very cute couple. Miss January is pouting near the phone, waiting for Ricky's call.

The bedroom is where most of the uniforms have gathered. It's filled with crates of wine and whiskey and stacks of small appliances—mixers, microwaves, toaster ovens, electric knives—still in their boxes, fresh off the truck. One of the cops is looking at a waffle iron as if it was the murder weapon.

"Apparently the profit margin on smack wasn't enough for Ricky," Crowley says. "He had to get into housewares."

"Some guys just can't pay retail."

"Too bad Muller's fiancée didn't register here," Crowley says. "You could have picked up a wedding present real cheap. You gave them a present together, I'm thinking? As a couple?"

"I think we got them spoons. Or forks. I forget. That doesn't mean we're getting married." I take a closer look at the whiskey. It's not my brand, which makes it easier to ignore. The wine is better quality, something Charles would appreciate more than me. Charles is a wine expert.

I learned this firsthand last June, when the four of us went to dinner at the 95th atop the Hancock building. It was the night Charles and Beth first met. Several things became apparent very early in the evening: Charles knew more about wine than the rest of us, he was the only one who'd eat veal, and he had a fear of heights—and elevators—that translated into nervous chatter. He and Beth hit it off immediately, sharing a lot of obscure jokes and multilingual puns, catching the waiter in mispronounced French. By dessert Alison was grinning like a Cheshire cat. And when Beth took Charles's hand on the elevator ride down, Alison poked me in the ribs. "See," she whispered to me. The whole thing seemed like a done deal after just one evening.

Crowley tells me I'm free to go. If I see Charles Muller I'm to call the station. "That is, if his fiancée doesn't kill him first." One or two techs are still working the stairs. I shake Crowley's hand, walk around them carefully.

"How come you never got married, Terry?" I ask him.

"Me? I got married. Then I got divorced, like any good cop. The marriage lasted six years, half the time I can't remember what she looked like."

"That happens."

"Except the night she left, dinner theater at Drury Lane, that I remember like yesterday. What we ate, where we parked. The dress she wore. And the songs from the show, the one where two guys find the village and nothing's changed."

"*Brigadoon,*" I say, heading down the steps.

"Yeah, that's right." Crowley watches an evidence tech bagging blood samples. Another tech is using tweezers to pull hair from the banister.

"*Brigadoon,* that's a nice show," Crowley says.

5

my friend Boone is working the late shift at Fields of Joy, a used sporting goods store on East 53rd. Cold winter nights bring out the fanatics—there are a dozen customers reliving their childhoods, swinging taped Louisville Sluggers, fingering worn Wilson gloves, showing yawning girlfriends the grip for a split-finger or straight change. It's an addiction I can relate to but try to keep under control. Cheering bleacher bums are the background noise. The walls are painted ivy green, the ceiling is sky blue.

Boone works several jobs while working on a dissertation that is entering its second decade. He handles engineering for the campus radio station, WHPK. His cousin owns a small UHF station in Hammond and Boone does voice-over commercials for truck-driving schools and personal-injury lawyers. "Phone the toll-free number today for your free brochure: No salesman will call; operators are standing by." He now has a business card that calls him the "Mellow Voice of Northwest Indiana." He works for me sometimes, too—he's good with electronics, and he's not bad with locks. He knows a lot of people on campus.

Right now Boone is arguing with a customer. Boone is always arguing with a customer. I'm not sure it's the best way to sell used sporting goods.

"You can't really compare them," he says to a man holding a catcher's mask, his brightly colored early-eighties White Sox cap worn backward. The colors have faded to dirty pastels. "Best single moment has to be game one, '59 World Series. Big Klu hits two homers, Early Wynn goes eight innings, the Sox beat the Dodgers eleven-zip in old Comiskey. Heaven on Earth."

"I need a minute, Boone," I say, and he nods, taking something out of the register and getting his coat. He's wearing baggy green pants, the kind with ten or twelve pockets, and an unraveling sweater. He's the only one in the place not wearing a baseball cap.

"But they lost the series in '59," the customer says as we leave. He throws down the catcher's mask as though he's going after a pop foul. "Best moment has to be game six, 1906. They beat the Cubs. How could you have a better moment than beating the Cubs in the World Series?"

We walk up the street to Hyde Park Liquors, where Boone tries to cash his paycheck.

"This is the last time, Boone," says the cashier, Doreen. Her eye liner is lime green. "If my boss catches me doing this, he'll slit my throat."

"Fives and singles, Doreen, I'm on the bus a lot lately."

He counts his change twice, then we walk next door to Valois restaurant. Boone inspects the steam trays full of fried chicken. He lets me pay for his dinner. I always end up buying Boone dinner, no matter what time of day it is.

"That guy's probably right," Boone says as we sit down. "But 1906 is just too long ago. If that's your best moment . . ." He shakes his head. "So what's on your mind?"

"Do you remember a party last year at Bartlett Gym?" I say. "With ice sculptures? You were working the bar at one point. It might have been a benefit for a literary magazine."

"Sure, that was the *Mermaid* party," he says, reaching for the salt. "Can you believe this? Sea salt, in this place? What's next, Amish chicken?"

"What can you tell me about it?"

"Let's see." He unfolds a cheap napkin and tucks it into his shirt. "The magazine was full of artsy porn, the band sucked, my date didn't show, and Alison was mad about something—you got really drunk and threw up in the bushes."

"What was the name of the magazine?"

"*Mermaid.* I just told you that."

"Who threw the party?"

"That was Pollard," Boone says. "Logan Pollard. He threw up in the bushes, too."

"Do you know if a girl named Tracy Lawrence was there?"

He dumps two tiny creams into his coffee. "Doesn't ring a bell," he says.

"What about this guy Pollard? Is he still around?"

"I don't think so. Not in Hyde Park anyways. I saw him at Jimmy's last year, arguing for latkes. He was always a pro-latkes guy. Myself, I favor the hamantasch." The University of Chicago is the only place that holds a debate each year between fans of the two Jewish delicacies. "He was tracing the history of the potato pancake through art history. Come to think of it, he owes me ten bucks. He'll probably pay me off in latkes. You want some chicken, Harding? Or okra?"

"No thanks. You feel like talking to this guy Pollard for me? Get your ten bucks back?"

He frowns. "Since when are you concerned with my ten bucks?"

"I'm collecting information," I say, "on a woman named Tracy Lawrence. I think she wrote something for *Mermaid.*"

"And that's your best lead, a party?" He pats his lips with a napkin, then tucks it back into his shirt. "Well, I doubt if Pollard will be much help. By then he was only in English part-time, then he switched to B-school and started doing speed full-time. . . . He used to tell me if he could only get enough Ritalin, he could run General Motors. The Ritalin ran out. The last I heard he was running the family business, Dreamlike Display, in South Holland."

"What the hell is Dreamlike Display?"

"They make mannequins. Somebody has to, right? I mean, they don't breed. I don't think so, anyways. Who knows what goes on in department stores after dark." He strolls back to the food line and returns with a piece of spice cake wrapped in cellophane. "I take it something happened to this Lawrence chick?"

I nod. I'm looking outside the restaurant. It's hard to see through the glare, but there's a car across the street that looks like the black Cadillac from the Midway, the one with the vanity plates. It still hasn't found a place to park; it's just sitting in the shadows with its parking lights on. When I step outside, it pulls away so quickly, it nearly sideswipes a cab. The KEWL ONE plate shows up when an SUV trails it through the intersection with its brights on.

Boone comes outside, handing me part of his spice cake on a napkin, as though we were at the reception with Beth and Charles. He's drinking coffee. It's very festive on 53rd Street. There's a holiday feeling in the air. All the gangs are wearing special colors. The bars are full of holiday shoppers.

"What's your best moment, Harding?" Boone says. The guy from the sporting goods store is arguing baseball with a drunken sidewalk Santa.

"With the Sox? Probably when I was fifteen, Gloria Anders invites me to opening day with her father. I'd never been to opening day before. Sixth inning he goes to the john, Gloria lets me kiss her. I was in love."

"It took you six innings to get up the nerve?"

"It took her father six innings to go to the john." I borrow a sip of Boone's coffee. The spice cake is gone. Boone and I head back down the street.

"I thought you had a wedding to go to," he says.

"It's been postponed."

"Someone get cold feet?"

"Something like that, yeah."

donnie Wilson is sitting in his private office in the South Loop reading *Gent,* one of a dozen skin magazines he gets at work. I think he writes them off. I don't think it's legal, but I've learned not to argue tax law with Donnie.

I started in this business with Donnie many years ago, but we parted company when I lost my license. He runs a corporate security firm now, very successful, very suburban. Every time I turn around he's opening another branch. He has lots of lawyers. He keeps them on retainer. He keeps the back issues of *Gent* in leatherette binders.

"Jesus fucking Christ," Donnie says, not raising his eyes.

"*Gent* magazine," I say. "Home of the D-cups."

Most of the jobs I do for Donnie are off the books, done for cash, no questions asked. I've landed in jail once or twice because of Donnie, but those lawyers of his always get me out. That's not because of friendship; it's just good business. I've learned not to argue business ethics with Donnie Wilson.

"You're still interested in this job?" he says, and I nod. My bank account is empty.

We're in a prairie-style corporate park, the new South Side. I think the mayor lives across the street. Donnie's playing orchestral Pink Floyd on his Bang & Olufsen stereo. The CD changer hangs vertically on the wall, six colored disks in clear plastic, a minijuke-box. The bass is a little loud. There's a lot of fine-grained wood in here, lots of expensive electronics, toys for adults, most of it just for show. A flat-screen TV hangs on the wall like a Dalí clock.

"Tara said you needed a plate run," he says, referring to his latest assistant, currently filing her nails in the outer office. She may be the reason Donnie's here so late on a Saturday night. "You working on another case? Something big?"

"They're all big, Donnie. Fraught with human drama." I run my hand along Donnie's desk. The wood gleams like a coffin. "This is new," I say. "I like this. What is this, walnut?"

"Rosewood. Brazilian rosewood." The television is on, the sound muted. The remote sits on the desk next to the cigar box. You could land jets with Donnie's remote. "You must be working on something, Harding—"

"I picked up a tail, that's all." I can't tell what's on the television, a travelogue or an exercise show. It might be CNN. A blonde in a leotard is doing jumping jacks on the Great Wall. Behind her are about fifty Chinese in prol-gray sweats. "I thought you had these suburban cops in your back pocket. If it's too much trouble . . . if this is too much for you . . ."

He marks his place in *Gent* with a tiny Post-it. "It's no trouble," he says. "I'll run the plate."

"Veneer?"

"It's solid rosewood, asshole."

I give him the Cadillac's plate, which he notes on a crisp piece of yellow memo paper. Donnie loves office supplies, likes having the proper form for every job. *While you were being tailed . . .*

"The job's strictly hardware," he says, taking two slim cigars from a humidor and holding them out to me like chopsticks. I shake my head. "A wiretap, three or four bugs. Very simple, you're in, you're out, nobody's home. Right in your neighborhood."

"How much?"

"More than you're worth." Donnie lights his cigar. "Enough, believe me. I'll have the money for you tomorrow afternoon." He walks me to the door, shakes my hand. Donnie has a very firm grip. "This tail, they got close enough so you could get the plate?"

"Yeah."

"They knew you made them?"

"I'm not sure they cared." He nods. The blonde is now bicycling through the Forbidden City. She waves to the few Chinese on the square. The camera shows us her warm smile and lingers on the sharp definition of her thighs.

6

When I catch up with Alison, it's almost two A.M. She's sitting in the living room of her apartment, shoes off, contacts out, but still wearing her black dress. It seems even more appropriate now. I hang up my coat, loosen my tie, fix us both a drink. Alison doesn't like scotch, but she accepts this one without comment.

"Beth's at home," Alison says, sitting back on the couch, curling her feet under her. "Her sister's there with her. And her kids. She doesn't know what to think. I wonder if she'll ever want to get married again."

The lights in the apartment are all turned on, as though she wanted sunlight. The shades are up. There are women's sport magazines stacked everywhere, a pair of blue rubber dumbbells on the rug. Alison recently moved from the second floor to the fifth, not for the view but the stairs. She likes the exercise.

"You said that the last time," I say. "After her divorce. She'll be okay. Especially with those kids."

"Yeah, her kids are great."

"Her sister lives in Chicago?"

She nods. "Park Forest. Henry Dahlgren stopped by, too, which I thought was nice. He seemed very concerned about Beth—"

"The shrink? Again? Maybe he's trolling for patients, like a lawyer chasing ambulances. Except shrinks chase heartbreak and depression." I go into the hall bathroom to wash up. "Was his wife with him?"

"Moira? No, I think Moira was on her way to the airport." She points me to the clean towels. "The house is full of wedding presents. It's just awful. And her daughter's on the phone trying to cancel the honeymoon reservations in Ireland so they can get some of the money back."

She watches me walk to the kitchen and back, turning off the lights. I pause at the dining-room window, looking out at Harper Avenue, before closing the drapes. That black Cadillac is still on my mind. It crossed our path today like a black cat. "You know, I never understood who was paying for all that. The wedding's bad enough. But a honeymoon in Ireland? Beth's filing chapter eleven, isn't she?"

"Charles has some money," she says. "He won that genius grant last year, remember? And Beth has an aunt that may or may not leave her something, she keeps changing her will." She sips the scotch, then looks at the glass to see what she's drinking. "He's out there somewhere right now, Harding. Probably scared to death."

"Did he move his stuff from Denver?"

"It's all in storage. You're wondering if he went back there. He might have, I guess. For some reason I think he's around here, close. He wouldn't know how to run." She stretches her legs out on the coffee table. "Do you believe the way Crowley was talking?"

I sit next to her on the couch, kick my shoes off. "They're trying to figure Charles out, Alison. Nobody knows much about him."

"You don't have to know very much to see what happened—if anything *did* happen. They took him up there to rob him. Charles fought back—"

"Probably."

"Probably?"

"I'm not arguing, Alison. I stood up for the guy with Crowley."

I can feel her body stiffen next to me. "He didn't do drugs, Harding. And the other idea's ludicrous."

"You haven't seen him in years," I say. "Remember?"

"What's that supposed to mean."

"Nothing. But either you know the guy or you don't."

She glares at me.

"You should keep your stories straight," I say. "That's all I'm saying."

"You sound like Crowley. I don't need this from you, too."

"Are you so sure Charles never used drugs? Because he has that kind of addictive personality, doesn't he? We know he was a drunk for years—"

"He was never a *drunk*." She says the word as though it has some clinical meaning that I'm missing. "And you're the last person in the world to talk about somebody's drinking problems."

"Not the last," I say. "Surely there must be one or two worse than me." When I tell her about the bill Charles has run up at the Tiki, she frowns, taking a sip of the scotch as if in sympathy. "That might just be the stress of the wedding and the move. . . ."

I nod. She's right, I am talking like Crowley. Something about Charles gets under my skin.

"He's going to need my help, Harding."

"Your help? Why you?"

"He's like a kid. You know that. I mean he's brilliant, but he can't even get a table at a restaurant. And he's a mark. He lets himself be talked into all sorts of stuff on the phone—CDs, insurance. He won't know how to cope with the cops in this town. I bet he hasn't even got a lawyer."

"He's a grown man, Alison. And isn't that Beth's job, to help him?"

"She'll need help, too," Alison says. "She's sort of spacey sometimes—they're academics, they don't know how this town really works."

I turn on Alison's ministereo, just Christmas music, something soothing. "You should stay out of it, Alison."

"Why don't you like him, Harding?"

"I don't really *dis*like him—"

"You think I slept with him."

"Did you?"

She goes to the window, holding her drink. She peeks through the drapes as though he might be right outside, listening. The radiator comes slowly alive in a corner of the room.

"I hate discussing this kind of thing with you, Harding. You think something that happened ten years ago is important to me. And it's not. I don't hold grudges like you do and I don't daydream about old lovers. I don't live in the past."

"You're saying I do?"

"You attach too much importance to things that are dead and buried. Charles and I were friends. He had a room in the house. I had a room. So did Tracy, so did a dozen others, off and on. Even Moira lived there for one summer—"

"Moira Dahlgren?" I say, surprised. "You never told me that."

"That's because it's *no big deal.* I don't even *like* her now. After you left I had to practically force myself to talk to her, to ask her about Tracy. But she hadn't heard from her in years either." I'm very aware that she never really answered my question about Charles. So is she.

The radio announcer runs through the carols he's just played. It's a long list. Alison looks at me from the window, debating how far to take this, hips tilted, weight on one foot, holding the glass with two fingers.

"I've got some pictures from that summer," she finally says. "With Tracy and Moira." She pauses. "Would you like to see them?"

"Very much."

There's a small yellow Kodak packet, fading snapshots of three women—all of them in bathing suits, lying on their backs on the deck of a sailboat, oiled and tanned, or propped on one elbow, smiling, giggling, squinting into the sun. Alison's wearing a black bikini I've never seen before. I'd forgotten how skinny she was then, pre-workout, pre-creatine. Her smile's the same, though. So is the life flashing in her green eyes.

"That's Tracy," she says, sitting beside me. Her fingernail runs along the length of Tracy's body. "Moira's in the one-piece." Moira in college was just as thin as now but with shorter hair under a sombrero-like sun hat.

Tracy's face and hair are a bit like Alison's, but their bodies are much different—Tracy's is less athletic, much curvier. And softer somehow than Alison's. She's spilling out of her bikini. Her smile has a knowing, mischievous look to it that's very sexual. "She looks cute, doesn't she?" Alison says.

"Tracy? Cute isn't exactly the word I'd use."

"I meant Moira. Moira used to be cute. I'm not sure what happened to her." She takes the pictures away from me, smiling a bit. "Of the three of us, Moira was the wildest one by far."

"She's wearing the most conservative suit."

"That was for the pictures, to hide her tattoos and belly ring from her parents. She spent the rest of the weekend in a thong. Or less. So did I, actually . . ."

"Now you're just teasing me."

"I'm not," she protests, laughing for the first time tonight. "There was no one around, we were just having fun. You can't do that on campus, there's always people watching. . . ."

"Where were these taken?" I say.

"A house near the Dunes. Moira's uncle owned it or something. We spent a weekend there over Labor Day; we were just supposed to study for the GRE. It was not a good idea."

"Was Charles there with you, too?"

"No, no, just us three. Ladies only. A neighbor took the pictures."

"You look like you had a good time."

"Oh, we had a great time. We just didn't study very much." She puts the photos back in the packet. Their edges still peek out at me.

She starts to go and I get up awkwardly, and we kiss, standing in the middle of the room, one of her hands still holding the glass. Her other hand draws circles on my shirt. Later tonight or tomorrow I'll tell her about Donnie's job, Crowley's request for help in finding info on Tracy. Not now.

"I'm going to bed," she says. "Are you coming?"

"I think I'll have one more."

"Suit yourself. Don't stay up too late."

"You know, Alison, I'm a little surprised you never told me about Moira Dahlgren before. Or that summer . . . or those pictures."

"That was just one summer, Harding," she says, smiling. "There were lots of summers."

She heads for the bathroom. I switch radio stations and plug in the earphones. I'm drinking from the bottle now. There's an all-night show on one of the classic rock stations that mimics the underground FM stations of the late sixties. They're playing Soft Machine, Lothar and the Hand People, Captain Beefheart, Earth Opera, the Incredible String Band.

First girl ever I loved

I get the pictures back out, the ones of Alison and Moira and Tracy. I don't remember hearing their names back then, but then those days are a little hazy now. Alison was still in college, majoring in art history, learning photography, while I stumbled about, looking for someone who would hire an ex-con. All I knew how to do was tail people, watch people, hunt people down. I was drinking a lot then, something I'd picked up in the army, where a CIA case officer taught us electronics and ended each session in a bar bragging about the NARV officers and Saigon politicians he'd bugged and blackmailed—after a few mai-tais he'd reconstruct the Ho Chi Minh Trail electronic wall on the bar counter using matches and little umbrellas. Like so many other things then, it was, he'd tell you, a theoretically brilliant Company idea ruined by the idiots in Defense.

I forgot the theory, but not the surveillance tricks I'd learned in CID. Not the drinking. After college Alison became a photographer, opened a gallery, managed a camera shop. Along the way she got into personal training, began to spend more and more time in the gym, taught self-defense classes on campus. Just to be near her I would sometimes play the guest villain in these classes, allow myself to be covered with padding and then pummeled and tossed around on the mats. I was working for other private detectives by then, doing their legwork, handling the nuts and bolts of missing-persons or divorce work, sitting long hours in rented vans, installing cameras in a lot of bedrooms. Watching people.

There were times when I carried the job over to my normal life. I remember watching Alison coming out of Doc Films with two other women, all three dressed in jeans and halters; I followed them to the Medici, even watched them for a few minutes through the windows before realizing what an ass I was making of myself. I once saw her with another man at a concert, watched them holding hands, and thought about the different ways I could tap her phones or bug her bedroom.

I'm embarrassed to think of that now. I can attribute it to the alcohol, use the eighteen months I did in prison as an excuse. But she's probably right about me caring more about the past than she does. Part of that is the way I think of myself. I can't carry a gun. I can't get a P.I. license. There's no name for what I do now. I'm an ex-con. An ex-detective.

i'm drifting. Most of the bottle is gone. I've reached the point in the night where I customarily review my sins. It's a long list. I don't look for absolution; it's more like counting sheep. Once in a while I think about those pictures that Crowley showed us.

When Alison comes back out, she's still wearing the long dress. She sits on the couch. She yawns. She turns her body gently toward mine and then puts her head on my lap. I rub her shoulders while she says a few more things about Charles and Tracy and we talk for a few minutes before my hands go farther down her back and find the low end of her dress and then we don't talk anymore.

my legal residence is on the North Side of Chicago. I have an apartment there, four rooms that once belonged to a dentist. They're small and cramped. I have my work files there and most of my clothes. My gun, a Sig 9mm, stays there, buried in the sock drawer. There's beer in the refrigerator, a bottle of Wild Turkey under the sink. The medicine chest in the bathroom has razor blades and aspirin. I stay there one or two nights a week, when I'm working on the North Side, or when Alison's out of town, or when she's just tired of me, which given my personality you'd think would occur more often. My landlord, Minas, collects my mail. My answering machine collects my calls. Otherwise the place pretty much runs itself.

Every once in a while Alison and I talk about moving in together. Sometimes the discussion revolves around how silly it is to pay two sets of bills or how much time we could save not having to drive back and forth. It's easier to frame the argument this way, I think, in terms of convenience rather than emotional commitment. I guess there are worse reasons for moving in together than saving time on a commute.

We've never talked about marriage. The commute would have to be a lot farther to justify that.

Sunday morning starts slowly. The clock-radio reminds me how much my head hurts. Diana Ross is singing about a love hangover. I help Alison open PowerFemmes, shutting off the alarm system I installed that's blinking in the locker room.

Alison has personal training sessions with clients scheduled for most of the day. A couple of her students are getting ready for local competitions. Women's bodybuilding is all over the map these days—men go strictly for size, but women have to remain "feminine," and are divided about what that means. Alison has both kinds of clients, some training for Ms. Power Chicago who want their muscles cut and defined like men. And she has clients training for Ms. Fitness Chicago, who are more into aerobics and staying lean, and think the lifters are gross. The common denominator is Alison and the intensity of her workouts. Alison is lean but very strong.

The rooms always have a stale, musty feel until we get the air-conditioning on, like a movie theater at the first show. There were Realtors here before we moved in, a record store before that. Alison wanted a bare-bones look, which certainly fit her budget. Other than full-length mirrors she left the walls bare. The weights and most of the equipment we bought used from another gym in Lawndale. We sniffed everything before we bought it, then hauled it to Hyde Park in a rented milk truck. We scrubbed everything with Lysol, and you can still smell that before the air-conditioning begins circulating the air.

One night a week the place goes coed, which gives the women a chance to drag their boyfriends or husbands away from their books to see what goes on in here. It was conceived as good marketing strategy, good community PR, but I think Alison considers it good deterrence—a lot of the women who train here followed Alison from the self-defense classes she holds on campus, in church basements. Alison teaches kick boxing and judo; she lettered in four sports at Chicago. She's a Title IX poster girl. Her classes in self-defense—"relationship counterterrorism"—are for women who've decided to hit back. I think Alison decided to hit back the second the doctor slapped her.

She always starts each self-defense class with a table full of books.

"Most of you are students or scholars, and there are studies here on rape from just about any perspective—they can give you profiles of the

potential rapists, they can give you patterns, they can give you crime statistics. . . . I think they're all a waste of time. You can be attacked anywhere, anytime, by anyone."

"We're meeting Beth for an early dinner," she says, removing her windbreaker, tucking her mesh top into red running shorts. "Just the three of us. Her idea." That's as close as she's come to mentioning Charles. We woke up at different times, ate breakfast separately. It was a short night. Neither one of us slept very well. I ingested six cups of coffee before leaving the apartment, listened to Dusty Springfield singing Jacques Brel. Very melancholy. I look like death warmed over. Alison did sit-ups, drank water, swallowed designer proteins, listened to Metallica and Nine Inch Nails. Alison looks fine.

"We should have a good crowd tonight for coed night," she says. "I've picked up a lot of new members lately. A whole class just for stomach crunches." She charges a lot for personal sessions, says it's therapeutic and makes her students work harder. I think Freud said the same thing about analysis. I don't know Freud's view on stomach crunches.

A woman comes to the office door, knocks lightly. She's deeply tanned despite the season, muscular beyond belief. Her black hair's pulled back into braids. She's wearing cutoff shorts and a Power-Femmes tank top. "Sorry I'm early," she says to Alison. "I'll just get started, do some stretching."

"I'll be right out," Alison says. "We want to get your back worked on today. Michelle? Have you met my friend Harding?"

Michelle and I shake hands. She has bright eyes, a friendly smile. Alison tells her to be sure to limber up first, especially the hamstrings. We both watch Michelle walk away. I might hold my gaze a little longer.

"Down, boy," Alison says to me. "She's seriously married."

"I was just admiring her . . . symmetry. That's what you call it, right?" Actually, Michelle looks a bit like Alison, though her body's on another level. "Where are we meeting Beth?"

"The faculty club."

"Isn't that an odd place for her to choose?"

"She's not gonna wear a bag over her head, Harding. Besides, there's nobody there on Sunday nights. And it'll do her good to get out." She comes over to my side of the desk. "Have you talked to Boone yet?"

"Not since last night."

"I was trying to think of somebody to call about Tracy . . . I could just go over to the Women's Center and ask around, see if anyone knew her—"

"Let me see what I can find out first," I tell her.

I help her move the mats out; I put a new bottle of water on the dispenser. I check the bathroom to make sure it's clean. I make sure there are lots of towels. They go through a lot of towels here. By noon there are a dozen women working off the excesses of the weekend. Pat Benatar is blasting from the speakers. The room is a curious mixture of perfume and sweat. The grunt level is very high. There are one or two women in matched outfits, but most are dressed like guys in gym class—shorts, tank tops, sweatshirts cut at the shoulders. The only spandex in the room is on the cleaning woman, vacuuming the front room, her image reflected in six different mirrors. It's one of my least favorite exercises, the Hoover Sweep.

It's Convocation Sunday; the quarter's over next week. I walk to the Co-op and look through the *Trib* and the *New York Times* and then sit for a minute at a little café in the middle of the store. I'm back to my normal style of dress, if you can call it a style—blue jeans, work shirt, brown bomber jacket. On weekends everyone in Hyde Park seems to shop at the Co-op, the store is full of students and faculty. A group of shoppers is debating the merits of the new produce-sprinkling system. It's an impassioned debate, as are most arguments in Hyde Park. Even a woman handing out SnackWells samples in little paper cups is struggling to stay behind her card table.

I carry a very cheap cell phone, but I don't trust it; I use pay phones whenever I can. I use one now to call Boone at his apartment on Cornell Avenue. He says he talked to a friend in the humanities department about Tracy Lawrence but came up empty. The magazine known as *Mermaid* may or may not have ever seen the light of day.

"If it did, they'd have it at Regenstein," he says. "In the journals collection."

"What about Logan Pollard?"

"Pollard I talked to, but it turns out his ex was the one that drug him to that party, she was the one into 'zines and maybe into the editor, too—"

"Who was the editor?"

"He didn't know. Pollard's not a real friendly guy to begin with. And since he associates all that with his ex, he's not real happy strolling down memory lane."

"Maybe we should try the ex."

"She moved to Brazil."

"Wonderful."

"If you wanna take a run at Pollard yourself, be my guest. Try the CyberBeanery in Wicker Park, that's where I found him, and I got the feeling he's there a lot. I think he reads poetry at the Friday-night slams."

"Another poet? Just what I need."

"This place is caffeine and computers. It's a great place to pick up chicks. Chicks love poetry. The whole place is addictive. Have you ever fucked around in a chat room?"

"No."

"You can be anyone you wanna be. Night before last I was Tanya, exotic goddess of the east. I spoke in pig Russian."

"That must have turned on the kids. Why don't you just sign on as yourself?"

"I'm myself all day. I get tired of myself."

"How'd it go?"

"I struck out," he says. Boone is the only cyberslut who cannot get laid.

i walk down Lake Park past the white Art Deco university bank building. It's a dull day, typical for Hyde Park. The only sign it's Sunday is the church bells that serenade you outside the Cove while you wait for the accordion fence to be unlocked, the taps hooked up, the bottles opened.

On Kimbark I pass the redbrick building where Alison and I once shared a closet-size efficiency: seventy-two dollars a month including heat and parking. Paid in cash, from tips Alison made waitressing and the minimum wage I made pumping gas at a two-pump Texaco on Cottage Grove. The probation office found me the job. That was the last time we lived together full-time. It was a small apartment. It got a little crowded.

Regenstein Library is open and fairly deserted for a Sunday; the campus must be emptying out. The guard barely looks at my ID despite the hours I spent constructing it. I check their computer to see if Tracy's published anything in books or journals, but there's nothing there. Something like *Mermaid* might have been off the radar, though. As leads go, this one is fairly obscure. But I assume Crowley and the cops are checking the obvious ones.

The journals are temporarily buried in the basement, where the air smells like it's been recycled a few too many times. *Mermaid* did indeed see print, though for only one issue. It's bound now with a dozen other failed campus periodicals in library orange.

I take the book to a carrel that smells like body odor and sweat and skim the pages of *Mermaid*. The pages are sea-blue, glossy; the type is difficult to read, needlessly obscured by photos or drawings. There's nothing by Tracy listed in the table of contents. But the centerfold is a garish picture with dolls and two nude women, posed in frozen tableau, their bodies deconstructed into parts. The whole thing's superimposed over bits of dialogue. It might be bad poetry, it might be from a chat room.

> do you remember where we were
> fucking baby
> which time
> uh the second i think
> because i wrote for a while thinking you were still there
> sorry
> all alone jesus i hate being alone
> i know, i know
> that's okay i'm just trying to remember
> should we start
> you can start anywhere . . . i can start if you want
> —
>
> —
>
> are you there
> are you there
> are you there

One of the women is Tracy; the other—younger, with dyed red hair, a lip piercing—gets a model credit at the bottom of the page. Her name's Gretchen Moss. The copyright date on the magazine is last December.

There's no credit for the photography. There's no editor listed either, which is strange—just a faculty adviser, half a dozen contributors, and a "special thanks to Crystal Royce." A girl at the reference desk loans me a campus directory; Crystal Royce and Gretchen Moss are the only ones still listed. The other contributors must have graduated. The faculty adviser must have moved on to yet another one-year appointment.

I'm not sure how important any of this is. It's the closest I've gotten to Tracy. That doesn't mean it's important to anybody else.

When I call Gretchen Moss and mention Tracy, the name takes a few seconds to register before she says, Oh, how is Tracy, doing these days? She says she can meet me in the lobby of her dorm, Woodward Court, if I want to talk, though she sounds slightly baffled by the idea.

The woman who merited a "special thanks," Crystal Royce, has two numbers listed in the campus directory. The first lands me at the development office, which probably means that Crystal helped finance *Mermaid*. I leave a message. The second lands me in her bed, where I sense I've interrupted something.

"Tracy Lawrence?" she says in a breathy, sexy voice that I don't think is for my benefit. "And you said your name was—darling, just a second, please . . . I don't think I know any Tracy Lawrence."

I mention *Mermaid,* her name on the masthead.

"Oh God, baby, don't do that while I'm on the phone," she says, "save it for later, pretty pul-lease—"

I remind her about the photographs.

"Oh God, yes, those pictures," she says. "I tried to tell him they should leave those pictures out, but some people you simply cannot talk to—not you, darling, I love the way *you* talk to me—"

"Who did you tell this to?"

"The editor, of course. Why? And why does this interest you?"

"I'm doing a piece for the *Reader* on college sex. Who was the editor?"

"No, wait, baby, *pul-lease,* Mama's almost done—"

"Ms. Royce? There's no editor listed."

"Pollard," she says. "His name was Pollard. And I told him not to run those pictures, but some people—baby, please, if you do that one more time, I will simply go *through the roof*—"

"What about the women in the pictures, do you remember anything—"

But she doesn't answer. Baby hangs up the phone.

So Pollard lied to Boone about *Mermaid*. He even constructed a little improvised tale about his wife and the editor. It's a strange thing to lie about. I change a dollar in the coffee room, photocopy the masthead and the pictures, and then put the heavy orange volume on the cart. I'm told that art enriches the spirit, but the illustration is too reminiscent of Tracy's crime-scene photos. It's good to get back outside into the fresh air.

Woodlawn Avenue south of 57th reminds me of Embassy Row, beautiful homes now used as offices. Frank Lloyd Wright's Robie House is on 58th Street, sadly in need of repairs. The brick is crumbling. Air conditioners are jammed into the narrow windows.

Across the street is Woodward Court, a late-fifties dorm on its last legs. I show the girl at the desk a fake staff ID, ask her to ring Gretchen Moss, then sit on a backless couch, wondering why anyone would build such a thing. The campus cop on duty knows me well enough to nod hello.

In a few minutes Gretchen Moss comes down a narrow hallway wearing a hooded sweatshirt, jeans, and a school football jacket— maroon and white—and carrying a purple backpack. She regards me suspiciously, which is perfectly understandable. She wants to stay by the desk, so we sit on the backless couch.

"I only have a minute or two," she says, pushing her backpack under the couch. "I'm meeting someone at Court Theatre." She's the girl in the photograph all right, with the dyed red hair, black roots. She still has the lip piercing, and she's added two or three in her eyebrows. Her breath smells like she's just had a cigarette. "It's weird you asking about Tracy, I always wondered what happened to her. . . ."

"Were you good friends?"

"No, not really—we worked together at a veggie place for a month or so. But this was, like, a year and a half ago. I was still a freshman. Why?"

"The police are trying to figure out where she's been the last few months."

"Police?" She's pulling on a strand of her red hair. Her finger-nails are painted shiny black, with little white half-moons. "Did something happen to her?"

"She was killed last October."

"Shit, really?" A group of girls walks by, Gretchen waves at them nervously. "I didn't know. . . ."

"What was the name of the restaurant?"

"Casa Cucumber," she says. "Killed? Like, murdered?" I nod. She looks at me a bit differently now. "You didn't say you were a policeman."

"I'm not, Gretchen. Just a private detective."

There's a radio playing, tuned to the campus station. Usually they play modern stuff, but some goofball named Screaming Larry is doing a three-day marathon of seventies music as a reunion fund-raiser. He's on 1978: Patti Smith's "Because the Night." I am a big Patti fan.

They can't hurt you now,
can't hurt you now

"You know, I was at the launch party for *Mermaid* magazine, Gretchen, but I don't remember you being there. Or Tracy. And I talked to Logan Pollard, but I guess his wife left for South America or something."

She stares at me a second. The strand of red hair is wrapped around her finger.

"Were those pictures Tracy's idea? The ones with the two of you and the dolls?"

"You talked to Pollard?" she says.

"There's no photographer listed—or editor, for that matter—"

"How did you get in here?" she says, looking around for the guard. "They make you show an ID—are you a student? Because you're kinda old to be a student. So how did you get in?" Before I can answer, she's on her feet, slinging the backpack protectively over

73

her shoulder. I have to hurry to catch up with her outside on the sidewalk.

"Look, I've got Mace and pepper spray," she says, backing away from me, looking me in the eyes. "And I know how to defend myself. Okay? I took a class."

"If you took it in Hyde Park, my girlfriend Alison probably taught it."

"At the Women's Center? Tall, black-haired chick?" I nod, and she relaxes a bit. I don't crowd her. I do show her a phony PI license. She's more spooked by what I said than by my presence. Was it Pollard's name?

"Sorry to get weird on you," she says, setting off again in her Doc Martens.

"No problem."

"She was fairly awesome. She's really your girlfriend?"

I nod.

"You're kinda old to have a girlfriend," she says.

"Well . . . I can't argue with you there."

We walk past the Oriental Institute toward the main quadrangle. This is the last week before winter break, and most students are either taking exams or packing U-Hauls. Gretchen tells me about her classes and a paper on Hegel she has to absolutely, positively finish today by five P.M. I wait until we're nearly to Botany Pond before returning to the subject of *Mermaid.* She seems surprised that Pollard didn't tell me everything since he was the editor and publisher and photographer.

"There was an ad in the *Maroon* calling for contributions. I sent in a couple of things, pretty bad, I guess, but Logan called me and told me how promising they were, et cetera . . . lots of bullshit. He wanted what he wanted. I didn't know any better, I was just a freshman." She says this as though the intervening year had been a lifetime. "Of course nothing of mine ever got into the magazine . . . other than my naked butt."

"Pollard was in the English department?"

"I guess."

"And Tracy?"

"We were both waiting tables. It was pretty clear he'd handed us both the same line of B.S. When she saw the pictures, she went ballistic. He just superimposed that shot of me onto the dolls. It's a really cheesy fix." She shakes her head. "If I'd known he was such a jerk, I wouldn't have posed for those shots—"

" 'Those'?"

"We had a couple of sessions," she says.

"Where was Tracy living then?"

"I dunno. She was dating Pollard, she might have been living with him. They showed up together a lot at the restaurant."

"Casa Cucumber." She nods. I remember the place, a misguided attempt at an upscale vegetarian restaurant. People will only pay so much for lentil loaf. It was on the near North Side. They had a nice bar, though, where I downed more than a few organic wheat beers. Which means I might have seen Tracy then . . .

"Was Pollard photographing Tracy, too?" I say. She stops to light a cigarette and pulls the hood up around her neck.

"From what I could gather," she says, "Pollard was photographing a lot of women, if you know what I mean. Though Tracy was definitely his favorite. What she saw in him I have no idea."

Traffic is stopped on 57th Street; there's been some kind of small fender-bender near the crosswalk. Sometimes it's hard to see on days like this, despite the raw sun. Gretchen adjusts the backpack on her shoulder and stands just outside Hull Gate watching the two parties arguing over who had the right-of-way.

"Where did Pollard photograph you?" I say.

"Me? In my room, in the quads. Wherever. There was only the one nude and of course that's the one he used."

"And Tracy?"

"I don't know where he did her. His place maybe. I think she mentioned that her session with Pollard got a little strange."

"How so?"

She shrugs. "She didn't say any more than that." She hasn't seen Tracy since then, doesn't know where she'd been living.

I'm focused on Gretchen and so it takes me a minute to notice the long line of cars on 57th, another to pick out the black Cadillac with the same vanity plate: KEWL ONE. The windows are partly tinted, partly dirty. I can't see who's driving. Somebody's keeping an eye on me, and they don't seem to mind me noticing them.

It's happened before—I do a lot of missing-persons work, skip traces, bail jumpers, and there's often a relative or girlfriend unhappy with my efforts. My number's in the book, and I'm not hard to find.

"There's somebody else you could talk to," she says. "The hostess at Casa Cucumber—she knew Tracy better than I did, and I think she's still around; I saw her at the Medici a couple of Sundays ago."

The Cadillac pulls around the accident. I can't go after it without spooking Gretchen. "What's her name?"

"Crystal Royce," she says, pulling her backpack up tighter. "Just don't mention my name, we didn't really get along. She's sort of a slut, in a retro-fifties dumb-blonde way. And please don't mention me to Logan Pollard. Ever." She squints across the street at Regenstein Library and puts out her cigarette. The theater is still another block beyond. The black Cadillac has moved on. I have more questions, but Gretchen is already crossing the street. "I think I can make it from here," she says, meaning it's time for me to go. And she walks away a bit faster than before.

8

The coffee bars are staking out their niches. There's a string of them along Milwaukee Avenue in Wicker Park, tucked between the galleries: Kerouac's, Buddy Greco's. Kerouac's is fifties hip, beatnik. Buddy's, two doors down, is postbeat. Instead of Dylan and the Weavers and Farinas, they're playing the MOR pop that clogged up the Grammys in the sixties: Andy Williams, Anita Kerr, Jack Jones, Vikki Carr. The cashier's fourteen or fifteen, dressed like Lana Cantrell in mini and with Joey Heatherton hair. Lana herself, long forgotten, is on the Dual turntable, remembering when the world was young.

Ah, the apple trees. . .

There's a new tea boutique across the street, a caffeine-free zone down the block. And then there's the CyberBeanery. Its gimmick is computers. It's full of high school students, web-footed friends networking. A stenciled sign on the front window curls from a printer, and the words curl upward, too, like the prologue to *Star Wars*. Friday night is the weekly VR Poetry Slam. *Words Screaming 'Cross the Skies* hyper-hypertext.

The clerk is behind the counter, fussing with the cappuccino machine. He has a steel-blue apron strapped to his torso like a bulletproof vest; plastic "trainee" badges pinned to both shoulder straps; two earrings; and piercings in his eyebrows. There may be more, but I don't want to think about it. I'm hoping the badges aren't pinned directly to his shoulders.

"Hey," he says, nodding with polite interest, the blank look of commerce. He has wild Jerry Garcia hair, steel wool combed and forced into a part.

"Tall latte," I say.

"How about a fresh scone to go with that? Six varieties, baked fresh—"

"I think just the coffee."

Logan Pollard sits at a corner table studying a *Wall Street Journal.* I might have seen him at the *Mermaid* party, but I wouldn't know him without the corporate ID clipped to his jacket. Boone said he was a speed freak, but he looks more like an accountant. These days the two aren't mutually exclusive. He's very thin, with black hair freshly cut but still curling slightly behind his thick horn-rims. He's wearing light blue trousers with a Haggar sport coat, part of their spring collection circa 1974. I had one just like it in high school.

The clerk gets my order and hands me a small mouse-shaped card. I should have worn my screen-saver tie. "You get a free hour on the computer," he says. "As a first-time customer." I can't quite place the music that's playing; it might be Tangerine Dream or Orb, it might be Brian Eno's *Music for Airports.* Everything's bathed in white noise.

Pollard folds his *Wall Street Journal* and brings an oversize white mug up for a refill. He must be six-nine, but thin and awkward, all elbows and knees, what a basketball coach would consider a "project." He's well past recruiting age, though. And he walks with a slight limp, favoring his right foot.

"One more for the road, Jamie," he says to the clerk, pushing the mug forward like it was a shot glass with long Uriah Heep fingers. Jamie nods, gets Pollard his refill of Kenya blend, piles six brown sugars like sandbags.

When I tell Jamie I'll need some help getting on-line, he hesitates. "I'm more the coffee dude," he explains. "The computer dude should be here by five—"

"I can help," Pollard says softly, shaking his head. His eyes meet mine. It's the kind of moment often shared by responsible adults in the presence of shiftless teenagers. "I'm in here so much they should be paying me anyway. You want me to use the IBM or the Toshiba, Jamie?"

Jamie says as far as he's concerned either one would be cool. Pollard walks slowly to a small workstation, puts his white Cyber-Beanery mug carefully on a black coaster, pulls up a second chair. The mug lists the winners of recent poetry slams, with Pollard's name at the top.

"You must be into computers to spend so much time here," I say.

"Not really. I like the coffee." Some of the high school kids watch Pollard. They give him a wide berth. There are only one or two girls here today, the demographics of a video arcade. "I do come here for the poetry slams sometimes and read a little something." He pauses, rubbing his pants. "Let's see now, we just need a user name. Something real, something made up. Something you'll remember."

"My name's Harding," I say.

"We can use that," he says. "Logan Pollard." He doesn't extend a hand. "Though I suspect my corporate ID precedes me . . ."

"Dreamlike Display?"

"You haven't heard of us?" he says dryly. "We're on the cutting edge of mannequin technology—we make them, break them down, recycle them. We have the power of life and death over the little creatures." He unfolds his sentences like he unfolds his long body when he gets more coffee, slowly, deliberately.

"How does one get into the mannequin game?" I say.

"One inherits," he says. "One assumes one's family obligations, puts aside childish things, et cetera, et cetera . . ." He doesn't sound very happy about it.

"You know, we met once before," I say. "At a party in Hyde Park."

"My old stomping grounds," he says. "I don't get back there much. You sure you wouldn't want to use something else, a different name? Just for privacy's sake?"

"Harding's fine. I'm kind of used to it."

He types in something with long, graceful fingers. "Oddly enough, someone else was just asking me about those days. A coincidence? You're a friend of Boone's?"

"As a matter of fact, I am."

"Then you're the private detective. That's right. Harding. I remember now. You live with that woman, the exercise girl. Alison."

"You're partially right on both counts. How do you know Alison?"

He pauses. "Well, I don't know her per se," he says slowly, as though speaking to a child. "But when I lived in Hyde Park I became personally acquainted with her self-defense techniques."

"You took a class?"

"I dated a girl briefly, very, *very* briefly, who took a class." He gives me a small crooked smile, bends to raise the trouser leg from his right ankle. The sock was already sagging into Pollard's penny loafer. "Seven bones in my right foot were broken. That's a sixty-percent kill rate, or so I was told by the orthopedic surgeon who did the reconstruction. He was quite impressed. I was on crutches for two months. I used to like to cross-country ski. Impossible. And with these scars . . . I can't wear sandals anymore in the summer."

"She knows a lot of moves like that," I say. "Defensive moves."

"Some defensive move. My God. You could conquer the Huns with defensive moves like that."

"It still bothers you?"

"It still bothers me," he says. "Certain days, certain kinds of weather. You shatter bone like that, little tiny pieces, it never heals right." He finally drops the trouser leg. Sometimes his crooked little smile stays fixed to his face a bit longer than necessary. "Excuse me, I didn't mean to be so melodramatic. Unfortunately, it tends to remind me of that girl I was dating."

"Boone probably asked you about Tracy Lawrence," I say. "And that magazine you edited, *Mermaid.*"

"To be honest, Boone didn't make much sense," he says, watching three security cops file in from neighborhood stores, wearing three different uniforms. It's a rent-a-cop convention. Pollard appears to grow a little nervous. "Which is normal for Boone. To tell you the truth, I wasn't paying very close attention. He was rambling. Which again is normal for the man."

"But you knew Tracy, right? From the restaurant and from the magazine—I mean, I heard you were practically living together for a while there. . . ."

He doesn't answer, just picks at a button on his shirt.

"I was looking at a copy of *Mermaid,*" I say. "Those photos of Tracy are quite . . . provocative." He looks at me calmly, doesn't bite. "And someone told me there were other pictures of her—quite a few, in fact."

"You've been talking to Crystal Royce," Pollard says, rubbing his trousers. His fingers are always touching something: his clothes, the keyboard, the ceramic mug full of cold coffee. "Crystal will say anything. My involvement with that magazine was peripheral at best. I lent a hand when it became apparent no one else had a clue as to what the editorial focus should be. I helped select the pieces, nothing more."

"You photographed Gretchen Moss, didn't you? And Tracy?"

"Ah." He swivels in his chair to look at me. "It was Gretchen who told you this, I assume." The look on his face makes me wish I'd kept her out of it. "Beware of Miss Gretchen. Gretchen has issues."

"With you?"

"With men in general." He gets up and takes his coffee mug back to his own table. He limps a little more than he did before. He says something to Jamie, who's cleaning the monitors now, yellow Windex bottles strapped on like six-guns. I wait until I see him gathering his things together, then I follow him out a side door. I ask him how well he knew Tracy Lawrence.

"Are you playing detective with me?" he says, turning up his coat collar. We're on Milwaukee walking toward the Double Door. The wind's blowing very hard. I'm not used to looking up—I'm six-two in my socks—but Pollard looms over me like an underfed giant. "Asking all these questions—I don't *like* answering questions—"

"Tracy Lawrence was murdered, Pollard," I say, grabbing his arm. "I'm trying to find out what she's been doing the past few years. When somebody lies about knowing her, I'm naturally curious."

He stops and stares at me. His reaction is more surprised than Gretchen's, but he may just be a better actor. "You should have just told me that up front," he says, pulling his arm away. "I didn't know. I'm sorry." He looks around as though he's forgotten where he was headed. "Look, I lost some money on that magazine. So did a few other investors. I thought maybe you were working for one of them."

"So what can you tell me about Tracy?"

"Not very much, I'm afraid. We went out once or twice for coffee when she was working at that dreadful vegan place. Gretchen and Crystal both worked there, too, but I suppose you know that already."

"How does Crystal Royce fit into this?"

"She worked for the development office then. She managed to get us a little grant for *Mermaid,* that's all. And she introduced me to Tracy. She liked putting writers together. She's sort of a writers' groupie, actually. A poor man's Lady Gregory."

"Where was Tracy living?"

"She had a place in Lincoln Park, on Cleveland, I think . . . I'm not sure. She was working on a prose poem that unfortunately wasn't very good—as that little collage she submitted to *Mermaid* demonstrates. Using dialogue and chat-room transcripts . . . it was dated even then. I published it mostly as a favor."

"She did that herself? You didn't photograph her?"

He shakes his head. "Not Tracy. I did photograph Gretchen but only at her request. She had some misguided idea that she might be a model. Like Tracy with her writing. Everyone has delusions of grandeur, Harding, as I'm sure you know. Sooner or later reality sets in."

"It hasn't hit me yet." He's swaying a bit, either from the wind or something he's taken. His eyes look dull. "When was the last time you saw her?"

"God, a year at least. As I recall, she was moving to Paris or Morocco or somewhere. Another expatriate artiste." We pause for a light at North Avenue, then cross against traffic. "Do they know who killed her?"

"They have a few suspects. She was killed in Galena or East Dubuque—at least that's where they found the body."

"Never been there," he says. "But then I rarely travel, unless it's with the imagination. Or the computer. I escort different people now, in those rooms—"

"Chat rooms."

"I correct their spelling," he says, "and their grammar. And I lead them. . . . They have no imagination. I give them a cheap thrill."

"What does it do for you, Pollard?"

He stops walking, puts one gloved hand before his mouth. "Oh, it's a diversion," he says. "It can be amusing. One gets bored. I certainly don't find it stimulating in any erotic sense."

"No?"

"Oh no . . . I need flesh and bone for that," he says.

9

donnie Wilson is waiting for me at a client's place in Beverly. He's been hired to protect the Lowry Stone and Gravel Works. There must be a lot of money in gravel or Donnie wouldn't have been lured this far south. There's certainly a lot of gravel. There are giant teepees full of sand. There are mountains of loose rock. A cartoonish mural in the lobby shows muscular men using heavy steel cranes and front loaders—it's the kind of hard work I try to avoid. I imagine they go home very tired, take long showers, sleep well. They probably have to empty their shoes a lot, too.

Donnie completes his business with the gravel guys and then we take a little walk through the grounds. Even though it's Sunday there are workmen milling about. "We're going deer hunting next weekend," he says to me. "The second season starts tomorrow. You wanna come?"

"I'll pass. Since when did you know how to hunt deer?"

"I do what the clients do," he says. "If they want me to hunt, I can hunt." He's dressed business casual today, his South Side look; usually he's in Armani or Kenneth Cole. "Deer, squirrel, whatever. Bow and arrow if they want to play cowboys and Indians. I can play badminton in little white shorts if that's what they want. Long as they pay me." There's always a pedometer clipped to his thin leather belt, a SmartStep monitor watch on his wrist—Donnie waits for the massive coronary that took his father at forty, lives each day listening to his heart. I think sometimes it must feel like a rock.

"They're giving me that 'one shot' bullshit," he says. "Gotta kill the deer with one shot. Some kind of Zen shit. Asking don't I need to do that in my line of work."

"They got that from the movie."

"I told them when I shoot at something that's armed, I go for one shot. Your ethnic with a semi-auto I put down with one shot. With Bambi I don't see the fucking urgency."

I nod, waiting.

"So . . . you're still interested in this job I mentioned?"

"I'm interested. I wouldn't be here if I wasn't. But I haven't heard anything about the money."

"The money's good," Donnie says. "For what you have to do, the money's damn good." He runs through it quickly. There's a businessman, an ex-wife, lots and lots of alimony. The client wants details: what's she doing, who's she doing, what's she saying. The money is indeed very good: two grand. I know the building, a high-rise on 47th Street called Lake Village East. It's the kind of work I've done for Donnie dozens of times.

I assume it's one of the gravel guys, but Donnie doesn't go into details. He likes to run the show, and he likes to keep me away from the clients. I have no problem with that. Everything he wants me to do is more or less illegal, of course. That's why he wants me for the job. That's why he's paying two grand.

"Oh, yeah, before I forget," Donnie says, pausing to scrape some mud off his Cole Haans with a mica-colored stone. "I ran that plate for you."

"I hope it wasn't too much trouble."

"Nah, I used Lake Forest, they've got nothing to do up there anyway." His hands are dirty now; I think he'd like a Handi Wipe. He settles for a Kleenex. "Our first branch on the North Shore. They needed somebody to protect all that old money. I felt it was my civic duty." The name he gives me is Travis Savick. "Mr. Savick lives in Uptown." That's a fairly rough neighborhood; lots of gangs, lots of addicts. Donnie doesn't have an office there.

"Does that help you?" he says.

"Not really, but thanks." Actually, the name does have a distinctly redneck sound to it. A lot of Appalachian whites live in Uptown. And the last two cases I worked on were bail jumpers who ran south.

He checks the monitor on his belt, frowns at the readout. He asks how Alison is doing, whether the gym is making any money. And then, almost as an afterthought, he takes out a pair of reading glasses and unfolds them while handing me another sheet of paper. This one is a badly Xeroxed picture of a woman's neck, the face above cropped off, a black necklace being the center of attention. "If you run across this inside the ex-wife's—now, don't tear the place apart—but if you happen to see it, bring it along. Okay?" The reading glasses look a bit small for Donnie's face. "He thinks she keeps it in the bedroom dresser, bottom drawer. In a sock, if you can believe that."

I stare at the Xerox, hoping the picture and the job might come into better focus somehow. "You didn't mention the necklace last time," I say. Donnie has me off-balance again, one of his better management skills. "What's it worth?"

"The client says very little. It was a gift he regrets. Since you're going inside for the wiretaps he thought he'd like it back."

"Uh-huh."

"He says it has sentimental value."

"It also turns the job from breaking and entering into burglary."

"Harding, you know as well as I do, they classify every break-in that way whether or not you lift something, so why not lift something? As long as it doesn't lift you into a major felony."

"And this doesn't."

"Absolutely not. You place the bugs, run the wires, let me know the frequencies. If you have to leave an amp somewhere, let me know that, too."

"You don't want me running the surveillance, making the tapes?"

He shakes his head. "Set the thing up, make sure it's running.

We want the phones, we want the living room, we want the bedroom. And we need it soon. I'm leaving town tomorrow."

"Well, I can take a look at it tonight, but I can't promise anything. I sure don't have anything that will transmit from a high-rise."

He kicks a stone across the snow. He checks the wrist monitor and the one on his belt, and this time gives a contented little grunt.

"I'm supplying the hardware," he says. "So you won't have any worries there. Brand-new stuff, state-of-the-art. Just make damn sure you wipe it down." We agree to meet again on Thursday, when Donnie gets back. I get half the money now, half then. There might be a bonus, it depends on the client.

We're at the front gate. I thought we were just wandering aimlessly around the grounds, but Donnie has led us right to his car. He pops the trunk on his silver Lexus and hands me a green Field's shopping bag. The equipment inside is still shrink-wrapped, though minus any tie to Donnie. It looks much newer, more expensive than I'm used to. I hope it comes with instructions.

10

S unday night Beth joins us for dinner at the Quadrangle Club. The first-floor bar is full, but the dining room's half empty. It's a little depressing. The front of the building always reminds me of a funeral home: moody lighting, a very somber green awning over the sidewalk. Alison reminds me that we're here to cheer Beth up, don't dwell on Charles. Don't mention Tracy. She's wearing a long, tight black skirt and a one-button black silk jacket. The jacket, and its neckline, will stay with me for a while.

"No news," Beth says glumly, sipping a glass of wine. She's wearing a dress, lots of polka dots, with cowboy boots and a beaded necklace. Her blond hair looks flat, as though she'd spent the afternoon in bed. "He could be in Argentina by now. I just don't understand it—we were so happy, everything was so perfect . . ."

"What's good here?" Alison says, examining the small menu card. "I never eat here."

"What did the police have to say?" I ask Beth.

"They asked a lot of bizarre questions," she says. "Like they knew something I didn't know."

"The police always talk like that," Alison says. "They never know anything."

"When was the last time anyone saw him at the frat house?"

"Friday night, the middle of the night," Beth says. "He got a phone call. There's no phone in his room so they had to go up and wake him, that's the only reason they remember it. And that's it. He didn't come down for breakfast on Saturday . . . and no one saw him leave."

"Look, there's Professor Sprier," Alison says. "Dining alone, the poor dear. Yoo-hoo, Professor Sprier. Hello."

He responds with a wave of his fork.

"His wife left him," Beth says.

"Really? I'm so behind on my gossip."

"Another marriage on the rocks," Beth says. "I read in the *Sun-Times* today that fewer and fewer people are getting married, and those that do are less happy than ever before."

"That's the *Sun-Times*," Alison says. "Who reads the *Sun-Times?*"

"Sixty-three percent report feelings of dissatisfaction," Beth says. "Forty-three percent general malaise."

"They make those statistics up," Alison says. "You know that from your friend in urban sociology—"

"Ben Friedman."

"Ben Friedman, right. He publishes those crazy books about the joys of concealed handguns and nobody checks. Nobody reads the data. Nobody can interpret it except other statisticians. It's too boring to fact-check. And now can we talk about something more interesting? Like dinner? Harding?"

"I'm starving," I say.

"What are we eating?" Alison says, handing us the little order cards and tiny, putt-putt golf pencils.

"The stroganoff is good," Beth says. "Avoid the fish."

We write down our orders and hand the cards to the waiter.

"The police keep asking me about drugs," Beth says. "My first husband—I don't think either of you ever met him—"

"I saw the mug shots," Alison says.

"—was arrested once for drugs. They stopped his car and found some coke, so they keep asking me about that."

"Which has nothing to do with anything," Alison says.

"Charles has never had so much as a speeding ticket," Beth says. I'm watching her, slightly amazed at her attitude. She's still defending him despite everything that's happened.

"They always ask these questions," Alison says. "It's just routine."

"Plus they keep coming back to this week Charles spent in the hospital—again, I really don't see the relevance, and I thought medical records were private—plus I *told* them it wasn't a week, just a weekend, he checked himself out and the doctors said it was okay."

"You knew about this?" I ask Alison, but she shakes her head.

"When was this, Beth?" I say.

"Last January," Beth says. "Charles and I shared everything on that retreat we took in Wisconsin. We knew we had to be totally honest if the relationship was going to work. I told him I understood. Everyone gets depressed in the winter. It's such a tiny thing."

"That's where he proposed to you, isn't it?" Alison says. "On your birthday?"

Beth nods. "In the gazebo, he was down on one knee—"

"I thought that was *so* romantic," Alison says.

"Excuse me, but Charles was in a psychiatric ward?" I say.

"Only because that's where the rehab ward was. He checked himself right out, it was just one slip. I don't know how the police even knew about it."

I wonder what else the cops know about Charles. If I know Crowley, he's circulating Charles's name out of state, just to see what turns up. A short stretch in a psych ward doesn't look so bad on a poet's résumé, but to a cop it's more than just suspicious. It's abnormal.

Alison says she has to use the ladies' room. As she stands she turns to me and whispers, "Change the subject." I watch her walk from the room. As she leaves she mutters something else. It could be "More wine." It could be "Moron."

I pour Beth some more wine. "What are you teaching next quarter? Anything interesting?"

"Western Civ, we're lost in the Dark Ages. Grim death every-where."

"Beth . . . Alison's right. He'll be back soon."

She nods uncertainly.

"She's always right, about everything. But you know that—you grew up with her." I rearrange my silverware, a small-talk maneuver. "You were a couple years ahead of her, right? What was she like then?"

"Growing up? She was a handful," Beth says, smiling for the first time. "And I don't mean that in a cute way. She was always run-ning, just this bundle of energy, always moving. It could drive you crazy. She never shut up."

"Really?"

"I know, I know, she's sort of quiet now, isn't she? My theory is that she said absolutely everything she wanted to say by the age of ten. I'm half surprised she didn't just take some vow of silence and become a nun."

I consider this. But not for long. "I can't see Alison as a nun."

"But she was very religious then," Beth says. "For example, she never missed church. Never. I remember once she sent away for a series of books on the lives of the saints, her mom threw a fit when they started coming. But she read every one, cover to cover. Did you ever meet her mom?"

I shake my head.

"Alison looks just like her," Beth says. "Except for the long hair and tattoos. She gets her looks from her mom, her seriousness from her dad. Alison's focused, just like he was. Whether it's religion or working out, she never does anything halfway."

That's something I know about. Alison appears behind me. She's always sneaking up that way. "What were you saying about tat-toos?"

"I was telling Harding about your mom. That you look just like her."

"I don't," she says.

"Except for the long hair and tattoos," Beth says. "You do, Alison. You just don't want to admit it."

"I think it's you who looks like her mother, Beth," Alison says. "But that may just be due to the difference in our ages, dear."

It's my turn to use the rest room. What I really want to use is the phone, which is downstairs by the bar. I could use a scotch. I call Terry Crowley. It makes me feel like I'm back on probation, calling my parole officer.

"Charles Muller show up yet?" he says first thing, as though that's all that's on his mind.

"No."

"That's a hell of a thing," Crowley says. "Don't you think that's a hell of a thing?" He sounds short of breath. I wonder if they cut out everything they were supposed to.

"They don't know any more about what happened in that building?" I say.

"They know Ricky Lopez had more enemies than friends. Nobody wants to claim the body. There's supposed to be a brother, but nobody's heard from him. So he'll end up buried in a county lot. Where'd you say you was, the faculty club? What's for dinner over there tonight?"

"I'm having spaghetti. I've been warned off the fish."

"I had a nice piece of pike tonight that my brother Joey caught up in Sturgeon Bay—I couldn't taste it. Sometimes I can't smell nothing."

"Jesus."

"It's not like they cut something out of my nose, you know? But the doc says that don't matter. Everything's connected. You touch this nerve up here, something down here jumps."

"Who's handling the Lopez case now?"

"They're debating. Nobody wants it very much . . . it might end up in Narcotics, it might end up in Violent Crimes. It's not mine anymore, if that's what you mean."

"Have they pinned down the cause of death?"

"Blunt trauma," he says, wheezing just a bit. "His face collided with a fucking sidewalk. What the hell do you think cause of death is?"

"You don't have the lab work yet."

"Not yet," he admits. "The state lab is backed up. Did you find out anything about Tracy Lawrence?"

"A little, yeah. She was in Chicago eighteen months ago, living on the North Side, waitressing at a place called Casa Cucumber, working on a novel . . . and she may or may not have been living with a guy named Logan Pollard."

"That's it?"

"It's only been a day, Terry. I'm working on it. You might check out this guy Pollard, though. He knew Tracy from school."

"I hate that fucking college," he says.

"They won't talk to you?"

"They talk all night long," Crowley says. "They just don't say nothing."

"They're academics, Terry," I say. "They do that for a living." He coughs again. He sounds like he has bronchitis.

"You with Alison tonight?" he says. I tell him I am. "You tell her I did some checking out in Boulder and Denver. There was a woman attacked out there last June—she's leaving a restaurant, grabbed from behind, pulled into the bushes. Couldn't make an ID; he's wearing a ski mask, it's dark, et cetera, et cetera. But guess who's listed as a material witness? And gave a description of the alleged perp who for some reason they never could identify, much less find—"

"Charles Muller."

"You shoulda been a cop, Harding."

"When did you say this was, Terry?"

"Last June. Lemme see, I've got the date right here. Saturday, June twelfth." That's near the weekend when Charles met Beth in Hyde Park for the first time.

"They never made an arrest on that?"

"They looked real hard at the husband, who my source says was just this side of wacko. A professional astrologer. Told fortunes, read palms, the whole bit. But they never charged him. You tell Alison I would very much like to talk to old Charlie about all this, if and when he shows his face again. You tell her if he contacts her, she is to get in touch with me. Pronto."

"Did you talk to this woman, the one who was attacked?"

"No, I talked to the husband."

"The astrologer."

"Except he's not really an astrologer no more, he says. My source is out of date. He talks to dead people now, like a middle-man."

"You mean he's a medium."

"Medium, yeah. That's it. The first time he says it, I think he's telling me his suit size."

"Maybe the astrologer can help solve the case for you, Terry. Maybe he can talk to Ricky Lopez and ask him who threw him out the window."

"You want to watch your step with me right now, Harding. I feel like shit."

"So why bother with all this?"

"I smell something," he says. "I can't taste my food. I can't smell shit. But this fucking case . . . I dunno. I smell something here." An anthro professor I used to box out in pickup roundball stops me to say hello. He wants me as a ringer for a faculty team, but I think my full-court days are over. I'm wondering if I can get away with a quick scotch in the bar when my pager goes off. I don't recognize the number or the voice when I call it.

"Is this Mr. Harding?" he says.

I tell him it is.

"My name is Dahlgren. We met briefly at that unfortunate wedding, I believe. You were there with that delightful creature, Alison. Yes?"

"Yes to both, Professor. I was there. And she's delightful."

"I was wondering if I could have a word with you. Perhaps we could get together and have a cup of coffee."

"Now?" He has an irritating voice, at once mincing and cloying, the upper class trying to be seductive. Alison said he was a hypnotist, maybe he's trying to put me to sleep.

"If it's at all convenient," he says. "Sunday night is one of the few times I have some space in my schedule. Are you in Hyde Park now?"

"I'm having dinner at the faculty club."

"Well, then, you're five minutes from me. Have you had dessert yet? I have coffee and a cheesecake—both far superior to what they will serve you there. I only need a few minutes of your time. Could you indulge me, sir?"

When I return to the table, Alison squeezes my arm. "Everything okay?" she asks.

"Everything's fine." The food arrives. My spaghetti has meatballs. It smells like wine. "I'm apparently having dessert with Professor Dahlgren. He promised me cheesecake."

"Henry Dahlgren?" Beth says, spilling her drink. "Oh God. That has to be about Charles. They're having second thoughts about his appointment and they think Harding has some dirt. Oh God, oh God—"

"Beth, calm down," Alison says, mopping up the spilled wine. "This has nothing to do with Charles. Right, Harding?" I love the way she frames these questions as flat statements.

"Actually, no, Beth, it doesn't," I say. "It's a domestic matter, something about his wife. I shouldn't have even mentioned it."

"See?" Alison tells her. "What did I just say? He probably wants dirty pictures of that slut Moira for the divorce—in bed, on her knees—something perfectly innocent. Nothing to do with Charles's job."

Beth nods, partly reassured. "Henry deserves better," she says. "I never understood how he could put up with Moira, she seems like such a bitch."

"Well, people change. Moira didn't use to be a Moira," Alison says. "She used to be a Mo. She used to be nice."

A friend of Beth's, a faculty wife, stops by and says hello, patting her on the arm as she leaves.

"Everyone's being so nice," Beth says with a grimace. "I expect them to start bringing covered dishes. God. I thought this week would be the best week of my life . . . something to remember the rest of my life. Something to *change* my life. Make it better. And now . . ."

"Let's just eat," Alison says, "and try not to worry." She smiles at me.

"Good idea," I say. Beth nods.

"And let's say a prayer," Beth says, "that he's all right and he'll come back."

11

henry Dahlgren lives on South Blackstone Avenue in a two-story graystone that's small for the neighborhood. It's a beautiful house that hasn't been kept up very well. There are four or five large clay pots on the front porch with very dead flowers. The dirty windows look like leaded glass. The house doesn't match my memory of Dahlgren at the wedding: well dressed, in command. A very shiny gold-colored Audi sits in the driveway.

He greets me at the door as though we're old friends.

"Is your wife home by any chance?" I ask him as he takes my coat.

"I'm afraid not. Moira is . . . out for the evening. It will just be the two of us."

Dahlgren suggests we talk in the kitchen and I follow him there through a dining room filled with mission and southwestern furniture. We sit at a heavy pine table while he spoons some Stewarts into a gold filter. He seems to be in a hurry. There's a pair of black pottery salt and pepper shakers on the table, Indian baskets and sand paintings on the walls. I don't see any cheesecake.

"Cream and sugar?" he says.

"Black is fine."

"I can only drink one cup, otherwise I can't get to sleep." He's wearing a sport coat, light yellow shirt, and khaki pants. I sense that this is as informal as he gets. "I used to drink gallons of the stuff all day long. Of course I used to smoke cigars . . ."

"But no more?"

"My doctor says no." There's a beautifully refinished washstand with a rose marble top against the wall. Dahlgren turns on a small radio, finds a classical station. The signal wavers; Dahlgren moves the cord until he's satisfied with the sound. "Do you enjoy a good cigar, Harding?"

"On occasion."

"I try to limit myself to just one. But my self-discipline is severely tested whenever my source gets a new shipment of Cubans." The coffee is dripping now, too slowly for Dahlgren. He busies himself with cleaning a small plate at the sink.

"My dad smoked cigars," I say. "I don't think they were Cubans. I used to make banjos from the boxes with rubber bands. But I could never get the stink out of them."

"Bad associations?"

"Oh, you could write a book about my childhood, Professor."

"The past is a bitch," he says cheerfully. "Thank God for us, hmm, Harding? We both spend our time rooting around in other people's histories."

"But they never gave me tenure, Professor. And I suspect you're paid a bit better than I am. Alison said you did a lot of consulting?"

"I do, yes," he says, moving the glass carafe around as though that would make the coffee drip faster, tapping on the glass like a child with an aquarium. "I was always interested in diagnosis theory. Testing, evaluations, et cetera. You can pursue that in education, working on standardized tests and such, or you can move into the business world."

"I would think the business world would pay a bit more."

"Well, there are no school bond issues to deal with," he says, sitting down. "I've managed to expand my practice quite a bit in the last few years. I still teach, of course, but I'm affiliated with a very large firm. We have offices in the Loop, Oak Brook, Niles." He gets up once again to fetch more cream from the refrigerator. "Hypnotherapy is my main interest. Primarily teaching and research, although I do see a limited number of patients, mainly referrals. Have you ever been hypnotized?"

"No. I don't think I'd be a very good candidate."

"Not everyone is," he says. "The subject is often more important than the therapist." He pours the coffee, which is still dripping; some of it escapes onto the burner, and when he goes to wipe it up, he burns his finger, flinching for a split second before regaining control. "You know, I have a bit of experience myself in your line of work. Not as a detective, of course, but I have helped the police on occasion."

"Really."

"Oh yes. With memory improvement, recall. Helping a witness to remember a detail—the number on a license plate, for example. Or whether a suspect had brown or blond hair. That sort of thing. And I've done research on penal life, worked with prisoners, used hypnosis to try to change behavioral patterns. There is something inherently fascinating about criminally deviant behavior."

"But you don't make them take their clothes off or bark like a dog, I'm guessing." His voice is less irritating here than on the phone. A good shrink would need to have several voices, for different patients. I'm wondering what category Dahlgren puts me in. He looks like a man who makes a quick diagnosis.

Dahlgren looks around his table. I sense a mental checklist being examined. The coffee is poured. There's cream and sugar. He turns the radio off, puts on a CD of Renaissance or medieval music—I can't tell the difference. There are a lot of lutes. "Sunday nights are the only time I can relax," he says. He doesn't look very relaxed. He *sounds* relaxed, which is a neat trick; his voice is soothing even as he bounces around the kitchen. He finally turns the coffeemaker off and allows himself to sit down again.

"So," I say, and he nods as though I said something important. That's how shrinks make their living.

"I was wondering," he says, "what your take might be on the Charles Muller situation."

"I haven't given it much thought."

"Really?"

"Maybe I'm old-fashioned," I say. "But I think getting cold feet at the altar is perfectly understandable. I'm sure he'll come to his senses."

"And the entanglement with Mr. Lopez at that crack house?"

"I don't think he's involved with that. Do you?"

He crosses his legs. Even his casual pants have a sharp crease. "You must understand my situation, Harding. I'm charged by the dean to investigate every possibility."

"I didn't know there was an investigation."

"Sub rosa," he says. "It's a very important appointment, you see."

"I'm not sure what I can tell you, Professor. How did you get saddled with this? Why isn't the chairman of the English department investigating?"

"It's not an English department appointment. Charles is being hired by the Committee on Social Thought. And a chair like this requires a multidiscipline committee. As to why I seem to be in charge . . . that's because I was demented enough to volunteer."

"I didn't know it was a full chair. Charles?"

"You may not be aware of just how good a reputation he has. Both as a poet and a scholar." He refills my cup. "Things have a way of escalating. We don't want the problem to get out of hand. If there are complications . . . peripheral involvements by other parties . . . addenda, as it were . . . I would want to know."

"Of course." It's double talk, but I've lived in Hyde Park long enough to speak the language. He asks me who's in charge of the Lopez case and I tell him to contact Terry Crowley at the Twenty-first Precinct. He writes this down. I think he underlines it.

Then he gets to the real reason he's invited me here. "I was wondering if I might ask a favor of you," he says.

I nod in what I consider a very noncommittal way. I dislike

open-ended questions like this. They usually end with me doing a lot of work.

"I was wondering if you could possibly find room in your schedule to take a trip—a *very* brief trip—to Denver just to have a look around . . . as a personal favor to me. I know this is terribly short notice, and I do apologize."

"You think he's gone back there?"

"I don't know. His phone's been disconnected, but that may not mean anything. He was moving, after all. But it would ease my mind a bit if you were to have a look-see."

The doorbell rings, and when Dahlgren answers it, I hear a woman's voice—at first I think it's his wife, Moira, so I follow him to the door, but then that voice joins with eight or nine others in a Christmas carol.

"I played my drum for him
pa rum pa pum pum"

The group forms a half-circle around Dahlgren's porch, all dressed in Victorian clothing, one with a pennywhistle, another with a small tin drum. A chimney sweep with a broom bows and smiles at me, a crazy gap-toothed grin; I smile back. He has charcoal on his face, a sweep's raggedly formal clothes, and something green between his teeth, a nice authentic touch. Of course he might have simply gone for the pizza Florentine at Edwardo's.

We have to wait for all the verses. The leader's a professor named Tibbins; he conducts with tiny hummingbirdlike motions. When the sweep sings, his broom swings slightly off the beat and a small ponytail swings from an oddly shaped Mohawk. His silver earring swings, too, a large oval ring you could do gymnastics with, and then the song ends and he bows again and everyone tramps across the lawn to the next house. Dahlgren closes the door. "Are you supposed to tip them?" he says.

"I think you're supposed to offer them wassail."

He takes a call on his cell phone, one of those small flip-top models some people practically take to bed with them. As he's talking, he gives me a small piece of oddly shaped stationery with Charles Muller's Denver address, plus several other names, on it. Female names. It looks like company stationery with the letterhead cut off.

"These are friends of Charles's," he says, dropping the phone back in his pocket. "Lady friends. I thought maybe . . . well, you know."

"I don't think I want to get into that side of it." He nods, disappointed. "Don't you know anyone in Denver who could do this for you?"

"Well, yes and no," he says. "But it's difficult . . ." He sighs. The weight of the world is on his shoulders tonight. "As I said, the dean is very concerned. No one wants to see the university tarnished. There have been several negative stories about us recently and we don't need another. You're an alumnus, aren't you?"

I nod. He's starting to sound like a fund-raiser.

"From another, more personal point of view . . . well, both Charles and Beth are friends of mine. I care for them a great deal. And lately . . . I tend to value friendship more and more."

I suppose by this he means life since separating from Moira. I can see where she'd leave a certain void. Her presence at the wedding yesterday had apparently surprised everyone. Her absence from this house is already apparent. It feels like a widower's house, too quiet, too spare.

I'm remembering Alison's description of Moira as the "wildest one" of the three, the way she wore that one-piece to hide her tattoos, with the implied behavior that contrasts sharply with her husband's. They make an odd couple, but I've learned not to judge people by reputation or rumor. I've looked into too many windows for that.

As for the "favor" he's asking, it's simple enough to do. He hasn't mentioned money, but I do a lot of work in Hyde Park—this is just networking, like Alison with her faculty wives. It can't hurt for the dean to think of me as someone who can be turned to in a mess like this. And my schedule isn't exactly overbooked right now.

Dahlgren tells me he'd like me to leave tonight. "So I have something to tell the dean tomorrow at our meeting." He asks me if I'd like to phone the airport, then listens as I make the arrangements. I'm tempted to fly business class, so I can sleep on the plane, but Donnie's two grand will only go so far. Thank God I took that job; Donnie's the only one who's paying me.

He cleans up the kitchen again, rinses the cups, whistling Christmas carols. I feel like I've been through a job interview. But that may just be the way he talks to everyone. Alison mentioned something about him being in the military, and there's a bit of the retired general in him.

He puts a few things away in a hutch, and as he's straightening the drawer I see a flash of silver. It looks like a small gun, maybe a Beretta, but I don't have time to tell. It might just be something decorative.

"How did Beth seem to you at dinner tonight?" he says, drying his hands.

"As good as could be expected."

"Are the wedding plans on hold?"

"I think it's safe to assume that, yes."

We walk out through the living room, and he asks me if I've ever been to Colorado or New Mexico. I shake my head. "I'm just a city kid," I say. "But it looks like you've been there."

"Ah, yes. You mean the decorating. Well, Moira did that. She became infatuated with the Native American 'look' when she started sculpting."

"She's an artist?"

"Oh, yes," he says. "She paints, too. That's one of her works on the wall in the dining room behind you."

It's a brightly colored landscape—at least I think it is. It's one of those landscapes you could hang four different ways. Right now it's hanging behind a dying poinsettia plant.

I tell him it's very nice.

He nods, straightens the painting, and then steps back to examine his work. "I think that's better," he says, then gives it one final nudge.

"Perfect?" he asks me.

"Perfect."

"She thinks she's an artist," he says. "How do women get these ideas?"

12

ake Village East is a modern high-rise designed by Harry Weese, the architect responsible for Marina City. It sits like a lighthouse on 47th Street just west of the Metra tracks, facing the lake. Buildings like this can be tough to break into—there's usually a doorman, plus a lobby door to get past—and once you're upstairs, you're just standing in the hallway with very little cover.

The only advantage in tackling a high-rise is the sense of security everyone gets from being anonymous. No one thinks they'll be the one singled out for a break-in. So they often skimp on internal security. I had a friend who lived in this building some years back, a woman with short red hair who sang in Music of the Baroque and fixed me dinner dressed in lingerie and a long white apron. I remember her bed, I remember her eyes. I remember the basic floor plan, where the elevators are.

There aren't many people on the streets tonight. But it's not the kind of neighborhood where you do much Christmas shopping. I cruise around the block once or twice, looking for patrol cars, then park the 4Runner across the street at a new grocery store, where I fill a cart with large, light items: napkins, Kleenex, paper towels, a cheap flashlight, batteries, several pairs of gloves. The checker thinks I'm stocking up for a storm.

Then I take the bags back to my car and rearrange them with Donnie's equipment on the bottom and enough groceries sticking out to make the bags look heavy. When I carry them into the lobby, half hiding my face, struggling to keep them from falling, the secu-rity guard offers to help; a lady holds the lobby door for me. I don't even have to press the elevator button.

No one gets off with me on ten, which is a break, and when I take the stairs back down to nine, the small hallway is empty. There are only six apartments to a floor. The one I want is at the end of the hall, which if my memory serves me means it's a two-bedroom. I knock very lightly, listen a second, then pick the lock and take my groceries inside.

There's no one here. But the wineglasses in the sink and the smell of perfume tell me I've just missed a party. Whoever lives here lives very simply. There aren't many dishes. The refrigerator is empty, though there's ice in the freezer. The living room is a mixture of Scandinavian and Sears. The bedroom is better furnished, with a queen-size bed and a large mirror. I use a pair of gloves, which I think are meant for gardening, and the flashlight, and I install the hardware Donnie gave me. It's easy to use, though half the size of what I'm used to.

The necklace is right where Donnie said it would be, in the dresser's bottom drawer, wrapped in a small white sock that's cov-ered with hearts and cupids. I don't know enough about jewelry to estimate its value, but it doesn't look like anything special—black strands linked together like a spiderweb. I think they call it a choker. I slip it into my pocket.

The rest of the things in the drawer are actually more interest-ing: teddies, panties, bras, not everyday, very sexy and brightly col-ored. There's a black teddy that would look good on Alison.

On the way out I dump everything I bought at the grocery store down the trash chute. There's a different security guard on duty now. He barely glances at me. I leave a message for Donnie. The whole job takes less than an hour.

• • •

alison's not answering her cell phone; I suspect she turned it off at dinner. The line at PowerFemmes is busy. I need to stop at my place on the North Side and pack a few things for the flight, but first I drive along Hyde Park Boulevard. A light snow is falling. It's only twenty-four hours since Ricky Lopez was killed, but there's nothing in the alley to suggest a crime had been committed. All the windows are dark.

I go into the lobby and copy down the names of the tenants. Crowley said only a few apartments were still occupied, officially anyway; on cold nights there might be short-term tenants—addicts, winos. The landlord wants to rehab; he's not renewing leases. He'll be thrilled to hear about Ricky Lopez.

I walk back upstairs to the top floor, just like I did last night. The building seems deserted. The door to Ricky Lopez's apartment is locked. One flight down the door has a business card stapled to the wood, with everything scratched out. There's a bit of light coming from under the door. I knock, but no one answers. I think someone's here, but it's just a feeling. I knock again, then I walk back downstairs and make another trip around the building.

There's a two-car garage out back, an oddity in this neighborhood without a house attached. Four diamond-shaped windows are spaced out across the wooden door. I wonder who owns the garage. I wonder what they charge for the space. Everything's expensive in this neighborhood. Everything has a price.

There are bags of garbage in a Dumpster behind the garage. The cops have been through them already. The couple I saw arguing last night must have reconciled; I see their shadows on the kitchen walls, slow dancing. *"Silhouettes on the Shade."* The shirt she threw out is here in the trash, lipstick on the collar, the buttons torn off, along with pictures of the two of them she'd ripped in half; Kodak divorce. Tearing up their old life.

I try to picture Charles walking up this street, dressed for his wedding, writing free verse in his head, when Lopez the drug dealer spots him. Was Charles wearing a watch? Something to tempt Lopez besides the obvious, a gullible professor, an easy mark. But it was broad daylight. Was Charles buying drugs from Lopez? Crowley's right. None of this makes any sense. I walk around the building again and try to find the windows that match that sixth-floor apartment. Everything's dark.

I walk across the street and find the address that used to be Grand Terrace. The university still holds the mortgage, but the building's rental now, high-priced, utilities extra. The porch is fixed. The neighborhood's quiet. I wonder which window was Alison's. Which one was Tracy's. Which one was Charles's. Which door was open. As a game, I pick a third-floor window—lights on, drapes pulled—and try to imagine Alison living there behind those drapes. Walking through those rooms. Studying. Talking. Making plans. Making love. It's odd to think of her in there with Charles, or Tracy, or Moira. Where was I? It doesn't seem like ten years ago, it seems like today, like they're in there right now.

I'm sitting in my car, looking at the Xeroxed pages from *Mermaid* and listening to the radio, when a car pulls up behind me, nudging my rear bumper. It's Alison in her old Karmann Ghia. We both drive old cars: My 4Runner is pre-SUV, built like a tank and larger than it needs to be. Her Karmann Ghia is from another era. She's eating strawberry ice cream. Her eyes are a little red again.

"I saw you on Lake Park," she says, getting in. "Want a lick?"

"When have I ever said no to that?" She's changed her clothes; a different coat, a micro-mini. I give her a padded envelope with the necklace inside, ask her to put it in the PowerFemmes safe for a few days.

"I take it this was Donnie's job?" she says.

"Part of it." She doesn't ask me any questions, just puts the envelope by her purse, stretches out her legs. She has to trust me the way I have to trust Donnie. "And it's a good thing I got started on it. Henry Dahlgren asked me to fly to Denver. On behalf of the dean and some committee."

"That's why he called? He hired you?"

"Money didn't come up. But I said yes. Tell Beth I'm doing it for her, okay? Leave Dahlgren and the dean out of it. So she doesn't worry so much."

"They wouldn't have had time to discuss it today, Harding," she says. "It's Sunday."

"You're saying Dahlgren is doing this on his own?"

She nods.

"Maybe you're right. I can tell you this much. He lied about the cheesecake."

She looks at the page from *Mermaid* with Tracy's collage and reads the text. I tell her what I learned today about Pollard, Crystal Royce, and Gretchen Moss, that Tracy was waiting tables on the near North Side early last year. "That recently, that close?" she says, frowning. "I didn't know that. . . ."

"Crowley knows all three of you lived at Grand Terrace," I say. "So he might try calling you." She nods. "I tried calling you myself earlier, to tell you about the trip, but I couldn't get through."

"Yeah, it was a madhouse at the gym," she says. "Plus there was a bunch of wrong numbers."

"Oh?"

"Nobody there each time, so of course I thought it was Charles each time, afraid to speak. . . . Pretty silly, right?"

"Has that happened a lot lately?"

"No, just tonight." The radio's barely on, but a song I can't stand comes on and I reach to turn it down.

Is she really going out with him?

"You don't like that song?" she says, curling up against me. Her perfume is starting to smell like strawberry ice cream. "Joe Jackson?"

"I just heard it too often, at a bad time in my life."

"Well, you have to reclaim things, Harding," she says. "Like with a sad movie that reminds you of someone. You like the movie, but every time you watch it, your heart breaks again."

"So?"

"So reclaim the fucking movie, make it yours—watch it fifty times if you have to, with someone who's important to you *now*." She's so tough sometimes. I watch her finish her ice cream, turn the radio back up. "You want to stop back at my place?"

"I don't think I have time."

She frowns, crossing her legs at the ankles, flexing her thighs. "You're leaving right now? Tonight?"

"I've got a four-thirty flight."

She nods. She's drumming her fingers on the dash. "So how much time do we have?"

"Depends on the traffic on the Drive and then on the Kennedy . . . there's some kind of construction out by the junction, I think."

"Lock the doors," she says, already pulling off her jacket. "If you're done with the traffic report." She's unbuttoning her blouse. She climbs into the backseat. She pulls me back there, too. I protest for maybe half a second. The pages from *Mermaid* fall to the floor.

Her hands unsnap my jacket. She puts her hand down inside my jeans and kisses me on the mouth. Part of me is watching for pedestrians and traffic, and part of me doesn't give a damn who's watching. Alison's passion draws me into her world. For her nothing else exists. And for a little while there on the backseat of my car, nothing else exists for me either. She turns the radio up loud.

"Come on, come on," she says.

13

i catch the four-thirty flight to Denver. I sleep through most of it.
Everyone but me seems to hate Denver's airport. I think it has
a certain suburban shopping-mall charm. Of course I'm used to
O'Hare, which makes Denver International seem serene. And I
didn't have to pay for the damn thing, which always contributes to a
certain detachment.

I pick up my rented Blazer around eight A.M. and sit in the lot
studying a map the Avis girl gave me. I had her outline the shortest
path to Broomfield, the area of town where Charles lived, but right
now it doesn't look like the shortest route to me. She may have been
upset when I turned down all the insurance upgrades.

The drive from the airport isn't bad, though it takes me half an
hour just to reach the city. One of the first things I pass is the old airport, now closed. I understand a little better why people hate the
new one. The temperature's mid-forties, climbing to seventy-five
later today; I don't know how people dress around here. I always see
the Beautiful People skiing on television, in Vail or Aspen, wearing
brightly colored, very expensive down coats. They seem to like
headbands. They always have their sunglasses up on their heads.

Charles's apartment building looks like a remodeled coop—it's a
U-shaped courtyard with a new black iron gate out front. I don't see
a camera. I don't see anyone watching the building.

There's no super listed, so I ring four or five apartments until
someone buzzes the gate open. It's not the best time of day to do
this. The only people around now are probably here all day: older,

watchful. But someone must just want the damn noise to stop. I wait in the shadows long enough for the person to lose interest. Then I walk inside.

There are four entrances to the building, all locked, but someone soon comes out, a middle-aged woman dragging a portable grocery cart. She looks down as soon as she sees me. I smile and slip past her.

The building smells musty, but there are worse smells. Charles lives on the first floor. Someone has a television on very loud; I can hear *Jeopardy!* in the hallway. The category is Breaking and Entering. The deadbolt's not on. I'm able to manage my way around the other lock with a set of picks I brought along and almost lost coming through the metal detector at the airport. I told the security guard they were hairpins. "Sometimes I pin it up," I told him. "Like this. What do you think?" He waved me on. He had a slight perm himself.

I pull the shades down. I use gloves.

It's small, what would have been a one-bedroom but the rehabbers got trendy and ripped out all the walls, creating a sort of miniloft. I have no idea why the place doesn't fall down. The kitchen is designer-quality—custom cabinets, stainless-steel appliances, a marble-covered island—and everything's as clean as you'd see in a magazine ad.

The rest of the place is spotless, too. The furniture's all solid wood and creamy leather. It's not how I pictured Charles living. I thought poets lived in huts. Or garrets. I didn't know they liked Corian and Dacor. There's no sign the police have been here. Nothing's been disturbed. And nothing's been packed. Either Charles was saving his strength for his honeymoon or he wasn't moving out quite as soon as Alison said.

I start a cursory search. I look through his medicine cabinet. I check the end table by his bed. I look under the kitchen sink. Those are my three favorite spots for finding unmentionables. I look under the bed and under the mattress. I go through the clothes in his closet, paw through his pockets. I get a chair and look on the closet's upper shelves. There's not even any dust. As far as I can tell, Charles is clean.

There aren't many books here, which surprises me. A couple of literary biographies are stacked neatly on the coffee table. Maybe he keeps them in Boulder, at his office. Maybe he keeps his whiskey there, too. There's nothing unusual here. Nothing out of place.

Charles has a beautiful cherry hutch with a drop leaf he must use for a desk. The bottom of the hutch has a nice collection of Chinese porcelain. In the top drawer there are place mats and silver tableware and an address book, one of those oversize kind from a museum catalog, full of Monets and Manets. I've got one just like it at home somewhere, stuffed in a drawer. It's not going to fit in my pocket, but I don't need to steal it. The pages are blank.

The second drawer is locked. It's also more cluttered. There are envelopes and stationery and blue books—student themes, graded, never returned. It's like finding a stash of letters in a mailman's closet. There's no computer in the room, but there's a small floppy in a plastic case underneath them.

It's not a bad place to hide something. The themes would put most people asleep before they got any further. Unfortunately for Charles, I was trained in college to read Boethius and Hume, so the student themes are only a momentary distraction.

Everything else in the room is neat and tidy. This drawer is full of loose ends. It's the drawer you use to clean off your desk at the end of the day. There are rubber bands and paper clips and matches and dust made from art-gum eraser shavings; abandoned bits of paper, hair, tobacco. There's a pack of French cigarettes. There's a legal pad with notes for a poem that make absolutely no sense. And there's a single sheet of curling paper that reminds me again of Crowley. I half expect to see the business cards on it. Instead I find what looks like parts of a transcript in narrow Times computer script. It has a familiar ring to it.

you are in a private room
Chaucer enters the room
Ladywriter enters the room

hi
hello
how are you tonight
horny
as usual (g)
we were cut off last night
my server went down
can we resume at the same spot
okay
do you remember where we were
fucking baby
which time
the second i think
because i wrote for a while thinking you were still there
sorry
that's okay i'm just trying to remember
you can start anywhere. . . . i can start if you want
yes
is that okay
yes you start this time
okay
okay
—

are you there
are you there
yes sorry
that's okay I know what you're doing
(blush) you're right
as usual
did you get the attachment i sent

yes
what do you think
mmmmm very sexy
i have more i could send
i'd like to see more
i'll send them which address
not here
ICQ?
no use my other email
okay
the peace station one
you're there again
yes
i could bring them there it's so close
no I like keeping it separate
you do
yes
oh god tracy i can't wait
—
okay
okay
—
are you there
are you there
are you there

It's incomplete, a cut-and-paste job. Part of it was in *Mermaid,* of course. I'm wondering now if this really was a chat-room transcript or something Tracy created.

There are a handful of old pictures in here, too. There's a shot of Moira sitting in the kitchen at Grand Terrace, smoking, reading a paperback. She's wearing a bathrobe and floppy white socks; her hair looks dirty. Someone's standing behind her, but all you can see are her legs. There's a picture of Alison and Tracy reading in Regenstein Library, both slumped in matching chairs, running shoes propped against the desk, red pencils in hand. Tracy is very pretty, with an oval face, dark brown hair that she wore in bangs. Their faces are turned just slightly toward each other and their gym shoes are touching at the toes. And there's a picture of all three girls in their bikinis, from that weekend at the Dunes, I guess, though Alison didn't show me this shot. It's more explicit—Tracy's sunbathing topless, with Alison sleeping beside her. Tracy's breasts are very full, but for some reason it's Alison, curled beside her, a lazy look on her face, who's the sexier of the two. Moira must have taken the picture.

It's very odd finding the pictures here. It would be different if they were in an album, but seeing them loose . . . it's as though nothing's happened since then. Nothing worth photographing, anyway. I keep the transcript and the floppy and the pictures. I put everything back the way I found it. I don't know if anyone sees me when I leave. I'm pretty sure no one hears me since even I can't hear the sounds I'm making. All I can hear is *Jeopardy!*

There's a bar on the corner with an early lunch crowd and a fax machine. I show my picture of Charles around, but no one's seen him for a while. I feel like having a drink, but it's ten-thirty in the morning. It's later in Chicago. I order scotch on Central Time, then fax the transcript to PowerFemmes. And then I call Alison at home. I tell her there's no sign of Charles. I leave out most of the breaking-and-entering parts of the story. She confirms that the Lopez case is stalled, the university wants Charles kept out of it until there's hard proof he acted in something other than self-defense.

"If he was even there," she says. "I mean, what do they really have? A tall man in a dark suit . . ."

"You're right. It might have been Abraham Lincoln."

She says Beth talked to the dean in Boulder early this morning. They said Charles moved out of his office two weeks ago, turned in all his keys. That saves me a drive I wasn't looking forward to. Breaking into university buildings requires more resources—and more friends—than I've brought with me.

"Beth is having major mood swings right now," she says. "She hates Charles for not showing up, but she's scared to death something happened to him—"

"Listen to this, Alison." I read her the transcript. There's a long silence. "Sound familiar?"

"That's what you showed me last night, isn't it? From *Mermaid*?"

"You bet it is. But this is the long version, and Tracy's picture was in the same drawer, the same *locked* drawer. Along with yours."

"Okay. So what?"

"So he must have kept up with Tracy a little better than you did. It mentions 'attachments'—they were sending pictures back and forth. Gretchen Moss said someone took a bunch of pictures of Tracy. I'm thinking they were nudes, like the one in *Mermaid*."

"I thought you said Pollard took those."

"He denies it. Maybe Charles took them. Or maybe Pollard took them and Tracy was showing them to Charles. The point is, Tracy and Charles were having some sort of relationship. And if he was fucking Tracy, on-line or in real life, I think you'd better tell Crowley. And get out of the way."

"That transcript isn't enough to justify that, Harding. They might just have been exchanging work files—they're both writers, remember? Did you ever think that maybe Tracy just wanted Charles's opinion on something?"

"I talked to Crowley last night," I say. "He's been digging around in Charles's past. There was a woman attacked in Denver last June."

"So?"

"So Charles was questioned. Not as a suspect—as a material witness. He gave them a preliminary sketch of the guy. Who never turned up. The case is still unsolved."

"So what?"

"So Crowley asked if Charles had returned. I said no. That's all I said. But that was before reading this stuff."

"When are you coming home?" she says.

"Soon. Late afternoon, early evening." I'm thinking of the place mentioned in the transcript, Peace Station. It sounds like Tracy was living there, temporarily at least.

i could bring them there it's so close

The bartender asks me if I need a refill. I tell him I'm switching to black coffee.

"What are you going to tell Henry Dahlgren?" Alison says.

"Just that he's not here. You want vague, I can be vague. Don't worry."

"Because I might see him tonight, he's taking Beth and her kids out to buy a Christmas tree, I might tag along. She's in a state of shock this morning. She's going to need our help. Charlie—damn, I mean Charles—too, as soon as he turns up. Okay?"

"Okay, Alison." It's always nice to be needed.

I call Dahlgren and get his service. I leave a vague message. Maybe he's out scouting Christmas trees. I call my office and check my own messages. The ones from bill collectors are less than vague. But the last message is from Gretchen Moss. She sounds out of breath.

Listen, I just wanted to tell you to forget that stuff I told you, okay? Don't mention me to Pollard whatever you do, just leave my name out of it. I don't want to get involved with that guy ever again.

I sit at the bar another ten minutes or so, drinking coffee, rereading the transcript.

are you there
are you there

I check the time, then call the airport and push my flight back to nine P.M. I call the rental agency and tell them I'm keeping the Blazer an extra day. I add all the insurance upgrades, which makes the agent very happy. I ask if someone could tell me where Peace Station might be, and after about ten minutes on hold somebody new comes on the line. I think it's the woman who gave me the bad directions.

"Are you the one going to Peace Station?" she says.

"If I can find out where it is."

"It's not far, across the border in New Mexico. But it's not on the maps. You have to watch the signs. Get off the main highway." She gives me directions that I have no confidence in. But then she asks me if I'm returning the car to them directly and if I am could I buy a piece of pottery for her? At Peace Station? She'll pay me back, she'll give me a break on the insurance. They make the neatest stuff. "A bear would be cool. Or a unicorn. Anything except a wolf. I've got too many wolves."

The bartender gives me a large coffee to go. I feel stupid now for having read the damn transcript to Alison. By the time I call her back she's left for the gym. It's another ten minutes or so before I think about what I didn't find in that drawer: any pictures of Beth Reinhardt, the woman Charles was about to marry.

14

I swing west around Denver and head south.

It's snowing heavier now, but even full of clouds the sky's somehow brighter than Chicago's. The light's different, too. It might be because of the skyline. I'm used to midwestern hills. Out here the mountains are given majestic names, Native American names, spiritual names. In Chicago the mountains are named Hancock, or Sears, or Prudential.

Once I'm in New Mexico the roads get even slicker. The Blazer has four-wheel drive, but it handles like a box. I keep the speed below fifty. There's a single billboard for Peace Station Gifts. I don't think I'm lost, but when I cross the Rio Grande for the third time, I decide to stop at a gas station for directions.

The Navajo running the place has to call his wife at home and ask her for help. For a second I'm afraid I'm going to have to pick up some pottery for her, too. "Ten more miles," he says, smiling. Everyone's very friendly, without an agenda. It's refreshing. It would take some getting used to.

Peace Station sounds to me like a polar city: Little America. In fact, it's a tall, imposing mansion set on a New Mexico hillside; run-down, decaying, left to a commune. The ground slopes down to what in spring would be a running stream of fresh cold water, fed by the Sangre de Cristo Mountains. Right now it's a frozen creek bed.

"We use it as a marker for home runs," says my host, a woman named Sarah. "When we play Wiffle ball." She's somewhere beyond fifty, with long silver-gray hair. Her wrists are covered with beaded bracelets. She's a friend of Tracy's. They were keeping her room for her, hoping she'd return. "Everyone leaves for a while," Sarah explains. "Everyone usually returns."

She takes me first to the gift shop. They're out of unicorns and bears. I buy a cheetah for the Avis woman. I don't feel good about it. It looks an awful lot like a wolf. They also make very interesting jewelry, she says, made from recycled aluminum. I might like to take a catalog.

Sarah says Peace Station is a women's collective, designed to be a refuge. I don't ask her from what. Before I can see Tracy's room, I have to meet the rest of the group. There are twelve of them, all women. They're sitting in a circle, heads and palms upturned toward the sun. Alicia is leading them in prayer.

"Holy Father, one to one, all surrendering to your grace
We give thanks, we entreat thee enter the spirit of our community
with thy Holy Spirit—"

I've introduced myself as Tracy's uncle from Chicago, given Sarah a recent business card with my real name and address. She doesn't ask to see anything else. In fact, she looks at the card as though it were some sort of artifact and then leads me to the steep concrete steps that climb the hill to the house. There's a bench and a water fountain halfway up—it reminds me of the walk to Ricky Lopez's apartment. The addicts could probably use a way station like this on the third floor.

Tracy's room isn't locked. I stand uncomfortably for a second, not sure what I'm allowed to do. The furniture is unfinished pine. There are folded sweaters, soft jeans, cotton work shirts. It's like an L.L. Bean outlet store.

"How long was Tracy here?" I ask Sarah.

"Oh . . . just a few weeks this time."

"She'd been here before?"

"Several times. It's not unusual. People come and go. The door's always open." Sarah straightens the quilt at the foot of Tracy's bed, fluffs the pillows, adjusts the simple curtains. "You said she was missing?"

"It's probably nothing, but her family's concerned," I say, nodding. I don't like lying—I'm not all that good at it, for one thing—but people tend to freeze up when you start talking murder. "Would you happen to know where she went this time?"

"I'm afraid not. Someone gave her a ride to the bus stop. She only took a small suitcase. We assumed it was just for the weekend."

"And this was when exactly?"

"I believe it was October," she says, watching me. "Early October."

There are a few books on the desk, most notably a copy of *idée fixe: Poems by Charles Muller.* It's inscribed to Tracy. "With love, your Charles." And sitting on a bookshelf is a postcard from Galena, blank, as though Tracy just liked the picture. It's a picture of a hotel or a bed-and-breakfast, the DeSoto House. It does look very scenic.

"It's very generous of you, keeping her room like this."

"We liked Tracy very much," she says. "She was becoming an excellent potter. And the room was paid for in advance."

"By Tracy?"

"I'm not sure. . . ."

"Could you find out for me? I would really appreciate it."

She hesitates. "I suppose I could ask Alicia, she does our accounts," she says. "I suppose that wouldn't hurt. . . ."

When she's gone, I start looking through Tracy's things. There's no money or jewelry, nothing of any material value, which was probably why Sarah didn't mind leaving me alone. As for Tracy's writing . . . I can't find a computer or even any disks. There are no manuscripts, no unfinished drafts, no notebooks or files. She wasn't living here full-time, that's for sure.

"Are you finding anything that might help you?" Sarah says

from the doorway. I shake my head. "Alicia says Tracy paid with a third-party check. She remembers because the return address was a man's name—there was some confusion as to who was making the reservation. We don't allow men here."

I've been sitting on the bed; this makes me stand up. "Was the man's name Muller? Charles Muller?"

She says no, it was someone named Ben Andrews, of Taos.

"Tracy had a car," I say. "A purple Gremlin—"

"That's right, I'd forgotten. She had it the first time she came here, but not the second. She came by bus." She looks at my picture of Charles. She pulls her shawl tighter around her shoulders. "Tracy didn't list a home address, I'm afraid."

"Have you seen this man, Sarah?"

"He might have been here once, in the gift shop . . . I'm not sure." I can't tell if she's lying or just growing uncomfortable with my questions. She's moving quietly, with tiny steps, toward the door. "We're making some green tea if you'd like some—"

"Do you happen to have Ben Andrews's address in Taos?"

She says yes, she can give me that. I thank her for her help. I ask for directions and a rain check on the tea.

taos is another hour south. The sky now looks different: darker. The roads are filled with tractor-trailers. Mexican drug dealers use them as labs, making methamphetamine; it keeps the smell of urine away from nosy neighbors. I let them pass me. I keep my windows up.

I'm not used to the hills and the changing altitudes, the way the horizon keeps changing. My world usually stops a few blocks away. I pull over at a lookout and hunt for a radio station that isn't country and western. When a Cream song pours out of my tinny rental car speakers, I turn it up as far as I can.

And you see your girl's brown body
Dancing through the turquoise

123

Ben Andrews lives in an adobe built out of mud and old tires. It's sitting out on a pueblo, but the people walking nearby don't look like Indians, they look like hippies. A green station wagon even older than the tires sits with a newer Dodge. I don't see a Gremlin. There's an oval window that's more like a porthole near the front door, and when I knock, I can see an old man inside watching *Oprah* on a black-and-white TV. He has a bald head and a large handlebar mustache. He looks like a retired biker. His feet are resting on a beer case covered with promo stickers from the Grateful Dead, Hot Tuna, New Riders of the Purple Sage.

He invites me in. I give him my concerned relative speech, a business card; I ask him if he knows Tracy and he says yes, of course, they're good neighbors. Or were. "Tracy don't live there no more." He means the adobe about a hundred yards away, built like his. "Nobody lives there now. . . ."

He loans me the key. I have to get a flashlight from the Blazer. Tracy's adobe is older; at least the mud looks older. Her Goodyears look like retreads. The screen door's flapping in the wind. Inside it's very cold and dark. There's just one room, like Charles's apartment, but it's rehabbed differently. The furniture is simple wood plank, unfinished. There are no ashes in the kiva. The bathroom's out back. I decide not to investigate things that thoroughly. All I find are a few old paperbacks—*Cat's Cradle, Been Down So Long It Looks Like Up to Me, Stranger in a Strange Land*—and, under the washstand, part of a bulletin board facedown on the floor. It looks like it's been ripped from the wall.

Ben says Tracy lived next door "for maybe a year. Maybe a bit less. She was gone a lot, though." She rented the place from him, paid in cash, borrowed the green station wagon when she needed a car. Her mail went to a P.O. box. When I ask about Peace Station, he says no, he didn't know she ever went there. "I've heard about the pottery, that's all." And when I bring up the third-party check she used there, he grows silent, discovering a thread on his sweater to pull on.

"I was just trying to help her out," he finally says.

"By paying her rent at Peace Station?"

"No, no . . ." He waves this off. "I didn't know nothing about that. She needed money sometimes—and she'd sell me things. She wouldn't take a loan."

"What kind of things?"

"Oh, it started with the small stuff, books and tapes, knick-knacks. She was selling her clothes, too, I think, at a consignment store in Albuquerque."

"The check for Peace Station was for more than just knick-knacks."

"That would be for her car," he says, "which I had no need of. I sold it myself to somebody else. And then Tracy just used the station wagon. Like I said, I was just trying to help her out."

"Did she have a job, Ben?"

"Oh, sure, she had lots of jobs—waitressing, bartending . . . just shit to pay the bills. I think she might have done some dancing, too." He fills a teapot, lights the stove. "The only thing that mattered to her was her writing."

"I'd love to see what she was working on."

He nods, putting some things away in the tiny kitchen. The entire adobe isn't much bigger than an RV. "It seemed a little strange to me, the parts I read. I'm more into keeping a positive vibe. The Rapture's coming, you know."

"So I've heard."

"But there's a couple pages she left on my hard drive one day when her power was out. You wanna see that?"

I tell him yes. I ask him if she had any visitors out here. Boyfriends, girlfriends. He considers this as he sits down at his computer and flips on the printer. The desk doubles as an ironing board; there's a pair of chinos draped over the paper supply.

"Well, she wasn't a nun," Ben says. "But whether there was any-one special, I couldn't say." He has a picture of Tracy, taken last summer, sitting cross-legged on the floor of his adobe. You'd barely recognize her as the topless sunbather in the other photo. Her arms are thin, her skin is white. She looks frail, like one of the mesa winds would just blow her over. And her eyes are dull and distant. "You're not the first one to come looking for her, though."

"Oh?"

"Last month, early November," Ben says, tearing off a sheet of paper from an old dot-matrix printer. "He asked a lot of the same questions you're asking." Ben goes over to the window now, a spray bottle in his hand for watering his plants. Three of the planters are just coffee mugs—the familiar white of the CyberBeanery.

"Alfalfa," says Ben, nodding at the yellow-green sprouts. "Good for the sinuses. And totally natural."

I ask Ben about alfalfa and his sinus problems, and I tell him I have the same problems. He's sympathetic. "You need alfalfa," he says. Then I ask about the coffee mugs.

"Tracy gave me those," he says. "They came in the mail, she said, one at a time. She said it was somebody's idea of a bad joke. She didn't say who the joker was."

"Was it the same guy who was here asking questions?"

"Maybe. Except . . . No, I think the mugs came from Chicago . . . and this fellow was from Denver."

"Was his name Muller? Charles Muller?"

"That sounds about right," Ben says. He sniffs the alfalfa and sneezes. "She's not in any sort of trouble, is she?" I tell him no, I don't think so. "Because I gotta tell you, I kinda miss her. She was a smiling face around here. A real gentle spirit."

"Did she ever tell you what she was doing out here?"

He sets down his spray bottle. "On the mesa, you mean? It's cheap, man. And it's beautiful. You should see the summer sky—reds you would not believe, fifty different shades of blue. That's why there're so many painters here. And writers. Everyone's here for a reason."

"What's your reason, Ben?"

"Just tryin' to get centered. You know?"

"Uh-huh."

"Some people take vacations, go on a retreat. You look sorta stressed out yourself there, man. Maybe that's what you need."

"My whole life's a retreat," I say. I thank Ben for his time. He gives up the printout and the picture of Tracy for fifty bucks. Thank God he doesn't have a gift shop. Then I head north again with the ceramic cheetah and a mug of alfalfa beside me on the seat.

the roads are getting slick as I near Peace Station. I pull over and take out my maps. Neil Young is warbling on the radio.

You know how time fades away . . .

The mansion does indeed look like a refuge. The lights look inviting in the storm. The steps are covered with snow, the wind is pushing the porch swing. I find Sarah in the large kitchen scrubbing the remains of dinner—vegetable lasagna—from heavy Country French dishes.

"You're back," she says matter-of-factly, handing me a dish towel. I'm drying. A woman in a blue jumper moves over to make room. I get the feeling I'm Sarah's project. The other women are polite enough, but no one really looks me in the eye. "Did Mr. Andrews help you at all?"

"A little. But I'm confused about a couple of things. That's why I came back." I dry off a large platter and set it on an oak sideboard. There are stacks of blue dishes and silverware inside. "She was living in Taos, did you know that?"

She shakes her head. "But I knew it wasn't far away."

"That man I asked you about, Charles Muller? The one whose picture I showed you? He visited Tracy in Taos."

"I told you I might have seen him in the gift shop."

"Your gift shop is very interesting," I say. "But I doubt it would have brought Charles Muller down here from Denver."

"All right, yes, he did visit her here. He had dinner with us once or twice." The woman in the blue jumper leaves. We're alone in the kitchen. Sarah stands at the sink, facing away from me. I start to ask her a question, but she cuts me off.

"Tell me the truth, Mr. Harding, please. Are you really her uncle?"

I hesitate a tad too long. As I mentioned before, I'm not a very good liar. "I'm a friend, Sarah."

"Like Charles Muller?"

"I haven't yet figured out what kind of a friend Charles was to her. If you can enlighten me, I'd appreciate it."

"Maybe you should tell me why you're here first," she says.

I watch her wash the last dish and pull the plug. The water leaves behind a bubblebath of soap. "Tracy's disappeared," I say. "Her friends in Chicago are worried."

"Sometimes people want to be left alone."

"Was that the case with Tracy, though? Did she come here to be alone? Or to get away from someone?"

She hesitates, then sits down at the kitchen table and folds her hands. Her skin is red from the dishwater. "Women come here for different reasons, Mr. Harding. For some it's a shelter . . . they need a safe place."

"And Tracy?"

"I often felt Tracy was looking for something . . . or someone. We're quite remote out here, you know. It requires a certain spiritual independence."

"Her adobe in Taos was remote enough," I say. "Why would she come here?"

"For her work, perhaps. The book she was writing. Or for spiritual enrichment. It's a different kind of solitude here. You know you're not really alone, you're among friends." The wind howls, rattling the shingles. The metal gutters vibrate, a sound like someone is trying to peel back the roof. Sarah wraps her shawl around her, goes to the window over the sink, and parts the curtains. Clumps of snow are landing on the glass like dirt tossed on a coffin. "There's a storm coming," she says.

"Another one?"

"This one may be worse." She turns to face me. "Tracy's dead, isn't she, Mr. Harding?"

I don't answer her.

"I sensed it the moment you arrived. I knew something was wrong when she didn't write, but I was hoping . . . just hoping . . ."

"I'm sorry."

"When did it happen?"

"Halloween weekend. I don't know much more than that, I'm afraid."

"You think this man, Charles Muller . . ."

"Right now I don't know what to think." I put away the rest of the dishes, shut the glass doors to the kitchen cabinet. "I'm a private investigator, Sarah. My girlfriend went to college with Tracy, they're old friends. And the police aren't making much headway."

"So she was murdered?"

I nod.

"There was someone in her life," Sarah says. "I honestly don't know if it was Mr. Muller or someone else. I only know she had strong feelings about someone. And she was trying to come to grips with those feelings in different ways. By coming here, for example. And by writing about them."

"But you never read this book she was working on?"

"No," she says. "A lot of the women here keep journals . . . we respect one another's privacy."

"There's another man I'm investigating. . . ." I describe Logan Pollard to her. She shakes her head; she's not sure. "He sounds like a man who showed up once with a camera, watching the women play softball. But I'm not sure." She asks me how Tracy was killed, but I sense she doesn't really want to know. I certainly don't feel like telling her. "The police aren't releasing that yet," I say.

"She was safe here," Sarah says sadly. "She never should have left us. . . ."

A group of women comes to talk to Sarah and she tells them to shut the house down for the night. The chores are divided: secure the shutters, get more firewood, check the backup generators.

"We go to bed early here," Sarah says, apologizing.

It's my cue to leave. I get my coat. "I'll be on my way then."

"How far are you going?"

"Back to Denver, I guess. Or the nearest motel. Don't worry, I'm used to driving in snow, Sarah, I live in Chicago."

"But you don't know the roads," she says. "And this isn't Chicago. You can lose your perspective here, become snow-blind—and the drop-offs can be very steep. It might be better if you stayed with us. No one's using that room."

"I can stay here? In Tracy's bed?"

"For the one night, sure. Why not?"

I'm not sure why not. Except that room seems taken somehow. As though I would be intruding on someone. But the wind is howling, and it does indeed sound like a different wind than I'm used to. I'm out of my element here, out of place. The storm has already covered the path to my car.

My offer to pay something for the room is gently declined. "But there are one or two bills Tracy left behind . . ." The total comes to a little over three hundred. It's turning into an expensive room.

"Let me get you some more blankets," Sarah says. "There's a bathroom next door you can use. We keep spare toiletries in the top cupboard. There are probably a few razors up there, the throw-away kind."

"You're very kind."

She pauses in the doorway. "The rest of us have a little devotional later. . . . I doubt if you would be interested, but you're very welcome, of course."

"I think I'll just go to bed."

She nods. "Breakfast is at eight," she says. "If you get hungry later, there's fruit in the refrigerator. And if you need something from your car, you should probably get it now. We lock the doors at ten."

I do as she suggests and move my car closer to the main garage, in case I need it jumped in the morning. The snow swirls around my face like fireflies. The windchill must be twenty below. I call Alison from the kitchen and leave a message; I call the airline and change my flight again. My own machine is blank except for the message from Gretchen Moss.

Please don't tell Pollard about me.

Then I go upstairs.

There's no radio or TV in the room. Nothing to read but Charles's book of poems and the piece that Ben printed out for me. I'm expecting another prose poem or chat-room transcript, but this is what I find:

> He crossed the street at 56th Street, sloshing through standing water like an animal covering its tracks. He didn't know why he chose that spot, it just felt right. And when the woman left her house, he kept to the shadows, waiting for her to begin her jog, and then he broke into his own loping run, head down, trailing her by half a block, just another runner in dirty gray sweats and headband until the voice began to whisper in his ear, growing louder with each step, and he had to stop and say no no no—
>
> I don't want to do that.
>
> All right, the voice said. Okay. Just an idea. Something to consider. Do this and then I'll go away, leave you in peace. . . .
>
> And then his legs were moving . . . he knew the exact number of steps to the underpass and he counted them as he ran and waited for the traffic to disappear. . . . He waited for

the way her face would change when he did those things to her. . . .

The night passes swiftly. The sheets are cold. The building's quiet. At one point I hear a dog barking, then another. I get up and look out the window and see a wolf, the first time I've seen one outside a zoo. It's standing in the bushes, not really trying to hide. It paces in a circle for a moment, as though waiting for something just at the edge of the property. It's still there when I go back to bed.

my flight home on Tuesday is delayed several times. There are only two things to do in airports—read or drink. So I buy a very serious-looking hardcover and then spend most of the afternoon carting it, unopened, from bar to bar.

The flight itself is uneventful. My head starts throbbing somewhere over Nebraska. The airline magazine reads like *Forbes* or *Business Week*—stories of hard work, perseverance, good people doing good things. I find such stories very depressing, even without a headache. I try to sleep, but sleep won't come.

Every now and then the pilot announces that we're passing over something spectacular and I look out the window and stare into the clouds. When I put on the headphones, I find Gladys Knight using her imagination.

Got to make the best of a bad situation

At O'Hare I treat myself to a cab instead of using the El. By now I'm getting drunk. It's early evening. The whole day's been lost. Lake Michigan seems dark and deep, soaking up the moonlight. There are white lights in the trees in Lincoln Park. Belmont Avenue is full of potholes and my cab hits every one.

The Greek restaurant below my apartment is full of shining, happy people, a private party. "Anniversary," says Minas, the owner, also my landlord. "Thirty-five years." He says that's silver. I wonder what Alison and I have; ten years, off and on. Not much to show for ten years. Fool's gold maybe.

I climb the steps to my apartment. Halfway up, my neighbor Mrs. Loomis opens her door a crack and peers down at me. Then she quickly shuts the door. At the top of the stairs I find my own door wide open. "I think he left," Mrs. Loomis says through her door.

"What?"

"I think it's okay. I think he left." My gun's in the bedroom. But by the time I get to it I've gone through every room anyway. Mrs. Loomis was right—someone had indeed been here. My filing cabinets are open and folders are tossed on the desk. My computer is turned on. Chairs are slightly askew. Mrs. Loomis is persuaded to open her door, but all she can tell me is he wore white gym shoes. Mrs. Loomis likes to avoid eye contact. Minas is more helpful; he noticed a black car circling the block earlier tonight. It might have been a Cadillac.

I clean up the living room and put the files back, stopping to fix myself a drink. I turn on the radio. I'm debating whether or not to report this when my phone rings.

"It's Crowley," he says. "Am I disturbing you? Jeez, I hope I'm disturbing you."

"My place was broken into tonight," I say. "I'm already disturbed."

The computer's still on, so I insert the disk from Charles's apartment and find a series of pictures, the same ones I found in his drawer: Tracy, Moira, Alison. They're starting to look like sisters now—in my mind anyway. I'm trying to remember if there was anything on my own computer worth stealing.

"I've got a name you should check," I tell Crowley. "Travis Savick. He drives a black Cadillac; he wears white gym shoes." I'm mad at myself for not checking him out more than I did. I thought he might just be debris from an old case, but he's too persistent for that.

"Is this for the Tracy Lawrence thing? Or the Lopez thing?"

"It's for the Harding apartment thing," I say, finishing my drink. I should have brought the bottle in here. "Travis may have been my uninvited guest. And he's been on my tail since Saturday."

"Then you should file a report," he says. "The boys in Area Three know how to take a burglary report."

I tell him about my trip to Denver on behalf of the dean; I try to make it sound impressive, but cops don't impress easily.

"Muller's place in Denver was empty," I tell Crowley.

"Big surprise."

"But I found out where Tracy Lawrence has been living for the last year." I give him the Taos address, I give him parts of what Sarah told me, but I don't give him Peace Station. I don't like the idea of bothering Sarah. And I keep thinking of my talk with Alison yesterday. . . . *You want vague, I can do vague.*

At least one or two parts of the puzzle are in place. Tracy was living in Taos, working odd jobs, using Peace Station as a retreat or writers' colony. And both Pollard and Charles had known where she was. The goal here is to supply Crowley with just enough information so that he keeps me and the Wokowski card out of Tracy's case. Giving him too much just involves me further.

"By the way, you can forget about her car," I tell him. One of the files is locked; I put in every name I can think of as a password, but nothing works. "It was sold, then resold. She wasn't using it anyway."

I'm staring at the blinking computer screen, still waiting for my password. Things are moving that shouldn't be moving. I definitely had too much to drink on that plane. The radio is playing REM.

Did you never call? I waited for your call. . . .

"Is that why you wanted to talk to me, Terry?" I say. "To ask about Tracy?"

"Not exactly," he says.

I punch in a few more tries for a password. And then I try

Grand Terrace. And, just like that, the file opens. And I start talking to myself.

"What the fuck . . ."

It's what's called an animated gif file. The same pictures are here: Tracy, Alison, Moira. But once the file loads, the heads start moving, back and forth, onto different bodies. They look like paper dolls. Sometimes Alison's head is on all of them.

"There was a girl attacked in Hyde Park Sunday night," Crowley says. "Grabbed from behind, pulled into the bushes." He starts coughing, and when he continues, his voice has retreated to a raspy whisper. "She was lucky. A porch light went on and I guess she fought back, but you could still see the bruises on her neck."

"Is she all right?"

"They discharged her yesterday, she's back home in Kansas City by now."

"Yeah, but is she all right?"

"I'm not a fucking counselor, Harding." He says she's a student, her name's Gretchen Moss. He says one or two other things that I don't really hear. The figures on my computer screen are dancing like marionettes. Michael Stipe is singing "I'm sorry. I'm sorry."

"When did it happen?" I say.

"Eleven or so. At 56th and Kimbark. Weren't you in Hyde Park then?"

I tell him no, I'd left for the airport. He mentions that it's the same MO as the woman in Denver, the attack Charles witnessed, but I tell him to forget about Charles for a minute and pick up Logan Pollard and ask him about Gretchen Moss. I don't tell him where I'd been barely an hour earlier that night, just two blocks away, or what I'd been doing in the backseat of my car with Alison. . . .

Crowley mumbles goodbye and hangs up. I can't tell if he's pissed at me about something or just lonely. I sit for another few minutes looking at the computer file, trying to figure out which photos were used to create it. It reminds me of the collage in *Mermaid*. It scares me enough that I try calling Alison—I try PowerFemmes, I try her apartment. I try Beth's house. Nobody's home. Maybe that's a good sign; if the kids are gone, Beth's probably with them and Alison might have tagged along. I'm trying to remember what she said about buying a Christmas tree; was that last night or tonight?

I redial, pour myself a drink, then finish it quickly standing up, the way I eat most of my meals. I shake the ice in the glass when it's gone. I have another. I break a glass, so I get a broom and sweep it up. I decide to just drive down there now, to Hyde Park. I'm not sure I can sleep anyway. I turn off the computer, stick the disk back in the travel bag.

And so, a good half-hour after arriving home, I open my back door to take the trash out and see two things simultaneously. The lid to my trash can is off. The black Cadillac has returned to the alley. And someone to my right—who's been out here waiting patiently for me in the cold and the dark—is moving like a freight train way too quickly for me to see who it is or even to get my arms up to stop the heavy metal lid from being slammed against my face.

i'm out maybe ten minutes. Thank God the back door stayed open or I'd have frozen to death. There's a red crease in my face. I wash the blood off in the kitchen sink and put a Band-Aid over a cut that looks like it needs stitches. All I can think of is someone telling me not to wear white after Labor Day—I'm not sure if this applies to white gauze. My ribs are sore; I have a vague recollection of being kicked. I go through my apartment again. He took the cash from my wallet, left the credit cards and IDs. The only thing that's missing is my travel bag, sitting conveniently near the front door. The disk is gone, as are the pictures. I hope he enjoys the alfalfa.

I'm a little dizzy, so I sit on the couch and wait for Alison to call me back. I channel-surf past PBS and the Learning Channel for Telemundo, a world where all the women wear low-cut halters and hip-huggers and swing their hair a lot. I never meet women like this in real life. You don't find women in hip-huggers on PBS. I'm feeling very multicultural. When the phone rings, this time I have to interrupt my own voice on the answering machine. The voices overlap like a very bad madrigal. I'm feeling multipersonal.

"I'm looking for Harding." The voice is low and hard. There's country music in the background. I never realize how much I've been drinking until I have to carry on a conversation, something I'm not all that great at even when sober.

"I'm Harding," I say. "Who the hell is this?"

"Eddie Samuels, the Green Street Tavern. I got a friend of yours here with a hundred-dollar tab and a maxed-out Visa. I'm closing soon and it gets cold on the street. I'd hate to see him spend the night in jail. You wanna come pick him up?"

"If his name is Boone—"

"His name's not Boone. It's Muller."

"Charlie Muller? Jesus, put him on."

"Look, he's sleeping now. I'd just as soon not wake him up—he might start reciting poetry again. He says I should call you, so I called. Do you want the bastard or not?"

"Yeah, okay. I'll be there, I'll be there. Give me a minute."

"How soon can you get here? It's 230 South Main."

"You moved? I thought you were on Oak. Where the hell is Main?"

"From you? In Chicago? I would guess sixty-five, seventy miles, due west. You hit the river, you've gone too far. You're in Iowa. You don't wanna be in Iowa this late. There's nothing open in Iowa."

"What?"

"I'm calling from Galena, buddy. Galena, Illinois. You know where we are?"

I can hear the crowd from the party below spilling onto the street.

"Are you there?" says the bartender. "Hey. Fella. Are you there?"

16

I want to confess my sins," says Charles Muller, stumbling a bit on his shadow. He's very drunk, but the cold air is bringing him around. We're on a hilltop overlooking Galena, a nickel-postcard town, picturesque in summer, comatose in winter. There's a bit of snow coming down. The streetlights are brighter than the moon.

"The whole catalog," he says with a wave of his hand. "God knows I've got enough of them. Can I do that, Harding? Right now?"

"Let's just stick to the last forty-eight hours, Charles. I'd like to get home sometime before Christmas."

Beth stayed home with her children. Alison is below us somewhere—she's returning Charles's rental car, paying his bills, paying off the night manager at the DeSoto House, cleaning up the mess Charles made there. I think I'm supposed to clean up the mess Charles left in Chicago. That might be harder to do. When we found him at the Green Street Tavern, he looked dazed, unsure of where he was even. We walked him into the DeSoto House lobby, plopped him in a big reading chair next to the tour maps and postcards and a notice that the horse-drawn carriage rides had ended for the night. Alison took charge, though she was even more tired than I was. She wore a running suit under a long, elegant black coat. She was drinking black coffee, wearing sunglasses; she had one of her migraines. I couldn't see her eyes.

Charles has a poet's eyes, bloodshot, the color of a Bulls jersey; he's been drinking gin. He has headaches of his own right now.

"We have to sober him up," Alison said, "before we take him back to Beth. She shouldn't see him like this." I felt like arguing that this is exactly how she needs to see him but didn't; I was dead tired from the driving. There are no expressways to Galena. The roads are bad. It's the only tourist trap that discourages visitors. I should have stayed on the plane, I could have parachuted over Dubuque.

I'd had plenty of time during the drive to tell Alison about Taos and Peace Station. She told me about her evening in Park Forest, with Beth and her sister, watching rental movies. And she told me what she'd heard about Gretchen Moss. "No sexual assault, it never got that far, but you can guess where it was going. . . ." Gretchen couldn't give them a description. There are no suspects.

I reminded her that we'd been two blocks away from where it happened.

"I know that," she said. "Don't you think I know that?" What she didn't know, until now, was Gretchen's connection to Tracy Lawrence: both worked at Casa Cucumber, both appeared in *Mermaid,* and both knew Logan Pollard.

"That was her with Tracy? In that picture?" she says, and I nod.

"I'll find the guy if the cops don't," I told her, an empty promise out here in the darkness. All I could think of was Pollard and Gretchen's voice on my machine.

Please don't tell him.

"Let's just worry about Charles tonight," she said. "Let's get him home for Beth's sake. Help him, Harding. For me."

I decided, for tonight, to go along with her. I took Charles for a walk on a hill.

Charles is wearing a long gray topcoat. He was wearing it sitting in the bar, as though waiting for a ride home. Beneath the coat there's a brown tweed suit, yellow shirt, blue tie. Color sense isn't one of his stronger traits. There's some dandruff on his suit—either that or he's been eating doughnuts with powdered sugar.

"It really has been quite a week," Charles says. We're on High Street now, aptly named, walking aimlessly. He keeps talking in circles. I feel like a cop trying to get a drunk to walk a straight line. "It started with that damn bottle . . . maybe if I'd kept it inside the paper bag . . . maybe if they'd run out of ice—or didn't have a clean glass—any sort of barrier . . . maybe if I hadn't been *staring* at it since Monday night—then when the phone call came I could have managed, I could have coped better—"

"What phone call, Charles?"

He looks at me sideways. There's a seven-second delay as he tries to put a name with the face. "Alison said you're one, too," he says. "So you must know what it's like. The pressure builds up. That small room, alone all week, trying to write—"

"I'm not a writer."

"An alcoholic. That's why I had them call you. You would know."

"Just an amateur, Charles. I never went through a program. I can't mentor you."

He closes his eyes. He puts his hand on my arm and speaks in a conspiratorial whisper. "Even better. I don't trust those damn programs. They take your fucking soul. . . ."

He's much taller than me, with wide shoulders, but he stoops when he walks, even up here on the open hilltop, as though conditioned to finding everything in life made for smaller people. "Saturday, Charles. Why don't you just tell me what happened on Saturday?"

His eyes fly open, struggle to focus. "Yes," he says. "Why don't I do that."

We find an empty bench. There are a handful of tourists around, staring into windows, as though the restored buildings and museums would be open this late. Most of the town is on the Historic Preservation Registry, which may account for the bad plumbing. The bench is wrought iron, very uncomfortable. Charles likes the bench. I think there's a bit of the Calvinist in Charles.

"You have to go back to Thursday," he says. "That's when it started . . . when the seal came off the bottle." Friday night he couldn't sleep, alone all night in that empty bed, knowing when Saturday came there was no way he could get married. And he couldn't face Beth, didn't know what to say . . . so he rented a car. He drove out here. He's been here since Saturday, room eleven, the DeSoto House. Just drinking.

"Alone," he says, as though I'd asked.

"Why here?"

"It's very peaceful, don't you think? Very calming. Not so flat like Chicago, and the people have a genuine warmth to them—"

"You've been here before?"

He shakes his head. "Someone recommended it once. But really, Harding, I wasn't thinking straight."

"Were you drinking all day Friday?"

"Yes. And Thursday night. And I haven't slept since. I know you're wondering how I could have done this—"

"I'm wondering how you're still on your feet."

He was never in any building on Hyde Park Boulevard. He never heard of Lopez, he was baffled when Alison first brought it up. And it couldn't have been him—he was here, in Galena, drinking. He'd checked in, he'd registered. There'd be records to confirm it. Ask the desk clerk, he says. Ask the car-rental people.

"Why would they even consider me a suspect?" he says.

"You fit the general description. You disappeared right about that time. Cops look for patterns, Charles. And easy answers."

His eyes are glazed. I catch a glimpse of just how drunk he is, how skilled he is at coping with it.

"That's what writing poetry is like," he says. "Looking for patterns, digging for clues . . ."

He stretches out his long legs. His black loafers go a good foot beyond mine. Beth is waiting for us, I know. But I sense that this may be one of the few times I'll have Charles alone and in a talkative mood.

"What really happened, Charles? Where did you go?"

"You don't believe me?"

"You wouldn't drive all the way out here for no reason. If you just wanted to drink, you could have holed up in the South Shore Motel."

He says nothing.

"Why Galena, Charles?"

"You don't like me much, do you, Harding?"

"Charles, I'm trying real hard to like you. Alison wants me to help you. But you have to tell me the truth—"

"If I were to hire you," he says suddenly, "as a detective, would that mean you'd have to keep what we say secret?"

"Why would you want to hire me?"

"Just suppose I did . . . would this be confidential? Legally?"

"No," I say. "Not legally. We're not married. I'm not your lawyer or your priest."

"Oh," he says. His eyes close. His lips part. "My reasons for coming here, Harding, are quite mundane. And embarrassing to admit." He shakes his head. "The simple truth is that I'm forty-two years old, getting married, becoming a father, all for the first time. . . ."

"So this was an anxiety attack?"

"I ran," he admits. "That's what I do when I'm frightened."

"Why would you want to hire me, Charles? Because of the business with the drug dealer? I don't see how I could help you."

"No, it has to do with the phone call I mentioned . . . the phone call that sent me out here. Someone called and told me a friend of mine had been killed. A woman, someone Alison would know, too. I can't believe she's dead."

"Tracy Lawrence."

He seems genuinely surprised. I'm acquiring a portfolio of reaction shots. "How did you know?"

"The police told us Saturday afternoon. Who called you, Charles?"

"The police? Do they know who did it?"

"Stick with what happened here, Charles. Who called you?"

He pauses. "I didn't recognize the voice."

"Someone calls you up in the middle of the night to tell you a woman you barely know is dead, then hangs up?"

"Essentially, yes. Look, I'm not saying it makes any sense—I can't make much sense out of any of this right now—"

"Was it a man or a woman on the phone?"

"A man. A gloomy voice, probably disguised. *Memento Mori*. As if I would be dying soon, too. At least that's the way it seemed to me."

"So it was a threat, not just telling you about Tracy?"

"I took it that way, yes."

"And it connected you to Tracy."

"I don't know."

"How well did you know Tracy, Charles?"

"I hadn't seen her in years," he says.

"Really? You're sure about that?"

He gives me a quizzical look.

"I have a confession of my own to make, Charles. Everybody was worried about you—Beth, Alison, the university—so they asked me to fly to Denver. . . ."

I unfold the transcript from his drawer, the one I faxed to PowerFemmes. Charles looks at it carefully. It seems to catch him off guard that I have it. One thing a drunken poet can do is read.

"I can explain this," he says.

"I was sure you could."

"Tracy sent me this," he says. "She'd been talking to someone on the computer—she assumed it was me. This person, whoever it was, actually made plans to meet with her. When she finally called me to double-check the details—and I told her it wasn't me—she became frightened."

"Tracy sent you this? Or she sent it to you on the computer?"

"Why?"

"I'm just curious."

"She mailed it to me. I don't know how to do these things with computers. I don't even own one. The secretaries at the college type everything for me. I write in longhand." He hands me back the transcript. "She sent me a computer disk, too. Did you look at it?"

I tell him no.

He pauses. I can't tell if he's trying to remember the disk or trying to remember if he'd locked the drawer.

"I haven't either," he says. "Half out of fear, half because I'd have to ask someone to do it for me. She said there were pictures on it that she'd collected off the Internet, of herself and me and even Alison—others, too, people from Grand Terrace. Whoever is doing this knows a lot about me, and all of us, I think . . . from that time—and seems a bit . . . obsessed . . ." He stands, rather unsteadily, and puts his hand on my shoulder, then removes it, as though he's gotten too close. "I don't feel very well," he says.

"That's why we're still up here, Charles, instead of in my car. Can you tell me what this reference to Peace Station means?"

He hesitates. He's trying to focus on something. I can't tell if it's his story, or Peace Station, or me.

"That might be where she was staying. Living. I don't know."

"You don't know where she was living?"

"Why are you interrogating me about this, Harding?"

"Because Tracy died a few miles from here, Charles. And she lived about an hour away from you. In Taos. I talked to someone who saw you at Peace Station and someone else who saw you in Taos after she'd disappeared—he said you were nosing around there, asking about her. . . ."

"Okay," he says, more irritated than troubled. It's as if I'd caught him in an error in some philosophical proof. "All right. I knew she was living there. I just told you she was sending me those things. When I stopped hearing from her, I was naturally concerned."

"It would help if you'd stop lying, Charles."

"I'm not lying." He's so drunk it's hard to tell what he's really thinking. "You said she died near here?"

"The body was found near here. They don't know where she was killed yet."

"How did she die, Harding?"

"She was strangled," I say.

"Strangled . . . with what? With his hands?"

"I don't know." We start walking back toward town. I ask Charles about the pictures I found in his drawer from the Dunes and Grand Terrace. He says Tracy sent them, but his mind's on something else.

"Is that fast or slow, do you think?" he says.

"It's not fast enough," I say. He has to lean on me again, just to remain standing. "Why?"

"I can't help thinking of her last minutes, what she must have gone through. The terror she must have felt just then, right as she died—"

"Those are the minutes that killers live for, Charles."

"I've heard that somewhere. . . ." He looks around, as though waking up. "Where is Alison now, by the way?"

"Back at your hotel, getting your things together. We'll drive you back to Chicago, to Beth. Beth's been waiting for you."

"I suppose she's quite disappointed in me now, isn't she. . . ."

"I don't know."

"She can be unforgiving," he says.

It's an odd thing to say, and I don't know how to answer him.

"Beth loves you, Charles."

"What?" he says. "Oh, yes . . . Beth."

A bell chimes somewhere, whether for me or for Charles, I don't know. I've heard a lot of alibis in my time, but few compare to this one. Still, it seems too lame—and complicated—to be made up. And it was smart of him to call me instead of Beth—I do understand how the alcohol makes such stories seem plausible, even to yourself, even when you know they're not true. They *should* be true. The next few days should tell us more. Right now we're going back to Chicago, and Beth, and whatever it was he ran from on Saturday. He holds my arm; I hold the guardrail. We both walk back down the hill, taking tiny, tentative steps in the snow.

a lison meets us outside the hotel. She has the car warmed up. I help her put Charles in the backseat and then I take her aside.

"Did you talk to the desk clerk?" I ask her.

"I paid the bill. I stole some brochures. We didn't chitchat."

"What about his room? Anything there?"

"Some notes for a poem. Three empty bottles. A full ashtray. The clerk was with me the whole time, so I couldn't exactly pry up the floorboards."

"How's your head?"

"Splitting," she says.

"Because I'd love to drive to East Dubuque and look around."

"With Charles in tow?"

"He'll be sound asleep in the backseat in ten minutes."

"Not tonight, Harding. I can't make it." I put my arm around her. The right side of her face is burning up from her migraine. She gets in on the passenger side, frowning through the glass when I tell her I'll be right back.

The small lobby is lit by fake gaslight lamps and filled with imitation antiques, Early American reproductions. The wallpaper's peeling; that's not fake.

The desk clerk is a middle-aged man named Karl. "With a *K*," he tells me. It's a sore point with him. His badge has the *C* scratched out. He's having trouble getting his orange Flo-Writer to flow.

"Don't know why they give us these pens if they don't work,"

Karl says. The radio is tuned to an Iowa station; a newsman is discussing hog futures. If I understand the Board of Trade, these are hogs without any future.

Karl leaves the desk reluctantly when I tell him Charles left something in his room. We take the elevator, then he opens the door with an old-fashioned key.

"You worked here long, Karl?" I say, walking into the bathroom. I'm looking for some sign that Charles wasn't here alone. I go through the trash in the small waste can, check the drains for a woman's long hair, but come up empty.

"Eighteen years. I guess that's a long time to some." He watches me hunting through the medicine cabinet, pulling the shower curtain. "What is it he left behind?"

"A bottle of pills. I'm his doctor, Karl." I go through the chest of drawers and the end tables. The three bottles are still here—Charles was drinking gin. "Professor Muller's showing early signs of Alzheimer's: forgetfulness, loss of memory. For example, he says he drove here because it's a favorite spot, but my wife—the woman who paid his bill before?—doesn't think that's possible. I was wondering, have you ever seen him before this weekend?"

"Oh, sure," he says. "He was here before. I never forget a face." The bed hasn't been made; in fact, it looks as though housekeeping hasn't been here for several days. Karl watches me lifting the mattress, then hunting through a stack of newspapers. "What kind of doctor are you, by the way? The reason I ask is the day girl keeps calling in sick with morning sickness. Is there anything they can prescribe for that?"

There's nothing here. It's confusing. The room feels lived in, all right, but if someone just drove here without luggage and stayed this long, wouldn't there be bags from the pharmacy, toiletries bought in town—toothpaste, mouthwash? "I don't like to prescribe outside my specialty, Karl."

"What might that be?" he says politely.

"Brain tumors. Inoperable brain tumors."

"What do you do for someone like that?"

"Nothing to do," I say. "Gives me lots of free time. Would you have a registry I could see that would prove when he was here?"

"Don't need a registry," he says. "It was last August. During the fireworks."

"Was he alone?"

"With his wife that time," he says. "Looked a bit like the woman with you tonight. At first I thought it was her again."

"Do you remember her name?"

"Never talked to her," he says. "Never actually saw her out of their room, to tell you the truth, just like Mr. Muller this time. They were quiet, never made no noise at all. Why?"

"Just trying to complete my diagnosis." I wish I'd brought a picture of Tracy along. I take a final look around. There are some dirty dishes on a tray in the hall; silverware for one. Karl locks the room back up and we return to the lobby.

"About this girl with morning sickness—"

"I'd put her on the night shift," I say. "About that registry, is there any way I could see when Mr. Muller checked in?"

"Sure," he says, showing me the page for Saturday. It's in an old-fashioned ledger. For some reason Charles had signed in as "Mr. and Mrs. Charles Muller." But there's no time written there. And Karl with a K can't quite remember if it was morning or afternoon. A honky-tonk piano—"Down at Papa Joe's"—comes from the radio. Karl starts tapping his pencil on the desk. It's an infectious beat.

"Let me give you one of our deluxe suite coupons," he says. "In case you and your wife would like to be our guests some night."

"You said the woman Charles was with resembled my wife? How?"

"Oh, that might be me. She was a looker, like your wife . . . with real nice hair. And a nice figure."

"I think we probably will be back, Karl. We might not be as quiet as Charles, though. We might make some noise."

"Well, I hope you do," Karl says. "I certainly do."

. . .

It's just twelve miles to the river. The road curves and you don't feel the change in altitude, but suddenly you're on a modest cliff and the Mississippi is down below you.

If you killed someone in Galena, you could take this road to the bridge and there would be a hundred places to throw a body off. And the next day or the next month it would wash ashore. Unless it got hung up on something. . . . It's hard to tell from here how fast the current is.

The town of East Dubuque is at the foot of the hill. It has a business district that's mostly bars, liquor stores, and dance halls, all on one long street that runs parallel to the river. I think Al Capone used to do business there. It doesn't look like it's changed much. It reminds me of East Saint Louis or Covington, Kentucky—tiny midwestern sin cities, always just across the bridge.

I stop the car near a metal guardrail. Charles is sound asleep. Alison tried waking him occasionally, but he could only manage a few seconds before his eyes fluttered shut and he faded away. She keeps opening the glove compartment, slamming it shut, reopening it. Charles doesn't budge. The stereo is playing one of Alison's homemade tapes, *Best of Headbangers.* It's like a lullaby to Charles.

"The desk clerk said he's been here before," I say. "Last summer."

"Alone?"

"With Mrs. Muller. Who, according to the desk clerk Karl with a *K,* looked a lot like you. In fact, Karl with a *K* thought it *was* you."

"What did Charles tell you?"

"He said he's never been here before. Did the car-rental agency give you anything?"

"He rented it Saturday morning, like he said. In Chicago. That's all." She's quieter than normal. At first I think it's the migraine. But then I realize she's simply being careful with her words. Does she see me like Crowley now, interrogating her?

"What are we doing here now, Harding? Do you want to go down there and put your toe in the river, to say you've seen the Mississippi?"

I shrug. I'm used to Lake Michigan or smaller streams like the Chicago or Des Plaines. The Mississippi looks hostile, wide and dark and moving away from you, always pulling away. It's not the sort of river you skip stones across.

"It's a goddamn big river, isn't it?" I say.

"Beth's waiting," she says. "And I need a bed."

"He says Tracy sent the computer disk to him and the transcript. She was asking Charles for help. It's not much of a story."

"Unless it's the truth. Did Karl with a *K* happen to get the name of the woman who was here with him?"

"It was just Mrs. Charles Muller. And he says they hardly left their room. He thought they were real lovebirds. His term, not mine. But that could be Tracy."

"Tracy doesn't look like me."

"There's a resemblance." I pause. "I just wish we had time to look around Galena more . . . to ask around, see if anyone remembers them."

"We can come back with pictures of Tracy. I can't make it tonight. My head is godawful."

"Did you take a shot?"

"Yes, but it's not helping. Neither are these fucking roads." She takes off her sunglasses and rubs her eyes. "Did you ask Charles who called that night?"

"Well, that part is what I would call the weakest link in the chain. He claims he didn't recognize the voice, he was drunk as a fish, and there was something about *Memento Mori*—"

"*Memento Mori?*"

"You know. The Muriel Spark book."

"I know that. Leave it to Charles to insert a literary reference even in this." Her eyes close. The migraine is too much. I head for the bridge, intending to start back to Chicago, but make a wrong turn somewhere and end up on a small, unmarked road. It leads us to the water and a boat launch. Nothing fancy, just a gravel lot and a steep cement slide that goes right to the river. Right now it looks slick as glass.

The shoreline curves away just below us. The weeds are frozen; the black water laps softly against the rocks. Dubuque is across the river, but the lights from there are dull and foggy. The traffic on the bridge is the only real sign of life.

I've got a headache of my own, no migraine, just a dull ache from that trash-can lid. If Charles hadn't needed me, I might have started looking for Travis Savick tonight. I doubt if it's enough to interest Terry Crowley.

"What are you thinking about?" she says.

"The guy who kicked my butt. And stole the pictures I found in Charles's apartment—I wish you could have seen them."

She nods.

"Everyone has pictures of you, Alison."

"This surprises you?"

"They take trips, they move, they bring pictures of you along." She shrugs.

I sit for a moment, staring at the Mississippi. There are no street-lights out here; it's not like Chicago. The wilderness starts a few feet from the road. The darkness is everywhere. In the backseat Charles Muller begins snoring and shifting around in his sleep. Alison is drifting off, too, I think, beside me. She's tucked her head into her folded arm for a pillow. The snowflakes on the glass just a few inches from her skin melt as though from her heat. The radio is playing Joy Division.

Love will tear us apart . . .

I get out of the car. The icy snow stings my face. I slam the door shut and walk over to the weeds. On one side of the plateau is a wooden shack, built on the slope—I don't know if it was used for selling bait or soft drinks. For some reason it reminds me of a life-guard tower I saw in San Diego once and of a late November day Alison and I spent in California.

We were done with a case and had to hang around for another night to catch a cheaper flight home. This was in La Jolla, on one of those streets where every building's a crazy quilt of porches and decks in search of an ocean view. It was late afternoon. The Eagles were on the radio. I was drinking a Corona beer from the minibar and wondering how I could make the client pay for the beer and a ten-dollar jar of cashews and the souvenir T-shirt—with a seabird with spread wings in flight across the bay—Alison bought in the gift shop. From my hotel room I could see a half-dozen swimming pools, all David Hockney blue, edged with white recliners. The temperature was in the eighties. That's California. I guess you could live that way, but something about it isn't real. You'd have to know that somewhere, someone was freezing his ass off.

Alison was down there, on one of those recliners, by one of those pools, sunbathing, lying on her flat belly. She'd shed the gift-shop T-shirt; the top of her bikini was untied. Her skin glistened. The muscles in her back shifted whenever she changed position. Her head was tucked into her elbow and a few strands of her black hair lay on her arm. I can't remember how long I stood there look-ing. I can't remember what we did the rest of the day or what the job was or whether the client paid for the beer. Nothing's left from that day at all, except the beads of sweat on her arm, and the way her head was tucked into her elbow. . . .

It's funny how a memory like that can stay with you.

part two

18

Campus Security tries to disguise itself by hiding inside a quiet old building on Ellis Avenue, but it's the third- or fourth-largest police force in the state. I do enough work around campus that most of the guys know my face, if not my record. The ones who are ex-CPD aren't fond of PIs, though the fact that I'm an alumnus and my girlfriend hangs out with faculty confuses matters a bit. Most of them are just glad to find somebody lower on the law-enforcement food chain.

Willie Hendrix is manning the front desk this morning, and that's lucky for me. He owes me a favor. Willie's got a kid brother with a nasty crack habit and two strikes on his record. The rest of the Hendrix family gave up on the kid, but Willie found him a job at a hardware store, put him in rehab—I thought he was doing better until Willie called me last June, nearly in tears. One more bust and the kid would go down for a long, long time.

So I spent the rest of that night with Boone breaking into an Englewood True Value, replacing sixty-five dollars in cash, wiping prints, erasing the surveillance video. Every cent was returned, but I think Boone lifted some duct tape. You can never have too much duct tape.

"Travis Savick? Is he a student?" Willie looks like he's growing a mustache. It's in that awkward stage where you wish you could just stay at home.

"I doubt it, Willie." Of course, all I know about the guy is that he drives a black Cadillac, wears white gym shoes, and swings a mean garbage-can lid. Donnie Wilson could have helped me with this, but he's still out of town. "Can you check the state computers, maybe find me a picture?"

He frowns. "Not supposed to," he says. "Not without a reason. But yeah, I can." He sits down at a terminal and starts typing. He uses the two-finger technique. So do I. I once saw a chicken at a state fair type faster. "Name sounds familiar for some reason . . ."

The *Tribune* is opened to the Metro section. There's a small story about Tracy Lawrence, the first I've seen. It reads like a press release. The link to Chicago is fairly small; the only reason for the story is to fish for more leads, hoping someone will call.

"That's a terrible thing," Willie says, pointing to the story.

"I heard there was a girl attacked here Sunday night."

Willie nods. "You know, we tell them not to walk by themselves that late at night. They can take the campus bus, they can call us, we'll shadow them, whatever." He yells hi to another cop coming on duty. "Thank goodness she wasn't badly hurt."

"Someone taught her to fight back," I say. "Any leads? Physical evidence?"

He shakes his head. "We're helping CPD look at a couple names she gave them. And the desk clerk at Woodward says Gretchen met some guy earlier that day. We're hoping she feels better later today or tomorrow to give us a description. She couldn't say much the other night." It's always amazing how slowly these things come together. But sooner or later the guard will remember me or the desk clerk will pick my face from a book of mug shots. I need to talk to Gretchen, but I don't think Willie's the person to ask for her number.

Something on the monitor catches Willie's interest.

"You said you saw this guy on campus?" he says as the printer comes to life. "Where? On the quads?"

"All over. He's been tailing me since Saturday. Why, who is he?"

He tears the sheet off, but he doesn't share it with me. "I need to know if this is just something of yours, Harding—you know, one of your cases. Or if there're students and faculty involved."

"I don't know who's involved yet, Willie. I don't even know who in hell the guy is."

"Well, you know enough to have me check the state computer," he says, frowning. "You're right, he's got a record and he's done hard time . . . in fact, he's been inside most of his life, one way or another."

"For what?"

"The biggest stretch was sixteen years. Travis Savick, aka Trash . . . the nickname's what reminded me, it's been a while—"

"How'd he get his nickname?"

"The early busts were for rape and sexual assault, attempted murder, then he finally got over the hump. . . . This was after a stretch in Pontiac, his first week back when he's working for Streets and Sanitation, six-man truck, and he has words with a guy on his route, he's not separating the glass and the plastic or something, who the hell knows . . . there are words."

"He got sixteen years for arguing?"

"He got sixteen years for beating the guy to death with a fifty-five-gallon drum. My buddy was one of the arresting officers . . . it took four cops and five garbagemen to take him in. I would not mess with this guy, Harding."

"Do you have a picture of him?"

"It's on the printout," he says, tearing off part of it for me. It's a driver's license picture. Willie is watching me. I don't hide my recognition.

"Where have you seen him, Harding? On campus? I have to know."

"Believe it or not, he was singing Christmas carols last Sunday night."

"Come on."

"I saw him outside Henry Dahlgren's house." He frowns, writing this down. "And he broke into my place last night. You sound like you know him personally, too, Willie."

He starts to answer, then stops himself. I think it makes him nervous to be seen with me. "He went back inside on a narcotics charge; they've got him living in a halfway house. You want the address?" He writes it down for me, then folds the printout and puts it in his pocket.

"I owe you one, Willie."

"Not me, you don't. This conversation never happened."

the halfway house is in western Will County—it's a big, ramshackle place at the end of a cul-de-sac. The street's unplowed and the neighboring yards all have signs from Coldwell Banker saying NEWLY REDUCED / PRICED TO MOVE. No one wants one of these places in their backyard.

My own manslaughter conviction included a narcotics charge that was eventually thrown out, and I stayed in a halfway house after being released. Mine was a revamped motel called ShadyGrove— you could still find the name on stationery and pens in some of the rooms. There were dopers there, a child molester, a carjacker. It wasn't a bad place, but there was no grove around it and not much shade.

This place looks even less promising. The driveway hasn't been plowed. A stripped Schwinn rusts in the garden. There's no name or number on a large mailbox sitting in a gully. A steel I-beam stands tall next to it, sunk in concrete, scuffed by all the cars that have bounced off it over the years.

A kid as skinny as the I-beam opens the door. He mumbles hello. There's an older man in the kitchen washing up. His MASTER CHEF AT WORK apron is wrapped around a pale cardigan sweater. Both are dotted with red stains.

"Spaghetti," he says to me. "You like that Ragú?" I nod. It's always hard to tell the residents from the counselors in these places.

"Mr. Savick around?"

"Travis?" He peers at me. "No, I don't believe so. Kevin, have you seen Travis today?"

The skinny kid shakes his head. He's spinning a baseball cap on his head, tapping his right foot. His T-shirt hangs an inch or two below his sweatshirt. His baggy jeans are barely hanging on.

"I'm afraid our Travis isn't here very much these days." The old guy's covering for Travis, but not with much conviction. It's unusual for a violent con like Travis to be sent to a place like this, even with the drug charge. It tells me that Travis isn't stupid. He knows how to work the system. When I mention that the parole board referred me here with a job for Travis, the old man's tune changes just a bit.

"Well, he should be back any minute," he says. "I'm sure he just stepped out for something—a bag of chips or a newspaper—"

"I tried reaching him last night, too, and had no luck."

"I'm sure he was here. Right, Kevin?"

Kevin nods. I'd love to get into Travis's room, but this place is like the House of the Seven Gables: the steps curve up from a giant living room, where there are two or three men smoking and watching a small Sanyo TV with a cracked plastic shell. There's no way to casually slip upstairs.

The old guy wipes his hands and pauses to watch the TV. It looks like a soap. Two people are having a very earnest conversation in an Italian restaurant. I can tell it's Italian from the jug of wine and the candle on the table. Maybe they like Ragú, too.

"Everything stops around here when our story is on," the old guy says. "You get attached to the characters."

"There's not much else to do when you're inside," I say, nodding. "Hit the weights, stare at the ceiling. Wait for dinner."

"Exactly," he says with a smile. "We have to watch our story."

I tell him I've fallen behind.

"That's easy to do out here." He chuckles. He likes me better now; a fellow ex-con. "And things move fast. Just today we learned the McGuire twins have been living right down the hall from the stepfather who abandoned them."

"No kidding."

"Did you want to leave your name and a number? I'm sure Travis would be very interested in hearing about your job. He's not very happy with the one he has now, is he, Kevin?"

The kid shakes his head. He keeps tapping his right foot. He has the nervous energy of a junkie with too much time on his hands. It occurs to me that I'm in a roomful of ex-cons and I feel strangely at home.

"Where is he working now?" I say.

"I believe he's driving a truck for a doll company."

"Mannequins," the kid says, his first word since hello. He pulls his sweatshirt off to the sound of static electricity, revealing a big red Spider-Man crawling toward me.

"For Dreamlike Display?" I say. "In South Holland?"

"I think so," the old man says.

"Does Travis spend his nights somewhere else, by any chance?"

"Well, we have a curfew here," the old man says. "But it's not really enforced. And Travis works nights a lot. That's not against the rules, of course. If the employer okays it."

"Were you with him last night, Kevin?" I say.

"Me?" he says, already shaking his head. "I was here . . . watching TV."

"'Cept that time you went out for smokes," says one of the men. His eyebrows don't match; one's too overgrown. It looks like a caterpillar. He rises unsteadily to his feet and extends his hand. "I'm Mike and this here's Walt."

"We forgot our name tags," Walt says. He forgot his dentures, too, I think. Everyone's dressed for a different party.

"I was only gone an hour," the kid says, annoyed, "and I wasn't getting smokes, I was getting ice cream. And that ain't the stepfather. The stepfather was left-handed. We're supposed to think he's the stepfather, but he ain't. They're tricking us. They're always tricking us."

The kid's peering at me as though I might be his connection. On the TV there are two people in bed now. I can't tell if they're the same two people from the restaurant.

"I love a good story," the old man says.

it takes me a good hour to find Dreamlike Display in lovely South Holland. The factory is part of a paper plant and distribution center. There's a real stink in the air. I didn't know mannequins could smell so bad. There's no wind at all and with the extreme cold it feels like I'm swallowing ice cubes of the rancid smell with each breath.

A small display room is the only customer-friendly part of the operation. It's filled with mannequins and a single dotty clerk. The dressed figures—Blouse, Shirt/Suit, Bust, Dressmaker, Head, Hand, Pant/Sleeve, Shoe/Boot, Torsos—look like something from an old Sears catalog. So does the clerk. But somebody must buy them, the company fills the whole block.

There are no mannequins out on the factory floor, just huge molds and hissing steam and a lot of blue-collar workers; mostly Czech and Polish, I'd think, from the neighborhood and the sounds I hear mixed in with Americanized curses. It's the fashion industry at ground level, and it's not exactly haute couture.

Pollard comes off the floor to meet me in a tiny office he must share with the other managers. It's not exactly General Motors. I guess he didn't have quite enough Ritalin. The neon lights flicker. A radio is mumbling newsradio. There's a suitcase by his desk. It looks like it might hold a ventriloquist's dummy.

"If you want the tour, they do it at noon," Pollard says, a smile creeping onto his face. He sits down at his desk. His gray suit is off-the-rack Sears menswear. "A lot of school groups take it. We run through the whole process—designing the molds, creating the different model types—with slides of the finished products, window displays at Field's or Saks." He has a smell to him, too. It takes me a few minutes to place it: He smells like glue. He must be a hands-on manager.

"Do I get a dummy to take home with me?" I feel like throwing him up against the wall.

"You're welcome to what's in the recycling Dumpster," he says. "Other than that, no. And we don't call them dummies." His drug of choice still looks more like downers than speed. You might need painkillers to work at a place like this. Each time someone from the shop calls his name he reacts slowly, turning his head a second too late. "What can I do for you?"

I step closer to the desk, away from the noise. "I thought we could have another talk about Tracy Lawrence. Starting with *Mermaid* and how well you knew her then—"

"I've already answered that."

"—running right up to the present day. With stops in Taos and Peace Station." He looks at me but doesn't blink. "I was out in New Mexico yesterday, Logan."

"Do some skiing?" Pollard says pleasantly, his work face firmly in place. "Great skiing around there this time of year, supposedly."

"Your little poetry mugs are taking up space in her neighbor's adobe, Logan. They're filled with weeds, which I found appropriate. You knew she lived in Taos. Why didn't you tell me that on Sunday?"

He has a way of looking past you, as though something else is on his mind. "You asked me if I'd seen her. And I hadn't. Not in a long time. So what if I sent her a coffee mug?"

I push his paperwork back and sit on a corner of his desk, invading his space just a bit. When he reaches for the phone, I grab his hand. "Here's my problem, Logan," I say, twisting his wrist until he winces. "You knew Tracy, you knew Gretchen Moss, and I think you were doing more than having coffee with them. Now Tracy's dead, and on Sunday night Gretchen was assaulted, nearly killed."

"Let go," he says quietly. His hand is cold. "Look, I heard about

Gretchen. I tried sending her flowers, but she'd left campus—are you gonna let go?"

"Where were you Sunday night?"

"This is ridiculous—"

"Sunday night, between ten and midnight—where were you? It's a simple question." One of the secretaries is watching us now, and Pollard has to twist his body to avoid me turning his wrist over. "While you're at it, what about last Halloween, where were you then? You'll have to tell the police, Logan. You might as well tell me."

"Let go," he says, his voice rising to a little boy's cry. When I do, he pulls his hand back quickly, rubbing his fingers. It takes him just a second to regain his manager's composure. "As if the police would be interested in your idle speculation. You're a criminal." Those long, cold fingers now straighten his tie and smooth down his hair. "I think this concludes our little discussion." He presses a button on his phone. "Mr. Jones?"

"The police might be interested in your hiring practices, though," I say. "For example . . . why you've got violent ex-cons working for you."

"What on earth are you talking about?"

"Travis Savick. His friends call him Trash." He stares at me. "He's been following me since last Saturday, since I heard about Tracy. And he saw me talking to Gretchen, just before I talked to you."

"You've been talking to Crystal Royce, haven't you?" he says, the second time he's blamed his troubles on the hostess at Casa Cucumber. "That's where all this madness comes from—I owe her some money and now she's got you thinking I'm some kind of sociopath. Or is it your dyke girlfriend, the Amazon who broke my foot—is she still against me for some unknown reason?"

"You haven't explained what Travis is doing working for you."

"Who says he is? I never hired him—he scares the shit out of me, Harding, he's hated me ever since Crystal helped me with that damn magazine—"

"Gretchen warned me about you, Pollard," I say. "I was dumb not to listen."

He stands up. His hands are in his pockets. In these clothes you can see his profile better, how thin his legs are, the long slope of his back. His shoulders slump a bit like Charles's, but without the bulk. He looks like some kind of crane.

Two very large workmen appear at the door. Mr. Jones must have brought along Mr. Smith. Mr. Smith has brought a wrench. I decide it's time to go. Maybe the police can talk to Pollard. I told Crowley about him last night, but I'm not sure how seriously he took it.

"When do you get off?" I ask Pollard. "Five? Six? Because we will continue this discussion later."

"You're wasting your time." He's a little frightened now, but you can only see it in his eyes. The rest of him is locked down tight. "And I'm leaving on a business trip, so you're going to be waiting for me a long, long time."

"That's one of my strengths as an investigator, Pollard. I've got absolutely nothing better to do than wait."

19

rowley has the day off. He lives near Goose Island. I find him in his kitchen eating a fried-egg sandwich, drinking a canned Bloody Mary. He's wearing a blue shirt with frayed cuffs and loose polyester slacks. He has a napkin tucked into his shirt collar. He seemed bigger somehow the last time I saw him. Off-duty, he shrinks, his voice grows weaker.

"So your friend showed up," he says. The television is on, with the sound turned off. The sink is full of dishes. There's a *TV Guide* face down on the couch. The rest of the place is bare and empty. I get the feeling that the whole place would be a mess if there was anything here to mess up.

"You got him home safe and sound . . . tucked him into his bed?"

"He'd been drinking," I admit.

He hitches up his pants. He's wearing old loafers that are on their last legs and a wide belt that's on its last notch. The circular scar on his face seems deeper as his face grows thinner. "What'd he tell you exactly about his little vacation?"

"Not much. He spent the time holed up in his room. 'Wedding Bell Blues.' I'm sure he'd tell you the same story."

Crowley shakes his head. "They won't let me talk to him."

"Who, his lawyers?"

"The school. My boss. What happened in Dubuque is Dubuque's concern, what happened in Denver is Denver's concern." Crowley leans against the Formica counter. He has a bowl of stewed prunes that doesn't seem to interest him very much. "What happened on Hyde Park Boulevard is something no one's real concerned about. Nothing's tied to nothing. Even this Gretchen Moss attack—they call that isolated."

I nod. I wonder when somebody had the time to decide all this. Charles has only been back in town six or seven hours.

"He's got an alibi for the Lopez murder, Terry. There's no use pursuing that. It never made any sense to begin with."

"Maybe so," he says.

"You're not looking at him for the Gretchen Moss attack, are you?"

"Not officially," he says. "He's got a story for Sunday night, too, supposedly."

"Did you talk to Gretchen before she left for Kansas City?" I ask him.

"Not personally, no. I like to give a victim forty-eight hours, wait for the nightmares to kick in before I interrogate them."

"You're such a considerate guy, Terry."

He shrugs, picks something off his shirt. "It's my nature, I can't help myself."

He drains his Bloody Mary, then sets the can in the sink as though he might rinse it out and reuse it. Yellow prescription bottles are lined up against the wall like salt and pepper shakers. "That stuff you turned up on the Lawrence girl helps, though," he says. "I passed it on to my buddy in East Dubuque. It's real interesting that Charles lived so close to Tracy. And now you think this guy Pollard was involved with her, too?"

I show him the pages I copied from *Mermaid* magazine. It's a little artsy for him, but the basic message gets through. "Pollard took these? Of both girls?"

I nod.

"You believe in coincidence, Harding?"

I shake my head.

"Usually if something turns up in a certain place, there's a reason for it, am I right?"

"Usually, yeah. Are you talking about Charles? Or Pollard?"

He shakes his head, going to the refrigerator. The top shelf has a gallon of milk, the plastic caved in on one side. The middle shelf is filled with more Bloody Mary cans. He takes one out and shakes it. "I was looking at the list of what they found in the Lopez apartment. And your business card was there. The old one, the Wokowski one. The same one Tracy Lawrence had."

I stare at him. "That's fucking nuts, Terry."

"It's a coincidence, isn't it? He had it taped up right behind Miss December. We pulled a couple real good prints off it. Pulled quite a few off Miss December, too, but that's another story." The can's defective; Crowley uses a screwdriver to get it open, pounding it with the palm of his hand. He pours it into a juice glass. "Unfortunately, it's too late to talk to Ricky about it. He's in the ground as of this morning." He crosses himself. It looks like he's blessing the Bloody Mary. "Without Muller as a suspect—you said he's not a suspect, right?—then they might start looking for someone else to pin this on."

"Just because my card was there? You sound like I need a lawyer."

"No, I'm trying to help you, Harding, soze you *don't* need a lawyer. Look, I appreciate you helping me. And I *am* listening to you. After you mentioned Pollard and Savick last night, I ran their names. Savick has a record and he did hard time—"

"For rape and murder. I know, I heard about the nickname. But that's not all. I just found out this morning that Savick *works* for Pollard as a truck driver. Of course Pollard denies even knowing him."

Crowley goes into the bedroom for a handkerchief, then comes into the living room and slowly lowers himself into a recliner. "He's got a record, though," he says.

"Pollard? Really? For what?"

"A bunch of misdemeanors that sound like he was looking through people's windows. He never did time, it was suspended—his girlfriend filed the complaints, but she left for Africa before there was a trial. So he got counseling."

"Brazil."

"So you knew that, too."

"I knew where she went, I didn't know why."

He lights a cigarette and puts his legs up on the recliner. "You want us to like him for the Lawrence thing, you'll have to supply a motive."

"Since when do you need a motive for chopping up a woman and dumping her in the river? He was fucking her, Terry. Gretchen as much as said so. Maybe Tracy wanted to leave. Maybe she saw a side of Pollard he didn't want exposed."

"The writing thing again." He tries to get comfortable in the chair. He's not having much luck. "The main problem with the Lawrence case is they still don't have a crime scene, still don't have a murder weapon."

"So look harder at Pollard. Get somebody to talk to him at least. Throw a scare into him. And pull Travis in, that's easy enough."

"He's done nothing wrong."

"He broke into my place, stole everything I brought back from Taos. And I saw him on campus Sunday night in an old formal suit just like the one you're so obsessed with in the Lopez case—"

"Can you put him in the building?"

"You know I can't. You couldn't put Charles there either. That didn't stop you from convicting him." He doesn't answer this. He's getting tired of my questions. "Travis went inside on a narcotics charge a couple months ago."

"Yeah, so?" he says.

"Who bailed him out?"

He lets me see the rap sheet. The bail bondsman was Eddie Willis on West Randolph. The co-signer was Crystal Royce. Crowley must see something on my face. "Why, you know her?"

I shake my head. "We spoke once on the phone. But her name keeps coming up." I wonder if that's where Travis is spending his nights and parking his Cadillac.

He unsnaps a prescription bottle, swallows two pills with the last of his Bloody Mary. "Harding, if there was something substantial on either one of these guys, we would pull them in. But you're never gonna get an interview based on this, much less a search warrant."

I nod. I came here hoping for help with Pollard and Travis. Instead I find I'm a suspect in the Lopez killing. "You've got no leads in that case at all?" He shakes his head. "What about the canvassing they did on that block? Known associates, customers . . ."

"They can't find anyone who knows much. Or wants to talk. There's a boyfriend, apparently, Davey or Daryl or something, but he's dropped from sight. It didn't strike me as a crime of passion."

"Did anyone talk to Ricky's brother, the one coming in to pay for the burial?"

"From what I understand, no. That never happened. Roscoe Brothers Funeral Home was left holding the bag, so to speak—the brother either said no or whatever, he didn't feel like coming to Chicago. Apparently there is a rift in the Lopez family. So I guess Ricky won't get no headstone."

"The county buried him?"

"Why, you wanna pay your respects? That's damn sentimental of you, Harding. Brings a tear to my eye just to think about it."

"You're pretty sentimental yourself, Crowley."

"I literally can't help myself," he says.

Willie Hendrix is having his lunch at his desk. "Tuna again," he says, unwrapping the tinfoil very deliberately, as though he was on the bomb squad. The police scanner squawks from the next room. "Nonfat mayo, no eggs, no salt. This is what happens when my wife watches *ER*—she hears about heart valves and cardiac arrest and now I don't get any salt." He takes a bite, grimaces, and then looks around the squad room as though there might be a spice rack. "What's your interest in this woman, Harding?"

"She bailed Travis out of jail. I know she works for the university. I'm a little surprised you didn't mention her before, Willie, when you read me his record." He unwraps another foil package. "Is that what Travis was doing in Hyde Park besides following me? Does he live with her? Are they a couple?"

"Kosher pickles," he says. "She knows I like the sweet ones, the butter chips. And she gives me dill." He takes a bite anyway and winces, then wipes his fingers on a napkin. "Crystal used to work on campus, in development, fund-raising; she did a lot of entertaining. She doesn't work here anymore. Is this going to come back and bite me on the ass, Harding?"

"Just tell me about Crystal Royce. And how she knows Travis."

He sighs, leaning back in his chair, trying to avoid a beam of sunlight. "Travis is her brother—half brother, to be precise. I don't think they're close. I've never seen him on campus, not since he killed that guy. That's why I asked you where you saw him. He's trouble."

"He sounds like a psychopath. A fifty-gallon drum?"

Willie shrugs. "There may have been more to it than that. He had a better lawyer than you'd expect. And they got enough suppressed that Travis pled to man one. He kept his mouth shut, did his time."

"You're saying it was a job?"

"He sure came out richer than when he went in," Willie says.

"And Crystal?"

"Well, I never thought Crystal had anything to do with that side of Travis. For example, she was the one that turned him in on the narcotics rap."

"And then she bailed him out. What's her relationship with a guy named Logan Pollard?"

He shrugs. "I don't know Mr. Pollard," he says, unwrapping his dessert. It looks like a bran muffin. Willie pokes at it with his index finger. "But then I don't know all of Crystal's friends. And Crystal has lots of friends."

"Oh? Is that why you wondered if my questions would come back and bite you on the ass?"

"Let's just say there were rumors about some of the parties she threw. Rumors about a 'love nest' she kept off-campus. Her fundraising got sort of personal at times, if you know what I mean."

"She was hooking? Really?"

"More like accepting gifts in exchange for services rendered. She's been the 'other woman' in more than one local divorce. And she has friends. I've seen her with board members, I've seen her accompanying professors to out-of-town seminars. Alumni trips. She's never gotten in trouble because there's always somebody there to vouch for her."

"Who's bailing her out these days?"

He doesn't answer, just taps his pencil.

"Come on, Willie—"

"Okay . . . but you didn't hear this from me. A shrink named Dahlgren."

"Henry Dahlgren? No kidding." A cop brings a McDonald's bag into the squad room. Willie watches him unwrap the sandwiches. I think he might go for his gun. "I didn't know Dahlgren had such eclectic tastes."

"Crystal's never been charged with anything, Harding. Most of us think what she does is pretty harmless."

"So you look the other way because she's doing faculty instead of walking on 53rd Street?"

He shrugs. "You can only spend so much time in the library," he says.

professor Henry Dahlgren is sitting with a folded *New York Times* and an unfolded taco salad in Hutchinson Commons, a long, beautiful room now used as a fast-food cafeteria. Behind Dahlgren is a large formal oil painting of Edward Levi, who was president when I was in school. I had lunch with Levi once, part of the college's attempt at letting us meet and connect with the more distinguished faculty. Years later, Gerald Ford appointed Levi attorney general and I was in prison, and I often saw his name on various legal forms. I saw his picture on the warden's desk once. I felt we were connected.

"Crystal Royce?" Dahlgren says, spearing a tomato wedge with his fork. "I can't quite place the name."

"That happens, Professor."

"But you say I know the woman?"

"Apparently so." Dahlgren is dressed in a very nice gray pin-stripe suit today. There's a trace of mousse in his hair. He's one of those guys who always looks like he just got a haircut.

"May I ask how you know about this?"

"You can ask all you want. It's the Socratic method."

"But you won't tell me?"

"I don't think it matters much." There's always a slight echo in here from the wood paneling and high vaulted ceiling. The light comes from far above, filtered down through dust and years of student yawns.

Dahlgren pushes his tray away. I guess I've spoiled his appetite.

"I thought we were friends," he says.

"We shared some coffee, Professor. That doesn't make us blood brothers." Maybe if he'd brought out the cheesecake I'd feel different. He rises slowly from the table, rearranging the items on his tray. "But I helped you out by flying to Denver. I brought Charles back from Galena. So why don't you help me out with this?"

We walk out to the hallway of the Reynolds Club. Dahlgren picks up one of the free papers stacked by the front door.

"Beth called me this morning," he says. "I think she's worried that Charles is drinking again. Full-time, not just last weekend."

"She said that?"

"Not directly. She wouldn't . . . she's protecting him. Beth is sometimes too maternal. She has a generous heart." He pauses. "I do want to thank you for what you've done. Bringing him back. I haven't spoken to you since Sunday night, the day after he disappeared. Do you mind talking about this?"

"We can talk about Charles if you want."

"He was in very bad shape when you brought him back, yes?"

I shrug.

"I told the trustees I felt that his 'lost weekend' was an isolated instance, one of those rare dark nights of the soul we all experience at some point in our lives. Something that happens out of loneliness or fear. . . . Do you understand me, Harding?"

"I'm trying to keep up." The doors to WHPK must be open. The all-seventies marathon continues.

What's your name, little girl, what's your name

"The point is, there is no reason to publicly crucify someone for such an atypical action. We can work these things out in private. We're grown men, after all. These are isolated instances . . . of aberrant behavior."

"Are we still talking about Charles, Professor?"

"That woman you mentioned just now—"

"Crystal Royce."

"Again, officially I can't quite place the name—"

"That happens sometimes," I say, "with isolated instances of aberrant behavior. Sometimes it's hard to remember the names."

We're standing in the middle of the hallway, islands in a stream of book bags and briefcases. Dahlgren's oblivious to the kids moving around us.

"I met Crystal last spring at an alumni function. I mistook her for a faculty wife. I found her charming. We shared a drink. We became friends." He pauses. "Why does any of this interest you?"

"I'm investigating the murder of Tracy Lawrence. She was a

classmate of Moira's, maybe you've met her." He shakes his head, says Moira may have mentioned her. It doesn't sound like a ringing endorsement.

"I think Crystal's brother, Travis, may be involved in the murder. So when I heard how close you two were, naturally I was curious. Does Moira know about Crystal, Professor?"

He starts to answer, then thinks better of it. "That's really none of your business."

"Are you afraid she'll use Crystal against you in the divorce?"

"Of course not." He smiles at me, a concession to someone half a step slower. "With Moira's past she'd be hard-pressed making that an issue. Believe me. You can ask her yourself if you wish."

"I'd love to. But I don't know how to reach her. I take it she's not living in Hyde Park?"

"Not at the moment, no." He says nothing for a while. Then something occurs to him. He walks closer to Mandel Hall, away from the flow of traffic. There's a bench, but he doesn't sit down. "Perhaps it's fortuitous, our meeting like this. Because the truth is, Harding, my wife is . . . avoiding me right now. For reasons of her own."

"This is all very touching, Professor."

"She won't return my calls. She has moods like this sometimes. It can't be helped. But she might talk to you. And she'll be in town for a day or so, for a gallery show—did I tell you she painted?" He has an ad in his briefcase torn from *North Shore* magazine. It's another landscape, much better than the one in his house. The colors—soft oranges, deep browns, a rich blue sky that's like a canopy—have a sensuous quality even the cheap reproduction can't quite hide. It's a different sky than the one I saw in New Mexico. The painting is called *Mexican Moonlight,* like the song from Concrete Blonde.

Oh, amigo
here we do things slow

Dahlgren seems proud of the painting. Maybe that's why he's carrying the ad around. It's also helped him redirect the conversation away from Crystal Royce. "Why won't Moira talk to you?"

He folds up the ad, returns it to a slot in his briefcase. "It usually means she's found someone new. A new plaything." He snaps the briefcase shut. "She usually stays at the Palmer House. The gallery is on Wells. Perhaps if you were to act as an intermediary—"

"And tell her what?"

"Make sure she's safe. Tell her I'm worried about her. It's Christmas, after all. I'd like very much to see her. Despite what you've heard, the divorce isn't inevitable. I still have hopes of getting back together."

"Professor—"

"It's late. And I have a class to teach," he says, walking away from me very quickly. He's done it again, hired me without mentioning money. Lunch is over.

20

there have been UFO sightings all over southern Illinois the past few days. Even the cops have spotted strange flashing lights, so of course the newscasters are joking that Santa left the North Pole early. The TV pictures look like Frisbeed hubcaps or lids.

My head still aches a bit from my own close encounter with a trash-can lid, so I stop at the Walgreens on 55th for some aspirin and stand in the checkout line by the display for Doug Fir, the singing Christmas tree. Dick Van Dyke is on the cover of *TV Guide*—the old Dick Van Dyke, the black-and-white Dick Van Dyke, the one who lived in New Rochelle with Laura and Richie. He's in color on the cover.

Alison's in her office at PowerFemmes. She's sitting at her desk, wearing very tight black micromesh and sweatpants but looking very businesslike. The desk may have something to do with that. I need to get one for my office.

The gym's crowded and very lively; everyone's excited about the upcoming show. The two women I'm watching are contrasts, both sides of the current female-bodybuilding vogue. One is lean and athletic; the other has bulked up. You use lighter weights, do more reps, or you go for muscle. I smile at both women. I try not to take sides. The stereo is blasting Earth, Wind and Fire.

After the love has gone
How could you lead me on

Alison goes out to spot Michelle, the woman I met the other day. She's doing dumbbell curls, then deep-knee bends, then squats. There's more weight on the bar than I'd care to try. The muscles in her shoulders and back are impressive. They're also vaguely erotic. Michelle has bulked up. She must be competing in the show tomorrow.

"Six," says Alison, hands just above the bar on Michelle's shoulders. "Seven. Michelle, watch your posture." I wander out to the gym floor, watching Michelle's posture. "Charles was here before, Harding, on his way to see a lawyer. You should stop in and say hello." I nod. I had the same idea, though I wasn't quite as enthused about it as she is. "Maybe you two guys could do something together."

"Like what? Go bowling?" Actually, I have a few errands to run this afternoon. I hadn't thought of taking Charles along, but it might be oddly appropriate.

Alison waits while Michelle changes position on the bench, toweling off her shoulders. "He invited us over late tonight."

"I've got plans for late tonight."

"Hey, fella," she says. "So do I."

"They include you."

"They damn well better."

Apparently Charles was questioned briefly by the police, with a university lawyer present, at an office they've given him in Gates-Blake. Whatever he told them must have satisfied them.

"Nine . . . ten. Michelle, you're doing great. Remember to squeeze your quads each time."

"How's Beth taking all this?"

"She's doing better. Compared to husbands one and two, Charles still looks relatively tame. But she wasn't thrilled that he called us first, and she wasn't thrilled he'd been drinking. So everything's in limbo." She takes off her sweatpants, adjusts the micro-mesh hugging her rear. It snaps back against her skin. "I think if he enters some kind of program, she *might* take him back. Henry gave her the names of a couple that he recommends. But right now Charles is on probation."

Michelle is doing set after set, her eyes fixed on the ceiling. I think she wants to say something, but it's like trying to have a conversation while sitting in the dentist's chair.

I ask Alison again about Logan Pollard. Does she remember him at all? Or the woman she trained, who apparently broke every bone in his foot? She says no. She has lots of students. "Michelle . . . don't forget to breathe." She's putting on gloves, getting ready to do a set herself. "Maybe we can have dinner out, Harding, and talk about all this."

"I don't mind cooking something."

"Meaning you're broke," she says, smiling. "Don't worry, I'm teaching nonviolent resistance to a group of seniors; there's usually a granny who's not so nonviolent and wants to learn a choke hold. I can pick up an extra fifty." She touches my face with a glove. She smells great, but I pull back a little. It might be me getting the choke hold.

Before I leave I call around campus and dig up Gretchen Moss's home number in Kansas City, then I perform my management duties: emptying the trash, replacing a washer in a leak-proof faucet. The floodlight over the rear door is out, and when I'm climbing the ladder to replace it, I notice a series of scratches around the door frame and more around the lock. They're only noticeable when the sun hits the metal a certain way. I can't tell how recent they are.

Alison's busy with two other women now, both new clients, and she listens to me impatiently. She knew the light was out, she says. There are scratches everywhere.

"Did you get any more of those phone calls you mentioned on Sunday night? Where nobody's there?"

"Maybe," she says.

"Why didn't you tell me?"

"They were just wrong numbers," she says. She's busy, focused on her students, she can't talk now. This isn't the time or place to talk about Travis anyway. I check the locks again and run a quick test of the security system. The scratches on the door don't bother me as much as the floodlight, which has a single crack in its glass. The cold weather might have done that, I tell myself, though I know it's also possible that someone tapped it once, very hard, to short it out.

there's a new car in the Reinhardt driveway, a silver BMW. And there's a new Christmas tree in the front window with Popsicle-colored ornaments and lots of tinsel. Beth Reinhardt answers the door with a cell phone in her hand; I haven't seen her since the night we had dinner at the faculty club. She's wearing blue jeans and a red ski sweater with alternating rows of downhill racers and evergreens. The timberline stops just below her neck.

"I'm on hold," she says, letting me into the foyer, "trying to order something for Christmas. They're already out of stock on half the sizes and the good colors, I'll end up with an eighteen in lime—"

"How are things, Beth?"

"Things are proceeding," she says with a slight shrug. "Nobody slept very much. Charles is over at the gym, that's his cure for a hangover, I guess." She uses the edge of the cell phone to push her hair away from her face. "I have to thank you again for bringing him back. It's embarrassing to me, having you doing my dirty work."

"That's pretty much what I do for a living, Beth." She's putting on a good face, but her eyes show how tired she is, what this week has cost her. "The tree looks good. And the car's new, too, isn't it?"

"Charles rented it. It seems a bit much, but what the hell." She pauses. "He wanted to buy it for me, but I said no. And now he wants to take me skiing this weekend. It seems like too much too soon. You know. He's trying too hard. It worries me. I'm thinking of asking Alison to go. If she said yes, would you come along?"

I tell her I'll certainly think about it, though skiing to me is just an expensive way to fall down a hill. Her connection finally comes through. She mouths a goodbye and then walks back through the living room, trying to talk over a rather insistent grandfather clock. One of Beth's daughters, Cindy, is watching TV. There's a floral centerpiece on the table, early Christmas cards on the living-room mantel, toys and Nintendo and schoolbooks everywhere. The whole house is a casual mess, lived-in and warm and very friendly. It's not a world I've ever lived in.

Charles Muller is fast-walking on the track at Stagg Field. There are indoor tracks at Bartlett and the Field House, but Charles seems intent on proving something out here. He has a headband that looks like an old handkerchief, a long maroon scarf, heavy sweats, ice crystals in his beard. His running shoes aren't new, but they've spent more time indoors, propped on a footstool.

He doesn't have a gym bag or a change of clothes, and when he climbs into the 4Runner, he's still toweling off.

"Trying to sweat it out?" I say. His eyes look a little better today. More like a hungover rabbit's. "You know, Charles, when you run at the Field House, you can use their showers."

"I like it better outdoors," he says, pulling off the headband. "You can feel it more in here." He pats his chest, but I can't tell if he means his lungs or his heart.

"It feels more like penance that way, I guess. Is this part of your new regimen, starting over, et cetera? For Beth?"

He nods, draping the towel around his neck. "I'm that close to losing her, Harding."

"A shot glass away."

"I'm serious, Harding. I've stopped drinking."

"Uh-huh. How's life at the frat house?"

"It's fine. I'm not there a lot. Between Beth's and the library and the lectures I'm preparing—"

"I didn't know you were teaching already."

"Not a class, just a little talk they invited me to give tomorrow on the Romantic poets—Keats, Shelley, Wordsworth. I might lecture next quarter on Homer. So there's lots to do. You said you had some errands? Are you stopping at the grocery? I'd like to get some wheat germ and some yogurt."

"Maybe later." I pause before deciding to keep the nature of the errands to myself. "Right now I'm on a little odyssey of my own."

Crowley's description of the current state of the Lopez case wasn't encouraging. I knew the cops would do a routine investigation: talk to the neighbors, pull in known associates, hope for fingerprints or blood evidence to close the case for them. I needed to find out more about Lopez, and the best way to do that was to look into his past.

You can find previous addresses in old phone books, but Ricky Lopez is too common a name; it would take forever sorting through them. I thought about waiting for Donnie Wilson to come back to town—I'd already left messages asking for more records on Pollard and Travis and even Henry Dahlgren—but then I remembered the stack of *BoyzWorld* magazines in Ricky's living room, arranged chronologically. He must have been a loyal subscriber. So I called the circulation department. I'm often mistaken for a cop, usually undercover narcotics or vice. I have a good cop voice, I think. *BoyzWorld* must think so, too. They gave me three old addresses for Ricky.

Charles and I take Cottage Grove south, threading our way through ComEd trucks and orange barrels. I turn on WHPK and catch Screaming Larry introducing Chicago's own Chi-Lites from 1971. They're on a search, too.

Have you seen her
Tell me have you seen her

"I spoke with my lawyer this morning," Charles says, still a bit red-faced from his bout on the jogging track. "It's all going to work out, I think. The business with Ricky Lopez, I mean. That was all a misunderstanding."

"That's great." We pass Washington Park, leaving the campus behind. "I did want to ask you something, though, Charles." He nods, pushing his unruly hair down a bit. He must have run straight from Beth's; he didn't even have a coat. "You said you'd never been to Galena before, but the hotel clerk seemed to remember you."

At 63rd Street the road narrows to one lane. We're in a long line of cars, waiting for a road worker to flag us on. Charles takes a while to answer my question and when he does, he asks if he can smoke one of his foul French cigarettes. I crack open my window. "The clerk's right. I'd been there before. Last summer. With a woman. This is something that I had to finish, before my marriage. Clearing the deck, so to speak. It was not serious . . . *amour de rencontre*. Someone I knew before. You understand?"

I nod. A Santa Claus approaches, collecting for a nameless charity. He hasn't bothered with a fake beard. I give him a dollar, smelling the liquor on his breath.

"It was already over and yet not quite over. . . . I never told Beth about this and I'd prefer not to, especially not now with all that's transpired." He smiles. "It would hurt Beth unnecessarily. I'm sure you understand."

I nod. "Did the police ask you who called you in the middle of the night?"

"Not really. I didn't see any need to explain that."

"Yeah . . . They wouldn't have appreciated the Muriel Spark reference, I'm guessing."

"Exactly."

Slowly the traffic begins to move again. I put the 4Runner back in gear.

"You know who the caller was, don't you?" I say.

"What makes you say that?"

"Your story doesn't make any sense. The memento mori stuff . . . please."

"The idea of your own mortality doesn't frighten you?"

"Someone I know, telling me something I believed was true, would frighten me more. A stranger's voice wouldn't have sent me scurrying to Galena. I let it pass last night, but that doesn't mean I bought it."

He says nothing. He's watching the scenery, pulling on his lip.

"It wouldn't by any chance be the same person you just mentioned, would it?"

"What makes you say that?"

"Because I think you might have been with her again last weekend. None of this is my business, Charles. God knows I don't care who you sleep with. But you should be careful, handing out half a story. Especially to the police. They have a nose for that sort of thing. They like connecting the dots."

"I thought you were on my side, Harding."

"Charles, I defended you to the police. I agree, it made no sense to link you to the Lopez thing. But that doesn't mean your little lost weekend makes any more sense." I pause. "And if you were meeting Tracy Lawrence there last summer, you'd better tell me now."

He nods. I park the car on 74th Street near a flimsy row house. Ricky Lopez lived here three years ago. I don't have much luck at first—only two units are occupied and neither tenant will so much as open the door. I ring every bell in a neighboring building with similar luck. But a woman across the street directs me to a small house at the end of the block and there I talk to a woman named Sylvie, who holds a crying baby while she tries to determine if I'm from Child Welfare. I ask about Ricky, which brings forth a string of expletives from Sylvie and a bit of drool from the baby. Sylvie hasn't seen Ricky in months. She asks if I'm Ricky's new daddy. I tell her no. The baby waves goodbye as the door closes.

The street's deserted. There are two junked cars, a trash barrel used as a space heater for warming your hands. In the summer there would be people sitting on the porches, hanging out in the alleys. You flash a twenty and somebody remembers a face, somebody points you to somebody else. You might get lucky, you might get mugged. In this weather you have to knock on doors. Information is hard to come by.

Charles looks worried as I approach the car. "I'm wondering if this is such a good idea," he says. "Bothering these people . . ." He locks the doors as soon as I'm inside.

I turn the heater up a notch and unfold a city map. The next two addresses are both southwest of here. A gust of wind blows some dry snow across our windshield. "So what exactly did this person say on the phone, Charles?"

He sighs. He thought the subject had been dropped. "I'm not sure that it really matters—"

"Humor me."

He runs his hands through his hair. "What I said about memento mori . . . that was true. He told me about Tracy's death and said that I'd better watch out or else."

"Or else what?"

"Or else . . . the same thing that happened to Tracy would happen again. And again."

"That doesn't make a lot of sense, Charles. He was threatening you? Or somebody else? Was he threatening Beth?"

"No, he never mentioned Beth." He pauses. "He did mention Alison."

I put the map down and turn in my seat. "Charles—"

"I know, I know. I should have told you this last night."

"You should have told me this the night he called. What the fuck were you thinking, Charles? Running away like that?"

"I'm not proud of myself, Harding." It reminds me of his words last night.

That's what I do, Harding . . . I run.

"What exactly did he say about Alison? And tell me all of it,

Charles, because I'm getting tired of this habit you have, of giving me three-quarters of a story."

"It was just something like: I know about you, I know about all of you from Grand Terrace, and I know about Alison . . . I was watching you then, I'm watching you now—something like that. He said I should get out of Hyde Park."

"Somebody threatens Alison and you don't think to tell us?" I say, raising my voice. He nods, slumping in his seat. "That's why you wanted to hire me?"

He nods. The more I yell at him, the more he slumps. He shrinks when he's sober. I try to get more out of him as I drive to the second address; he insists I've heard everything. After I've parked and slammed the door shut and walked half a block, I call Alison on my cell phone. Those scratches on the back door bother me more than ever now, but the fact that she'll be at the gym all day relieves my mind somewhat. Anyone looking for trouble there would find it. I remind her to keep the back door locked, to stay out of the alley after dark. I'll be there to help her close up.

This address is part of a large tenement, but only one person answers the door and it's another woman with another crying baby—she crosses herself each time she says "Ricardo." As we talk her eyes keep going to Charles, who's just sitting in the car, scribbling in his notebook. We must look like cops.

"Any luck?" Charles says when I return. I shake my head. I've walked off most of my anger. There's a doughnut shop a block away; I get us six assorted in a cardboard box and two very strong coffees. He's putting on a brave face, but I know what he really wants. There are bars on every corner.

We drive west to Englewood, a rough neighborhood with a high murder rate. Ricky Lopez lived here in a decaying three-flat; he must have been down on his luck. The building hasn't been worked on since Ricky was here, maybe since he was born. There's a grocery cart in the flower bed. Most of the linoleum in the lobby is gone, replaced by a mulch of cigarette wrappers, newspapers, chicken bones, French fry boxes. It's like the undergrowth in a rain forest. I have trouble getting the lobby door open.

The man renting Ricky's apartment has never heard of him. He invites me in for soup, which is the best offer I've had all day, and directs me across the hall when I politely decline. There I find a large woman in a bright pink dress who remembers Ricky but thought he moved to Detroit. "Him and his boyfriend," she says, giving me a second look. I'm on my way out, struggling again with the lobby door, when a small boy tugs at my sleeve and tells me, "Mr. Ricky's dead."

"I heard that, too," I say, crouching to talk to him. He's bundled head to foot in winter clothes. "I was looking for somebody who might have known him."

"We don't know nothing about that," his mother says, scooping him up. "Come along, Jesse."

"I'm not a policeman—"

"Mister, I don't care what you is. If you want Ricky Lopez, we have no business with you. The man was a philanderer, a drug dealer, and—hold your ears, Jesse—a sodomite." The boy does indeed hold his ears, smiling up at me. I give his mother twenty dollars. "The day Oak Woods took his miserable body was a better day than the one before."

"Oak Woods Cemetery?" I say, making her repeat it. "I thought the county had to bury him. Somebody paid for his burial?"

"A *much* better day than the day before," she says again, closing the front door with one practiced push.

Charles is scribbling in his notebook again. Two of the doughnuts are missing. I take the lid off my coffee and start back toward Hyde Park, running into a lot of traffic around the Dan Ryan. WHPK slowly comes within range, playing Steely Dan.

Well the danger on the rocks is surely past
Still I remain tied to the mast

"This was fun today," Charles says, looking out the window. I can sense he sees things differently than I do, as a poet or a painter naturally would. His notepad is filled with isolated words and images, colors, details. "I'm not sure how much longer I'll be around here."

"What are you talking about?"

"I talked to Henry Dahlgren today," he says. "Henry implied that I'd better get my act together quickly if I want to keep the appointment. There's a departmental meeting next week at which my name may come up."

"That's just a formality."

"No, I think he wants me to leave." We're on Cottage Grove again, heading north. "I think he wants me to resign my position and kiss Beth goodbye and get the hell out of town."

"What makes you say that?"

"Did you know he used to date Beth? When he was first separated from Moira?"

"He took her to a faculty dinner or something. Alison mentioned it. I don't think they were *dating*."

He shakes his head. I sense that he sees this differently, too. "He took her kids to the Ice Capades last week; he bought the family's Christmas tree—did you see the damn tree he bought them?"

"Henry Dahlgren is the one who brought you here, Charles. He's worried, that's only natural. . . . He's got a lot invested in you. The last thing he wants is for you to fail."

"I'm not so sure," Charles says. We're stuck in traffic on Garfield Boulevard. I swing down a block and run into the same backup.

"What possible reason could he have for hurting you?"

"Sometimes personal matters hold sway. Overshadows what's reasonable."

"Speak English, Charles."

He finishes his coffee. "I had an affair once. With Moira."

I do a bad job of hiding my surprise. "When was this?"

"Four or five years ago. I took a teaching job at Southern Illinois, where Henry was doing research—Carbondale, one of those small college towns where there's nothing to do. . . . And we just had this wild affair for the three months I was there. And then I didn't see her again for a long time. But I never forgot her."

I can tell he'd really like a drink now. He looks like he wants to bolt from the car. I keep a flask in the glove compartment—the way he's going, I'm surprised he can't smell it.

"You're worried about an affair that ended four years ago?"

"You don't understand. Henry took it very hard. And besides . . . it didn't really end there."

"*She* was the one you were with at the DeSoto House last summer?" He nods, not looking at me. It does make sense; the desk clerk said the woman looked like Alison. Moira certainly comes closer to that than Tracy. "Why didn't you just admit all this up front, Charles?"

"Because everything I say goes straight from you to Alison. And Alison tells Beth."

"Maybe Beth deserves to know. Maybe you should be telling Beth about these things yourself—"

"Beth wouldn't understand," Charles says, shaking his head. "She can't stand Moira. Moira . . . rubs people the wrong way. They don't understand her. Her husband certainly doesn't."

"And Dahlgren knows? About you and his wife?"

Charles just nods, staring out the window. "Oh, he knows," he says. "Dahlgren knows."

I'm sick of sitting in traffic like this. The weather's not helping. The storm they've been predicting for days is finally here. They won't get the snow plows out in time for rush hour. I take a chance and slip down an alley and cut through to a street that's mercifully clear of cars.

"So why did Dahlgren help you get the appointment?" I say.

"I've wondered about that myself. It surprised me when I heard from him. But he may have thought the affair was over." He turns to face me. His glasses are tilted slightly. "Henry himself has some rather strange tastes," he says.

"Like what?"

"He used to frequent the closest thing we had to a whorehouse. Three women lived there, ostensibly tutors—the athletic department used them—but some of the faculty liked to visit late at night, Henry in particular. That's partly what drove Moira to me, I think. The time he was spending there. I was so happy with Moira, I couldn't have cared less what he was doing."

"It's hard to picture." It's hard to picture Henry with someone named Crystal Royce, too, though the mental image I've constructed of her may be all wrong. I'll find out for sure in about an hour. Crystal's meeting me downtown. I hope the traffic's better on the Drive than it is here. I keep trying different routes just to move a few miles.

"You're completely at ease in these neighborhoods, aren't you?" he says. "I taught a class once in community college with some rough characters, but nothing like this. . . ."

"I grew up here, Charles." It occurs to me that I have no idea where Charles was born, no image of him prior to Grand Terrace. It's like he was born there. He has a flat midwestern accent, but not one that I'm familiar with. When I ask him about it, he says "Bainbridge, Ohio" as if reciting a prison sentence.

"Population eight thousand," he says. "Just a stretch of Dairy Queens, Little League, Sunday school. And I went to college at Otterbein, another small Ohio town."

"Coming to Hyde Park must have been a change."

"My God, yes," he says, watching the scenery pass. "It seemed like paradise. Especially that one year at Grand Terrace . . ." He shakes his head. "Everyone else just saw the gray buildings and the cold weather, but to me it was freedom. I started writing seriously then for the first time. That time's just a blur now. It went so fast. An island paradise, within the university, within the city . . . and then it ended. Does Alison remember it that way?"

"I don't think so." He recites part of a poem in a low voice. He says it's from Shelley.

"It is an isle under Ionian skies,
Beautiful as a wreck of Paradise."

"Have you ever had a time like that in your life, a perfect moment?"

"I went to Woodstock. It rained a lot."

"You're not much of a romantic, Harding."

"I just believe in understatement. A poet should appreciate that." I recite the closest thing to poetry I know.

"You call someplace paradise . . . kiss it goodbye"

"That's from the Eagles," I tell him. Glenn Frey is the desperado of romantic poets.

I've driven him to Beth's. The Christmas tree lights are flickering on and off. When he gets out of the car, I see one of Beth's daughters watching from a bedroom window. "Harding, that was most enjoyable today, whatever it was we were doing. It felt like an adventure."

I nod.

"Who were we looking for today, anyway?"

"It's just a case I'm on," I tell him.

"So this is detective work?"

"This is detective work," I say.

22

the doorbell at Roscoe Brothers Funeral Home is loud enough to wake the dead. The neighborhood around here keeps changing, but the Roscoes are flexible—there are Christmas lights, Hanukkah candles, and Kwanza decorations displayed in the bay windows. The front parlor is filled with poinsettias along with a lot of cut flowers. There's no shortage of wreaths for the door.

When I was a kid, my Little League team was sponsored by the Roscoe brothers—Sal, Saul, and Sylvester—and we would often celebrate our victories with a party in the basement of the funeral home, sneaking beers from the refrigerator and climbing into empty coffins. In those days their front yard at Christmas always featured a wicker crèche with a manger and live animals—a goat, a donkey that brayed in the middle of services—but the neighborhood changed; somebody stole the goat for dinner and the donkey for God knows what. The crèche is still there, downsized, with plaster of Paris animals. The donkey is chained to the water main.

A young woman named Ms. Whirlpool answers the door. Her hair is swirled to the side of her head. I can't tell if it's brushed that way or if she just slept on it funny.

"Richie Lopez?" she says, frowning a bit. "Are you sure he's staying with us?"

"Richard Lopez. I was told he had a brief stay here before moving on. I was wondering if you could tell me what happened to him."

"I see. Are you a relative of the deceased?"

I nod. "But I was in Greece for the olive season. The news

reached me rather late." I try looking over her shoulder as she opens a scrapbook-size accounts ledger. "He passed away last Saturday and you might have moved him from the county morgue to Oak Woods Cemetery."

"Oh, yes . . . Mr. Lopez." She reads something to herself while talking to me. "We weren't sure why we'd even been called—that is, no one had contacted us from the family."

"And for that I certainly apologize. But when the olives are ripe, one must go where the olives are. You understand. The olives wait for no man."

"Very true," Ms. Whirlpool says.

"Do you know what happened to him?"

"He stayed with us for a night. There was no service of any kind. He was going back to the county when someone arranged his burial."

"Could you tell me who that was? And where the burial was? I'd like very much to pay my respects. To the loved one." I have to use that expression at least once.

She flips through some index cards. "The Loyola Shelter paid for the ambulance that moved him. That's all I have listed here."

She has the shelter's phone number, which she writes on a Roscoe Brothers grief brochure. The cover has a very moving picture of an ocean sunset. It looks like a vacation planner.

"Thank you so much for your time and for all you did for Ricky," I tell her.

She closes the ledger. "The paper is specially treated . . . in case you happen to get it wet, the ink won't run."

"Thanks, I always cry at these occasions."

the traffic north on the Kennedy drives me onto the local streets miles before my destination. The snow tapers off close to the lake. I drive east on Peterson, past Wolfy's and a fondue restaurant I had a very bad experience at. I can't remember if it was the food or Alison's mood. I know we both drank a lot, and somewhere during the second bottle of wine it occurred to me that those little bread cubes wouldn't be enough to slow down the effects of alcohol. I also have a vague memory of Alison threatening me with a fondue fork.

The Loyola Shelter is more a bureaucracy than a physical structure; they rent storefronts in poor neighborhoods, providing temporary beds and soup kitchens during the winter months. A volunteer at their small office directs me to the shelter's director, Michael Glass, who lives in a large, white stucco house not far from the bend in Sheridan Road, the graveyard of the old Granada Theatre, bulldozed into a tacky strip mall. The house would be a lot cheaper in Bridgeport or anywhere else on the South Side. You pay for location, of course, though what you're getting for your dollar around here isn't immediately clear. There's gang graffiti on the overpass and still no place to park.

The front facade of the house is crowned with a pair of rust-colored gables. The porch is covered with frozen pumpkins and Christmas lights. The window is decorated with bunches of thistles and flowers and what basically look like artfully arranged weeds. I ring the doorbell and a small cat pushes the drapes aside.

"Hey," I say, kneeling by the window. "Is your daddy home?"

A tall man with a weathered face steps onto the porch, carrying some packages and sparing me any more conversation with the cat. He is wearing a tan trench coat with the collar turned up. The packages all have a return sticker with a holly wreath and "Flowers Under Glass" written in green script.

"Help you with something?" he says.

"I was looking for Michael Glass." Let's see—the Roscoe brothers, Ricky Lopez, his ex-girlfriend, the mysterious sister—I wish there was an easier way to explain this. I need a genealogical chart, and it's not even my family. And all because a ten-year-old business card of mine had showed up in a crack house. "I was hoping for some information about a funeral service—"

"I'm Michael Glass. A funeral service? What did you want to know?"

"A friend of mine was buried last week, Ricky Lopez. I know he didn't have any family, but the funeral home told me your shelter paid for his burial and service and I wanted to thank whoever did that."

"I see." He looks at me curiously. For some reason he reminds me of Sarah at Peace Station, the questioning look she had. "Excuse me, but you don't really look like a friend of Mr. Lopez."

"More like an acquaintance, really. We went to school together."

"Really."

"St. Anthony's. We were altar boys."

He shakes his head. "I used to be a priest, Mr. . . ."

"Harding."

" . . . a parish priest, Mr. Harding, which means I've listened to lots and lots of stories in my life. We'll get along much better if you just tell me the truth."

I nod. It's a new concept. "I'm a private detective. I'm trying to find out who paid for the funeral because I want to ask him about Ricky."

He nods.

"I'm trying to find his killer."

He pauses, waiting. He's very good at this listening thing.

"I'm also sort of a suspect in the murder. Just to be truthful."

"But you didn't kill him."

"No."

"Would you like to come inside?"

"You look like you were headed out . . ."

"Just to the post office. It can wait."

He walks to a small rolltop desk, sets his mail down neatly. It's a nice living room, full of knickknacks. The flowers help, large arrangements on every table. It takes me a second to realize they're artificial, either silk or plastic.

"I have a shop in Winnetka," he explains. "A florist shop, but I like flowers around the home year-round."

"Mine always die."

"They take nurturing," he says. "This city is hard on all types of beauty, I think." The cat rubs against his flannel trousers, round and round. "Tell me, do you enjoy it? Being a private detective?"

"I'm not sure anyone's ever asked me that before."

"So perhaps you've never had to think about it. I was just wondering, because you don't look particularly happy."

"Now you sound more like a shrink than a priest."

"Ex-priest," he says, smiling at me. "I'm fairly good at reading faces, telling fortunes." He looks at me as though reading mine. It doesn't take him long. "So . . . Ricky Lopez. Have a seat, please."

He points me to an old rocking chair.

"We operate shelters in Woodlawn," he says. "One of our volunteers, a young man who we've grown very fond of, told us about a friend of his who'd died recently. It seems the friend was about to be buried in a county plot without any blessing. He asked us to intervene. It's not normally something I would do, but I didn't see the harm in it."

"Can you tell me his name?"

"Well, I can't do that since that's why he wanted us to intervene. So he wouldn't be connected to Mr. Lopez."

"All I want to do is talk to him."

"I can give him your name and phone number. Okay? If he wants to speak with you, he will. I'm sorry, but that's the best I can do."

"He's afraid of something?"

"He's very afraid, yes. Of someone."

"Then you're taking a chance, aren't you, Father? The someone could be me."

"No, I told you before . . . I've listened to a lot of stories." He shakes my hand, looking in my eyes. "You're not a killer," he says.

He walks me to the porch. I thank him and say goodbye. Even the best fortune-tellers miss one once in a while.

23

i t's called Lady Dahlia," Crystal Royce says, offering me her
wrist. "What do you think? It's a new fragrance for me."

We're in Café Spiagga at a small table overlooking Michigan
Avenue. Crystal has been Christmas shopping. She has a brown bag
from Bloomingdale's filled with little totes from Ultimo, Hermès,
Marilyn Miglin.

"Are we eating? I hope so . . . I'm starved," she says. I motion
for a waiter, who interprets this as a call for another drink. When he
brings it, I ask for a menu. Crystal gives the waiter a happy smile, as
though they are old friends. "They used to have this fabulous
bruschetta here, outrageously expensive. I reeked of garlic for days
afterward, I think."

"That might be Spiagga," I say. "The restaurant part. Next door."

"Oh, you think so?"

"If it's out of my price range, it's next door." Crystal is more or
less as I pictured her—mid-thirties, blond, with a midsummer tan.
She's dressed in a winter dress that even Alison would approve of—
long and black and slit to show her legs when she strides across the
room. Her hair hangs just past her shoulders, and her blue eyes follow every word you say. "Thanks for meeting me, Ms. Royce."

"Crystal. I'm desperately trying to get some Christmas shopping
done—I hope to be on the beach in Jamaica by next week—but
Henry Dahlgren called and begged me to talk to you. What was I to
do? I never could say no to Henry."

I doubt if Henry begged, but it's hard to argue with Crystal. "Did he tell you what this is about?"

"He said you wanted to ask me about Logan Pollard. Are you the one who called me last Sunday?"

"Yes, and I apologize for interrupting . . . whatever I was interrupting." Even as I'm saying it, I'm wondering if it was Dahlgren with her. She sees my thoughts and smiles.

"We needed a breather anyway," she says. Crystal orders a Caesar salad and one of the luncheon specials, pasta with sun-dried tomatoes and pine nuts. I stick with my drink. I hope I have enough money to pay for the pine nuts.

"I really don't know how I can help you, Harding," she says.

"You could tell me a little about your relationship with Logan Pollard and Tracy Lawrence."

"My relationship?"

"When you were working at Casa Cucumber with Gretchen Moss—"

"That was ages ago, Harding."

"Why did you get a special thanks on the masthead of *Mermaid*?"

"I helped Logan obtain some funding. Originally the magazine was supposed to be an outlet for student work, but Logan wasn't interested in that. He had no trouble taking the college's money, though. The administration let them print one issue, then closed it down."

"Gretchen Moss said he promised a lot more than he delivered. She said both she and Tracy were led on about certain things—"

"Yes, but they were big girls, Harding. Besides, once Logan read the pieces Tracy submitted, he had no intention of publishing them."

"He did publish one."

"That thing with the body parts? I think Logan did that himself. It was a waste of space, don't you think?"

"I think it was odd, yes."

"The rest of her stuff was even worse, from what I understand."

"Did you read any of it?"

"Just a story about a serial killer. I don't like that sort of thing." Her salad arrives. She asks the waiter if maybe she could have just a *tiny* glass of Chardonnay. "We talked a lot at work, you know; between shifts, late at night, after the dinner crowd thinned out. Tracy was definitely tired of having her work rejected. I think she was trying to write something more commercial. Supposedly, there was an entire manuscript circulating, very violent, set in Hyde Park."

"But you never saw it."

"I only know how Logan reacted to it when he read it."

"And have you seen Tracy in these past few months?" She shakes her head. "Your brother Travis has been working for Pollard, did you know that?"

"I really don't keep tabs on Travis," she says, moving an anchovy to the side of her salad plate. "We were never very close. I don't know where he's living, for example. I didn't know he had a job. At least now when he calls for money I won't have to feel guilty about hanging up on him."

"Did you introduce them?"

"Not formally," she says, laughing. "But I might have mentioned Travis to Logan at some point—perhaps as an interesting 'type,' someone to write about. I don't think they liked each other, to tell you the truth."

"How did you come to help Pollard with the magazine?"

She pauses. "You're asking a lot of questions, Harding."

"I'm sorry."

The waiter brings her wine. She takes a sip, her tongue lingering on the rim of the glass. "I just hope you don't see me as a different kind of interesting 'type.'"

"I think you're very interesting, Crystal, but in all the right ways, believe me. And I'm grateful for whatever information you can give me."

"I helped him with the magazine because he often helped me.

When certain friends would come to see me . . . he would be their cover. In case their little wives became suspicious. And Logan was my driver."

"Well, Logan now runs the family business in South Holland. And Tracy Lawrence is dead. She was murdered last October."

She reaches for her purse. I think she wants a cigarette, but you can't smoke in here. "I didn't know that."

"It was in today's paper. She was stabbed to death, her body mutilated, thrown into the river. Something a serial killer might do."

She orders another glass of Chardonnay from the waiter. "You don't think Logan did that."

I shrug. "You know him better than I do, Crystal."

"I don't think Logan is capable of something like that. I mean, he is a little socially backward, but he never seemed violent."

"You never saw him lose his temper?"

"Well . . ." Her pasta arrives; the waiter cautions her that the plate is very hot. "Yes, of course he got mad occasionally—"

"Because of the magazine?"

"Because of the magazine, sure, but also in his role helping me. It was rather demeaning at times, at least I think he saw it that way."

"Why did he do it?"

"I'm not sure. For the money, I suppose. He was at a low point—he'd given up on school, his uncle was still alive and running the business, and Logan was determined not to end up there." The waiter asks Crystal if she'd like some freshly ground pepper, and she touches his arm when she says yes. "Tell me, Harding. Henry says you have a girlfriend, but he's not sure if it's serious. Is that true?"

"Partly true. It's often more comical than serious. Her name's Alison, she runs the women's gym on 57th Street, PowerFemmes."

"Oh, I know her," she says. "Tall, dark hair, devastating green eyes . . . I've seen her at some parties. She's very intense, isn't she?"

"Which party?"

"Oh, who can keep them straight?" she says, smiling.

"I wasn't aware Hyde Park was such a party town."

"It's not," she says. "You have to create your own fun. Be creative. You know?"

"And is Henry Dahlgren much of a party guy?"

"Henry is . . . Henry is just very sweet," she says.

"I can't quite picture him having very much fun, but I guess it would take a professional to loosen that tie of his—"

Her smile freezes. "Mr. Harding. I don't think you know what you're saying. I'll excuse you this time."

"I'm sorry."

"I don't know what people have told you, but I'm not that kind of woman."

"I'd love to hear what kind of woman you really are, Crystal."

"Someone who appreciates . . . intellectual stimulation," she says. "I have friends. They show their appreciation for me in different ways. Buying me gifts. Taking me places. There are a lot of lonely men in this neighborhood, Harding. Most of them are married."

"Like Henry Dahlgren."

"Like Henry Dahlgren," she agrees. "Although he won't be married much longer, from what I understand. If you knew his wife, Moira, you might understand why."

"I've met her. She seemed a bit out of place in Hyde Park."

"Exactly."

"But then . . . excuse me, Crystal, so do you."

"Why do you think I have so many friends?" she says, laughing. "These men are bored, Harding. I know how to talk to them, I don't embarrass them in social situations—and yet I'm very different from their wives. What did Henry tell you about Tracy?"

"Nothing. I didn't know he knew her."

"Oh," she says, realizing she misspoke. "I must be confusing something—"

"Henry Dahlgren knew Tracy Lawrence? How?"

"You should ask Henry."

"Oh, I will now, believe me."

"But now you'll make too much of this," she protests. "I didn't mean to imply there was any kind of . . . relationship there. Just that I saw them together once or twice."

"You must know more than that."

"I don't really," she protests. "I don't know *everything* that goes on in this neighborhood, Harding."

"Where did you see them?"

She sighs. "If I tell you a bit more, will you promise to keep it a secret?"

"I'll try."

"I don't like to have my little soirees in my own home. And I do not frequent hotels. I have another place—an apartment, off campus, where there's a bit of privacy."

"You saw Henry Dahlgren and Tracy there . . . in this apartment?"

She nods.

"When was this?"

"Last spring. Please, you must keep this a secret."

"Where is this apartment?"

"Lake Village East," she says. "On 47th Street. You know the one?"

I tell her I do.

"It's a dump," she says. "I don't live there, but it comes in handy for certain occasions." She smiles at me. It's a smile that's full of possibilities. "Maybe you can see it for yourself sometime . . ."

"What's the apartment number? In case I'm in the neighborhood."

She smiles, writes it down on my napkin. "So you don't forget," she says slyly, tucking it into my shirt pocket. I'm not likely to forget; I've been there once already. Was it Crystal's necklace I had stolen? And for whom?

She asks me again about my "girlfriend," extracts a promise to call her sometime. She puts her hand across the table and touches mine. I can smell her perfume. It smells like citrus. "Now tell me, Harding, please. Do you think we have time for dessert?" she says.

· · ·

My own apartment greets me like a jilted lover. I haven't been home since I drove to Galena. There's a message on my machine from Moira Dahlgren, answering calls I made to the Palmer House—she says she'll meet me tomorrow night for a drink.

I dial the number for Gretchen Moss. A woman answers; her mother presumably. She cuts me off mid-sentence, says "Don't call here again," and hangs up. I start to dial again, then stop. They've got enough aggravation right now without me. Then I install a new lock on the back door, one of those super-duper deadbolts they advertise on late-night TV. Maybe Boone does the voice-over. I'm smart enough to know that the lock isn't the problem, the door is only as secure as its hinges and frame. I'm not smart enough to reinforce them. The lock is a Band-Aid, but it will do for now.

I go through my files, looking for some reference to the Wokowski cards that keep turning up. My files aren't really organized that way. They're designed to hide information, not show it. Some are written in a shorthand I can no longer even read.

But I do remember where I stored the cards themselves: in a shoe box in my bedroom closet. The shoe box is there, but the string that was tied around it is gone. So are the cards. I kept a pair of formal black shoes near that box, shoes I wore to a funeral last March. I don't remember the string being untied then.

So whoever took the cards had been in my apartment this year. That limits it to friends, clients, neighbors, repairmen. . . .

I go through my mail, make one or two calls, pay a few bills. There's an alumni magazine in my mail, and when I thumb through the back to see who else from my class is now a CEO or a corporate mogul, I see a picture of a group of travelers—faculty mostly—on the deck of a large boat. Henry Dahlgren is there, in badly fitting cruisewear, and so is Crystal, in a tiny white bikini. The bikini fits her fine. Crystal is holding a highball glass and Dahlgren is holding her. "Sailing through the Aegean" is the caption.

I'm looking at Crystal in her white bikini when the phone rings. "I keep thinking of Tracy Lawrence," Crystal says. "And Logan Pollard. You mentioned those pictures . . ."

"Yes?"

"I suppose you've checked his house? And that creepy place where he works?"

"Not yet."

"I told you that he drove me back and forth for a while last spring. I didn't tell you that he tried to get fresh with me once. More than fresh . . ."

"Go on."

She sighs. "He was supposed to be driving me straight to a party, but instead we stopped at this old building. It was just filthy inside and filled with old mannequins—"

"He drove you to South Holland?"

"No, it was Evergreen Park. His factory. Off 95th Street somewhere, behind a bank. You haven't been there?"

I tell her no.

"I don't think I'm remembering it wrong. But then I wasn't really noticing the scenery . . . It wasn't exactly the Gold Coast. I was just hoping I'd get home alive." She hangs up on that note. She has a way of making you think you're sharing a secret, even if it's just something from the menu. Her words about Pollard had a different tone, though. Something scared her.

I'm several days behind on my sleep and finally I just crash on the sofa. It's cold in the apartment, so I use my coat for a blanket. I should have slept at Alison's. Alison's bed is always warmer than mine even when she's not in it. I couldn't tell you why.

Around six o'clock I wake up with a stiff neck and a nasty taste in my mouth. I shower and shave; I make some coffee and drink it by the TV. There's a circus on A&E, where the Flying Wallendas are performing a stunt called the pyramid, all six of them on the wire at once. If one of them goes, says the announcer, excited, they all go. They're a very close family.

24

at the gym there's only Alison and Michelle now. I let myself in the back door, checking to see if there are any new scratches, any signs of tampering with the alarms. I run a fuller check on the security system. Everything seems okay. I get some fruit juice from a small refrigerator and the *Trib* and sit at her desk.

I hear my name, tell Alison hello, and start talking about my day before I realize it's Michelle. Their voices are a bit similar. Michelle's wearing a black muscle shirt tucked into cutoff Daisy Dukes, black Nike socks and shoes. Her arms are covered with sweat. "I'll just take a quick shower and leave you guys alone," she says.

"Take a long shower," I say, trying not to stare at her body. "We're not going anywhere. You're getting ready for the pageant?"

"The contest, yeah. The prelims are tomorrow afternoon, the finals Friday evening. I don't think I have a chance, but Alison wants me to compete. She thinks I'm ready. I'm not so sure."

"Listen to Alison," I say. "She's always right."

"That must make your relationship fun," she says, smiling.

"Oh, we don't have a relationship," I say. "She's training me, too. For what, I haven't discovered yet."

"She must think you're ready. Or she wouldn't waste her time with you. That's what she says about me, anyway."

"Oh, I'm ready," I say.

"Have a good workout," she says.

· · ·

When Michelle leaves, I go out into the front room. Alison is there, alone, working out to Prince.

Let's go crazy

She stands five feet ten inches. Her hair is tied back. She is wearing as little as possible, the object being to show her body, not in any erotic way although that's hard to avoid. It's called a workout bikini. The top flattens her breasts and pulls tight in the back. The bottom is cut a little higher than it needs to be on each side. And she's wearing tight white leg warmers that reach to mid-thigh. Her arms aren't as muscular as Michelle's, just toned, but if she flexes the definition appears. It's the body of a lifelong athlete. She looks like a college track star.

"When was the last time you had a serious workout, fella?" she says to me.

"Too long."

"Come here and spot me."

She always does things on her own terms. She used to be heavily into Goth. She still wears black, but now her arms are tan year-round. She thinks her best feature is her back. She works hard on it. I think her best feature is her flat belly and abdominals, but she says no, everyone has that. The ones who win the contests score points with details. They've worked their calves to exhaustion. Muscles no one normally notices, they've spent hours and hours on.

She's in a corner of the room, facing floor-length mirrors, doing flat-bench flyes and dumbbell lunges in descending sets, working her chest and legs. For some reason I remember the picture of her with Tracy and Moira at the Dunes. Alison's body is so different from the other two women's, especially Tracy's. There's something hard and unyielding about it.

She's still holding the dumbbells when I kiss her. They drop from her hands. "I need a shower," she says. Her hair flops forward into my eyes when I undo the rubber band. We sit on the bench facing each other. She kicks off her shoes. Her clothes are pure white. Her eyes are malachite green. She wraps her legs around me.

"No," I say, tasting the sweat on her neck. "You don't."

afterward we sit on the floor against the mirrors. Our knees are touching. "I've got big feet," she says. She's down to just the leggings, ribbed white cotton, stirrup straps around both heels. I'm down to a towel. I lower one leg and turn to kiss her.

"I love this room," she says. "Especially at night. With all the lights turned on and the music blasting."

When u were mine

"It's very peaceful here, don't you think?" she says, lying down on her back. The muscles in her stomach are like small ridges under perfect skin. "I always feel safe here, like I'm home."

"Those are the places I distrust the most."

"What a pleasant thought, Harding." She's learned to dismiss my negativity without too much trouble.

"You know what I mean. Tell me about Grand Terrace."

"What do you want to know?"

"Everything."

She gets up and walks across the room to adjust the thermostat. The leggings are like white stockings hugging her thighs, ending a hand's width away from her firm rear. When she walks back, she's smiling at my attempt to maintain eye contact. "I lived there for two years. There were eleven others. Nine women, two men. It wasn't a commune, but we were close. The insanity of that school pushes you together. It's like boot camp sometimes, the stress. You have to relieve the stress. So Grand Terrace was an island in all that. . . ." We're shoulder to shoulder now, sitting against the wall, staring at our reflections in the mirrors. Her fingers are scratching my arms, my chest, absentmindedly. "You know some of the people, their names at least. Tracy, Charles, Moira."

"What were the . . . sleeping arrangements?"

"My, we're direct tonight, aren't we."

"All right, Alison."

"Ever since this started, when we heard about Tracy, you've had one question—you think I don't know that?"

"Why not just answer it?"

"I'm not sure it will help us."

"You're the great believer in honesty."

"But you're not. I've accommodated myself to your low standards."

"Very funny."

She turns toward me, props herself up on one elbow. "I'm serious. Men always say, 'Tell me the truth.' You tell them the truth, they fall apart."

"Men say that about women."

"Not about me." She pauses. "Okay. You understand the reason I'm not more forthcoming about this stuff has nothing to do with being ashamed of what I did."

"I know that." Actually, it's hard to picture Alison being ashamed of anything involving sex. This room, these mirrors and bright lights are unforgiving, but Alison seems perfectly at ease being naked here.

"Good. Then ask away."

"Did you sleep with Tracy?"

"Yes."

"That's all? No details?"

"I don't kiss and tell," she says with a grin. "Besides, if you're looking for some sort of comparison, all I can say is, that's not somewhere you want to go, baby."

"I was wondering if it was serious."

"We were kids, Harding," she says. "Everything's serious . . . nothing lasts."

I'm reminded of last Saturday, after she'd seen the crime scene pictures of Tracy and downplayed her relationship with her.

"You told me you were just friends," I say.

"I'm aware of that. I was having a hard enough time dealing with those pictures without dealing with your jealousy at the same time."

"Sorry." I'm reminded once again why I love this woman. Even in the middle of a sexual confession, she takes the high ground away from me.

"What about Moira?"

"Did I sleep with her? Yes. But we were never really close, not like Tracy. Sex was just play for Moira then, maybe it still is." She pulls her bikini bottom over to cover her chest. "Tracy got more emotional."

"Did you sleep with Charles?"

"No."

"No?"

"We were more like buddies. I don't think he even wanted to. If he did, he never pushed it."

"You never picked up any signals?"

"Not that I'm aware of. But a lot of time . . . I try to ignore those kinds of signals when they come from men."

"Not always."

"No," she agrees. "Not always. When ex-cons try to pick me up on a Greyhound bus, I'm such a pushover."

"Anything else I should know? What about Beth?"

"Beth went to college in California. Beth didn't live here then. Beth is straight as an arrow."

"I know. I just thought I'd ask. I'm close to getting the phone book out and just going through it alphabetically."

"Were you faithful to me? The whole time we've known each other?"

I pause, thinking of former girlfriends—lawyers, strippers, bartenders, grad students. I almost use her own words against her. *That's not somewhere you want to go . . .*

"We weren't close all the time," I say.

"Exactly."

"Whenever we were close, I was completely faithful."

"Me, too," she says.

"So I guess this is a good reason to move in together."

"I'm ready," she says. "I've always been ready."

"A lot of couples have met, married, had kids, and gotten divorced in the time it's taken us to get to this point."

"Hey, nobody said you were a quick study, Harding," she says.

"You never said these things before."

"I always know what I want," she says. "I've always wanted you. But I don't always feel so close to you. I see you better now."

"Because I'm half-naked?"

"Because you reveal yourself when you make love," she says.

"How?"

"You can't hide."

"Hookers do it all the time."

"Hookers aren't making love."

"You're getting tantric on me again, Alison."

"Come here, baby," she says softly, motioning with her finger. She has thin velvet ropes that she gives me with open hands.

It must be tantric. It gets me moving.

The ropes loop over her wrists and tie her to the horizontal bar just over her head. I move the pin so there's too much weight to budge . . . I kiss her and slide down her chest to her flat belly and then her legs. Her thighs tighten and she pulls on the weight with each movement of my mouth until she groans and the damn weight lifts an inch or two off the ground and hangs there for an impossibly long second before it comes crashing down.

a t ten o'clock Alison and I are parked outside Dreamlike Display, snuggling in the backseat, drinking rum from a flask and listening to Midnight Oil on XRT. The view of the monochromatic factory through the snowy windshield is like a black-and-white drive-in movie. The wind is howling bloody murder.

Your dreamworld is just about to end

We'd gone for a drink at the Tiki, carried our little umbrella concoctions back to the car, and then driven to Logan Pollard's home on South Cottage Grove, about a block from the factory, a tidy little bungalow that didn't match the person I talked to. I wondered whether he'd inherited it along with the business. It looked just like my cousin Jerry's house in Bridgeport.

The driveway was shoveled, the sidewalks were clear, and a local squad car made a slow pass around the block, so I didn't feel like breaking in. And there didn't seem to be any reason to. The drapes were open. I could see into every room in the house. There were red and green electric candles in the windows, a string of lights across the porch, a Christmas tree in the living room. It reminded me of Charles Muller's Denver condo—neither place looked like anyone actually carried on the messy day-to-day business of living in them.

It started to snow harder as we sat there, heavy, wet flakes that quickly covered the car before the wind sent them swirling again.

"I thought you said Pollard hung out in Wicker Park," Alison said.

"I know. It's kind of a ways from here, isn't it."

"In miles and in attitude," she said. She wound down her window and tossed the remains of her kamikaze into the snow, making a faint red mark. I told her what Crystal Royce had said about Dahlgren and Tracy. I showed her the picture I'd found in the alumni magazine. She didn't know Crystal. She didn't much like her bikini. "Implants," she said.

The squad car never made a second pass, so I went in through a basement door, gambling that there was no alarm. I only stayed a few minutes. I was looking for something of Tracy's—maybe that book she was working on. I didn't find anything. The basement smelled like gas. Upstairs, the bed was made. The suits were hung according to color. The books were arranged by height. There were painkillers and sleeping tablets in the medicine cabinet and more by the bed, stray pills mixed with paper clips in a desk drawer. Something was bothering Pollard. I doubt if Dalmane and Percocet were enough to quell it.

The radio played the Doors as we drove the four blocks to Dreamlike Display.

She's a twentieth century fox

I tried to picture Pollard living in a house that may have been his parents', sleeping in their bed, walking this way to work every morning, the same path his father had taken. Hanging up the same Christmas decorations his father had, buying the same kind of tree, fussing with the same lights. Using the same stained recipe cards his mother had used. Logan's Favorite Christmas Cookies . . .

I was noticing the little details on each bungalow, efforts to make them just a little different. Lawn ornaments, aluminum siding. It didn't really work. My street in Back of the Yards was the same way.

"You grew up in a neighborhood like this, didn't you?" Alison said, reading my mind. "What was Christmas like?"

"Well, on Christmas Eve my mother took us to early mass," I said. "We stopped at the cousins' and the grandparents'. We opened our presents. Listened to Christmas music on WGN. And then there was the traditional ceremony of looking for my old man. My mom had the holiday hours for all of the bars written on a prayer card."

"Don't you have any happy memories?" she says.

"That is a happy memory."

Dreamlike Display is just as quiet as the house. I park across the street in a snow-covered lot that may or may not be paved. We get out of the car and flinch a bit at the drop in windchill. The hard-packed snow feels like slick concrete. Alison's wearing a heavier down coat than normal, plus thick black carpenter's pants, a tiny little belt, a hooded black sweater, a boy's black wool cap. Her field glasses are around her neck. She looks like a cat burglar who hopes to do a little birdwatching. I'm wearing an old blue peacoat I got at the army-navy store and Spalding boots that cost me all of twenty bucks.

"There's a gate over there," I say, but neither one of us moves.

"You were here already, right?" she says, chewing gum. "Earlier today when they threw you out?"

"Yeah. But I didn't really notice the security."

"You didn't notice," she says.

"No."

"It's a constant mystery to me why you're not more successful in this business, Harding."

First we walk down an adjacent street, on a narrow path beside a high chain-link fence. We hold hands. With any luck we just look like two goofy lovers.

"The fence isn't wired," she says.

"Doesn't look that way." There's a side gate that's locked with a heavy steel chain wrapped around the fence poles a half-dozen times. A metal KEEP OUT sign hangs from a single nail, swinging in the wind. The front gate looks easier to manage. It's just a simple padlock, and when I get it open, there's rust on my gloves.

Alison closes the gate behind us, lifting it back onto its track, and then she sticks her gum on the side of the padlock.

"That's for luck," she says.

"Since when?"

"Since right now. This is how traditions are started, Harding. I've decided we need more ritual in our relationship. More ethos."

We walk to the main building. The grounds are fairly dark. They must never need an evening shift. There are a half-dozen alarm stickers on the office window, peeling off like old parking permits. I actually did notice the security this morning, what there was of it. I find it's best to downplay my advance planning around Alison. She's more impressed by off-the-cuff improvisation than plodding investigation. She likes artists more than academics.

I can see the row of mannequins sitting above the counter. They're not wearing jewelry now, as though this was a Tiffany's window after hours.

"For example," she says as we trace the phone lines, "we never celebrate our anniversary."

"Did you bring the wire cutters?"

She shakes them before my face. There are a dozen or more cables, all interlinked with temporary switches and patches holding things together. It's like an outlet in a small apartment, with eighteen things plugged into it. Every time the factory changed companies, the technician must have just added a new connector. I don't know how a repairman could figure any of it out. I'm not even sure how it works.

"In fact, I think you only remember the date because it's the day you got out of prison."

"Alison, how much have you had to drink?"

"Why?"

"You hate anniversaries, you hate birthdays, you don't celebrate Christmas. Every year you tell me not to buy you a Christmas present."

We cut the phone lines and the alarm, then return to our car to see if anyone shows up. It's the trial-and-error method of investigation, which I know always impresses the hell out of Alison. But there are so many old lines, it's hard to tell which are still live.

"You met me in my Wicca phase," she says. "I've moved on."

We wait twenty minutes. I empty the flask, she empties her pack of gum. Alison uses my cell phone to check her machine. Then we retrace our steps to the main gate. The snow hasn't been disturbed here. We're leaving a lot of footprints.

"Did you bring a gun?" she says.

"No."

"What if there are guard dogs?"

"We run," I say. "It's a little tradition of my own."

the main building is laid out like a run-down car dealership, with a showroom up front, then rows of tiny offices, and the physical plant behind.

I find the office where Pollard met me this morning, pick the lock on the door, and then go through the things on Pollard's desk. There are a lot of memos, reports, and catalogs. None of the drawers are even locked. Rows of red binders sit on a sagging wall shelf.

"Don't they ever dust?" Alison says.

It's a totally nondescript office, anonymous, bland. If Pollard brought anything of himself here, he took it with him when he left. At least that's my first impression. The only hints of another life are the poetry journals squeezed between the trade magazines, the empty Percocet bottles in the drawer.

What I really came here for was Pollard's daily calendar, and I find a copy in his secretary's desk. Like a lot of people she doesn't quite trust the one on her computer and keeps a second one the old-fashioned way. Pollard's days away from work are marked in little purple X's. The mood probably brightened a bit on those days.

"What was June twelfth?" Alison says, watching me.

"The night that woman was attacked in Denver. Pollard was out of town, it doesn't say where."

She sees where I'm going with this. "What about Halloween weekend?"

I page through the calendar, filled with color photographs of cats. "He was here Friday. There's nothing about the weekend. But he was off Monday and Tuesday."

"Maybe all that candy gave him a bellyache," she says.

Alison leads the way back through the factory, takes the metal steps down to the main floor. There's a distant rumbling from the boiler room. Half the floor is automated, the other half filled with individual workstations, where the customizing is done. It's all very low tech and not very clean.

"How do they make money?" she says, shaking her head.

"I don't know." I'm remembering how noisy it was earlier today—all the hammering and sawing, the hissing of the air pumps, the constant loud hum from the generators—and wondering how someone who wanted to be a poet could stand such a place.

We come out near the loading dock. There's an L-shaped extension to one of the outer buildings, almost like a small ranch house. All the windows are bricked up. I think the factory must date to the Pullman days, when they'd need someone here 24/7. This may have been the night watchman's quarters.

I don't see an alarm. The lock's not hard to pick. There's one room, barely furnished; a cot with sheets, an army blanket. A folding table. There's a small space heater in the corner. The power's on.

"Look at this," Alison says. She's in a small bathroom. The garbage can has several red Slim Jim wrappers. The faucet in the sink has a slow drip. "Why would they leave the water on back here?"

She shines her flashlight at the mat. A cockroach scurries toward the baseboards. There's some garbage under there that I bring out with the tip of my boot: balled-up paper bags, fast-food receipts with recent dates, more Slim Jim wrappers.

"Someone's been staying here," she says, and I nod, thinking about Travis Savick and what the old man at the halfway house had said: *Travis works nights. . . . He's not here that much these days.*

We lock up. It's snowing harder, and the temperature is really dropping now. I should have worn a heavier coat. The light is sodium yellow. An eighteen-wheeler groans on a nearby street, its air brakes hissing.

"It's a beautiful night, don't you think?" she says, shivering. "In an Edward Hopper sort of way?"

"You see too much beauty in the world, Alison."

"I never knew that was a problem."

We walk back to the car a different way, near a construction site. Black canvas flaps in the wind. Two-by-fours form icy crosses. A sky-blue Porta Potty tilts in fresh snow. "Many, many moons ago," I say, "when I was trying to get my business going again after prison—"

"Oh, goody," she says. "It's story time."

"—I took this case, my first case that involved more than a phony insurance claim, and I was tailing a guy in southern Indiana. Very beautiful country, lots of horses. Amish country, I think. This guy skipped on some payments; it's a long story and doesn't matter much. Doesn't matter much how he got to that field, that day." Another truck drives past and we both move into the shadows. "All that matters is I found him. This was late summer. I was maybe a football field away from him, behind some trees. He'd pulled off the road, for no reason far as I could tell, and he was eating peaches, one after the other. He had them in a paper sack. The sky was perfectly blue, not a cloud anywhere. I was feeling very good about myself. And then I heard a thunderclap. He heard it, too. We both looked up in the sky. He dropped the bag of peaches. Or I thought he did. The next thunderclap took his head right off. I mean it was just . . . gone. And then the rest of him fell backward, almost an after-thought, into the grass."

"You led them to him?"

I nod.

"Did they arrest the guys?"

"They don't arrest guys like that, Alison. The shooter was probably in Miami by midnight. They arrested *me,* hoping I'd flip. But I didn't know anything—the shooter was behind me somewhere, I never saw him. And the guys who hired me were long gone. They sent me a bonus, though. Which I took and spent on setting up an office, getting started again. And I learned a lesson about tailing people. And what can happen on a perfectly beautiful day."

"You are a real mood setter, Harding. A girl could just lose herself in stories like that."

I shrug.

She shivers. "It's not *that* beautiful around here," she says.

We relock the gate, throw some snow on our footprints, then take the Calumet north. There's just enough snow on the roads to make people nervous. It takes a good hour to reach Evergreen Park.

"She said it was near a bank?" Alison says, thumbing through the Yellow Pages I lifted at a gas station. Harold Melvin and the Blue Notes are riding with us.

If you don't know me by now . . .

"There are only about fifty banks in this neighborhood," she says.

"I know. Crystal wasn't very precise." There's a Harris and LaSalle and a First Federal and a dozen others with bland corporate names. "I think there used to be a Musicraft store around here somewhere—"

"There used to be a Musicraft period. You dragged me out here to buy stereo equipment."

"I did? I forgot."

"Women remember being tortured, Harding."

We're on 95th when I see a promising spot—a string of four old buildings a block from a Midwest Savings. There's a Mobil station nearby, behind a huge billboard.

We take the long way around, circling the gas station and the bank to see who else might be around. It's surprisingly deserted. The main business district stops just a few blocks away. Maybe nobody wanted to build next to Pollard's little eyesore.

There's no lock on the fence, just four buildings sitting two by two, taking up most of a city block. None of them look connected to any alarms. Once we're in the center of the buildings, the soft yellow light from the street lamps and the chill finding its way through my clothes and the sound of our boots crunching on the brittle snow make me feel like we're on the moon. The windows are so grimy we can't see much inside. The buildings look forgotten, but the doors are locked tight. Alison holds the flashlight while I pick the lock.

"So Pollard's out of town now?" she says.

"I guess. Why?" I take off my gloves, trying to get a better feel. "You're afraid he's gonna pop up here tonight?"

She shakes her head. The cold air comes from her lips like smoke. "I wouldn't mind talking to him, that's all," she says.

"About this?" I say, surprised.

"About Tracy," she says. "Apparently he knew her better than I did. Maybe Charles did, too."

This is harder than it should be. The lock is newer than the door. When it finally yields, I slip the tools back into my pocket, blowing on my hands like a relief pitcher. The door swings open easily.

"I thought it was a really good sign," she says. "Charles running at Stagg Field."

"Charles has been full of surprises today," I say. The room's filled with old furniture and documents—there are steel shelves with boxes of old invoices, bills of lading, shipment tracers, old catalogs. There's no order to it. It looks like somebody just got tired of having all this crap in the main building and shipped it over here one day.

We walk to the next building, our big winter coats throwing shadows on the sidewalk. This one is empty. I'm glad Alison isn't pressing me on why we're here, what we're looking for. I'm not really sure. I just have a sense Pollard is hiding something.

"I told you about the phone call, that someone threatened you. According to Charles, anyway." She nods, runs her hand through her hair. I can't tell how seriously she's taking this threat. "But I haven't had the chance to tell you the rest of it. Charles thinks Dahlgren wants him to leave."

"Why?" she says.

"Do you get the feeling Henry is more than a little interested in Beth?"

"They're friends," she says. "He's jealous of Henry Dahlgren?"

"That's part of it. Four or five years ago Henry and Charles were both teaching downstate, at Southern Ilinois. That's how they first met."

We cross a slippery patch of ice, holding hands. She pulls her hood up around her face. "I knew Charles taught at the U of I, at Champagne-Urbana, I didn't know he taught in Carbondale. And I knew their paths overlapped somewhere, I never knew where."

The third building has concrete floors and looks like a machines' graveyard. There are old die punches, steel presses, sanders, small conveyers.

"Oh, their paths overlapped, all right," I say.

She pushes the hood back. "No . . . Charles? With Moira?"

Some of the machines are still oily, sawdust clinging to the valves and gears. They don't look as if they came together, more like one by one they were moved back here as they fell from grace.

"I was given the lowdown from Charles. Moira is apparently quite the temptress. And Henry has a few eccentricities of his own."

"I don't believe it."

Our boots kick up particles of dust that hang in the beam of our flashlights. Every once in a while I hear a car from the street. Alison stops me as we step outside.

"Did you hear something?" Alison says.

I shake my head. "Like what?"

"Someone coughing. Just once." We turn off the flashlights, stand frozen for a minute. The only sound I hear is the wind.

"Let's check this last one and get out of here," I say.

This building is larger than the others and split into two rooms with offices on the second floor that overlook what once must have been a workspace. There are more machines here, some with plastic covers—they look like drill presses and cutters. The blades have been removed. The same metal shelves are in here, but this time they're filled with dolls. Hundreds of them—some in boxes, some just sitting out, their legs hanging over the edges. They're all old and decaying: the wooden ones probably have termites or carpenter ants by now; the ones without boxes seem like disinterred corpses needing burial. Some are missing arms or legs or eyes.

"We need a doll hospital," Alison says.

One of the strange things about the room is that the boxes are stacked so that the dolls are standing up, facing outward. The effect is that of standing onstage surrounded by tiers of doll spectators. They all look like they're waiting for something. All their eyes are open.

"Weird," Alison says. "You'd think they would just throw this shit out." She pulls a green tarp off a bushel basket of mannequin parts—arms, legs, torsos—that must have been cut up by the machines. Why, I don't know. They're piled in the basket like a fruit display.

"Maybe Pollard has a sentimental attachment to some of them." It smells like Clorox in here. Now I hear a noise, like someone clearing his throat. I can't tell if it's outside or upstairs.

We both freeze. A shadow moves across the skylight. The ceiling creaks. The ladder to the second floor makes too much noise to be very subtle. I push a trapdoor up with my shoulder and shine my flashlight around the attic. Dull metal reflects the light back at me— more equipment but dismantled this time. There are footprints here, some recent. The floor is wet in spots. Alison climbs up behind me.

That's when I hear the noise on the roof and the ice hitting the ground as someone scrambles over the shingles, and instead of going down the ladder, I move toward the noise and a skylight, and the floorboards creak and crack—before I can say or do anything, the floor gives way and takes Alison to the ground. She lands on the tables with a dozen or so dolls, bodies painted brown to simulate summer skin, faces covered with lacquer. The metal objects that fell are sheathed metal machine saws. They've been washed of dust, but there's something brown between the teeth.

I pull Alison to her feet, brush off her coat, pick tiny plastic doll fingers and toes from her hair. Her glasses are covered with dust.

"You're right, this is sort of kinky," she whispers.

Now we can see where the Clorox smell is coming from, a large washed-out spot beneath one of the shattered tables. Someone was cleaning up. We go outside just as a tall figure in a black coat moves toward the back fence and then climbs it like a gorilla, pulling his weight up with long arms. A car starts. Through the window I see the black Cadillac turn on its lights and pull away.

26

We catch up with him on South Kedzie. He's about a quarter-mile ahead and driving very slowly. The roads out here are in bad shape and we're skidding a lot. We cross the railroad tracks, heading east on 95th Street.

"You know this guy?" she says, feeding a roll of film into a camera.

"We met briefly." I reach under the seat to see if there's anything left from my last surveillance job. There are a couple of trackers and a cheap monitor, but they don't do much good if they're not on the car. "I think he's the guy who hit me the other night. And he's been tailing me. He works for Pollard; his sister's Crystal Royce. Don't ask me what that adds up to."

"He's turning, Harding."

"I see, I see." We drive north on Western through a forest preserve. A few blocks later the Cadillac slows and then again changes direction. He must be lost. "Willie Hendrix knows him. He said Travis did a nice job selling a hit as manslaughter. Did the time, never told them who hired him. So he knows how to take directions."

"What's east of Evergreen Park?" Alison says, wiping steam from the windshield.

"Let's see . . . We're headed for the Ryan, I guess. Chicago State, lots of railroad tracks. And then the Skyway."

"Great." She unwraps a new stick of Juicy Fruit, buckles her seat belt.

"Beyond that there's Hammond, Gary . . . Fort Wayne . . ."

"I am not going to Indiana tonight, Harding. I don't have my toothbrush. Or my pajamas."

"They have pajamas in Indiana, Alison. I'll buy you pajamas." Every time I try to get out of low gear, the 4Runner slides sideways. The Blackhawks couldn't be skating any better than we are tonight.

After a half-hour or so, the Cadillac stops for gas at an Amoco truck stop and we sit and watch Travis jawing with the clerk. He's carrying his coat now, wearing baggy jeans and a white T-shirt. It's the first good look I've gotten of him. His upper body's chiseled, his arms stretching the cotton T. I tell Alison about last Sunday, when he was dressed like something out of Dickens, singing carols. I don't think he'd fit through anyone's chimney.

"What do you think he was doing there?" Alison says.

"At Dahlgren's? Besides singing? I don't know. But that coat could have been the tux people claim to have seen on the man at the Lopez place. Though why he'd let me see him in it, I don't know."

"You said he tailed you in the open, too. That's either intimidation or stupidity."

"I don't think he's stupid," I say. "I think we found Tracy's crime scene tonight, though. Those saws are the first thing I've seen that could have made those cuts in the photos."

The more I watch him, the more nervous I get. Even without knowing his record, I'd know he'd done serious time. It's something you can spot when you've done some yourself. And he has one of those physiques that bother me the most. He was born that way. He takes it for granted. I don't.

"So do we have a plan?" she says.

He picks up a six-pack of Miller, curls it like a dumbbell, and leans against the counter. The clerk rings up his beer, then gives him his change along with the bathroom key. If he'd just stay on foot, we'd have no problem. He sticks out like a cell phone tower.

"Harding? Is there a plan?"

I'm watching him add some protein to his purchase, a package of Slim Jims in a festive red-and-green package.

"It would be nice to see where he goes, though following him in this weather's a little dicey." He walks the same way he climbed that fence, like a gorilla, as if the muscles get in the way of simple movement. He's awkward as hell, but then he's not trying out for the Joffrey.

"You could talk to him," she says, watching him tear open the Slim Jims with his teeth. Slim Jim cravings are worse than smack.

"I could talk to him, yeah. I don't see myself beating a confession out of him."

I tell her to call Crowley or 911, then I go inside and stare at the magazine rack. The kid at the counter is watching me. I order something called a double Oasis burger just to give the kid something to do, vegetable protein deep-fried in olive oil, couscous and lentils instead of fries. When even the truck stops turn third world, you know things are changing.

The bathroom door squeaks. He's standing at the first urinal. His mouth twists into a smile.

"Hell of a storm," he says. His voice is a little higher than you'd expect. I wash my hands, realizing how dumb it was to walk in here. I feel like I'm being led by the nose.

He zips up and shoves me out of the way, harder than he needs to, but then it's the little things like that that make his life worth living. I feel like a wiry tight end colliding with a middle linebacker. Outside, he's at the counter, wiping his hands on his jeans. There's a cut on his right arm and an orangish-red splash of rust around his knees, where he must have slid off the roof.

"I hope you didn't hurt yourself," I say. Through the windows I can see Alison leaving the 4Runner, circling around behind the Caddy. It's snowing heavily now. I'd like to keep him here until Crowley arrives, but I don't have a gun. I doubt he'd succumb to my boyish charm.

Another car pulls into the lot and Alison drops to one knee behind the Caddy as though tying her shoelace. It strikes me as a silly idea—who kneels in this kind of weather—when I realize she must have put one of those old trackers on the bumper.

He puts his coat on. The clerk bags his beer and Slim Jims, and I put my hand on his shoulder to keep him from turning. He looks at it like it's something that died. "I don't want any trouble," he says in that high voice.

"I just wanted to thank you," I say, "for those Christmas carols you sang. That chimney-sweep outfit must have been a bitch to put together. What are you, an alto? Soprano?"

They're having a nice promotion at the gas station, something called a Mary Ellen doll, ten bucks with a fill-up, a holiday gift from the fine folks at Amoco. A row of them is near the register, in green and red boxes, with Mary Ellen's face shining through the cellophane. He takes one down, pokes his finger through the wrapping, pulls the doll from its box, and then twists its head off. The cheap plastic protests only slightly. He tosses the doll's head to me as though we're playing catch.

"Merry Christmas," he says. He's right in my face. I try to look tough. But my left foot's itching to move back a step, like a batter who can't stay in the box against high heat.

I'm expecting him to take a swing at me, but nothing happens. He just picks up his bag and leaves. Alison gets in his way for no good reason; he pushes her aside and she loses her balance. I help her up, brush the snow off her. "Shit, he's big, isn't he," she says. When we get back to the 4Runner, Alison plugs a Watchman-size monitor into the cigarette lighter. A red dot blinks on and off in sync with the Caddy fishtailing back onto the highway.

"Bingo," Alison says. Two more cars pass, then we pull in behind him.

"Did you reach Crowley?" I say.

She shakes her head. "No, 911. They'll know it was me, right?"

"Yeah." I wonder whose jurisdiction this is. I'm not even sure where the county line is around here. "What about the inside of the car? Did you get a look?" She says no. "I was hoping the guy behind this might be with him."

"Why does it have to be a guy?" she says. "Maybe it's a woman." Visibility is about a hundred feet. We can just see the Caddy's rear lights. Each time I think I'm catching up, the Caddy zooms ahead.

"I have a bad feeling about this, Harding," Alison says. "I think we're definitely going to Indiana."

I feel like we're driving in circles. I'm going to have to stop for gas soon. But there's a long, dark stretch of road near the Indiana border and a railroad crossing, and when we come out of a fog of snow, we see the red flashing lights about a half-mile ahead and the Caddy pulling around them to cross the tracks. I hit the gas hard, but Alison yells "No!" and I see the train on my left side just as I hit the brakes. We hit a patch of ice and I feel the 4Runner start to swerve. Turn into the skid, I say to myself, but there's too much ice. I turn too hard. The car spins around like a toy—it feels like we're in a video game or a movie—and for a minute or so we sit there stunned, straddling two lanes, facing the wrong way, looking backward into the darkness as the train roars by behind us.

the cops keep us until two. We've been interviewed, finger-printed, poked, and prodded, but not charged. We have Crowley to thank for that. Alison's 911 call brought both CPD and county cops to Evergreen Park—it looked like a simple breaking and entering until Crowley showed up, sealing the place off, bringing in the crime scene techs. The South Holland police did the same thing with the night watchman's quarters at Dreamlike Display. It took a while to get everyone on the same page, linking both places to a woman's body fished from the Mississippi two months earlier. Crowley got them to focus on Travis and Pollard. Unfortunately, Pollard was nowhere to be found.

They brought in Travis—he came willingly, an amused look on his face—but it was his word against ours that he'd even been near the place. This is why he avoided a fight, of course. Two of his halfway-house buddies supplied enough of an alibi to keep him out of jail. It will take days to determine if those blades we found mean anything at all. In the end, it was just two ex-cons with shaky stories.

So we retreated to Alison's apartment; tired, thirsty, grumpy. Alison's back is stiffening up a bit from the fall she took. She refused the ambulance and X rays. She might regret that by morning. Right now she's lying on the couch, waiting for aspirin and muscle relaxants to kick in, watching *Lost Horizon* on cable—the early version, I think, no one's singing yet. She's wearing one of my old terry-cloth bathrobes. I turn off most of the lights and then stand in the kitchen and drink a shot of bourbon and then I call my machine. There's a message from Father Mike, the florist. He says the man I wanted to talk to—the man who paid for Ricky's funeral and burial—will meet me tomorrow. His name's Davey.

I wash out the shot glass, turn out the kitchen light, sit beside Alison in one of the armchairs. She's sound asleep. Shangri-La flickers on the screen. When the phone rings, I think it's Jane Wyatt.

"Harding?" It's Beth, sounding like she dialed the wrong number.

"How are you, Beth?" I say sleepily.

"Well . . . not good. I think I'm turning into my mother."

"What's wrong?"

"He took a drive," she says.

"Charles?"

"Charles."

"Did you want to talk to Alison, Beth?"

"Maybe I shouldn't worry. Do you think I should worry?"

"How long has he been gone, Beth?"

"I've lost track. A long time . . . he said we needed a Christmas tree."

"At this hour? I thought you had a Christmas tree."

"We do. I'm afraid he's drinking somewhere. I thought maybe Alison could go with me to look for him."

Alison's dead to the world. "Let me do it. Give me ten minutes."

"You must think I'm acting like a fool. Worrying like this. I should just kick his ass out. . . ."

"Let me find him first, Beth. Okay? Then you can kick him out."

i make the same search I made last Saturday, limited now to bars with late licenses. It's a pub crawl I've made myself many times. The snow keeps falling. This time of night everything seems frozen just a little harder. The thin yellow light from the street lamps is like an Arctic sun.

The 4Runner slides a bit when I make a loop around the Midway. For the hell of it I drive by a Christmas-tree lot, closed and dark, the Scotch pines sleeping in the snow. I'm wide awake now, mostly from the cold, and I'm starting to wonder if I need to hit the surrounding neighborhoods when a bartender on South Shore remembers seeing Charles.

"The writer guy," he says.

"He was here?"

"For an hour or so, yeah," he says, wiping the bar with a dirty-looking rag. "Sitting right there, scribbling on something. Drinking one Guinness after another. Paid with a fifty, left a fifty-cent tip, that's why I remember. And he kept picking pine needles off his coat and flicking them on the floor. I told him, Don't do that. Those needles are sharp, it's a safety hazard."

"I don't suppose he told you where he was going next."

"He asked me if there were any Christmas trees for sale in Jackson Park. I said, What are you, nuts?"

"Thanks," I say, leaving a ten.

"They don't sell trees in Jackson Park."

"I know."

"So what is he, nuts?"

"As soon as I get a diagnosis, I'll let you know."

the new BMW is sitting behind the Museum of Science and Industry. I don't know if Charles intended to go to the museum or whether he was looking for a tree. I find him on the rear steps, by the Columbia basin, half frozen, scribbling in a notebook. He can't have been out here too long or he'd be blue. But he might not have noticed. I have to say his name several times to get his attention.

"Let's go home, Charles," I say, sitting down next to him.

"Harding?"

"Yeah, Charles. It's me. Come on, buddy—"

"Harding . . . Good, I'm glad you came. You want a drink?"

He has a flask that's more like a canteen, the cap already off; it sloshes onto the snow when he hands it to me. I screw the cap back on.

"I found a good tree," he says. "I had a little trouble with it, though. I should have brought an ax. I don't think Beth owns an ax."

"You have a tree already, Charles. In Beth's house."

He's wearing a heavy coat but no gloves or hat. His thin blue trousers are shiny at both knees. His rear end must be frozen. "That one wasn't quite perfect, Harding. It wasn't as *straight* as it could have been for one thing—"

"So you came out here in the middle of the night?"

"I think it's important," he says, intent on making his point, "to get the right tree. For the children. For our first Christmas together— it should be *our tree.*"

"Beth's waiting for you, Charles. You're scaring her half to death."

He stands up reluctantly. His knees crack. He loses his balance and I grab his arm. "We should go then," he says. "Except . . . I think I drove."

"I'll get your car in the morning if it hasn't been towed by then."

He takes a few tiny steps and then stops abruptly. "What about the tree? My tree, the perfect tree. Should we get the tree now or in the morning?"

"Let's wait until morning." I pause. "You didn't really chop one down, did you?"

"I lost my hat," he says, not listening, going through his pockets as though that's where he left it. "I must have forgotten to bring it back. Beth gave me that hat. It has tiny angels on it. It's my Christmas hat. Harding, we have to find that hat. Please . . ."

There are various stages of drunkenness. He's not as bad as he was the other night. I tell him to stay where he is, then I head off in the direction he's indicated, following his footsteps in the snow. I know this area fairly well—I used to jog through here each morning, back when I used to get up before noon, back when I used to jog. It's pretty in summer. There's a Japanese garden with a wooden bridge, lots of flowers, lots of wildlife.

It takes me about five minutes to find the tree he selected, another five to find his damn hat. There's a hatchet here, too; it's very dull, but Charles made a good start on the tree. I have to admit, he chose the best one. I think it's a Scotch pine. His footprints wander in and out of the woods, as though he'd been here for a while, hunting. There are sled tracks, too, also going in and out.

He's sound asleep when I get back.

"Let's go, Charles," I say, helping him up. He staggers a bit. He doesn't say much in the car. His shoes are muddy. He has a little piece of leaf in his beard that I brush off. I straighten his shirt collar the way Alison does for me sometimes. I put the hatchet under the seat.

I'm assuming this may delay the wedding a bit further, if Beth doesn't just kick his ass all the way back to Denver. When Alison got calls like this—"Harding's too drunk to drive"—she'd just hang up or say "Let him walk." Sometimes I'd find my clothes on the sidewalk. Once she changed the locks. But you never know. Charles may have found a woman willing to put up with his various falls from grace. Beth's had such bad luck with men, she might be determined to make this one work out, no matter what. And maybe she sees something in Charles that I don't. I see an alcoholic writer, a step from collapse. She might see happiness. She might see Shangri-La.

When I pull into Beth's drive, Charles simply gets out and goes inside. Beth waves at me from the window, a bathrobe clutched around her. I'm afraid to look at her, I don't want her seeing what's on my mind.

28

donnie Wilson is out by the first row of the grandstand at Hawthorne Race Course. No one's bothered to shovel the snow. It's nine A.M. The temperature's nineteen degrees. The Thoroughbreds aren't running this week.

Donnie's wearing leather driving gloves, a black cashmere scarf, and the kind of coat I see in display windows on Michigan Avenue when I'm trying to catch a cab after dinner at Eli's. There's just enough fur around the collar to let you know it's damn expensive fur.

"How's your Christmas shopping coming, Harding?" he says.

I tell him I haven't really had a chance to get started.

"You know what I did this year? Sent everybody one of those lobsters. You open the box, there's a live lobster. Throw it in a pot and you've got dinner."

He's leaning on the railing, as though waiting for the last race to start. Donnie usually gets what he wants; it wouldn't surprise me to see something—Thoroughbreds, greyhounds, snowmobiles—coming around the turn.

"This used to be one of my favorite spots," he says. "Right up there, first row of the grandstand. Won my first trifecta. Bet a lot of paychecks I couldn't afford to lose. I met my first wife here, did you know that?"

I shake my head. Donnie and I go way back, but there are definite gaps in our friendship. I don't think I ever met the first Mrs. Donnie Wilson.

"Katherine," he says. "I called her Katie. You never heard me mention Katie?"

"I don't think so."

"She was a flight attendant for United."

"How'd that turn out?"

"Not good," he says. "I lost a few paychecks on her, too."

We wander back toward the stables, out of the wind and out of sight. Donnie's carrying a small briefcase. There are still one or two horses here, in heated stalls, beds of fresh straw. Someone must board them over the winter. A garden hose is running into a rusty drain in the concrete floor.

"Watch where you walk," Donnie says.

The barn smells like fresh hay and old leather. Saddles are draped on sawhorses, bridles hang from the walls. We stop by one of the jockeys' dressing rooms, empty now. Donnie looks closely at the wall before deciding he can stand next to it. He gives me the same kind of look.

"Heard your name quite a bit this morning on the scanner," he says.

"I know," I say. "And I usually try so hard to avoid the limelight. Let's talk about that job I did for you last Sunday. And that necklace I lifted."

He considers this. "The taps are working fine. The client's happy. What's your problem?"

"Well, for one thing, you should have told me I was breaking into Crystal Royce's apartment, Donnie. And stealing her necklace." He frowns. "After you ran that plate for me—the Cadillac, Travis Savick, remember? Travis is Crystal's brother. And they're both mixed up in a case I'm working."

"And what case is that?"

"You talk to me first, Donnie. Who was I really working for that night? Who was the client?"

"You know the way we operate, Harding. Cash on delivery . . . no questions." He unsnaps his briefcase. He shows me an envelope full of hundred-dollar bills. It looks like Monopoly money. "Did you bring the necklace?"

"Don't change the subject."

"By the way, I got that information you wanted," he says. "Those phone records, which were damn hard to get on short notice—"

"Don't change the subject, Donnie," I repeat, irritated.

"I'm not changing the subject," he says. "Let's see . . . Logan Pollard, Henry Dahlgren. You wanted Henry Dahlgren's phone records? I called a buddy in the county sheriff's office, I got you Henry Dahlgren's phone records. I am not changing the subject."

"Meaning what?"

"Meaning, in pulling Henry Dahlgren's phone records, I found myself confronted with a serious ethical dilemma."

"Well, that would be uncharted waters for you, Donnie. What's the dilemma?"

"We do security for Dahlgren's company," he says. "They're in three different malls now, office parks; we handle the alarms, vet the new employees. It's a nice retainer. If one of the partners needs a favor, we try to accommodate."

I catch myself staring. "You're saying it was Dahlgren paying you?"

"I talked to him once or twice," Donnie says. "He seemed like a nice guy."

"I was working for Dahlgren? Did he know I'd be the one doing the job?"

"I don't think so. I never mentioned you. You're not exactly listed in our annual reports, Harding."

"I thought it had something to do with the gravel guys. I thought I was working for them."

"Nah, that's something else," he says. "I've been helping them with the various aldermen as they come up for reelection. I've been all over the fucking city." He grins. "Fifty wards, they all need gravel. You have to spread it around."

"So what was this other job really about? What was I doing in there?"

"Just what I asked. Picking up that trinket for Henry. Which he gave to this hooker in a moment of passion and never should have, et cetera, et cetera."

"You believed that?"

He shrugs. "I've heard worse."

Well, of course he has, and so have I, but rarely from an assistant dean and tenured professor. Still, like my friend Willie Hendrix says, you can only spend so much time in the library. Crystal Royce does have a certain charm. If Henry was having trouble in his marriage, I can see him falling for her, giving her the necklace; I have no trouble believing he'd go to Donnie for help and that Donnie would turn to me. I don't mind being used in such situations as long as I get paid. I've more or less built a career on such things.

But that doesn't explain the wiretaps and bugs I installed in Crystal's apartment. I point this out to Donnie, who's fingering a jockey's yellow and green silk shirt as though he's at Barneys. "The wiretaps are another story, Harding."

"I thought they might be."

"See, I found Miss Royce's story fascinating," he says. "I've never heard of her before. She's never shown up on my radar. Have you ever heard of a hooker without a rap sheet? Or a rep? When Dahlgren told me how she had everybody in the college up there at one time or another—"

"The taps were for you? Jesus, Donnie."

"You don't approve?"

"You might have told me."

"I'm telling you now, Harding. Why is this bothering you so much?"

"Because I'm looking at Dahlgren for something else. Trying to find out if he's dirty. That's why I asked you for his phone records. What did you think when I asked for them?"

"I thought, Gee, this puts me in a serious ethical dilemma." He remembers the folder and gives it to me. "What are you looking at him for? Not that business last night?"

"I'm not sure. He's mixed up with a case I'm helping Crowley with. A woman named Tracy Lawrence got dumped in the Mississippi."

"I saw that in the papers."

"Dahlgren told you about Crystal; he didn't mention her brother?"

"Word of honor, no, Harding. I never made the connection." He pauses. "You're looking at *Dahlgren* for that? Are you sure? I think the only thing he's guilty of is leading a dull life."

"I don't think he killed anybody," I say. "But I think he knows more than he's telling me about Crystal and Travis. Did you run Logan Pollard?"

He nods. "I did him first. There was no ethical dilemma."

There are pages of phone records, in very tiny print, with names and addresses supplied by one of Donnie's assistants. It will take me a while to plow through them. But a couple of things jump out at me right away. Dahlgren was calling Tracy during the months she lived in Chicago and worked at Casa Cucumber. The calls came from his house and stopped when she moved west. The time frame corresponds to when Moira was still living there. It could have been her making the calls.

Pollard was calling Tracy Lawrence starting last year, when she lived in Chicago and worked at Casa Cucumber. Later he was calling her in Taos. I expected that. But I didn't expect to find out where Pollard was living ten years ago. Donnie had found his old addresses and one of them was Lopez's building on Hyde Park Boulevard. He was living there—top floor, Ricky Lopez's apartment—when Alison was across the street at Grand Terrace.

"I didn't ask you to find all this stuff," I tell him, and he shrugs.

"That's how I've advanced so far in the world of criminal justice," he says. "Anticipating the needs of my clients. Plus I've got these interns from DePaul with nothing to do." He tilts his head a tad, a small smile on his face. "So are you gonna give me the neck-lace, Harding, or what?"

I hand him the padded envelope. He hands me the money. "I was afraid maybe you lost the damn thing," he says. "There's no insurance on it." We shake hands and then head back toward the grandstand. A horse trailer backs up the access road, warning lights blinking.

"I thought it just had sentimental value," I say.

"Yeah, but that's always the hardest shit to replace, isn't it?" he says.

One of the horses whinnies behind us, as though startled. We both turn, but it's just some guy pushing a broom. Donnie's hand is on his fur collar. I can't tell if he's going for his gun or checking his heartbeat.

"Watch where you walk, Harding," Donnie says.

the bodybuilding competition takes place at a junior college on the far southwest side. There are prelims all day, combined with a fitness pageant and health fair. The drive from Hawthorne takes me through Cicero lunch traffic. I park beside a football field and follow hand-lettered signs to a theater that's used for band concerts and musicals and the kind of student assemblies I used to sleep through. Right now the place is less than half full.

"That will change," Alison says. She says her back is better. She's wearing jeans and a PowerFemmes T-shirt; her hair's pulled back, and she has a White Sox cap that nearly comes down to her glasses. It's her no-nonsense look. "When they get closer to the heavyweights."

I look at the large women posing on the stage. "These are the lightweights?"

She nods, chewing gum. "Your category," she says.

She tells me what is going on right now backstage: everyone nervously oiling themselves, pumping up with dumbbells, sneaking glances at the next person's obliques. Despite the time of year everyone's completely tanned, some dark brown.

"Actually, women go through this every day of their lives," Alison says. "Being judged by their bodies . . ."

The event is co-sponsored by a number of gyms, partly to promote the fitness industry, partly to let some of the less experienced women see what it's like before the real contests start in the spring. Alison has three women competing in the fitness part, but I think she's most excited by Michelle's chances in the bodybuilding. "This is a good first step for her," she says. "It takes guts to walk out there the first time."

"Where is Michelle?" I say, looking around.

"At PowerFemmes. I told her not to come too early. Some of the veterans like to play mind games, psyche you out." She loaned her car to Michelle, rode out here with her fitness contestants. They're all wearing spandex, cute headbands, and showing a lot of leg and a little cleavage.

I walk outside to get some bottled water from my car and use the pay phones in the lobby. I want to talk to Dahlgren and ask him about those phone records, but his secretary says he's seeing patients all day. I try Gretchen Moss again; this time I get the father. They're protecting her, as they should.

There are booths lining the back row of the theater like a carnival midway, where sales reps are pushing everything from workout shoes to soy milk, showing how their bench or leg press or rowing machine improves upon the original. Several women insist I try their new, improved endurance-enhancer power bars. By the time I return to Alison, I have a cute white-plastic bag full of free samples—shampoo, snack bars, vitamins, deodorant. Lots of deodorant.

"We're having dinner with Beth and Charles," she says. "In Wicker Park." They're still talking about this skiing trip, trying to convince us to go along. It seems odd to me; you'd think they'd want some time together. I'm not thrilled at the idea of seeing Charles again.

I tell her I'm having trouble getting through to Gretchen Moss.

"It's that cheap phone you use. Where did you find it, in a box of Cracker Jacks?"

"It's not the phone, Alison. It's her parents." I give her the number and ask her to try it for me later.

I'm reading the program, ogling the pictures of the women and the ads for sports bras when one of the volunteer ushers comes up to Alison and tells her there's a man hanging around backstage without a pass.

"There should be a security guard back there," Alison says with a frown. I sit up. "We paid for two guards. Is he bothering anyone?"

"No, just sort of pacing, like he's waiting for someone." The volunteers are wearing lime-green running suits. This one looks like she could compete herself. "I asked him to move, but he didn't answer. I wasn't sure what to do."

"He's probably just a boyfriend or a husband," Alison says, getting up. "I'll speak to him." She walks up the center aisle, talking to the volunteer. It's amazing to me how many friends Alison has made in the business. She's only had the gym a year or so.

They're nearly to the stage when the curtains near the left exit sign begin rustling. Someone screams. I run up the aisle and catch up with Alison backstage. The women are in a protective circle around the one who screamed, a thirtyish brunette who is full of nervous laughter now.

"He just spooked me," she says. "I'm all right."

"He didn't hurt you?"

"No, no . . . I'm sorry, it's nothing. I came out of the bathroom and he just surprised me, being there. I don't know why I screamed."

"What did he look like?" Alison says.

"Tall, white. I don't know . . . he looked weird. He was wearing a green coat. And his eyes were kind of wild. Like he was on drugs."

"Creep," says one. The competitive feeling has left the room; the women have closed ranks. I'm the only man back here, and I'm getting a few looks.

Alison asks if anyone saw where the creep went and we're directed down a back stairs. One way leads outside, the other toward the college gym. I push the first door open. I don't see any footprints in the snow, but it's so icy here there's really no way to tell. There's just a long alley that turns to the right and must lead back to the street.

"It could have been Pollard," Alison says. "Or Travis. Or just an anonymous creep."

"You better get the security guards," I say. "Let me take a look around."

"Be careful," she says.

The alley's been treated with blue salt that doesn't seem to have done much good. I try each door I pass; nothing opens. A downspout that's separated from the wall swings in the wind. If the intruder went this way, he went all the way to the street.

There are footprints farther on, but the janitors must use this path; I can't tell which way the intruder went. The alley turns into a service drive and then a parking lot. I have to climb a fence to get back to the college. I'm on the athletic field, on a gravel track circling the baseball diamond, when I see the back door closing. When I get there, it's still unlocked.

It opens with a squeal. There's a long stairway that opens into a small old-fashioned gym, the kind you find on the west side where neighborhood kids learn to box. I flip a light switch, but nothing happens. Every step I take makes an echo. The floor is worn hardwood. The air is very close.

There are side rooms off the main area, where the weights and mats are, and there's a running track around the balcony. By now I'm thinking it's Travis and wishing I'd called the police or brought a gun. If he came this way, he could be up above me on the track. He could be anywhere.

I go through the hallway connecting the gym to the theater. The two buildings share rest rooms and a hallway with display cases. So there are football jerseys and programs from *La Cage aux Folles* jostling for position in the same trophy case. The men's rest room is empty. I knock on the women's and hear a female voice.

I'm on my way back through the hallway to the theater when something moves in the shadows to my right and there's a flash of light reflected in the display case. It's Pollard and he's faster than I would have predicted; he has a gun in my back before I can even turn around. He tells me to put my hands up on the display case. I'm guessing he doesn't want to discuss the orchestrations for *La Cage*.

He pats me down badly, a technique borrowed from TV dramas. "Sit down," he says. He's sweating like a racehorse. If I had to guess, I'd say he was back on speed, maybe moved on to crystal meth. It's a different look for him than the Dalmane. "I just want to . . . just want to *talk* to you," he says.

"You could have phoned. I'm in the book."

He waits until I sit against the wall and then moves a few feet away, looking past me in that way he has. His clothes are different from what I've seen him wear previously—layers of shirts with unbuttoned sleeves; trousers without a belt. But what's most remarkable is the difference in his speech. The long, slowly unfolding sentences are gone. His words come in spurts, a speedster's rap. It might make a nice poem for the slam.

"You have to talk to them," he says, "and *now,* Harding, because this whole mess started with you, that day you came into the café asking questions, all those questions, about Crystal, that bitch Tracy, your fucking *girlfriend, Mermaid* magazine. No one cared a shit when it was published and now suddenly there are all these *questions*—who took the *pictures,* why'd I take the *pictures*—that's why I followed you here, you can talk to them, they *know* you, they'll listen to you. The police, I mean. This whole mess started with *you.*"

"Yeah, the cops are great buddies of mine." The floor's uncomfortable, but each time I shift my weight, the gun jerks toward my face. It looks like an old revolver that's been sitting in a bureau for fifty years. Pollard's finger is on the trigger. The safety is off. "I think this is where I'm supposed to say just turn yourself in, things will be okay."

This doesn't calm him much. His whole body looks on edge; his lips are chapped, the skin cracked and peeling. His hair's uncombed. He paces in front of me like a manic prosecutor, limping slightly, one hand rubbing his coat.

"Things will *not* be fucking okay, Harding," he says, the words tumbling out, "things are royally, royally fucked up, okay? My lawyer says they want to *question* me, *interrogate* me, about Tracy, they want samples of my blood, they want to search, invade my privacy. And this is all your fault, it started with *your* questions, your digging up those pictures. What did you tell them about me? Harding? What did you say?"

A door slams. His gun hand moves enough that I duck. He's too far away from me to do anything. I have to get him closer. "Are they here already?" he says, perhaps paranoid from crystal meth. "The police? Did you call the police?"

"No. Relax, Logan. No one's coming. Put the gun down."

"What did you tell them?" he demands.

"I didn't tell them anything—"

"Why are you *harassing* me, you and that fucking dyke Alison?"

"Okay, all right. You want to know what I told them? I told them you've known Tracy since Grand Terrace and Gretchen for years, and now guess what, Tracy is dead and Gretchen's lucky to be alive—"

"Gretchen? Gretchen is your fault," he says. "Gretchen was talking to *you,* asshole, that's *your* fault, what happened to her. I haven't seen Gretchen fucking Moss in *years.*"

"Then you paid Travis, you sent Travis, you've had him on my ass all week—"

"That's what this detective is saying, Crowley, *you* told him that."

"Why are you doing all this, Logan, calling up Charles Muller and threatening him and threatening Alison? Why did you kill Tracy Lawrence, Logan?"

"You're nuts, Harding, you are insane—"

"Where are the other pictures you took, Logan, of Tracy and Gretchen? And what about this book Tracy was writing about a psychopath? Did you read it, did it strike a bit too close to home—"

"There are no pictures!" he says, more bothered by this than anything else. *"Quit asking about the fucking pictures—"*

"I know all about you, Logan."

"You know *nothing*—"

"I know you were talking to Tracy in New Mexico—I've got the phone records, Logan—"

"—acting so smug the other day, as if I didn't know what you wanted—"

"I know you were arrested, something you never mentioned. I know you like looking in people's windows."

"—as if you could *manipulate me* the way you do some pathetic lowlife—as if you know more about *me*—"

"Tell me what you know, Logan," I say, drawing him closer, so close I can smell the chemicals seeping through his skin and watch the drops of sweat congeal on his face. "If you mean Grand Terrace, Alison, and Tracy, that's nothing new, I know all that—"

"But you don't know the *details*," he hisses, "how they looked in *bed* together, they were in fucking *love,* Harding, and half the things they did, I'm guessing she never told you. Do you really think she looks that way at you? How will you ever fucking know?"

Another door slams; this one is closer. I think I hear footsteps. Pollard sees my reaction. It's enough to spook him, and when he commits himself to following my gaze, I go for his gun. He's stronger than I anticipated; adrenaline will do that. I'm not sure which annoys me more—the little struggle he puts up before I knock him out or the fact that the gun's not even loaded.

the local police take Pollard into custody. They listen to my story. I tell them to contact Detective Crowley at the CPD; they nod. These things sometimes take time. Meanwhile, Pollard will be charged with illegal possession of a weapon and several minor misdemeanors. They won't get a coherent story out of him until he comes down. Right now he's bouncing off the walls.

Alison huddles with some of the other promoters; they decide to go on with the competition. Both security guards are now very visible, patrolling the perimeter of the theater. I talk to both of them, telling them which exits I want checked. I give them a description of Travis. A local cop promises to swing by on his patrol.

Alison backs me up on everything, which helps a good deal. "I'm supposed to meet this guy Davey," I tell her. "But I can stick around if you want."

"Go, go," she says with a wave of her hand. "I'm okay here. And don't look so worried. Pollard's in jail. You did good." Travis is the unspoken fear. Neither one of us addresses it.

She reminds me about dinner with Beth and Charles, at Onkyo, in Wicker Park. Michelle still has her car, but even if she's late a couple of other friends can drop her off.

"Her event's running late," Alison says. On the way out I have another quick look around, whether to ease my guilt about leaving or my annoyance at Pollard for surprising me, I don't know. I'm doubly annoyed at myself, though. I'm still thinking more about what Pollard said about Grand Terrace—and Alison—than about the look in his eye or even the gun in his hand.

30

Sometimes Chicago seems to be filled with graveyards. If you've lived here your whole life, you've visited enough of them that the green spaces on the city maps begin to look like the swimming pools in a John Cheever story. You could travel across the city stopping at each one and remember this friend, that cousin. Today we're at Oak Woods Cemetery on 67th Street. It's a new stop for me.

The grounds are covered with a foot of snow, the headstones are white-topped, the flowers nailed to the graves. There's a six-foot brick wall surrounding the grounds. The ornate iron gates are closed. Nobody's going anywhere.

I get directions and a map from a woman in the office, then set off on foot along the circular drive. Former mayor Harold Washington is buried here; so is Jesse Owens and lots of other notables. It's a beautiful place. If you have to be dead, it's not a bad way to go.

In the center of Linden Hill a young man stands twirling an umbrella over a newly turned grave. He's nineteen or twenty, with a thin mustache. He crosses himself, eyes closed, and then pulls an old baseball cap out of his cheap jacket. He walks toward me with his hands jammed into his pants pockets.

"Davey?"

"Just walk with me," he says, head down. "Like you're a mourner."

I fall into step beside him. We stroll to a more secluded section, where the monuments are like small houses, the mausoleums drifting icebergs come to rest.

He looks around the grounds nervously, keeping his back to the brick wall.

"My name's Harding—"

"I know who you are," he says in a nasal voice. "Father Mike told me. And I've seen you before. You were there that night, the night Ricky died, with that chick, with the cops."

"But I'm not a cop," I say. "And I didn't see you that night."

He pulls out a pack of cigarettes, offers me one. I tell him no. His gloves are worn through at the knuckles. His fingers shake when he holds the match.

"If you're not a cop, what were you doing there?" he says.

"What did Father Mike tell you?"

"That you're looking for Ricky's killer. And you're a suspect yourself."

"I'm a private detective, Davey. I'm only a suspect because they found something of mine in Ricky's apartment. Something that must have been planted there. Were you in that apartment a lot?"

He doesn't answer this.

"Can you tell me why you paid for his burial?"

He takes a long drag on the cigarette, shaking his head. "That's none of your business," he says. This isn't starting out well.

"What about last Saturday night when Ricky was killed. Do you know who was there?"

"I can't help you with that," he says.

"Father Mike thought you might be able to."

He bites his lip, says nothing.

"Look, Davey. You and Ricky must have been close, right? That's why you spent the money for the burial. You want to do right by him. And you want the killer to pay, don't you?"

"I never said I knew who killed him," he says, getting upset. "What makes you think I know who killed him?"

"Father Mike said so."

He looks into my eyes. "He didn't say that."

"He said you were frightened of someone. If that's the case, then maybe I can help."

"Yeah, right," he says with a small laugh. "Everybody wants to help. You just wanna help *yourself.* And get the cops off you. You don't care about me."

"Even if you're right, the only way I can clear myself is by finding Ricky's killer." He's pacing now, first toward the path, then back to me. "You must want my help, Davey, or you wouldn't have shown up here."

"Father Mike said I should talk to you. I've got nightmares. I can't sleep." He's looking at me, sizing me up. "If I tell you what I know, what's to keep me from ending up like Ricky?"

"Because the guy who did it will be in jail."

"And he'll get right back out and come after me."

I shake my head. "It sounds like murder one, Davey. No bail. He won't be getting out."

"What if he does?" Davey insists. "What if they screw up his trial like that guy on death row and they set him free? What if he escapes?"

"Then you come to me. He won't hurt you."

He shakes his head. "You can't stop somebody like that."

"I can stop him." He looks at me, rubbing his hands together. I'm not sure he believes me. I'm not sure I believe it myself. "But I need a name, Davey. Who was up there that night with Ricky?"

"No way," he says. "I won't do that. I won't have you leaving here and telling people that I gave up the man's name. Because then I'd be dead. I'd be fucking dead."

A hearse pulls up to the gate. It stops at the office and the driver gets out, stretches, adjusts his tie and topcoat. "I've brought a few pictures, Davey," I tell him. "Could you just look at them and let me know somehow if I'm on the right track?"

"No names?" he says, watching the hearse. The other mourners are lined up on 67th Street, a row of Plymouths, Fords, Chevys, lights on, American flags fixed to their antennas. I'm afraid Davey's going to bolt, so I turn his attention to the pictures: Travis, Pollard, Dahlgren, Charles. He looks at them all. His face never changes expression.

"I never said I saw him," he says. The hearse driver comes out of the office, holding the same map they gave me. The funeral procession inches forward toward the circular drive.

"What can you tell me about that night, Davey?" I say.

He pauses. "I know Ricky was expecting someone. We were supposed to go out and then he canceled at the last minute. He said it would be worth his while to stay home."

"Someone was paying him?"

"I guess."

"Was he fencing those boxes of mixers and toasters at his place?"

"That . . . that was nothing."

"And he was dealing?"

"He was always dealing," Davey says, watching the line of cars. "This was something bigger."

"Do you recognize any of these men, Davey?"

He doesn't answer.

"Davey, please. Father Mike said you could help me."

"That's the only reason I'm here," he says softly. "Father Mike says it will help . . . if I tell somebody. Because right now I can't sleep." The procession of cars has stopped at one of the farther hills. The mourners stop and talk before the service starts.

"Davey, I'm gonna put these pictures away one at a time. We'll say the ones I put away are the men you didn't see up there. Okay?"

He nods.

"That way, you're not telling me anything."

"Okay."

"Ready?" I say. He nods.

I reach for Travis's picture and he stops me.

"This was the man?"

He shakes his head.

"Did I misunderstand something?" I say. "Let me start again."

He picks up Dahlgren's picture and puts it in my pocket.

"Okay, then this man you've never seen up there, never seen before, is that right?" He nods. "Then let's make my other pocket for the ones you have seen, okay?"

"All of them," he says.

I stare at him. He's looking around the cemetery nervously. Snowflakes are wetting the pictures, and I wipe them dry with the cuff of my coat.

"You're sure? All three?"

He nods.

"All of them that day, that Saturday?"

"I don't know about that."

"What does that mean?"

"I only saw one of them there on Saturday. But I wasn't there much that day. I had church work. And the other two I've seen many times."

I pick up Charles's picture. "This man? You've seen him in the building many times?"

He nods.

"And this man?" I show him Pollard.

"Many times."

"What were they doing there?"

"They had business with Ricky. I don't know any more."

"Drug business? They were buying drugs?" He shrugs. "But you said only one of them was there on Saturday when Ricky was killed. . . . It must have been this man." He nods when I point to Travis. "Was he wearing a black suit?"

"Just pants and a white shirt. And a coat. But I don't know who was up there when it happened. I wasn't there."

"Okay."

"I didn't see it happen."

"I believe you."

"If anyone asks, you tell them I wasn't there, I don't know nothing. I won't talk to the cops, I won't help them."

I give him a minute to calm down. "I have a friend, a detective—a real good guy, Davey, he wouldn't bust you on this or anything else—"

"I won't talk to the cops." He looks like he's about to run. I give him my card and put my arm around his shoulders. He's trembling; he needs another cigarette.

"If you think of anything else, give me a call. Okay?" He nods. "If you need help with something, if somebody bothers you, let me know."

"All right."

"Could I know your last name?"

He hesitates. "Garcia."

I offer him my hand. "Davey, I think what you did here—getting Ricky into Oak Woods instead of being in a county plot, with no name, no tombstone—that was a very classy thing to do. You're a good friend, Davey. I hope I have a friend like you."

The sun's going down. There are a half-circle of mourners on a distant hill, their backs to us, just black silhouettes. "He wouldn't care," Davey says, crossing himself, his eyes turning away. "He was a goddamn bastard."

31

We meet Beth and Charles at Onkyo, a trendy restaurant in Wicker Park. I think we're the only ones in the place over thirty. Alison is dressed totally in black, so we barely make the quota on that. Her pants are leather, very tight, very sexy. She's wearing a Harley jacket. There are a lot of artists in this neighborhood, of course, but I doubt they can afford to eat at Onkyo.

Conversation is forced. The food is designer and minimalist, on square plates. The wine is French and overpriced. Charles orders the wine but doesn't drink. The rest of us do our best to finish two bottles. On the way out one of the waiters giggles at the way Charles is dressed—plaid shirt, wrinkled sport coat, salt-stained brown loafers. I feel like taking him aside and telling him: You want artistic? You want Bukowski, on-the-edge poetic madness? This is the real thing, fella. This is what it looks like.

There's a blues club two blocks away; Beth wants to go and no one wants to disappoint her. Alison whispers that she spoke to Gretchen Moss very briefly; she's agreed to talk to me. Charles walks beside me, pulling on a pair of brown gloves. He apologizes for last night, says he doesn't remember much of what happened.

"I guess I shot myself in the foot again," he says.

"Did you get your car back okay?"

"Yes, Beth got it . . . with Henry Dahlgren." He says Dahlgren's name as though it's a new strain of virus.

"What made you start drinking again, Charles? You seemed okay in the afternoon, when we took our drive."

"Afternoons aren't the problem, Harding," he says. "It's late at night, when I'm trying to work . . . that's when I have problems."

Despite the cold, there are small groups of people outside the club. Some are buying tickets; most are buying designer drugs, not something you see much at a blues club. Charles points out the poetry slam signs in the window. I make at least three pushers as I'm escorting Beth in the door.

"It's not too late to rent a cabin with us this weekend," Beth says to me. She's wearing a white parka and soft-leather brown boots. She looks ready for après-ski right now. "I'm not sure Charles can ski, but I think it's good to get away for a while. This place is sort of rustic, and he needs a change of scenery."

I don't answer right away. She asks me if something's wrong.

"You're amazing, Beth," I say.

"Why?"

"After all the shit Charles has pulled . . ."

"I'm no saint, just a historian," Beth says. "I take the long view."

"Sure, but still . . ."

"It's a disease, Harding," she says, turning serious. "You of all people should know that. And it can be cured. There's a good man underneath all that pain. What if Alison had given up on you?"

It's a question I've never been able to answer.

I get us a table near the back. Alison hates smoke and this place is very smoky. Charles takes the chair with his back to the stage, either to facilitate conversation or as a critical statement on the proceedings. "This is just stand-up comedy," he muttered on seeing the signs for the slam.

"These are very big in Hyde Park, too," Beth says. "These poetry slams." A waitress takes our orders. It's tough to know what to drink around Charles. Beth and Alison get more wine; I'd like a beer but settle for cranberry juice. Charles has ginger ale. "Dennis Gould's son competes in a slam. Dennis thinks it's terrific."

"Dennis Gould is a moron," Charles says.

"He won a Nobel Prize," Beth says.

"In economics. Bean counting."

"Don't be grumpy, Charles," Alison says.

I excuse myself and find the bar and the guy who seems to be running things. He points to a green blackboard, where tonight's drink specials are listed along with the poetry slam standings. Pollard's name is listed first, below the Wordgasm Martini.

"He's usually late," the guy says.

"Do you know him very well?" I say.

"Yeah, we've talked," he says. "He's cool 'cause he's a bit more . . . cerebral than some of the others here. Most of the people here . . . they compose out of the moment, you know? It's street poetry. Logan's stuff is more polished." He's polishing it in jail tonight.

My cell phone's acting up, so I use a pay phone near the men's john to call Gretchen Moss in Kansas City. Her voice is soft; there's a lot of noise in the bar, even back here. I ask her how she's doing. I apologize several times.

She tells me that she's fine, she left school with one paper left to finish, she's been working on that, getting ready for Christmas. I tell her I usually did my papers the night before they were due. There's a nervous pause, then I ask her if she minds telling me about last Sunday night.

"Okay," she says.

"Are you sure? Maybe it's better not to talk about it."

"Actually, I'm supposed to talk about it, and believe me, I've gone over it fifty times with fifty different people. That's supposed to take the importance away. Make it, like, routine." There's a pause; I hear her lighting a cigarette. "As if," she says.

"I know the only reason you called me back is because of Alison."

"That's true," she says. "What she taught me probably saved my life."

"But anything you could tell me I'd very much appreciate."

Her voice is very small somehow. I don't think it's a bad connection. All I can think about is those fingermarks on her neck. "Didn't the police tell you what happened?"

"Just the barest outline." A waitress finds me, brings me my cranberry juice. "Remember I asked you about Tracy Lawrence? I'm still trying to figure out what happened to her. And as far as the police go, I'm sort of out of the loop."

"See . . . nobody I talked to mentioned Tracy. Not the campus police, not the Chicago police. They didn't even know who she was, much less that she was dead or murdered."

"But you brought it up?"

"Well . . . I'd just talked to you. It was in my head. And I might have—*might* have—given them the impression that you were involved somehow. I didn't mean to and if I did . . . well, I'm sorry."

"Tell me what happened Sunday night."

There's a noise, as though she's changing hands, maybe settling back in her chair. "I was in my dorm, watching TV, and I got a phone call, eleven o'clock or so. By now it's obvious how dumb I was, but see, I'm in this study group with this guy named Tim and the caller said Tim had been trying to reach me, Tim wanted to meet me at the Medici for a hamburger, and I was bored and, besides, this guy Tim is sort of cute."

"But it wasn't Tim who called."

She sighs. "No, that's the dumb part, he said he was Greg, this *other* guy in the study group who I never noticed and wouldn't recognize his voice in a million years. This was really, really dumb, Alison would shoot me, I know . . ."

"So you left your dorm around eleven, walked up Woodlawn to 57th?"

She says yes. "I think he was waiting in the playground. I told the police I felt like someone was following me then. I should have called security, I know that now, but each time I turned, there was nobody there . . . and the Medici was just a couple more blocks. I was thinking Tim would be there, we'd have a good time, maybe next quarter we'd go out. I was gonna cross Dorchester when he grabbed me . . ."

She stops, and I realize I've been listening so closely, I haven't noticed the anger in her voice until now. The anger seems directed at herself.

"He grabbed me by the neck from behind, so I never saw him—real strong hands, real powerful, he was pulling me toward some bushes when I started using my elbows the way Alison taught me. I was trying to turn around so I could kick him in the balls, but all I could do was swing at him. It was awkward as hell, but a couple of them must have landed, enough that he was getting pissed at me and I was able to yell until the hands got tighter and I thought I heard a switchblade open, but then a light when on somewhere and he just dropped me and took off."

"Did you see his clothes at all?"

"No. One of those creepy ski masks on his face, that's it. I was so stupid, so fucking stupid—all I could think about was I can't go into those bushes, if he gets me into those bushes then I'm dead."

"What about his shoes?"

"Just some kind of guy shoes. You know, like my father would wear."

"Not white gym shoes."

She says no. I tell her that Alison and I would love to take her to dinner after school starts again. She says she's feeling better—really better—but she's not sure if she's coming back to school next quarter. She's seeing a shrink now. She's not sleeping very well.

I go back to the bar. Someone onstage is announcing the night's first performer, a poet named Sergei. Charles comes up and puts his arm around my shoulders, the way I did with Davey Garcia. He smells like aftershave.

"Do you know this policeman named Crowley very well?" he says.

I tell him I do.

"Is he honest, do you think?"

"Within limits, sure. He's a cop. Why?"

"He's pestering my lawyers for an interview. I'm not sure what to do." He makes it sound like Crowley's a stringer for *Time*. "I'm not even sure what he wants to talk about."

There's a rock band playing, which I thought was an opening act, but the music grows quieter and the lead singer, Sergei, starts reciting, holding the microphone uncomfortably close. "This is a new haiku," Sergei the poet says, "called 'Retch.'"

"Did he say 'Retch'?" Charles says to me, and I nod. "Jesus, what a circus." He looks like he might retch himself.

The bartender pours me another cranberry juice, telling me the juice is all-natural, from organic bogs. I tell him I can taste the difference. I think I can taste the bog. *Retch* might be the word for the night.

I've waited till now to talk seriously with Charles. He's a bit more relaxed than he was at dinner—as relaxed as he'll get without drinking. I wish I could buy him a double whiskey, something for him to hold in his hands and focus on. Instead I ask him to tell me about Ricky Lopez.

"There's nothing to tell, Harding."

"You've never been up there before. To see Lopez."

"Why would I be doing that?"

"That's what I want to know, Charles. And that's what the police will want to know once they tie you to that building."

Birds retch we jump
Birds retch we run
Why are we afraid of birds

"Birds don't retch," Charles mutters under his breath. "Jesus Christ."

"Sssh," the bartender says.

"Well, it makes no sense," Charles says, louder this time. Sergei the poet stops and yells at Charles to shut the fuck up.

"Crowley didn't mention that," Charles says to me.

"Crowley doesn't know what I know. Someone has gone on record as having seen you up there last summer, Charles. Several times."

"Last Saturday, when he was killed?"

"Did I say last Saturday? But you lie about one thing, you could be lying about everything. That's the way cops think, Charles."

He looks into my eyes. When he stands up straight, he's a good two inches taller than me, and I'm six-two. But he slouches so much, you don't notice his size. "Do you think I'm lying?"

"Charles, it rarely matters what I think."

The truth is, I can't tell with Charles. Even when he's telling you the truth, he parcels it out so much you feel you're getting the runaround.

He stares at the stage. "It is possible," he says, "to be less than truthful about certain details . . . in order to avoid hurting people . . . while being true to the basic story, don't you think?"

"That's gibberish," I say. "Were you up there buying drugs?"

"No. I was up there—no more than three times—trying to settle a dispute between Lopez and Tracy."

"Tracy bought drugs from Lopez?"

He nods. "Tracy was living somewhere near here all summer, I don't know where exactly. When she wasn't in Taos, I mean. And when I came to Hyde Park, I would see her at a friend's apartment."

"This was while you were also seeing Beth, of course. And Moira Dahlgren, too?"

"But I wasn't seeing Beth. I mean . . . not like with the others. Beth was different."

"You mean you weren't fucking Beth. Yet." He flinches at this, as though I've broken some sort of taboo. It's a virgin/whore distinction with Tracy in the latter category. Charles had a very busy summer. "Charles, no one at that commune Tracy stayed at, Peace Station, mentioned she was on drugs."

"Well, they probably wouldn't have allowed her to stay if they knew. She was good at concealing it. But that's why she was always out of money, always borrowing money. She tried to sell me a gold pin that belonged to her mother once. I wouldn't do it."

"You don't know where Tracy was staying last summer?"

"She didn't want to tell me. I know it sounds silly, but she was very secretive that way. She would phone me to say that she'd be in Hyde Park on such and such a date and so I would make arrangements to be there, too."

I nod. I motion for the bartender and trade in my cranberry juice for a double scotch neat. I buy the same for Charles. "Alison didn't know she was here," I say.

"I don't think she wanted to see Alison. Or any of her old friends. She was embarrassed about the drugs, her lack of success—"

"But she wanted to see you."

He tries sipping the scotch, then just pours it back. His tongue collects what's left on his lips. "Maybe I accepted her the way she was. God knows I've got enough problems of my own not to go judging someone else."

"How did Tracy hook up with Ricky Lopez?"

"I don't know. How do junkies find their dealers? I got the impression someone introduced her to him, one of his other customers."

"You supplied her with money?"

"Sometimes." I think I hear the sound of Charles shooting himself in the other foot.

"Oh, Beth is going to love this, Charles. Alison, too."

"I was only trying to help her. She—don't laugh—said she was in love with me."

"Did it ever occur to you that the only reason she came back to Hyde Park was to score more drugs? And that you were just her bankroller?"

"I don't believe that. She came here to see me, Harding. The drugs were secondary."

"If there's one thing I know to be true, Charles, it's that drugs are never secondary. What was she using?"

"Coke for a while. Then speed, a lot of speed."

"Methamphetamine?"

"Yes."

"How much did she owe?"

"I'd gotten it down to a reasonable amount—"

"How much?"

"Five thousand."

"Was she buying from someone else besides Lopez?"

"Probably, but she only let me see a part of that side of her, so I don't know. Why do you ask?"

"Logan Pollard uses meth, too. I'm wondering if she bought from him. Or if they both got high at Ricky's place. This friend's apartment where you met Tracy? Where was it?"

"That can't matter now."

"Indulge me, Charles."

"It was a friend of Tracy's. I don't even know her name. She was never home when we were there."

"You must remember the address."

"It was that high-rise at 47th Street," he says.

"Ninth floor?"

"Yes, how did you know that?"

"It's a busy spot lately," I say.

Sergei the poet leaves the stage to scattered applause and makes his way to a table close to where we're standing. When he sees Charles, his eyes light up.

"Hey, man," he says. "What the fuck was that all about?"

Charles turns slowly, as though it takes him a second to locate Sergei in his sights.

"You shouldn't criticize, man, if you don't have the balls to do it yourself."

"Sorry," Charles says, offering his hand. "You're right, of course. The word just seemed wrong."

"It's the name of my band. Retch. And my girlfriend, Amber, she likes birds. Okay? It's just a fucking poem, man." A cute redhead turns and smiles at us when she hears her name. Charles smiles back, grabs a cocktail napkin, and starts scribbling. He's finished by the time they reach the door.

Amber eyes in storefront glass
What if seagulls retch our past lives
Swoop and spin and tell us things we did not know.

The girl says thanks. "Not bad," Sergei the poet says.

"It stinks," Charles says. "I'd never commit to paper."

Charles insists on settling the bill. I'm not going to argue with him. Alison and Beth walk outside and I follow. Charles catches up midblock.

I ask him if he knew whose apartment that was, the one where he had met Tracy. He says no. "You never met Crystal Royce, Charles? Or her brother?"

"Is that who owned it? No, I don't know them. There was never anyone there. And Tracy had a key."

"I suppose you met Moira Dahlgren there once or twice, too? In addition to your dates in Galena?"

"No," he says. "I told you, the thing with Moira was over."

"Did you ever see Henry Dahlgren there with Tracy?"

He gives me a strange look, as though what I'm saying could be any stranger than the story he's just recounted. "Henry with Tracy? God, no."

We drove here in separate cars and I'm trying to remember which side street I left mine on when the women cross Milwaukee against the light, caught up in some conversation. Charles and I wait for the light to change.

"Moira Dahlgren's in town tonight, Charles."

"I didn't know that. But we haven't spoken in a while." His eyes squint a bit, looking into the wind. "Moira's lost to me now," he says.

That's when a red Mustang pulls up and blocks our path. The driver's a guy I saw out front with the dealers earlier. I'm watching him and wishing the light would change, so I don't notice what's going on across the street until Charles pulls on my sleeve. There are two guys walking with Alison and Beth, circling them. Charles takes off before I can say a word and then the Mustang's door opens, so close it hits my leg.

"You have a problem?" the driver says to me. Alison is trying to ignore the guys and get Beth to her car, but the guys finally plant themselves in their path and I see one of them reach for Alison's bracelet while the other reaches for Beth's purse. The driver of the Mustang gets out, holding a knife. A guy in the backseat is covering me with a 9mm.

"No problem," I say, trying to follow Charles, but the driver pushes me back. I can see Beth turning, looking for us; I can see the panic in her eyes, and when she sees Charles, she waves to him and he breaks into a long, loping trot. Alison puts up with the one guy as long as possible before hitting him. She knows you have to put the guy down, and she does that. But the other guy has a switchblade and he slices through Beth's purse handle. That little victory keeps him from running off. He is sort of shadowing Beth, keeping away from Alison, when Charles shows up behind him. Charles ignores the knife, fights like a schoolboy, more or less; he grabs him from behind by the neck and then spins him around and slams him against the storefront. The knife hits the sidewalk; Alison kicks it away. One guy helps the other up, then starts down the alley. But the first guy stays for a second, just staring at Alison, as if daring her to make a move, his fingers twitching at his side, wishing for the knife, before a crowd pushes forward and he finally backs down, following his friend. The dealer gives me a final shove and gets back into the Mustang. The last thing I see is the guy in the backseat with the 9mm blowing me a kiss through the rear window.

The whole thing takes less than two minutes. The small crowd has gathered around Beth and Alison, urging them to call the police. But I move everyone to Beth's car. I have no wish to get my name on more paperwork. Nobody's hurt, Beth's minus a purse, but by now it's in a Dumpster somewhere.

"How much cash were you carrying?" I ask her.

"Maybe twenty," she says.

"I just used most of it paying the bill," Charles says, still breathing hard.

"My hero," Beth says, smiling at Charles, kissing him.

"That was dumb, Charles," Alison says. "Really dumb. He had a knife."

"I know," Charles says, oddly pleased with himself. "It was dumb, wasn't it? Almost mindless."

Beth wants to stop at a club like Crobar, but I have my date with Moira Dahlgren, so I beg off.

"I need my sleep, Beth," I say. Alison wants to go back to the competition. Beth and Charles say they'll drive her, keep her company, which makes me feel better. Alison's not frightened by what happened. But I'm writing down the license plate from the red Mustang. There was something odd about that attack. Not just the way they tried to separate the men from the women; I've seen that done before. It was more the look on the first guy's face and his failure to run. The purse snatching seemed less important than confronting Alison.

"Harding needs his warm milk and Geritol," Alison says.

"Charles," I say, "maybe we should have found women our own age."

"Oh, what fun would that be?" he says.

32

I meet Moira Dahlgren in the lobby of the Palmer House. She's having a drink with someone who might have been a male model in an earlier life: late twenties, tennis sweater, bottle-blond hair in a Robert Redford cut. He's fixed now in a perpetual state of boredom. He doesn't get up when she does, doesn't help her with her coat. He leaves those things to me.

"Don't forget me, babe," he says, already glancing at a blonde nearby.

"That was Tyler," she says when we're outside.

"He looked like a Tyler. Or a Lance."

She's wearing cute little black mittens, black boots, another short, slinky dress under knee-length fur. Silver bracelets slide on her small wrists. "It's such a beautiful night. Would you mind if we just took a short walk and window-shopped?"

"No, that's fine."

We walk north on State Street to Carson's. She's right, it is indeed a beautiful night. "You're the private detective," she says, as though this explained what I was doing here. I nod. We pause briefly before Carson's windows, which seem to be featuring talking bunnies. "Did my husband send you here for some reason?"

"He's worried about you," I say, and she smiles at that. "He thinks you're avoiding him."

"How clever of him," she says, lighting a cigarette. She has a nervous habit—or a slight affectation—of running her fingers through her copper-colored hair, shaking it free. As mannerisms go, it's fairly sexy.

There are a lot of street-corner Santas and musicians out to-night, hoping to cash in on the season. A tenor sax player I usually see on the Lake Street subway platform has surfaced on Madison, playing "The Shadow of Your Smile." As we cross the street, the various instruments start to overlap: flute, trumpet, a one-man band playing "Silent Night" on spoons and knee cymbals. Moira and I weave our way through the late-evening crowds to this soundtrack. It makes me feel like Frederic Forrest with Cindy Williams in *The Conversation*.

"The last time we met I didn't get a chance to tell you how sorry I was about Tracy Lawrence."

She regards me blankly, taking a long drag on her cigarette. "Thank you," she says finally.

"I know how close you were to her in college."

"That was a long time ago, Harding. Don't tell me Alison sits and pines over Tracy."

"No," I say. "She doesn't."

"I wouldn't think so."

I watch her stand and smoke. The silence doesn't bother her. She stares at the window display. "Why go through all this now, Harding? She's gone."

"I'm trying to find out who killed her. I guess I thought her friends would want to help."

"What have you learned so far?"

"Not a hell of a lot, Moira. Everyone liked her, no one seems to have gotten close to her." I pause. Those phone calls from Dahlgren's house to Taos are on my mind. "For some reason, I don't think that applies to you."

"Alison got close to her," she says. "Alison got very close to her. You know she was living in Hyde Park until February, I assume. You know she was working as a waitress. You know she was writing non-stop."

I nod. "And I know about *Mermaid* magazine and Logan Pollard. But I can't tell what their relationship was. Or if anything from that time period even means anything. She was killed eight months later."

"Pollard . . . Is he a suspect?"

"He's in jail. You heard about Gretchen Moss? That she was attacked last Sunday night?"

"No, I hadn't heard that. I've been out of town. Gretchen Moss?"

"She worked with Tracy at the restaurant. And she posed in one of those pictures in *Mermaid* that Pollard took."

"But Tracy barely knew her. You think she is involved somehow?"

I shake my head. "I think she was attacked because she was talking to me."

"Lovely," she says, shivering and looking around her. "I'm glad I'm leaving town again tomorrow."

I tell her about my search for Tracy, which began last Sunday, and how it had led me here. I might be telling her more than I should. But I want her to open up to me.

"Let's go back to my original question," I say. "When was the last time you saw her?"

"Let's see, it was around Halloween. I was visiting her at her place in New Mexico."

"Did you do that often?"

"Whenever I was flying to the coast, I would stop in and see her. I had friends in California."

"That's when she disappeared, you know. Halloween weekend."

"No, I didn't know that," she says. It takes a second to sink in. "You're saying what? That I was one of the last people to see her?"

"That depends on what you did that weekend."

"Nothing. We had dinner in Taos, shopped a bit, and then stopped in Santa Fe so I could buy some boots. That was the only reason I was there, actually. And then I drove her to the airport in Albuquerque. Tuesday night. I flew west, she flew east."

"She was flying to Chicago?"

"Yes."

"Was someone meeting her here?"

"Not that I know of."

"I don't suppose you'd remember the flight number."

"God, no."

"Did anyone else know she was flying then?"

"I don't know. It wasn't a big deal at the time. I was only out there to buy some new boots."

"Was there a reason she moved to New Mexico?"

"I think it was just another place to try. She'd lived all over Europe the past couple of years. Maybe she thought it would be a good place to write."

"I've heard that she was writing a book about a serial killer, but no one seems to have read much of it."

"Neither did I. She kept those things to herself. Her work, her art. But I'd be surprised if that was her real subject."

"Why?"

"I don't know. She had other things on her mind, I think. We all have our obsessions, Harding." She won't say anything further.

"She wasn't running away from someone?"

"Like who?"

"I don't know. Logan Pollard. Charles Muller."

"She and Charles were never serious."

"Do you mind if I ask you . . . how close you were? With Tracy?"

She turns the silver bracelets nervously around her wrist. "We were friends."

"Were you close enough to know if she was using drugs? And who she was buying them from?"

"I never saw her . . . using. Injecting, snorting, whatever. I know she was high sometimes."

"Just sometimes?"

"All right, most of the time. Especially later in the summer. She was a writer, an artist. It's not that uncommon."

"You're an artist, too, Moira."

"Not like Tracy," she says, shaking her head. "And I wasn't unhappy, like Tracy was. . . ."

We're looking at the Christmas windows at Field's, but we've started at the wrong end. All the little mice and rabbits had a night full of adventures, but you'd never know it here. There are large dollhouses with tiny sleeping mice and rabbits, all tucked in on Christmas Eve, wearing stocking caps and scarves. If we want to see what mischief they got into, we'll have to walk down to Randolph Street, to the first window.

"What do they do with all this after Christmas?" she says.

"Put it in storage, I guess. There's a funny museum in Wisconsin that displays a lot of the old stuff." A Santa sneaks into the window, then returns offstage. "There's someone else involved in this, a man named Savick, an ex-con who works for Pollard at Dreamlike Display. Do you know him, by any chance? Or his sister, Crystal Royce?"

She frowns, doesn't answer for a bit.

"I've met Crystal," she says.

"Were you and Crystal both involved with Tracy last spring?"

She doesn't answer. I've seen so many photographs of this woman lately—old photographs admittedly—that I somehow feel I know her better than I do.

"I don't know why I should trust you," she says.

"You're probably like me, you don't like trusting anyone. But Tracy's dead. I don't see the point in keeping secrets."

"Tracy and I were friends," she says again. "I don't see the need for graphic details."

"Was your husband a similar type of friend to her?"

"Tracy, with Henry? Please."

"I've been told you had an affair with Charles Muller that began when he taught downstate—"

"Look, Harding, you found me here with Tyler, and I can just imagine some of the stories you've heard about me—"

"I didn't mean to imply—"

"—but most of what people say is hurtful and mean and I

stopped caring what they thought about me a long time ago. I'm not a friend of Crystal's. Or a fan of hers. Our paths crossed a few times, but Hyde Park's like a small town."

"But did you keep seeing Charles? Were you with him last summer in Galena, for example?"

She says yes. "We thought we'd see if there was anything left. There wasn't." She pauses. "It was his idea, not mine. I know he was seeing Tracy then, but that's all I know. And that's all I feel like saying."

"Can you at least tell me where you and Tracy met when she came to Chicago? You moved out of the house on South Blackstone in February—"

"I had an apartment. My husband was the one who rented it."

"Isn't that odd?"

"We were still friends, Harding. And he put it under some subsidiary of his business so he could write it off somehow. Don't tell him I told you that, please."

"Where was this apartment?"

"In Lake Village East."

"At 4700 South Lake Park?"

She nods.

"What apartment?" I say.

"Nine C." Her eyes have a dark look to them despite her pale skin. She's still trying to decide if it was a good idea to talk to me.

"You and Charles were both involved with Tracy all last summer," I say. "Didn't that seem odd?"

"That we found the same woman attractive? No, Harding, it didn't. We'd known each other for years, remember. And I sometimes think Charles was making up for lost opportunities."

"How so?"

"None of us slept with him in college. At least I know Tracy didn't and I didn't. If Alison did, she never told me."

"Just one more question. Forgive me if this seems frivolous. The year you spent at Grand Terrace, your senior year—what are your memories of that time?"

"God . . ." She runs her fingers through her hair. "Trying to get enough credits to graduate. Begging professors for letters of recommendation; I was going to grad school. Driving to the North Side on Saturday nights to go dancing. Endless hours in the library . . ."

"That's it?"

She nods. "Why, what were you expecting?"

"Charles remembers that time as a sort of hedonistic free-for-all. Like that weekend you spent with Alison and Tracy at a cabin."

"Oh, yes," she says. "The famous cabin. You know what I remember about that? Sand everywhere. No food, nothing but Triscuits and a failed attempt at making a chocolate mousse. There were mosquitoes everywhere. And the beach stank of rotten fish."

"You don't look all that unhappy in the pictures."

"We were kids, Harding. It was an adventure. That doesn't mean I'd want to do it again." She smiles, mostly to herself. "Charles spent every waking moment up in his room reading or writing poems—and he remembers it as hedonistic?"

"The cabin belonged to your aunt?"

"God, no. Some second cousin of Tracy's." She's like Alison, she wants to pull the conversation back to the present. "You said my husband hired you?"

I nod. I don't say for what. Apparently he hired me to break into his own apartment. It's getting difficult to tell just who was sleeping with whom in that apartment. It reminds me of Grand Terrace.

"How much did he pay you?"

"Two thousand," I say, "plus expenses. You seem surprised. It's pretty standard."

"I'm not surprised, I'm touched," she says. "He never spent that much on me before."

• • •

i'm in Miller's Pub on Wabash nursing a scotch and making a few notes when my cell phone rings. The voice is very familiar and very welcome.

"Crowley is looking for you," Alison says.

"What's he want?"

"You think he'd tell me? This is men's business, Harding. You want his number?"

I tell her yes. He must have lost my cell phone number. I think he hates the damn things as much as I do. "Are you home? How'd the competition go?"

"Okay. I pushed PowerFemmes. Two of my fitness babes qualified for the finals. And I'm at the gym now, closing up."

"What about Michelle?"

"She didn't show. I don't blame her. I chickened out the first time I had to do one of these. After throwing up all night the night before. She'll be okay. We'll just work that much harder."

"Did Beth and Charles stay with you?"

"All the time, lover. I was closely guarded. But I missed you."

"Listen, Alison. Did you ever hear anything about Tracy being on drugs?"

"We all smoked grass, you know that."

"Anything stronger?"

"Who are you talking to?"

"Just tell me the truth, Alison."

This annoys her, but she answers. "I saw her use coke. I saw her sniff heroin *once,* only *once.* Just to try it. I never saw any needles."

"Did she use drugs that weekend you were at the Dunes? With Moira?"

"I don't remember—"

"Where was that place located, Alison?"

"At the Dunes? Harding, I spent a weekend there ten years ago." I hear some voices in the background: women leaving the gym, saying good night.

"You don't remember anything? A street, a landmark?"

"No. I mean we stopped at Phil Smidt's for frog legs, but that was on the way. There was a lighthouse nearby—or a lookout tower. It might have been Chesterton. That sounds right . . . Moira was reading Chesterton then for a senior paper, so we made jokes about that. She might know where the place is; her family owned it."

This surprises me. "She says Tracy's cousin owned it."

"So you're with Moira? She's back in town?"

"I'm in Miller's Pub alone, Alison. Moira is back at the Palmer House by now, with Tyler. Or Lance."

"Harding, about Tracy . . . lots of kids used drugs."

"I know."

"So what's this about?"

"I'll tell you about it later."

"There's something else to tell?"

"Actually, no," I say. "I just thought it sounded good to end the conversation that way."

"Call Crowley."

"I'm calling Crowley," I say.

But Crowley doesn't answer. I leave a message, but I get the feeling the desk sergeant doesn't much care where he's gone.

33

northern Indiana is Chicago's New Jersey, the brunt of jokes, but once you get past Hammond and Gary, following the tollway around the curve of the lake, you find long stretches of wilderness as pretty as anything in New England. The snow is still piled along the roads out here, covering the shoulders like a wrap of white mink. The branches of the evergreens sag like disjointed arms.

I have a good map of Indiana and another of the Dunes Park, but I still get lost a few times. Nothing's numbered very well, and the houses are set far back from the road. It takes me several hours and two stops at local antiques shops for directions to find the lookout tower Alison mentioned. At one point I'm driving through acres of pine trees when Lake Michigan suddenly appears. For some reason it's not frozen. The moon seems very close. Somehow, even at night, the water looks astonishingly clear and blue. You'd never know it's the same lake that washes up on the 63rd Street Beach.

Tracy's cousin's house is close enough to the Dunes to be battered by the sand and the lake-effect snow, but it's not on the water. It looks like a run-down Tudor and sits about a quarter-mile from the road, wrapped in rows of cottonwoods and white pine. There are two other cabins nearby but both look like summer homes, shut for the season. One has a sign advertising comforters and apple jelly. The other is being guarded by a pair of decorative geese, wearing bonnets and carrying wicker baskets.

I park as far from the driveway as I can and take a walk around the house. A mailbox out by the road is full of junk mail and spider-webs. It's too cold for spiders. No one's been at the house in a while.

There's a tiny front porch with warped boards showing the sand and silt underneath. The front door is locked and the curtains are drawn. There's a small stone porch out back, with a path that leads toward the woods. The beach and the boat dock would be beyond that. I can tell where the girls would have been sitting. I can picture them again on that boat. I can see the same trees that were in the pictures. The lock on the back door is so flimsy, I use a credit card to get in.

It opens to what they call a great room in the real estate ads. There's a stone fireplace set in a redbrick wall; large, round wool rugs; cheap oak furniture. It's very cold in here. I have a flashlight, but I have to keep it low, away from the windows. The power's off. The phone is dead.

It's a large house for one person, two floors, but I think most of the house is taken up by this main room. The second floor looks more like a balcony. There's no basement, of course; not with this water table. Even in winter you can smell the lake, marinated over time into the hardwood floors and beams. The wind is blowing hard enough to rattle the flue in the chimney.

I put on a pair of gloves. The kitchen has staples: salt, sugar, cof-fee, boxes of Wheat Chex. There are bags of lentils and red beans with small mice holes gnawed through the plastic. I open the refrig-erator and a bad smell makes me close it quickly. But then I open it again. There's no milk or eggs, nothing that would spoil quickly. No leftover dishes. Just cans of juice. The smell is coming from the freezer, where a package of ground beef is slowly rotting.

Brown rusty water drips from the tap when I turn it on, proba-bly from a well or a cistern. Still, I wonder how long the place has been vacant. I wonder why the pipes didn't freeze and flood the place. The fact that there's no mail, no old newspapers, means either that someone has been collecting them or had them stopped. I'm already thinking that this is where Tracy lived last summer.

I'm something of a connoisseur of bad smells. I've walked through a lot of crime scenes. As I take the steep, creaky steps to the second floor, I smell something I recognize. There's an open area at the top of the stairs with a desk, a rowing machine, and two dark, still closets with open doors. They're empty. The single bedroom is quiet. The smell comes from here.

The trail of blood leads to the bed. I open some wooden blinds. The moonlight shows more blood. There's blood everywhere. It's been here awhile, but it disturbs me nonetheless; I curse myself for walking in here. I reach for a gun I don't have, something I often do when I see blood. The bathroom door is partially closed. I kick it open with my right foot, so hard it just bangs on the wall and starts to close again.

There's no body, but there are bits of flesh and hair, and even more blood in the bathtub. Plastic bottles of shampoo are lined up neatly in a straight row on a ledge. The cold kept the smell down, but it's still fairly disgusting in here. I have to walk outside to get the stench from my lungs.

When I return, I go through the whole house, looking for papers or mail. The noise from the flue draws my attention; I move the grill and open the glass doors and shine my light inside the fireplace. The remains of a fire are still here: black chips of wood, a bed of ashes. And two curled scraps of paper that must have swirled in the updraft before drifting down. There are probably others in the woods, mixed with the leaves and the sand. One scrap has a page number. The other has just a part of a sentence, which is meaningless without the context. I wonder if this is all that's left of Tracy's manuscript. I wonder who burned it here and forgot to close the flue.

I look around the bedroom again. I don't find anything connected to Charles, Travis, or Pollard. I do find a pair of blue silk panties, torn through the crotch. A cup of something—coffee?—beside the bed on a nightstand. Both items now seem unbearably fragile and sad. I put the panties on the bed. I feel Tracy's presence awakening as though I'd disturbed a ghost.

Inside the nightstand there are bottles of hand lotion and fingernail polish remover and some cotton balls. They're sitting with a small invitation-size envelope, a box of Kotex, and some hair curlers on sheets of paper that almost look like shelf-liner paper. In fact, they're figure drawings, pen-and-ink sketches of Tracy and Moira Dahlgren. They look like they were just tossed off one night but kept as something precious. Most are nudes done here in this bed. One of them has Moira's initials on the bottom with a September date.

Inside the envelope there's a letter typed in a script typeface. It's initialed, too: LP.

> *I'm only saying this once more. You can't publish this, you can't use real names and places, especially 32 Milwaukee—I told you that night when I let you inside. That was private, you've got no right. . . .*

I'm standing in the bathroom trying to make sense of the whole thing, as frozen as the crime scene, unsure of what to do next, when my cell phone buzzes. It makes me jump, as though I've been caught doing something. I always feel guilty. It comes from being in prison.

"Harding?"

It's Crowley.

When I look at the tub now, I can see the impressions left by struggling fingers. If you stand right here, you can see it . . . made by someone lying in the tub, her head under the faucet, her right arm reaching up . . . resisting . . . being forced down . . . how three slender, stretched-out fingers left a final impression in the blood, at the final heartbeat . . .

"We've got another body," he says.

34

there are nine or ten cops trampling through Jackson Park just south of the Museum of Science and Industry—CPD, campus security, even a state trooper who must have made the wrong turn off the Skyway. They've blocked both entrances to the park, shut down the Drive at 57th. The morning rush hour will be starting soon. It's just past four A.M.

A burly uniform in a heavy black jacket leads Alison and me through a small crowd to where Crowley is holding court. I don't think he's in charge; there are other detectives around. He's starting to look like one of those guys who retires but can't leave it alone. Crowley nods hello to Alison, barely glances at me. He's coughing, lighting a cigarette. He doesn't look like he should be smoking. He doesn't look like he should be out in the cold.

"We were just reminiscing," Crowley says, "me and Becker and Russo here—"

"LaRusso," the uniform says.

"—remembering the trees, the museum's Christmas display. Harding, you'd remember. And you grew up around here, too, didn't you, Alison?"

She nods.

The museum is closed now, of course; no one's waiting to crawl through the submarine or the coal mine. Behind the museum there's a half-frozen basin, and beyond that a large lagoon, split into east and west pools by Wooded Island. The museum itself is brightly lit, but once you get into the park, it's very dark. Fresh snow erased the prints that Charles and I made last night. The snow has stopped.

"My old man brought us down here every year," Crowley says. "On account of how educational it was. The different cultures. He'd lead us to the spic tree and say, Hey, where's the taco ornaments? Where's the refried beans?" LaRusso laughs, a cartoonish giggle. "Here's the Irish tree, yeah, it looks a little tipsy. The same jokes every fucking year."

There's a slick black tarp near Crowley's feet. The tarp's pulled casually across a body like a sheet on an unmade bed. You can see the outline of the shoulders beneath the plastic, where small ridges are slowly turning white with snow.

The ambulance arrives to take the body away. It backs up onto the sidewalk, red lights blinking on and off. The snow there is brittle ice and it cracks like hundreds of small bones under the weight of the ambulance.

"Every fucking year," Crowley says.

Alison's wearing a long black coat, a heavy scarf, and a woolen cap. She's the only one dressed for the weather. A uniform swings his arms, trying to stay warm. None of the men are wearing hats. We're all tough guys.

She's standing apart from us, watching the EMS techs. There's a small metal wicket on the ground marking the gas line. She's pushing against it with the tip of her boot. When the techs reach the body, she steps forward, pulls off her cap, and brushes her hair back from her face.

"Her name is Michelle Regan," Crowley tells her, "according to the driver's license. Age twenty-five, late of Flossmoor." He pauses. "You know her."

It's a statement, not a question. Alison doesn't argue. She's standing over the body with her head bowed but her shoulders back, her feet planted. The medical techs are waiting, but Crowley motions them back.

"What happened?" she finally says to Crowley.

"Well, she was stabbed, obviously, multiple times. As to the where and when, we're not sure. Things are a little muddled. There's a spot over on the bridge with some bloodstains. He might have drug the body . . . They're looking for tracks." He doesn't sound convinced. "We don't have a murder weapon."

"But you're guessing what?" I say.

Crowley shrugs. "Something big. Something fucking sharp."

"Like those tools we found the other night at Pollard's?"

"Maybe, yeah. Some of the wounds have that same jagged edge. Some of them don't." His face is as white as the sandblasted limestone of the museum. "Time of death looks like maybe two, three hours."

Alison flinches at this, and I have to admit my stomach drops, too. If Michelle was due at the competition in the late afternoon and not killed until one or two in the morning, then someone kept her alive a long time before ending his fun.

"Where's her husband?" Alison says.

"Out of town," Crowley says. "This according to a Flossmoor cop, who says the husband flew to Newark last Wednesday." He coughs again, so hard he has to turn away and bend slightly. "That is the sort of town I should be working in, where the cops have time to keep track of people's travel plans."

I still can't tell if he's in charge. There are two other detectives now sitting in a radio car—they're probably already bored with the case, arguing over who does the paperwork. Who has to go door-to-door in Woodlawn, never a fun way to start the day.

"The reason you're here, Alison, is we found some forms in her purse for a beauty pageant that you co-signed, entry forms for Ms. South Suburbs—"

"It was a bodybuilding contest," Alison says, "not a beauty pageant. She trained at my gym." When she steps away, I take a look at the body. If this was a funeral, it wouldn't be an open coffin. The body that Michelle worked so hard to perfect has been disfigured almost beyond recognition.

She was strangled to death, her neck broken. Her head is turned sideways in an impossible position. Some of the cuts seem made just to cut through muscle. There are so many stab wounds across her lower abdomen, it looks like someone simply tried to pull her apart. And there are wild, deep gashes on her shoulders and ankles. They go through the bone, as if being scored for dismemberment.

The other detectives want to talk to Alison. A sergeant takes her over to them. Once she's gone Crowley motions to the techs. They load Michelle's body onto a stretcher and carry her to the gurney.

"They look a little bit alike, her and Alison," Crowley says to me.

Alison's sitting in the car, her head down. She's listening more than talking. Whatever they're telling her, she doesn't want to hear. I know the look on her face. Part fear, part denial. She's holding that cap in her hands. I can't see her feet, but I imagine they're trying to push right through the floorboards.

"We found Alison's car on South Kimbark," Crowley tells me. "We have a witness who saw Michelle park the car and go around toward the back of PowerFemmes. That's all the witness saw. Apparently Michelle never made it inside. This is maybe two or three P.M.; the witness isn't sure."

"That's what they're telling Alison right now?"

"They're wondering if the killer made a mistake. Michelle was driving Alison's car, they sort of look the same, she parks by Alison's gym . . ."

I nod.

"Of course he should have known he'd made a mistake once he got up close," he says. "But by then it might have been too late."

I'm thinking of what Gretchen Moss said to me. *He grabbed me by the neck from behind, so I never saw him.*

Alison is walking back toward us. Her hands are in her pockets. The ambulance crosses in front of her like a black cat.

"You know, when I walked a beat on Stony Island, you'd find

trees cut down, lots of little teeth marks," LaRusso says. "Not unusual at all. You see that resin on the bottom of the trees? That's to keep the beavers away."

"What are you saying?" Crowley says. "She stood there for an hour like an oak tree and let them do that to her?"

"Postmortem," he says.

"You're always thinking," Crowley says. "I can't understand why you haven't made detective yet."

they bring us to the morgue. We sit in the hallway on a Naugahyde bench. It's as good a place as any to sit. There's an air of finality about the place that suits our mood. Crowley comes through the swinging doors and asks us if we want a Coke. He's buying.

He feeds his money into the pop machine, hands us each a can that feels lukewarm.

"Why are we here?" Alison says dully. It's been a long night. Things are starting to catch up with her. "I told you it was her."

"That was a field ID," Crowley says. "They want a morgue ID."

"They can't wait for her husband to come down here?"

Crowley shrugs, eases down into a metal folding chair, opens his Coke. He looks as tired as Alison, except his has a permanence to it. The weariness has now become a part of his life.

"They asked me if you would," he says. "I can tell them no."

She shrugs herself free of her coat, leans back against the concrete-block wall, as if she wants to be uncomfortable. I used to stare at Alison sometimes and have no idea what was going through her mind. I know her better now.

Crowley takes a drink of Coke, makes a face. "Is this Classic or the old stuff?"

"I think Classic is the old stuff," I say.

"Then what's regular Coke."

"I guess that's New Coke."

He nods. He takes another sip, makes another face. He looks at Alison.

"Like I said, I can tell them no," he says gently.

She says No, let's get it over with. I start to get up, but she shakes her head.

"I'd rather do it myself," she says. Her long black hair is pushed forward, partly covering her face. When she stands, the vinyl cushion slowly fills in the marks her fingernails made as she gripped the edge of the bench.

Crowley takes her back. It's an odd sight—she's probably stronger than he is, but he escorts her like the father of the bride. He wants her to lean on him.

When he comes back out, we sit and stare at each other. He's always slightly out of breath now, and the cheap neon doesn't do much for his skin color.

I tell him I was in the park Wednesday night with Charles Muller. I tell him about the hatchet. He asks what car Charles was driving, and I remember that it was Dahlgren who picked it up the next morning.

"Professor Dahlgren?" he says. I nod. "He's running interference a lot lately, keeping me away from Beth Reinhardt and Muller."

I tell him what happened to me today—part narrative, part confession. The day began with Donnie Wilson at Hawthorne Race Course. It seems like a long time ago now. I ask Crowley to run the red Mustang's plate. He doesn't say yes, he doesn't say no. He's not happy that I wandered through Tracy's cousin's house. "Tell me you wore gloves," he says.

"I wore gloves." I tell him I found someone who puts Travis in the building at the time of Ricky's murder. He's not happy that I can't give him the witness's name. I tell him about the tracker Alison left on Travis's black Cadillac. The frequency for the tracker is in my 4Runner, so Crowley can take it with him.

I keep watching the door to the morgue, waiting for Alison to return. Crowley wants to hear about what I found at the house at the Dunes, and that reminds me of the note in the nightstand.

> *...you can't use real names and places, especially 32 Milwaukee—I told you that night when I let you inside. That was private, you've got no right. . . .*

"If I found another address for Pollard, could you get a search warrant?"

"Another one? Probably not. The arrest was for gun possession and they've got the gun. They might charge him for some pills they found on him, but that's all. The shit you found in Evergreen Park we still don't know is his."

"The blades, the tools, had blood on them—"

"Yeah, but we still don't know *whose* blood—the state police lab has a two-week backlog." He coughs, covering his mouth with his coat sleeve. "We got some guy to show us how those blades work. They're used to cut fabric, and in the machine they cut straight down, very clean, but if a man was using them, as heavy as they are, they would tear and stretch. Pull the fabric apart. So I do think they might be the murder weapon. For Tracy, I mean, not Michelle. Michelle was just hacked apart, chopped down like one of those trees."

"And Pollard isn't talking. . . ."

"He's still pretty wired. Not so wired that he couldn't get a lawyer, though. But he hasn't made bail. He's not going anywhere."

Alison comes out, gives me a smile. It fades quickly.

"Take me home?" she says.

"Of course."

Crowley gets to his feet then doesn't move. Alison takes my arm as we walk down the hallway, trying to leave the dead air behind.

"That's not the way I wanted to remember her," she says.

35

at seven A.M. Alison and I are sitting in an Oak Lawn church. I've never been here before, don't recognize the name on the door or the saint on the altar. Alison isn't even Catholic. We're just sitting quietly in the last row, like tourists.

I'm thinking about all that's transpired the last few days. I feel like I'm in someone else's game with an agenda that's baffling and mysterious, but then that's often the way I feel at mass. I wonder how many answers were burned up in that fireplace, if Tracy's manuscript would have read like Scripture, showing us the way. The parishioners around us don't seem as lost—they're locals, probably here every day for six-thirty mass on the way to work. I hear yawns, smokers' coughs, morning voices. I hear two or three different languages in the responses.

Pollard sits in a cell, Travis is God knows where with an APB trailing him and the Cadillac. Charles spent the night all warm and cozy in bed with Beth. By now there's probably a crime scene unit on its way to the house at the Dunes. With any luck there'll be blood evidence, hair, fiber, something to show us who was there. I'm starting to wonder if Tracy was killed not for what she found out about someone but simply for who she was. An addict who owed a lot of money.

I want to talk to Dahlgren this morning and to Crystal Royce, but Alison wanted to stop here first. We're still wearing our coats. I know what's haunting her right now, what sends her to the front of the church in small, sad steps to take communion. . . .

They look a little bit alike, her and Alison . . .

"It's not your fault," I tell her as we're driving home. All around us there are people on their way to work—a normal day. The sky overhead is a bruised shade of gray.

"I know that," she says. "Don't you think I know that?"

We park on Harper Avenue. The wind is blowing her hair across her face. She barely notices. I push it gently back behind her ears, but she shakes her head and pushes my hand away. A red poster stapled to a telephone pole dances in the wind.

BREAKFAST WITH SANTA
ENJOY A SPECIAL HOLIDAY MEAL
WITH SANTA CLAUS
AT HARPER COURT

"We had the son of a bitch last night," she says. "He walked right by us. We should have taken him behind that goddamn convenience store and broken his fucking legs. And then Michelle would be alive—"

"You can't think that way, Alison. We didn't know." I don't add what she's probably thinking, too: neither one of us seemed up to stopping him alone.

"She was taken right outside my gym, Harding," Alison says. "*My gym.* It's supposed to be safe there. . . ."

She hands me her keys, follows me upstairs, pulls off her clothes in the hallway, and goes straight to bed. I check the doors and windows. Alison's apartment has a good security system. She doesn't usually turn it on, but I set it now, test it, reset it. I check the back door. I lock everything up tight.

There's a foot of snow on the ground. I take the 4Runner to the gas station and fill the tires, check the spare, and then run it through the car wash to get the salt off. I help a neighbor of Alison's shovel out her car, an old Buick buried like a snow dome, and then I do the sidewalks in front of the building. I sprinkle salt like Johnny Apple-seed. I walk over to the gym and do the same thing there. The exercise doesn't calm me exactly, but the cold air helps to clear my head.

At nine A.M. I meet Boone in a parking lot off Damen Avenue. I have the Friday papers and some take-out coffee. Boone's eating a chocolate muffin. He's wearing borrowed clothing from his store—a hockey jersey, cross-training Nikes, ski pants. Luckily his parka covers most of it. "I don't like it," he says, looking at a building across the street. "Midmorning, broad daylight? A busy street?"

He'd like it even less if he knew what I was basing this on, a single mention in an old letter. I've taken a short walk around the neighborhood, looking for ways inside. It won't be easy. Pollard has the first floor of a narrow, odd-shaped building. There are no windows on the side at all, a heavy utility door in back; the first floor was slightly below street level. All the tenants use a common door. I think the building was a shoe store originally, then a photographer's studio. Now it must belong to Pollard.

"You're losing your nerve," I say.

"I just don't see the fucking point, Harding. He's a murder suspect, isn't he? Call the police."

"They can't get a warrant. They've got nothing on him. They've got more on *me* right now than they do on Pollard." We're not far from the CyberBeanery, which might explain why he's there so often. "Besides, I've seen his house in South Holland, and I broke into his factory. I didn't see anything fancy."

"Then those places weren't important to him," Boone says. He's right, of course; I had the same thought. If this is his sacred spot, then it might be wired in a novel way. Boone is better at this sort of thing than I am.

Boone winds down his window; he has a fear of dying from carbon monoxide poisoning. It's the silent killer. "Somebody who knew Pollard in college said he started getting paranoid his senior year," Boone says. "He moved out of the dorm because he thought the university had the rooms bugged. And he set up his own burglar alarms in his apartment. The last place he lived in, there were little metal counters attached to every single door. You have to picture this."

"What kind of alarm was that?"

"It wasn't an alarm. It was so he'd know for sure that everybody who *came in* went *back out.* Nobody's hiding in the closets. This is one paranoid son of a bitch, Harding."

When I enter Alison's apartment, I hear the shower running. I turn off the alarm and then call through the door to let Alison know I'm home, but I get no response. I get a glass from the kitchen and pour myself a drink.

The bathroom is full of steam. Alison's glasses are on the sink. I step into the shower. She is standing under the water, her hands on the tile in front of her. I think she's crying, but I can't really tell. I put my arms around her and she leans back against me. When I enter her, she whimpers slightly. Neither one of us talks. She grinds against me, slightly mechanical. The only sound is the running water.

And then we're on the bathroom rug, both soaking wet, her long hair unbelievably black and shiny, and she moves on top of me, long, slow revolutions, her eyes closed. I'm not even sure she knows I'm there until she moves faster and her legs contract and she's pushing against me, harder, harder; she lowers her head and her eyes open, inches from mine, and she stays like that for a minute or so until a slow smile softens her pounding heartbeat.

36

enry Dahlgren is hypnotizing research subjects in Mitchell Hospital. A sign-up sheet outside the psychology department directed me here. EARN MONEY WHILE REVEALING YOUR DEEPEST DARKEST SECRETS!! The guinea pigs are foreign students who couldn't afford to go home for Christmas. Dahlgren pays them six dollars an hour to fall asleep.

His assistant points me to an old chair and a stack of even older magazines. *Travel Inns* describes a Wisconsin B&B that sounds good. It might be a nice stop before the ski resort. I tear out the page. When Dahlgren has a break, we take the elevator to the cafeteria. He still has his lab coat on. Maybe it makes him feel like a doctor. The Clinique girls at Field's wear them, too, of course. So did the butcher in my old neighborhood, an awful Ukrainian who handed out meatballs at Halloween.

"My wife called me late last night," he says, taking a chair. He seems tired, not quite the bundle of energy I'm used to. His white shirt isn't quite as crisp as it might be. "I suppose I have you to thank for that."

I nod, watching as he rearranges the items on his tray, just as he did the other day at Hutch Commons. A green Granny Smith apple wobbles on his tray. "I told her you were worried about her."

He asks me about Alison and what happened in Jackson Park. I tell him about Michelle, her friendship with Alison. I don't tell him Alison might have been the target. I don't tell him about finding Tracy's cousin's house at the Dunes.

"Moira and I decided we should try to remain friends," he says. "That was always my intention, of course." He scoots his chair in a bit closer to the table. "Tell me something, Harding, if you don't mind. Was she alone when you saw her?"

I tell him yes. There's no point bringing in Tyler or Lance into this.

"And how did she seem? Happy?" he says, picking up the apple and checking it for spots or worms or something, then polishing it on his lab coat. "Did she seem happy to you?"

"She seemed happy." I pause. "Are you all right, Professor?"

"Me? Yes, of course. Why, do I look that bad?"

"You look tired. And distracted."

"I haven't been sleeping well," he says. "End-of-quarter work-load. Papers to grade." He puts the apple aside. "I should have looked at this better," he murmurs. "There's a bruise . . . here. See?"

I nod. I don't see the bruise.

"What did you two talk about last night, Harding? Anything you can share?"

"We talked about Tracy Lawrence."

"Ahh."

"Moira told me you rented an apartment for her after she moved out, an apartment that a lot of different people have used."

"The lease runs out soon."

"Why did you rent it in the first place?"

"It does seem a bit odd, I know," he says. "But the truth is, Moira and I have lived apart for years now, even when sharing the same house . . . the same bed. I've known for years that she was hav-ing affairs. With both sexes. As long as she was discreet and kept up appearances, I tolerated it." He sees something on my face. "You don't approve?"

"I didn't say that."

"Last year I became aware of a relationship that I deemed unhealthy. I told her so. Despite my feelings, she persisted. It became a point of contention between us. And ultimately led her to moving out, first to the apartment in Hyde Park and then . . . well, different places. And, finally, to our divorce."

"And the other party in this relationship?"

"There were two. Crystal Royce and Tracy Lawrence."

"Moira said as much. Why in hell didn't you tell me this before?"

"I didn't deem it . . . relevant."

"And you didn't approve of this relationship."

"I didn't deem it healthy," he says.

"Because of drugs?" He doesn't answer. "What was Crystal's role in all this?"

"As I understand it, she was the facilitator. For Moira I think it was just a fling. Moira has many such flings."

"You haven't explained why you rented the apartment for her."

He sighs. I watch him as he takes the apple back to the cafeteria line and exchanges it for another. He looks through all the apples before finding the perfect one.

"I told my wife it was a good business deal, a write-off. It was a motivation she could understand. The truth is, I did it to keep her close to me. I was worried about her."

"Come on, Professor."

"I was still in love with her. Then and now. Despite everything." Again he rubs the apple on a fold of his lab coat. "Oh, I know it won't work . . . there won't be a happy ending. We both have lawyers, the papers are being filed. But I wanted to put off her disappearance from my life as long as possible. She would have moved to New Mexico with Tracy. As it is, she still visited out there but stayed here most of the time."

"It must have bothered you, Professor, more than you're saying. Your wife with these other women."

He shrugs. His voice becomes softer. "She has certain proclivities that I don't pretend to understand. I try not to judge."

"That's the doctor talking," I say. "Not the husband. And she wasn't just sleeping with other women, was she?"

"What do you mean?"

"I heard something about Moira and Charles Muller."

"Who told you that? Charles?"

I shrug. "He seems to think you might be just as happy seeing him go as stay."

"I think that's the alcohol talking," he says, shaking his head. "My God, I've been trying to help him. Both of them. They're leaving on this ski trip later—I volunteered to help baby-sit the kids, I'm taking Beth's daughter Cindy to the orthodontist tomorrow."

"I also heard that Crystal wasn't the first of your extracurricular activities, that there was a house in Carbondale you were fond of frequenting . . ."

"I have to get back to my lab." He stands up stiffly and shakes my hand, starts to walk away. Then he stops. "Look, Harding, that was five years ago. It was a difficult time. We were living in a small town. My work wasn't going well. And I was discovering that my wife wasn't the woman I thought she was. If I strayed myself . . . it was only out of despair. Over the affair Charles was having with my wife . . ."

He hesitates, as if stuck in neutral, waiting for a better explanation to present itself. "Thank you for speaking with my wife," he says finally. "You said you thought she looked okay? She looked happy?"

"She looked good, Henry."

from Mitchell Hospital I drive to Lake Village East, stopping at the same grocery store as last Sunday night. I buy a couple of lottery tickets. I play Alison's birthday on both. Crystal buzzes me up. The same security guard is there from the other night. He nods, I nod. We're developing quite a rapport.

She's waiting for me when I get off the elevator, taking my hand like we're at a high school dance. She's wearing a yellow pantsuit designed to be simple and low-key. The rayon hugs her rear. The top two buttons on her blouse are undone. I can see how she'd make friends at academic functions.

"I think my phones are tapped," she whispers. She's wearing that same perfume. I still like it. "There are clicking noises when I'm on hold and just before the dialing starts. That's not supposed to happen, right?"

I shake my head. Not for what Donnie paid for those taps, it sure isn't. I hope he kept the warranty.

There are newspapers scattered about, copies of *Foreign Affairs, The New York Review of Books.* "Research," Crystal says with a wink. "A girl has to talk." She waits in the kitchen while I investigate the phones, waving my flashlight around in the air like a divining rod. I take one of the phones apart. The tap does seem a little loose. I tighten it up with a screwdriver.

"The police were here this morning," she says. "Very early this morning. A Detective Crowley, wanting to know about Travis."

"You haven't heard from him?" She shakes her head. I give the tap a final twist and replace the shell. I ask her if she's heard about the woman they found in Jackson Park.

She says yes. "Isn't it ghastly?"

"Remember the last time we spoke? And you suggested I find one of Logan Pollard's buildings? Your brother was there, too."

"This detective mentioned that." She comes closer, sitting on a corner of the sofa. "I didn't set you up, Harding. Really I didn't. As I told the detective, I don't like my brother. I've spent my life avoiding him."

"And yet you bailed him out."

"Not because I *wanted* to. All he ever wants is money. He frightens me, Harding. Is that so hard to comprehend?"

I shake my head. I'm not sure she's telling me the truth. It's possible to be afraid of Travis and still feed him information. "If you do hear from him, Crystal, would you call me? Even if you don't feel like calling the police?"

She nods, crossing her legs. Last night I walked through the house at the Dunes, feeling Tracy's presence. I don't feel the same thing here. I do find myself looking at innocent things, though—chairs, the sofa, the kitchen counter—and wondering what they witnessed, whose leg went here, whose hands grabbed there. I ask Crystal if Tracy had kept anything here last summer.

"Just the essentials," she says. "You know, underwear, stockings. That piece of driftwood on the mantel is hers. Nothing else, I'm afraid."

"Who has keys to this place?"

"Right now just me," she says. "I've changed the locks since then." That would explain why Henry Dahlgren couldn't just come up here and retrieve his necklace.

I check the other phones, make a few more adjustments with my screwdriver. I tell her the noises she heard were probably just static overloads. She walks me to the front door, gives me a brief kiss.

"Thanks ever so much," she says. "I was afraid to even *talk* in here."

"A girl has to talk," I say. "Crystal, it would have helped me if you'd been honest from the beginning about who paid the rent here."

She smiles. "That was just a harmless little fib, Harding. To shield Henry, he's such a dear. In my business, you have to tell a few." She thanks me again for making sure her phones aren't tapped. I nod. In my business you have to tell a few fibs, too.

37

beth and Charles are leaving for their skiing trip, loading up Beth's Camry while various kids and dogs play in the snow. Charles is wearing brand-new clothes from Urban Outfitters and Erehwon. His coat has lots of pockets and zippers. They've loaded their skis onto the overhead rack and filled the trunk with big furry boots and extra blankets, as though they're going to stay in a tent.

"Charles believes in being prepared," Beth says.

"We don't know what the accommodations are like," Charles protests. His ski cap still has a sales sticker attached. He's trimmed his beard. He cleans up okay, but the facial lines and world-weary eyes that come from drinking are harder to wash off.

"You guys are coming later, right?" Beth says, and I nod. Alison and I need a night to ourselves. Right now she's playing with one of the dogs, a white husky that looks as if it could be of use in the great white north of Wisconsin. She's wearing a rust-colored pullover and black jeans.

"Have you ever skied?" Charles says to me.

I shake my head.

"Really? Never?"

"My family rarely got to Aspen, Charles," I say. "And Wisconsin was strictly for summer. It never made much sense to my old man to drive even farther north in winter." He puts his arm around Beth. "The one time we did was for the turkey bowling in the Dells. Not for the skiing."

"It's actually a lot of fun, Harding," says Beth, who's wearing lots of fleece; she looks very cozy. "Even if you'd never tried. We'll put you on the beginners' slope."

"With the lame and infirm," Alison says, tossing a snowball at me. "Just don't get in their way."

"Turkey bowling?" Charles says. "What's turkey bowling?"

"Pretty much what it sounds like," I say. "With frozen turkeys. It's very big in Wisconsin."

"My kids would like that," Beth says. "They'd like it better with live turkeys."

There's a baby-sitter here, a student from Kenwood High, and Beth goes inside with Alison to give her more instructions, dogs and kids trailing behind.

"How's she doing?" Charles says, watching them go.

"Alison? She's . . . I don't know. Part of her is in a state of shock, I think. Part is in denial." For just a second I think he's been drinking—his eyes lose focus before he turns away from me and lights a cigarette.

"Beth said this woman . . . Michelle? Michelle was a close friend."

"Very close." I'm watching the way he avoids my eyes. Drinkers have a "tell" just like poker players. I haven't figured out Charles's yet. "It's a little early in the day, isn't it, Charles?"

He doesn't answer, tosses the cigarette in the snow. "I'm just nervous," he says. "I needed one. Just one."

"Right."

"The police called my lawyer this morning."

"You mean because of the other night . . . in Jackson Park. With the hatchet." He nods "Well, that would seem to be worth a phone call, Charles, yeah."

"I was drunk, Harding. I wasn't killing anyone. It was that damn Christmas tree that Dahlgren bought for the kids. Beth couldn't stop talking about it. Oh, what a great tree, what a great time the kids had . . ."

I understand the drink he had a bit better now. It's not the police making him nervous; it's Beth. And the prospect of three days alone with her.

"Pollard's in jail, and they're looking for Travis," I say. "When they get the two of them together, one of them will flip."

"You think it was Pollard who called me that night?" I nod. "Why would he want to hurt Alison?"

"I don't know that yet, Charles," I say. When Beth comes back outside, she's making her final goodbyes, kissing one of her kids, giving them lists. She's more organized than I'd realized. It makes me wonder how much of that flighty, spacey attitude is an act. Maybe Charles finds it sexy.

"Alison's trying to get me to try snowboarding," Beth tells me. "Did you know she almost tried out for the X Games once?"

"I'm too tall," Alison says. "You need a lower center of gravity."

"When did you learn to ski?" I say to Alison.

"In college, actually. That was the first time. With Moira and—"

"Tracy," Charles says. "We all decided to stay on campus over the Thanksgiving break. And then somebody got the idea to rent a car and drive to this resort in Minnesota."

"Feeling left out, Harding?" Beth says, smiling at me.

"A little. Charles, did I ever tell you about the week I spent in a cheap Mexican motel with Beth?"

"We should have done it," Beth says. "We'd have something on these guys the way they do on us."

"It's never too late, Beth. Get Charlie out of your room. Expect a knock on the door around midnight."

"What room?" Charles says. "What door? Didn't Alison tell you? We're roughing it, Harding."

"Going *au naturel*, baby," Alison says.

We walk back to Alison's apartment, picking up some groceries for dinner along the way. It's turning into a very strange day. It feels like a

Sunday, or the day of a funeral. The gym is closed in honor of Michelle. Her funeral is next week. I have some old records of mine—case files, tax forms—from my first years out of prison. The Grand Terrace years, the Wokowski card years. Alison starts chopping onions in the kitchen. I'm not the best recordkeeper. The content is so bland, the angels would weep. I'm weeping, too, though it might be the onions.

"Do you remember any of the cases I was working on when we were first dating?" I ask Alison as she's cooking. "Where I might have handed out that Wokowski card?"

"Hand me that bottle of Moselle from the refrigerator," she says. "And that's cooking wine, Harding. If you want a glass, open a new bottle." Whatever she's cooking it smells very good. The garlic has overtaken the onions. "I don't think you talked very much about your work then, Harding. You may have been going for an 'air of mystery' sort of thing. For a while I thought you might be a spy. And have a real job."

"I was doing a lot of surveillance work then. You taught me how to work that German camera I found in a pawn shop, remember?"

"The one with all those zooms. I remember. That camera was actually much easier to use than you realized, Harding. You made it too complicated," she says, stirring some red peppers in another skillet. "Maybe you're making this card thing too complicated as well."

"What do you mean?"

She shrugs. "What if they only had a minute or two alone in your apartment? While you were in the bathroom, say. Or on the phone."

"You're saying they just took the first cards they found?" She nods. I tell her I don't like it. It makes too much sense.

Boone calls me as we're sitting down to dinner.

"First of all," Boone says, "I had to size the place up, wait for it to get dark. Milwaukee Avenue's all commercial along there, lots of foot traffic, I had to blend into the neighborhood. You said he mentioned having visitors; I had to make sure they weren't there. And I had to cut the power to get in. Because of alarms."

"Okay."

"That meant cutting the phone lines, too. Since I didn't know how the alarms were rigged."

"I have no problem with any of this. What'd you find?"

"Well, it turned out the place wasn't wired. No alarms."

"That's strange. What else?"

"I think you'd better see for yourself."

"Boone—"

"No, you have to see it," he says. "Really. Both of you." He pauses. "Especially Alison."

38

ogan Pollard's apartment is one long room. A Realtor might call it a loft, but it's really more like a third-floor basement that's never been broken up into rooms. The floor is linoleum, the walls are roughed-in cement painted in alternating shades of blue. Boone has the flashlight. We're standing just inside the front door.

"Well, this was worth missing dinner for," Alison says. "And it's just like old times. Spending a quiet evening with my two favorite criminals."

"Nobody's broken any laws yet," Boone says.

"Boone, you broke into the man's apartment," she says.

"Well, yeah," Boone says. "There's that."

The only light is from an aquarium that separates the living area from the kitchen. Boone directs me to a switch above the stove. When I turn it on, I jump and reach for a gun I don't have. Boone laughs. The soft blue light from the aquarium now highlights a figure sitting at the kitchen table.

Alison comes forward to look.

The figure is five-ten, athletic-looking, with long black hair, wearing a track suit complete with black Reeboks. Her eyes are green. She's eating breakfast—she looks like she's been eating breakfast for a long time. Her arm is poised with a spoon halfway to her lips, her head slightly bent to receive it. The cereal bowl is filled with plastic fruit. It's like a George Segal sculpture. What's most unsettling about her is that she doesn't look bizarre or creepy. She's made up to look as beautiful as Alison looks. And she almost looks like she belongs here and might open her mouth to speak.

"I always wanted one of those," Boone says, moving around the kitchen. "My mother said no. I might mess up her precious Oriental rug. Which turned out to be not silk but some sort of rayon, made in a Bangkok sweatshop."

"You wanted a love doll?" I say.

"An aquarium. The love doll I probably could have had. As long as I kept it away from the Oriental rug."

"This is too weird," Alison says. She gingerly touches the doll's arm. It bends slightly. "But her body doesn't really look like mine, just her face."

"What's your shoe size?" Boone says.

"None of your damn business," she says, but she checks the size of the track suit. "Small feet, size-four dress," she says. "A male fantasy."

"Those aren't your sizes," I say.

"No kidding. I have big-ass feet."

"This looks like a preliminary model, actually," Boone says. "It's cheaper to just do the face, use one of the standard bodies. The really good ones are modeled on a real person. From a body cast."

"It's just a fucking rubber doll, Boone," says Alison, checking the bra size. "Thirty-four D. Another male fantasy. Does Pollard make these things in his factory?"

"I don't know."

"There are pictures in the desk drawer you might want to look at," Boone says. "And I booted up his PC, left a movie running for you. I didn't go any further. Once I saw RoboGirl, I thought I should call."

"Thanks, Boone."

"The pictures are sort of strange—"

"Stranger than this?"

"Different," he says. "Have fun. Don't forget to lock up."

• • •

alison finds the pictures Boone mentioned. They're in a portfolio like the one that was stolen from me. This is the unabridged version, though, with pictures I haven't seen. They're all new to Alison, and she turns the pictures slowly, one by one.

They're all of Tracy Lawrence, taken in the house at the Dunes. Some of them are nudes, with Tracy either asleep or drugged. Her eyes are closed. Her face looks like a death mask. She's been posed on an old couch, on the floor, in a dirty gray bathtub. Other shots have her awake and dressed in very sexy outfits, the kind Alison wore in her leather days. Her hair's been wetted down, so it looks darker and worn straight, like Alison's. Her expression—intense, staring at the camera—is a fair impression of Alison at certain intimate moments.

In still others she's posed in S&M scenes, handcuffed on a mattress. She's trying to look sexy, but she only looks scared. Of course, some guys find that sexy. . . .

"What do you make of this?" Alison says, her mood changing.

"I'm not sure. I thought Pollard was Tracy's boyfriend, maybe even stalking her. Now . . ." I shrug.

"Now it looks like he wants to be my boyfriend," she says. "Was Pollard even involved with Tracy? Or was he just using her for these pictures?"

"She might have done it for the money. For drugs."

It's hard not to think about the way Tracy once looked in the photo Alison had—how lush her body was, the way her suntanned breasts spilled out of that bikini. In these photos, her breasts are still full, but the rest of her body's become anorexic, thin-shouldered, pasty white. The change becomes even more noticeable when Alison finds more photos from Grand Terrace. These are the pictures Boone was talking about, not the others. These were taken with a telephoto lens.

"Oh, God, that's me," she murmurs. Blurred, distant images: Alison standing at her window, sitting at her desk, lying on her bed. "And that's Tracy." Her poses are similar to Alison's. In fact, a lot of the poses are exactly the same. The quality's not good, but that's part of the fetish. It makes them real.

"You should have closed your blinds," I say.

She doesn't like that. "That's all you can say? This isn't about me, Harding, okay?"

But those aren't the most powerful images. There's a whole series of pictures from the weekend they spent at the Dunes—on the beach, on the boat. In bed. There are one or two shots of Moira, but they seem incidental. The pictures of Tracy and Alison together seem endless. They're more explicit than the ones Alison showed me. The bikinis are long gone. In one of them Alison is wearing a short peach summer dress, kissing Tracy, her hand between her legs.

"What's the matter?" she says to me. I shake my head. For the first time the relationships formed at Grand Terrace become clear to me. Charles wasn't involved. Moira was unimportant. I'd asked Alison about sex and she'd told me about sex; she told me she'd slept with Tracy. She never told me she was in love with her.

There are dozens of chat-room transcripts here, too. Some of them describe actions and rooms from the pictures, as though both parties were familiar with them or even had them as they typed. I sit on Pollard's couch and read one as Alison continues to find more and more pictures.

> sitting on your bed
> yes
> in hyde park and it's raining and cozy
> yes
> you be alison
> all right
> i'm sitting beside you and i lean over and whisper how hot you look tonight
> yes i'm feeling hot
> you're always hot that turns me on and when i kiss your cheek i rest my hand
>   on your left thigh
> yes

and then you're staring straight ahead, trying to ignore me and i can see you
    in profile and see your eyes
yes
and my hand slides slowly up your thigh
no one can see us
no no one we're in your room who could possibly see us
i'm wearing a short black skirt no stockings and a black sweater and heels
yes you look so hot and my hand moves farther up
yes
you're not wearing panties
no i never do
oh alison
you like calling me that don't you. . . .

"Charles said someone was doing all this," I say. "Sending things to Tracy, pretending to be different people."

"Pretending to be me, you mean." She reads part of another one aloud, mockingly at first, though it turns darkly erotic despite her tone of voice. It makes me wonder how these would sound performed at a poetry slam. I suspect they'd be crowd pleasers. The same holds true for the stories I find in Pollard's bathroom, "living statuary fantasies." Sometimes the women lose the use of their arms or legs or slowly become numb and frozen. The woman is aware that she's losing control but can't resist. Sometimes the statues "wake up" in embarrassing situations. Sometimes they're dolls that come to life. It's not exactly *Coppélia*.

"Did Pollard strike you as a killer?" Alison says.

"There are all kinds of killers. But no, not really. He's more of a stalker. I can see him doing the photography and computer stuff, though. And hiring someone else to do the dirty work." As usual she's firmly in the present. I'm not thinking about Pollard.

She finds some bookmarks on the computer that seem to go with the stories—"newsgroups like alt.sleep, alt.robot . . . creepy stuff," she says. I start digging through Pollard's files and desk drawers and rummaging through his clothing, which is hanging on laundry racks, above a pile of shoes, and then looking through the metal kitchen cabinets. The doll is always in the corner of my eye. Once or twice I find myself turning to look at it. And when I find a tux mixed in with the clothes—with a scrap of paper in one pocket—I find myself reading the lines out loud, as much to the doll as to myself.

> There is a poetry
> of death
> *no slip and no panties, just bare brown legs*
> sleep, sleep,
> stay still
> *peach dress, white summer sandals*
> two golden legs at rest

"You found Charles's tuxedo?" Alison says, excited. She comes over and stands beside me.

"I guess it's his," I say. "It might be Pollard's. There's poetry in the pocket. He's a pocket poet." But it's the other item of clothing that I've found that interests her more.

"No way," she says, shaking her head, unfolding the same peach dress. The white sandals are here, too, scuffed and worn; one of the straps is broken. "I threw them away ten years ago. . . ."

She holds the dress up against her body. "He must have liked the way you looked in them," I say.

I keep looking through drawers. I'm looking for that book Tracy was writing. Alison's watching a movie on the computer, a filmed sex show from somebody's basement. There's a thin woman with long black hair, staring straight ahead. Her expression never changes. She might be thinking about her laundry. The crowd sits in folding chairs, very close to the stage. It's like Blue Man Group or Gallagher; they really needed some plastic covering. The man's sweating and looking straight ahead, too; at the woman's back, at her ass, at the wall. Maybe he has laundry, too.

It goes on for a long time, to very little point. The woman clearly looks enough like Alison to keep the movie in heavy rotation on Pollard's PC. I step outside for a minute to call Terry Crowley. He coughs several times before even saying hello, then listens while I describe what we've found here.

"Is that enough to hold him?" I say.

"It would be, if you were a cop with a warrant," he says. "Don't worry, he's not going anywhere real soon. He's having trouble making bail." He tells me he ran the red Mustang from the other night in Wicker Park. "It's registered to a Sunderman, Alan, of Harvey, Illinois. Mean anything to you?"

"Nothing."

"Well, it wouldn't. He's a small-time hood, sitting on half a dozen outstanding warrants. And he's already done time for auto theft. But what I find real interesting is he was moving through the system the same time as your boy Travis."

"They knew each other?"

"It looks like they might have crossed paths. One did time at Pontiac, the other one at Danville. But when they left the system they both spent some time in a transition center downstate. Outside Champagne-Urbana."

"Transition centers are just fancy names for minimal-security places, aren't they?"

"Last stop before parole. They give them jobs, let them take classes. Sunderman has a sister in St. Louis that Travis used to bang, so the cops down there are checking it out. Plus we found the Cadillac in Midway long-term parking, thanks to that tracker you put on it."

"Alison did that, actually."

"No shit. Well, tell her thanks. We'll find him, Harding. If I hear anything else I'll let you know."

I tell Crowley thanks. I tell him where we'll be the next few nights, in Wisconsin. I remember that fight after the poetry slam, how the last guy didn't want to leave even when they had the purse, how he just stared at Alison. I watch the traffic on Milwaukee for a minute or two, letting the cold seep into my skin, and then I go back inside.

"Look at these," Alison says, showing me some more recent photos: Alison leaving her apartment, coming out of PowerFemmes, walking to her car, a gym bag over her shoulder. Alison kissing me on campus outside Cobb Hall. Alison with me in the backseat of my car the night I left for Denver.

"I found a lease for this place, too," she says. "Travis signed it. He must have rented it for Pollard."

"Come on, let's get out of here," I tell Alison. I realize I'm looking past her as I talk to her, toward that damn doll. I imagine Pollard coming home to this each night—unlocking the door, setting his briefcase down, and then seeing her across the room, just as he left her, sitting there perfectly posed in her cool blue light.

Alison is staring at the porn movie again. Some of the photos are still laid out on the desk. She turns the computer off, puts the photos back. And then she shivers, and for the first time since we got here, she touches me, pulling my arm around her.

"Let's just nuke the whole place from the air," she says.

b y the time we're on the road to Wisconsin, the sun's disappeared and the falling snow is covering all the spots I shoveled. We have to thread our way north on the Kennedy and Edens
through postgame traffic, running from the Bulls. Expressways are
always carved from middle-class neighborhoods—the mansions
that fill the North Shore are far to the east, near the lake—so we
pass neat little subdivisions, office parks, county salt mounds. The
prettiest sight is an outlet mall in Racine lit with blue lights.

We swing west around Lake Geneva and lose the traffic, but the
roads are getting bad. We stop three or four times, driving far enough
off the highway that anyone following us would have to show themselves. Each time we stop, we check in with Beth and Charles. It's a
relief to get to the bed-and-breakfast near the Mississippi.

t he room turns out to be their most expensive suite—a third-floor
penthouse reserved mostly for honeymoons, anniversaries, adulter-
ous flings—decorated in earth tones. What that basically means is
that we have the attic of an old house all to ourselves. My best friend
in third grade, Bill Partlow, had the same deal when his parents
decided he shouldn't be rooming with his sisters anymore. His earth
tones came from the brown and yellow mud daubers who built nests
over his bed.

We have a hot tub, a stereo, a VCR. The tapes supplied are chick

films and love stories; the CDs are light classical and very moody—
Moods for Lovers, Romantic Moods, Passionate Moods. The water in
the hot tub is lukewarm.

I know all this because while Alison soaks in the tub I'm reading
the brochures and watching the rodeo on the Nashville Network. I
find it as relaxing as the hot tub. I used to think the bulls just bucked
and kicked in a random fashion, but the announcer says they move
in patterns, certain bulls move in certain ways. They're predictable.
It's hard to believe, watching an eight-hundred-pound animal snort
and twist as he kicks his rider into the air. The cowboy clowns run
into the ring to distract the bull; the rider dusts himself off, glaring
at the bull. I guess some of them throw in a little extra twist.

"I should call Beth," Alison says when she's getting dressed.

"Well, we have a phone. We have three phones, including one in
the bathroom. The brochure says so." She dials while sitting on the
edge of the bed, sliding on her shoes. She's wearing dark stockings, a
black leather blazer, and a longer skirt than normal, all concessions
to the cold, but her top is a concession to me: a skintight black
leather camisole.

There's no answer, but we just spoke with Beth an hour or so
ago; everything's fine, she said, the only problem is these damn
phone calls. "They must be skiing," Alison says.

We leave for the restaurant by the back stairs. The innkeeper is
shoveling snow. Alison takes my arm. I've never been on a honeymoon, but I imagine it's something like this, only warmer.

The restaurant calls itself a "supper club," but it's just a road-
house that overlooks the Mississippi. Some of the diners have binoc-
ulars. I'm so tired of looking into other people's windows, but these
are for watching bald eagles nest in nearby trees. I wonder if bald
eagles screw around like humans. It's our national bird.

The waiter's wearing a blue blazer that's never known the joys of
dry cleaning. Apparently we've arrived on an auspicious day: there's
a fish fry tonight. I think there's a fish fry every night.

I have a steak, rare. I drink two scotches before my salad arrives. Alison orders some kind of sea bass. Her face has a tired, pre-migraine look, but she says she's fine.

Our food arrives. I ask the waiter for another drink. He raises his eyebrows as though I've reached my limit.

"Whatcha thinking about?" I say.

"What else? Beth and Charles." I don't believe her, but I don't argue.

"Henry Dahlgren seems to like Beth," I say, and she nods. "Buying her a Christmas tree, baby-sitting the kids . . . I thought maybe she'd call off the wedding with Charles. She wants dull and stable, Dahlgren looks like the real thing."

"But she's in love with Charles," she says. "Do you think Charles will keep drinking?"

"Probably, yeah. As alcoholic's go, he looks like the real thing himself. There's nothing you can do about that."

"I keep thinking this is all my fault."

"Why? Because Pollard is nuts? And Travis will do anything for money?"

"Maybe it has something to do with me teaching Pollard's ex to kick—you said he seemed bitter about that."

"I don't think that had anything to do with it," I say.

"What made him go nuts like that after ten years?"

"Pollard? Some guys . . . you just flip a switch."

"I've been looking for that switch," she says.

"Oh, you have to hunt for mine," I say.

She doesn't like the vegetable medley with her fish. She scrapes it onto my plate. She steals my tender crisp asparagus. She pushes the hollandaise sauce off each piece with her fork.

"So what happens now?" she says.

"I guess I get the check."

"I mean when we get back to Chicago."

"Are we making this some sort of watershed event, a life

changer, that sort of thing? We watch Beth and Charles get married. We borrow some money to expand the gym."

She sips her wine, eyebrows slightly raised. I must have reached my limit on something else.

"Life goes on," I say.

"What about us?"

"Us? We live happily ever after."

"Do you want to work at the gym?"

"What would I do at your gym?"

"I don't know. You're one of the owners. You own half of it, Harding."

"In theory."

"I'm sick of theory," she says. "Do you want me to work with you? I don't have any major felonies on my record; I could get a PI license."

"You'd hate it."

"I like it sometimes, when I help you."

"You like it part-time. As a lark. You wouldn't like it as a career. I'm not sure it really is a career."

"I could do the parts you hate."

"I could do the parts you hate at the gym."

"See, that's the problem, I think," she says. "Between us we just about make up a normal person."

It's cold walking back to the bed-and-breakfast. We use the front door this time, sit for a few minutes in the parlor to warm up. It's jammed with dolls and pictures and Victorian furniture. The innkeeper has left a tray of peanut butter cookies.

I look through some of the brochures for local sight-seeing. Alison frowns at me.

"We're *not* going to the Trolley Museum," she says.

"What about the River Hall of Fame?"

She shakes her head.

"The House on a Rock?"

"No."

"I thought this was supposed to be a vacation," I say. I'm think-ing about our dinner conversation, the way we both dance around a subject as important as our future together. She's right, we do need more ethos, more ceremony.

The B&B is full tonight. Music drifts from the room below, one of those romantic CDs. The steps creak as we find our way to our dark room. Alison won't let me turn on the lights. Her hands are all over me. Her mouth is on my neck. I pull her in front of me.

"I am such a bad girl," she says, kissing me.

There's a thump behind us. Glass shatters and scatters like wind chimes.

The door bangs open. Alison is pulled away from me, out of my arms.

And then I am pulled backward and thrown across the room. My head hits the hot tub. I hear Alison screaming. There's a dead weight climbing over me, pulling at my hands, and then I can't tell where Alison is or which of us is screaming. Travis breaks two fin-gers on my left hand slowly, deliberately, as he whispers, *Happy Holidays, Happy Holidays . . . "*

After that he doesn't talk, doesn't make a sound other than grunts and heavy breathing that comes in spasms. The darkness is disorienting, and he keeps us apart; I can't see Alison, though I hear the fight she's putting up each time I come to. He works calmly, deliberately, dealing with both of us, going for my throat, being pulled off, going for Alison's, having one of us always in his grasp.

There is a point when I think it's over; I land several punches that finally connect and I feel his head snap back and I hear him groan and slump to the floor. His legs are over mine like heavy weights, and when I push them off and scoot backward on my elbows, I look for Alison in the darkness but see nothing, I whisper her name, but she doesn't answer. "I think I got him," I say, louder, and then his hands are on me again, slamming my head down, yanking me back on the rug until I'm near the banister, and Alison says "Harding?" as he kicks the wood and pulls me through it; I feel a shard of wood graze my jugular. If he could see better he'd end my life right there, but he is on the steps, pulling me through; my shoulders break through and I try to kick up but I can't, I am falling at his feet now and I can almost feel the tumble begin, down the long flight of stairs, when I hear him grunt and grunt again as Alison kicks him in the throat from above. That's when I manage to grab his arms and keep his hands down so he can't protect himself while Alison kicks him again in the same place even harder, and this time when he falls he doesn't get up. When I find his neck there's no pulse. His head is like a rag doll's.

The other guests come out one by one, the landlord calls the local police. We sit on the steps, trying to catch our breath. My hand is throbbing, Alison's right knee is swelling up. We're told that this is the first time something like this has ever happened here, *nothing* like this has ever happened here. Everyone's in pajamas and bathrobes. Alison tries to call Beth and Charles. There's no answer. She lets it ring a long time.

"Who knew we'd be here?" I say, going through Travis's pockets and finding a wallet with three of my Wokowski cards and a half-sheet of blue paper, the same kind Dahlgren gave me in his house, with the letterhead sliced off. Besides the names of the bed-and-breakfast and the ski lodge, there are times and abbreviations—*P 8 55 to Wood*—that could be schedules of when Alison leaves for work, what path she takes.

She leaves for PowerFemmes at 8, takes 55th to Woodlawn.

"Nobody," she says. "Nobody knew."

"I told Crowley," I say, wishing he was here. "You must have told somebody, Alison. He didn't follow us, we were watching like hawks—"

"Shit. The baby-sitter," she says, limping a bit now. "I told Beth's baby-sitter—"

"And she told Henry. It's Dahlgren. We've been looking the wrong way the whole time." I try to tell Alison we need to wait for the local cops, but she's already pushing through the crowd and running out the door to our car.

40

the 4Runner fishtails from one parking lot to another, prowling, searching for Beth's Camry or Dahlgren's Audi among the rows of Quonset huts and fake Swiss chalets that make up the Badger Run Resort, until Alison finally just abandons it and somehow beats me to the nearest door despite the damage Travis has done to her leg. She's in the hallway outside room eighteen, knocking on a run-down pine door while looking sweetly at a family checking in down the hall. She waves at the six-year-old. When they're inside their room, she kicks the door in.

"Fuck," she says at the impact, rubbing her knee. I wonder what Travis did to her. I check the bathroom first, the only place to hide. But they're not here. No bags, no clothes. No Beth, no Charles. The bed's made; the paper wrapping's on the bathroom glasses.

"You have a reservation?" says the clerk when we return to the lobby. His name's Nick. The dominant decorating theme is badgers— running, skiing, ice-skating. "Two nights minimum stay in season."

I tell him we're not checking in. "We're looking for two guests; the registration would be Muller or Reinhardt."

"Try the courtesy house phone, sir, right over there by the holiday elf." I take out my wallet, show him a fifty-dollar bill, and pull him away from the front desk to a large fake pine tree. A bellboy stands at attention beside the elf.

"Let's start over," I say. "Beth Reinhardt, Charles Muller. They were supposed to be in room eighteen. They checked in yesterday; they're not there now."

"They might be on the slopes," he says, frowning. "This is our Moonlight Madness Weekend. Late-night skiing, complimentary hot buttered rum."

"I'll check the bars," Alison says impatiently. She's limping more with each step. I'm starting to feel all the spots where Travis hit me; my left hand is throbbing.

"Did you say Muller?" the bellboy says. "They're the ones who moved to the Aspen Retreat, remember, Nick?"

"Oh, right, right," says Nick. "They moved to the Aspen Retreat?"

"Where the fuck is the Aspen Retreat?"

"Is this going to get me into trouble?" Nick says nervously.

"Not if you help me." It takes another fifty to convince him of this, plus one for the bellboy. I draw the line at giving money to the elf. "Which side of the lodge is it on?"

"It's not in the lodge. It's a cabin beyond the hill. It's for people who like their privacy, if you know what I mean."

"Enlighten me."

"There's only one cabin and only one way to get there—the ski lifts. The guests like it that way. Honeymooners love it. They have a full kitchen, completely stocked. Unless they request something, we leave them alone. That's what makes the Aspen Retreat special."

"There must be a road up there. How do you service the lifts? What if they break down?"

"There's an access road, but it's closed now. It's on the other side of the mountain and it's only open off-season." He's placing his fifties in a hidden section of his wallet. "Believe me, you don't want to go over there, you'll just get stuck and I've got no way to get you out."

"This is nuts," I say, frustrated. "You must have some way to get up there, you've got guests staying there."

"We use a Sno-Cat. We make one trip in the morning, one in the evening." He points to the big transporter, which probably sounds like an army tank and goes all of five miles an hour. Not the best way to sneak up on somebody. "Other than that, the guests use the lifts. We've had couples stay up there for a weekend and never open the door. It's what makes the experience so special."

"Do you have a map of the area?" I say.

He takes one from the desk. The elf is at the front desk now, waiting on people, not very happy with us.

"Where are we now?" I say, opening it on the bellboy's stand, finding the tiny dot that Nick points at. "This is a town over here? With an airport?" He nods. "There's an airport and you don't have a way to get there?"

"You can get there from *here,* sir, on the roads. You can't get there from the *cabin,* but that's by design."

"It's what makes it special."

"Exactly."

Alison comes back from her search, favoring one leg, shaking her head. "Beth's not answering her cell phone," she says. I know what she's thinking.

Not Beth, too, Harding . . .

"I think Dahlgren's here," Alison says. "There's an Audi parked sideways in the handicapped spot."

"That's Dahlgren." I ask for a map of the cabins; Nick gives me a very colorful brochure. I ask if there's a security guard on duty. He points to the elf. I tell Nick to call the county sheriff and the state police *now.*

"We better go," Alison says, and sticks her chewing gum on the bellboy's stand.

the lift attendant remembers Dahlgren—he was the jerk who wouldn't let him tear his ticket in half. I think he expects a tip, but I'm out of money.

The ride seems to take forever. We're the only ones without skis, but no one seems to find it odd. We sit next to each other in the gondola, our legs dangling. There are colored lights strung up and down the mountain. Somebody has fireworks. A few of the skiers have sparklers. The bravest or drunkest are leaving the paths and criss-crossing through the woods, where the trails are lit with candles.

"We had everything wrong, Harding," she says to me. "It was Dahlgren, not Pollard—he was right there in front of us the whole time. You said he was fucking Crystal Royce, that's how he met Travis."

"We don't know that yet. Not from just that piece of paper."

"Why else would he be up here?"

I don't have an answer. I remember one of the first things Dahlgren told me, though, about some work he'd done in prisons. Had he met Travis and Sunderman then? *There is something inherently fascinating about criminally deviant behavior.*

When we reach the top, we find a party in progress, a small shelter with a bar and tiny dance floor, disco music being pumped through outdoor speakers. Everyone's drinking. The music fades as we walk to the other side of the hill. There's not much cover on this side. The cabin's lights are on. There's smoke coming from the chimney. The roof is covered with snow. It looks scenic as hell.

"You don't have your field glasses, do you?" I say. She shakes her head. My gun is back at the bed-and-breakfast.

We follow a wind fence around to the rear of the cabin. There are two bedrooms, though the main one is really part of the living room, with a large hot tub and an open fireplace in between the rooms. The porch light is off. The back rooms are dark. We try those windows, but they're double-hung and locked tight.

"Is that someone on the bed?" I say, peering through the glass.

"I can't tell," she says. "No, I think it's just shadows."

There's a sliding glass door that looks down on the mountain. We can see through a fold of the drapes. The walls of the cabin are whitewashed stucco. The light comes from the television. Charles is sitting on the couch in his robe and slippers. I don't see Beth. But I do see Henry Dahlgren sitting in a rocker. He's holding the silver Beretta I saw at his house.

"Come on," Alison says, but I pull her back to the rear of the cabin.

"We can't rush him," I say. "He could shoot Charles. And Beth must be in there somewhere, I just can't see her from this angle."

"We can't wait for the county sheriff, Harding. I don't mind going in alone. Maybe if you made some noise over here by the window—"

"No. We'll do this together, but in a way that makes sense. You still have my cell phone?"

She nods, pulling it out of her jacket. We go a bit farther back, away from the cabin. At least the wind is blowing the other way. I call Donnie Wilson at home and tell him I need a favor regarding one of his clients. "Tell him you figured out what he's up to and you're at the lodge right now, he better come back and talk. Tell him you've got a man outside the cabin right now, so don't fool around—he's watching you, he can see you sitting in the goddamn rocking chair."

"What the fuck does that mean?" Donnie says.

"Just do it, okay? Get him to come outside. Tell him you need a payoff or something. *Now,* Donnie." I hang up before he can argue the point.

"Do you think this will work?" Alison says.

"Donnie can be very convincing," I say.

We go back by the window. We can see Dahlgren talking on his phone, still holding the gun. He's on his feet, pacing a bit. His clothes are rumpled. Now I understand where that distracted expression came from the other day. When he comes to our window, we have to lunge backward into the shadows and then circle the cabin.

The front door opens tentatively. The nose of the gun sticks out first. Alison doesn't wait, she grabs his wrist and twists it hard; the bone cracks, the gun drops to the snow. So does Dahlgren; I hit him just hard enough to knock him down. He looks like a snow angel. I empty his gun and then throw it aside.

Beth and Charles both come to the door. Beth looks stunned. She's clutching Charles's shoulder like it's a life preserver. I see a patrol car finally at the rear of the lodge, its lights flashing. The desk clerk must have believed me. I think they sent the fire trucks, too, and the ambulance.

Alison leans over Dahlgren, who is barely with us. Alison broke his wrist; I might have broken his jaw. "We're going to wait for the cops now, Henry," she says. "Okay? I know your wrist hurts, but if you move an inch, I swear to God I will break both your arms and you will feel pain you didn't think possible."

He tries to say something, but Alison doesn't feel like listening. When he struggles to get up, she knocks him out cold. I have to stop her from hitting him again.

"Thank God you two got here," Charles says. "He was ranting, not making any sense."

"I think he flipped," Beth says. She's not letting go of Charles, not now. This is the second time he's been her hero. "I can't believe he'd do all this and frame Charles just so he could have me. . . ."

"But one thing he said made sense," Charles says. "Pollard is one of his patients. Or was. Something about counseling he got after being arrested years ago—Henry was the doctor. Trying to cure him of being a Peeping Tom, bothering women."

The sheriff is at the lift now, about to take the slow ride toward us. I'm sure he appreciated the clerk's explanation of how special the Aspen Retreat was. Some of the skiers have come toward us, curious.

"Beth, you're going to freeze out here," Alison says.

"I'll take her inside," Charles says, putting his arm around her. For the first time they really look like a couple. At least they'll have something to tell the grandkids.

Alison's knee is bothering her more and more. Or maybe she's allowing herself to show it. Travis must have hurt her more than she let on. She needs a doctor or one of those ambulances. I check on Dahlgren, who is still out cold. I tell two of the bigger skiers to keep an eye on him until the deputy gets here; one of them plants his foot on Dahlgren's neck. And then we walk back to the lift. Alison is limping badly, cursing with each step.

"It's not broken but something snapped," she says. "Something's torn." I help her onto the lift and she cries out when she has to bend her leg to get on. She's sweating now. "My goddamn knee . . ." The lift starts moving, painfully slow. I give her my jacket. I bundle my scarf around her neck.

We're fifteen or twenty feet off the ground. I can see why people come here, it's very beautiful at night. There are a few lights on the other side of the hill, the airport maybe. The only sounds are from the lift and the icy crunch of the skiers.

"Isn't that Crowley?" Alison says, pointing to a lone figure on one of the lifts. "Coming toward us, over there?" She's right, it is Crowley. He's waving at us, wearing that same damn topcoat he wore at the Cove. He must have been tailing us or tailing Charles. . . .

I still have my cell phone, and when I answer it, I hear Donnie Wilson asking me if everything's okay.

"More or less, yeah. You did good, Donnie."

"I have no idea what I did." The lift moves slowly toward the lodge. "But maybe you can help me go through these fucking tapes I made at Crystal's. In exchange for this."

"That's not a fair exchange," I protest, laughing a bit. "You're talking about plowing through hours of recordings versus the one phone call you made tonight."

"Yeah, but this one was a lifesaver, you said."

"Not my life. Charles Muller and Beth Reinhardt, maybe you can con them into listening to the fucking tapes." Crowley is about thirty yards away, sitting all alone. He looks like an old man on a porch swing. "Right now I'm taking Alison to see a doctor, she hurt her knee. And then we're looking for a room with a very large bed." Alison hears this and smiles.

"Muller's there now?"

"Yeah."

"You're right, maybe he should be the one to sit through this shit, he can probably help me ID the names. He's all over these tapes, by the way."

The lift jerks; Alison winces. I turn around and see that the back door to the cabin is open.

"What are you talking about?"

"It sounds like he was using the apartment as a meeting place—"

"Charles? That was last summer with Tracy Lawrence—he was meeting a woman there—"

"No, this was last Friday," he says. Alison leans closer. "And it's not a woman. Listen to this. Are you sure he's being straight with you?"

"Lopez wasn't part of the deal—"

"Of course he wasn't, Travis, but there are always changes, improvisations. Just do it differently and keep me out of it."

"The deal was ten thousand for the girl, genius. . . . Lopez is extra. . . ."

The sky rushes toward me now, so fast I feel I'll be crushed up on this mountain, and Alison fumbles with the phone, demanding, *Was that who I think it was? . . . There must be some mistake, play it back, play it back,* as I undo my seat belt, telling her that's why it was so easy getting into Pollard's apartment, so easy for Charles to be a hero that night outside the bar, and she listens with her hands digging into my forearms. *I can't jump . . . I can't make it. . . . You'll have to bring him back again, Harding, bring him back . . .* and then the rest is lost with the jump, twenty feet or so to the hard-packed snow, and then another body tumbles from the sky and rolls toward me, and I hear Terry Crowley calling my name.

We climb the hill in silence. Crowley's not limping, but he's bent over from some pain in his abdomen. He can no longer stand up straight. We're well to the right of the cabin. I can see the deputy with Dahlgren; I can see Beth. I don't see Charles. But I know where he is and what he's doing.

That's what I do, Harding . . . I run, I always run. . . .

The snow's not packed up here. We pick up his tracks behind the cabin's rear door. They lead to the woods.

Crowley doesn't talk, just pulls on my sleeve and points to the nearest fence, running parallel to us. If he saw the same map I saw, he knows there are three such fences, the last being the gateway to that forbidden access road. But if what Nick said before is true, there's no way down the hill from that side. Crowley wants me to swing around and cut Charles off, box him in at that final fence.

Crowley hands me his piece, a lightweight .38. "I can't shoot worth a damn anymore," Crowley says, his voice gone. His eyes are tearing from the wind. I nod, checking the clip before slipping uphill, heading farther behind the cabin. I thought Charles would be going down the mountain, but Crowley's right; he's far ahead of me, running toward the marked-off area. I climb the fence, pulling myself up with one hand, and I watch him clawing on the snow, running sideways on the hill.

Even I can follow these tracks. I'm guessing he saw the sign for the road but didn't have the same conversation I had with the desk clerk. There's a second wire fence with NO TRESPASSING signs every fifty feet that follows the crest of the hill. He jumps the fence and I follow. I can no longer see Crowley.

This side isn't lit like the others. All we have is moonlight. And now I see why they fenced this area off. It's steep, all right, and you wouldn't want to walk here. It must be something in summer. The whole mountain is landfill, just packed garbage with a million-dollar system to draw off the gas and keep the smell down. The skiers never see this, of course. A lot of that machinery is over here. There's one final fence, tall wooden spikes leaning against the wind, snow-banks piled like soft pillows. The gate in the center is arched like a lovers' lane. Charles tries to climb the fence, trying to get a footing, jamming the tip of his shoe between the narrow boards, both his hands pawing the face like a mountain climber before losing his grasp and tumbling into the snow. When he stands up he's furious, lashing out at the storm, kicking the snow, and then he's attacking the gate, pulling at the chain, both his hands yanking a board off as some kind of scream comes from his throat. The board gives way and then another, and I'm about twenty yards away when Charles tries squeezing through the gate. Crowley is behind me on my right.

"Take the shot!" he yells at me. Charles's coat is caught on the wood. I'm searching his face for the person who could have done all these things, for another person, but he looks just like he did that night in Galena, on that other hill. His glasses are gone now; there's snow in his hair. And his face is flush from climbing up here; he's panting, like an animal caught in a trap. He tears himself loose, the fabric ripping apart. I don't shoot because I know there's nowhere for him to go. He disappears beyond the fence and in a split second he's gone. I hear him tumbling and falling down the man-made hill, creating an avalanche of trash. I hear him screaming. And then he finally comes to rest somewhere beneath the freshly packed snow and the garbage. And the screams stop.

Epilogue

the wedding is set for two P.M. on a Saturday in late May. Everything came together very fast. Beth changed caterers, moved
the reception to a smaller hall, and shifted the ceremony from
Bond Chapel to an enclosed shelter on the Point. She got lucky
with the weather—it's a beautiful day, clear and a bit chilly, with
the blue waters of Lake Michigan for a backdrop.

The shelter's used in summer for picnics and barbecues, but
today it looks like a Renaissance fair. There are lusty wenches and
rusty knights, a main room full of banners and decorations, very
retro music from the Three Merrye Fellows—lute, percussion,
flute—a hundred guests in rented costumes, a nervous bride. The
groom is late. Again.

"Has anyone seen him?" I say.

"Of course," Alison says. She's dressed in a long green velvet
dress with a black veil, kind of a Goth Maid Marian. I tried to kiss
her before and was quickly rebuffed. I might damage her makeup.
Alison rarely wears makeup, but this isn't Revlon, this is theater.
This is opening-night makeup.

"Henry had breakfast with Beth's kids at the House of Pan-
cakes," she says, crossing her legs with a slight wince. She had arthro-
scopic surgery on her knee, but it still bothers her. Muscle memory
takes a long time to heal. My own injuries healed faster. "He said he
needed time to run a few errands. Tie up the proverbial loose end."

"They reported no unusual signs? He didn't have a suitcase with
him, for example?"

"Confidence is high," she says. An English professor named

Tibbins is sitting directly in front of me. He was in that group of car-olers that Travis latched on to—I've quizzed him about it, so have the cops. All he knew was that Travis paid for the coffee.

"And he was a tenor," says Tibbins. "It's hard to get good tenors. He will be missed."

Alison rubs her shoe against my leg. "Maybe you should go look for him," she says. "Just in case he fell asleep or something. It would ease my mind." I nod.

The Three Merrye Fellows are launching into "Matty Groves" and getting lots of recognition applause when I leave the shelter and cross the drive to the parking lot. Dahlgren's house on South Black-stone has a SOLD sign on the lawn. I break in, gently, my footsteps echoing on the hardwood floors. Nobody's home. I stop at a liquor store on Cornell, buy a pint of scotch—I have no faith in wedding-reception open bars—and then start compiling a list of possible last-minute hideouts: Beth's house, Dahlgren's office in Mitchell, the new house they've bought in Kenwood. I can't help thinking of the times I did this for Charles Muller.

There's been a lot written about Charles, of course, with lots of experts weighing in on just what happened to him. Some attribute it to artistic excess, others to the alcohol. There's the usual nod to childhood trauma. Since most of what we found in that apartment on Milwaukee Avenue was kept out of the papers, no one knows quite how to connect the dots.

Alison thinks something happened to Charles after college, dur-ing the ten years she lost track of him. She wonders about the affair Charles had five years ago with Moira Dahlgren. There's a logic to it starting there. That's when he met Travis, teaching a class at the prison. Maybe Moira woke something up in Charles that should have lain dormant. Memories of Alison, for example. "A flash point," Ali-son calls it.

Myself—though I know firsthand what alcohol can do to a person, and God forbid I'd ever underestimate childhood trauma—I think Charles was a dead man the day he took those pictures at the Dunes. I'm told that one of the experts has found allusions in Charles's poetry to that day, to the three women, with references to everything from the holy trinity to the beauty of triangles. That sort of thing is over my head.

I know what loneliness feels like, though, and how it feels to be an outsider, older than the rest. I know how empty the campus can be on a summer night between quarters. I can picture Charles at Grand Terrace on that Friday night after the girls had left for the Dunes, standing on Hyde Park Boulevard, hands in pockets, unsure of what to do or where to go. I can picture him drinking, spending a restless night alone, and then driving down there the next day, ringing the doorbell, finding scattered clothes, trying to figure who slept where . . . touching the bedclothes . . . and then walking around to the back, to the path that leads to the beach, a cheap Kodak in his pocket.

Of course the problem with this is that none of the pictures or the poems capture what Charles saw that day at the Dunes. Maybe only a poet would have been so moved. Alison barely remembers the events of that day. When I pressed her, she recalled spending most of the weekend outside, either sunbathing or swimming or boating. Like Moira, she remembers finding a French cookbook in the kitchen; that they drove to the local grocers and bought wine with a phony ID. She remembers a soufflé, not a chocolate mousse. I've been in that house, of course, gone over the layout in my mind, as Charles must have. I don't ask her about the sleeping arrangements or where everyone ended up in that one-bedroom house; I don't ask her about the sex. It's not that I'm not curious. I just don't want to end up like Charles.

We reopened PowerFemmes in January, and when our neighbor Leon retired and shuttered the Clovernook Cleaners, we put a deposit on that space. Alison has elaborate projections that show it will pay for itself in the long run. She says she's thinking more like that now . . . for the long run.

Crystal Royce stopped by the gym one day, dressed in black fur. She told me Logan Pollard was getting out of the mannequin business. "For a creep he wasn't such a bad guy," she said to me. It looks like that's the extent of his crimes. He definitely slept with Tracy, bought drugs for her from Lopez, but I doubt if he was the only one. And, like Charles, he had a fascination with both Tracy and Alison during the Grand Terrace years, but in his case it was limited to watching. The voyeuristic photos from Grand Terrace are thought to be his; everything else in that apartment—including the peach dress—came from Charles. The fact that no one liked Pollard, especially Travis, made him easy to frame. Crystal moved away soon after that, by the way. I heard she moved to Cambridge, Massachusetts.

The only sad note, as spring approaches, was Terry Crowley's death from cancer. The last time I saw him he was very sick, entering the hospital for the final time, but I prefer to remember him as he was that day at the morgue, comforting Alison despite his own illness. The obituaries mentioned that he broke the Charles Muller case. I went to the funeral, but there were too many cops to get very close. I met his ex-wife there. I thought of *Brigadoon*.

Henry Dahlgren spent a week in the hospital recovering from that night at Badger Run. He turned out to have a fractured jaw along with a broken wrist and knife cuts and bruises. As for why he'd driven to the ski lodge that day—"a premonition," he said. He'd been helping Beth's kids that afternoon, hanging up the hats and coats that Beth and Charles had tried on and discarded for their trip. And he found a ski mask, similar to the one he'd heard about in the Gretchen Moss attack. Same color, same design. Was it even the one Charles had worn during the murders? No one could tell. It wasn't enough to make Dahlgren call the police, just enough to make him uneasy—it gnawed at him all afternoon, as he tried to read. Each time he called Beth, he got Charles. Each time he thought of calling me or Alison, it seemed ridiculous. It was his own *ideé fixe*, a lucky one, and it led him just in time to Beth's cabin.

I've been working an ugly skip trace for Donnie the past few months, but Alison kept me up to date with the neighborhood gossip. After the debacle with Charles, Beth fell into an understandable depression. Henry helped her a lot. His divorce from Moira came through, and after that they began to be seen together at faculty dinners.

They had a lot in common. He took her kids to Bulls games, took everyone to Florida for a week. I think that's where he proposed, at Disney World, during a fireworks show or a parade or something. She said yes. It's the Magic Kingdom.

An interesting sidelight to the whole affair was that Tracy's work was finally published. Not the missing book, which was never found, but a short sketch that Sarah found at Peace Station and included in one of their newsletters.

> She tagged along one Christmas, following Alyssa home to her grandparents' house in central Michigan, a beautiful farm with rolling hills . . . walked to the barn and fed the horses, black and sleek and shiny, a hundred dogs yapping happily around them. . . . She kissed her in the hay loft, trembling fingers on Alyssa's collar, reaching down inside her coat, the taste of lipstick, the smell of hay, the gifts beneath the Christmas tree, waiting just for them. . . . It felt like paradise and it felt like it would never end. . . .

"Was that the way it was?" I asked her. "You had grandparents in Michigan?"

Alison shook her head. "None of that ever happened, not to me, anyway." She couldn't recognize herself or Tracy anywhere.

I read the piece three or four times. The more I read it, the truer it sounded to me, and the more I could see Alison as Alyssa.

• • •

beth's house has a SOLD sign in her front yard as well. Henry Dahlgren is in the living room, sitting alone in a chair near the fireplace. He's wearing his overcoat, like Charles was when I picked him up in Galena, and holding a glass of sherry. This time there's a tux underneath, and he's holding a top hat I wouldn't be caught dead in, even on my wedding day. Dahlgren might be able to carry it off, though.

"Professor? Is something wrong?" The room seems much neater today, from the Realtors probably. The toys have been put away, the children's shoes and jackets moved upstairs.

"Just reflecting. After all that's happened lately . . . all this madness and death . . ." He holds the glass a bit stiffly, the result of what Alison did to his wrist on the mountaintop that night. I think the cast just came off last week.

"That's all over, Professor."

"Please, Harding. Call me Henry." I nod. I'm wondering if he was ever a Hank. He looks like he's trying to get used to the house, and the chair, and maybe this new life. I remember seeing Charles in this same chair in his bathrobe and slippers, not so long ago.

"Beth's waiting for you, Henry. And getting a little impatient, I would think."

He nods. "But I'm glad we have this minute to ourselves. Because there's something I wanted to give you." He hands me a narrow jewelry box. The necklace that I stole from the apartment in Lake Village East is inside, on velvet cardboard. "You should give this to Alison," he says.

"I don't understand—"

"It's a long story," he says. "I thought it belonged to my ex-wife. I saw her wear it once last summer. Apparently, it was an heirloom of Tracy Lawrence's, been in her family for years, but she sold it to Crystal Royce for drug money. I wanted it back, to give to Moira. . . . This was when I still hoped we might reconcile. I thought it would impress her. Crystal wouldn't return it, however." He pauses. "I did something very foolish to get it back."

"So did I," I say, and he smiles at me. That's as far as we're going to take this. He no longer wants the necklace; it belongs to the past. A church bell is ringing nearby, clear, sharp tones, competing with the yapping sound of a barking dog. "We'd better go," I tell Henry. "After what happened with Charles, there's a crowd of people at the Point putting down bets on you showing up or not."

"Well, then, let's go," he says, rising to his feet, "and show them they should have bet on me."

alison is outside the shelter in her green velvet dress, pacing in the cold. The slit goes to mid-thigh, and every time the wind blows, you can see her long legs and the sexy new pair of heels she bought. When she sees us pulling up in my car, she breaks out in a smile so wide that Henry and I both start to laugh. She shows him where to go and then attends to me, straightening my tie, brushing my hair back. Her fingernails are painted kelly green for the occasion; so are her toenails.

She reaches into my pocket for a piece of gum and finds the necklace. "How did you . . ." she begins, a sentence that goes nowhere. I take off the newer necklace she's wearing and put the old one on her. She has to find a mirror. She fingers it softly.

"This was Tracy's," she says.

"I thought it might have been. If it makes you too sad, you can take it off—"

"No, no," she says. "I want to wear it." I remember what she said that night in the car before we made love.

You have to reclaim things, Harding . . . make them yours.

"How do you feel?" I ask her.

"Strange. Like I'm marrying away one of my sisters. Like I'll never see her again. That's dumb, right?"

"They're just moving to Kenwood, Alison. But if she's the older sister, then maybe it's your turn."

She wets her fingers and tries to part my hair. "You have a way of backing into this, Harding."

"Into what."

"Talking about marriage and almost proposing."

"Maybe I'm waiting for you to propose to me. I don't want to seem easy, Alison. I want you to respect me in the morning."

"I barely respect you now," she says. "What's gonna change my mind by morning?" One of the bridesmaids walks by, gives Alison a hug. "If we do get married, we're staying married. Like my parents. No affairs, no messing around. No divorce."

"You're a tough broad, Alison, you know that?"

"You break the rules, Harding, and I'll kill you. Slowly, painfully. You do the same to me if I fuck up. Deal?"

"Deal."

There's a slight pause as this sinks in.

"What do we do now," she says, "shake hands on it or kiss?"

"I think you're always supposed to kiss the bride." Her lips taste like strawberries. She smells like Alison. I'm wondering what's underneath the green velvet dress besides the nail polish and the heels when a woman from the wedding party taps on the glass and says, "Come on, you guys, it's starting."

About the Author

JOHN WESSEL is the author of *This Far, No Further* and *Pretty Ballerina*. He lives with his wife in Lincolnshire, Illinois.